Praise for the *New York Times* Bestselling Books by the Bay Mysteries

Poisoned Prose

"A true whodunit . . . Adams's latest, like its predecessors, is rich with coastal color, an intriguing heroine, and a fine balance between the story line and the changing personal lives of the Bayside Book Writers. Like the good storyteller she is, Adams excels at varying her plots and developing her characters, and *Poisoned Prose* confirms her bona fides in the genre and the stature of this superior series."

—*Richmond Times-Dispatch*

"An excellent series with fun dialogue, likable characters, and themes that will resonate with readers long after the book is closed."

—*Kings River Life Magazine*

"Another fantastic story from this fantastic storyteller. You cannot go wrong with a book by Ellery Adams!!! I highly recommend each and every one!!!"

—*Escape with Dollycas into a Good Book*

Written in Stone

"*Written in Stone* is written with skill, as Adams continues to entertain her readers with a clever story and further develop Olivia, one of the most intriguing heroines of the genre and one created by a maturing and empathetic author."

—*Richmond Times-Dispatch*

"Well-paced mysteries, interesting back story, and good characters make this a must-read mystery."

—*The Mystery Reader*

continued . . .

The Last Word

"Adams concocts a fine plot . . . But the real appeal is her sundry and congenial characters, beginning with Olivia herself . . . [An] unusual and appealing series."

—*Richmond Times-Dispatch*

"I could actually feel the wind on my face, taste the salt of the ocean on my lips, and hear the waves crash upon the beach. *The Last Word* made me laugh, made me think, made me smile, and made me cry. *The Last Word*—in one word—AMAZING!"

—*The Best Reviews*

"The plot is complex, the narrative drive is strong, and the book is populated with interesting and intelligent people . . . Oyster Bay is the kind of place I'd love to get lost for an afternoon or two."

—*The Season*

A Deadly Cliché

"A very well-written mystery with interesting and surprising characters and a great setting. Readers will feel as if they are in Oyster Bay."

—*The Mystery Reader*

"Adams spins a good yarn, but the main attraction of the series is Olivia and her pals, each a person the reader wants to meet again and again."

—*Richmond Times-Dispatch*

"[A] terrific mystery that is multilayered, well-thought-out, and well presented."

—*Fresh Fiction*

"This series is one I hope to follow for a long time, full of fast-paced mysteries, budding romances, and good friends. An excellent combination!"

—*The Romance Readers Connection*

"[Ellery Adams] has already proven she has a gift for charm. Her characters are charismatic and alluring, and downright funny. Not to mention, the plot is an absolute masterpiece as far as offering the reader a true puzzle that they are thrilled to solve! . . . *A Deadly Cliché* is a solidly great, fun read!"
—*Once Upon a Romance*

A Killer Plot

"Ellery Adams's debut novel, *A Killer Plot*, is not only a great read, but a visceral experience. Olivia Limoges's investigation into a friend's murder will have you hearing the waves crash on the North Carolina shore. You might even feel the ocean winds stinging your cheeks. Visit Oyster Bay and you'll long to return again and again."
—Lorna Barrett, *New York Times* bestselling author of the Booktown Mysteries

"Adams's plot is indeed killer, her writing would make her the star of any support group, and her characters—especially Olivia and her standard poodle, Captain Haviland—are a diverse, intelligent bunch. *A Killer Plot* is a perfect excuse to go coastal."
—*Richmond-Times Dispatch*

"A fantastic start to a new series . . . With new friendships, possible romance(s), and promises of great things to come, *A Killer Plot* is one book you don't want to be caught dead missing."
—*The Best Reviews*

Berkley Prime Crime titles by Ellery Adams

Charmed Pie Shoppe Mysteries

PIES AND PREJUDICE
PEACH PIES AND ALIBIS
PECAN PIES AND HOMICIDES

Books by the Bay Mysteries

A KILLER PLOT
A DEADLY CLICHÉ
THE LAST WORD
WRITTEN IN STONE
POISONED PROSE
LETHAL LETTERS

Book Retreat Mysteries

MURDER IN THE MYSTERY SUITE

A BOOKS
BY THE BAY
MYSTERY

Lethal Letters

ELLERY ADAMS

BERKLEY PRIME CRIME, NEW YORK

THE BERKLEY PUBLISHING GROUP
Published by the Penguin Group
Penguin Group (USA) LLC
375 Hudson Street, New York, New York 10014

USA • Canada • UK • Ireland • Australia • New Zealand • India • South Africa • China

penguin.com

A Penguin Random House Company

LETHAL LETTERS

A Berkley Prime Crime Book / published by arrangement with the author

For information, address: The Berkley Publishing Group,
a division of Penguin Group (USA) LLC,
375 Hudson Street, New York, New York 10014.

ISBN: 978-0-425-27083-7

PUBLISHING HISTORY
Berkley Prime Crime mass-market edition / November 2014

PRINTED IN THE UNITED STATES OF AMERICA

10 9 8 7 6 5 4 3 2

Cover illustration by Kimberly Schamber.
Cover design by Rita Frangie.
Interior text design by Tiffany Estreicher.

To the amazing ladies next door:
Dianne, Dorothy, and Charlene

I would be a mermaid fair;
I would sing to myself the whole of the day;
With a comb of pearl I would comb my hair;
And still as I comb'd I would sing and say,
"Who is it loves me? who loves not me?"

—*FROM* ALFRED LORD TENNYSON'S, "THE MERMAID"

Chapter 1

Time will bring to light whatever is hidden; it will cover up and conceal whatever is now shining in splendor.

—HORACE

Olivia Limoges rolled the newest edition of *Bride* magazine into a tight cylinder and brought it down onto the counter with a resounding *thwack!*

"Enough! I don't want to hear another detail about your upcoming nuptials. You've turned into a groomzilla, Michel. Your obsession over the venue and your tux and the guest list is driving everyone in this kitchen insane." She pointed at a sous chef, who'd paused in the act of chopping onions to wipe his eyes with a dish towel. "That man is weeping, for heaven's sake."

"He always cries when he—" the head chef of The Boot Top Bistro began.

"It started with the tulips, right?" Olivia directed her remark at the sous chef. "Michel's supposed to be creating the finest cuisine of coastal North Carolina, but his soufflés are falling and his sauces are burning while he frets over whether to have blush-colored tulips, hot pink tulips, or lavender tulips at his reception." She turned back to Michel. "I will take a meat cleaver to the next tulip you bring into this restaurant, do you hear me?"

Michel opened his arms in a gesture of helplessness. "I want everything to be perfect!"

"Last summer you said that you wanted a simple, intimate affair. But your plans have grown grander and more absurd by the month. I wouldn't be surprised if Shelley was ready to call off the whole thing."

At the mention of his fiancée's name, Michel's petulant look instantly vanished, and he smiled widely. "She told me that I could have all the pomp and circumstance I wanted. Unlike you, she understands that I've waited my whole life for this day and I want—"

"White doves and stretch limos?" Olivia sighed. "This is about you and Shelley. It's a joining of two lives. A chance for the people who love you to share in your happiness. You don't need a chocolate fountain for a wedding to be beautiful. You only need you, the woman you want to spend the rest of your life with, and a few carefully chosen words."

Michel swiveled to face the rest of the kitchen staff. "Have I gone off the deep end?"

They nodded in unison.

"Has my food suffered?"

The line cook exchanged a nervous glance with the sous chef. Michel had a fiery temper and it was clear that no one wanted to say that his cooking hadn't been up to its usual standards. But Michel caught the furtive glance and instantly hid his face in his hands. "*Mon Dieu!* I have betrayed my art. And for what? Monogrammed napkins? Embossed invitations?"

"And tulips," Olivia added. She put a hand on Michel's forearm and gave it an affectionate squeeze. She was used to his theatrics, but this wasn't a good time for one of his meltdowns. They needed to review the possible menus for the historical society benefit dinner before showing them to the president. "You can stop looking around for the perfect venue. The Boot Top is your kingdom, Michel. Its kitchen is your beating heart. Have the reception here. I'm sure your colleagues would be delighted to prepare the food for your wedding feast."

Everyone wearing a chef's jacket or apron murmured his or her agreement.

Michel looked at them and sniffed. "Really? You'd do that for me?"

"Of course we would," Olivia answered on behalf of her staff. "That just leaves the cake."

Michel brightened. "Shelley and I always planned on making our own cake. I'll do the baking and she'll do the decorating. After all, no one can hold a candle to her when it comes to sweet confections."

Olivia thought of the Saint Patrick's Day display she'd seen in the front window of Decadence, Shelley's desserterie. Candy coins wrapped in gold foil spilled from a cauldron of solid chocolate. There was a forest of four-leaf-clover lollipops, marshmallow clouds, and a rainbow of candy fruit slices. Fondant leprechauns perched atop grasshopper cupcakes or cartwheeled across the frosted surfaces of crème de menthe brownies. "Shelley is truly gifted," Olivia said. "And so are you. Can we talk about the menu for the benefit now?"

"Only if you promise to come with me to the First Presbyterian Church before I get started on the dinner service," Michel said. "I promised to swing by with a copy of our program."

"I thought you didn't want a church wedding."

Michel shrugged. "*Maman* does. And since I am her only son, I did what she asked." Straightening, Michel barked out orders to the kitchen staff and they jumped to obey. Scooping the bridal magazine off the counter, he held it aloft as if it were a torch. "I am back, my friends. And I apologize for being so distracted. That's over now. You have my word as a gentleman and a chef. Spring is upon us and we will be busier than ever. We must uphold the reputation of The Boot Top Bistro. We must dazzle every diner!"

Smiling, Olivia grabbed her head chef by the elbow. "Let's talk in the bar and then we'll stop by the church. Which Saturday did you book?"

"I chose a Monday," Michel said. "The Boot Top is closed on Mondays. You won't lose any business and neither will Shelley. She and I will take Tuesday off and be back in the kitchen on Wednesday."

Olivia poked her head into her office and saw that her standard poodle, Captain Haviland, was fast asleep. She smiled indulgently and then led Michel through the dining room into the bar. "Why rush back to work?" Olivia asked. "What about your honeymoon?"

Michel sank into one of the leather club chairs. "We'll go when the tourist season is over. Mid-October maybe. I want to bring Shelley to Paris. We can visit our old haunts from culinary school and then travel to the Riviera, visiting vineyards as we make our way south. It's past time we updated The Boot Top's wine list." Michel gestured at the polished wood bar. "Not that Gabe isn't the finest tender in town, but his palate isn't sophisticated enough to be the restaurant's sommelier."

"Ah, the sacrifices you make for your job," Olivia said teasingly and placed a folder on the small table dividing her chair from Michel's.

Michel reached out and grabbed her hand. He tapped the platinum band embedded with dark sapphires on her ring finger, and said, "I'm not the only person in the room who should be making wedding plans. And yet I hear nothing of yours. Why not? What are you waiting for, *ma chérie*?"

Pulling her hand free, Olivia straightened the printed menus in the folder. "Mine will be a very quiet affair. Justice of the peace and a champagne toast. That's all. There's not much to organize."

Michel fixed her with an intent stare. "Then why aren't

you already married? Are you cohabiting, or is the chief still living out of a drawer? I know how much you treasure your independence, Olivia. But when you said 'yes,' you gave up your old life."

Olivia felt her cheeks grow warm. "It's complicated. When he's on duty, the chief needs to be close to town, so he stays at his place. My house is too far out. If there's a police emergency . . ." She shrugged, letting Michel reach his own conclusions. "And I don't like to spend the night in his house. His wife still has a presence there. She picked out the wallpaper and the towels, the dishes and the furniture. It's her home. It's a monument of their life together. Not to mention that it's too far from the water."

"We can't have our resident mermaid living away from the beach. Your scales would dry out." He gazed at her fondly.

Olivia shoved a printed menu under Michel's nose. "Let's focus on these menus now, shall we?"

An hour later, Olivia pulled her Range Rover into a private lot belonging to the First Presbyterian Church and opened the car door for Haviland. As he jumped out of the backseat and Michel alighted from the front, Olivia studied the Gothic Revival architecture, taking in its blocks of somber gray stone, pointed arches, and towering spire. It was one of the most imposing buildings in all of Oyster Bay.

A jarring mechanical noise erupted from inside the church. Michel winced and Haviland started barking.

"Is that a jackhammer?" Michel shouted.

"Maybe they're tuning the organ," Olivia yelled.

Haviland's barking increased in volume, and he retreated several steps. Olivia laid her hand on the poodle's head and tried to calm him, but he was clearly discomfited by the noise.

"I'm putting Haviland back in the car," she told Michel. "Go on. I'll catch up."

As soon as Haviland was safely inside the Range Rover, he stopped barking and stretched across the backseat. Olivia gave him a chew stick, promised she wouldn't be long, and crossed the parking lot. Drawing closer to the church, she noticed several commercial vans and a pickup parked near the building. A man in a hard hat came out of a door in the church's west wall and began rummaging through an aluminum toolbox in the bed of the pickup. After retrieving a pair of safety goggles and a crowbar, he disappeared into the church again.

Olivia found Michel in the sanctuary, standing next to a man wearing khakis and a blue dress shirt. Mercifully, the hammering sound had stopped.

Michel introduced her to Pastor Jeffries.

"Please call me Jon," the man said, offering Olivia his hand. His grip was warm and firm. Olivia liked both his handshake and his friendly brown eyes. They reminded her of Haviland's. "I can't believe we haven't met before," the pastor said. "Ours is a small town, but our paths have yet to cross." He smiled. "I guess I'm surprised because you're very active in community projects. Your name pops up all the time in the paper."

Michel put an arm around Olivia's shoulders. "My boss wrangles money from Oyster Bay's upper crust. You work in the trenches, Pastor. You probably aren't involved with the same charities."

"I suspect you're right," the pastor said amiably. "Until now. Miss Limoges and I are both supporting the upcoming historical society benefit. Not only is the historical society our next-door neighbor, but the society's founding family, the Drummonds, have been devoted patrons of this church for the past century."

Olivia let her gaze wander up the center aisle to the altar, and then over the polished pews to the stained glass windows. The colored glass was cracked in places and coated with a film of grime, making it hard for the light to pass through. Watery yellows and dull oranges spotted the sanctuary's red carpet, and Olivia wondered if the windows could withstand the force of the work being done in the room to the left of the vestibule.

Pastor Jeffries followed the direction of her gaze. "I was just telling Michel that we're in the middle of a minor construction project. At least, it started out as a minor project. The plan was to turn the cloakroom into a comfortable space for prayer and counseling, but as often happens during a renovation, the contractor and his crew encountered problems. Water damage, rotted floorboards, issues with the wiring. They've dug right down to the foundation stone." His eyes slid toward the large brass cross on the altar. "I spent half the morning praying that there wouldn't be any more surprises."

"Pastor Jeffries!" a man called from the doorway dividing the vestibule from the chapel. "You'd better come look at this. We found something buried in the wall."

"And people think the Lord lacks a sense of humor." The pastor winked, told his guests he'd return in a moment, and strode down the center aisle.

Michel sighed. "I hadn't pictured drop cloths and plaster dust as part of my wedding day décor."

"I'm sure the job will be completed by then." Olivia ran her fingers along the back of a polished pew. The sanctuary smelled of beeswax and lilies. Overall, it was a pleasant space. The walls were a soft white, velvet cushions in a deep cranberry hue covered the pews, and the entire room was illuminated by rows of brass chandeliers suspended from the high ceiling. Olivia swiveled, taking in the second-floor balcony and the gleaming organ pipes. Everything was simple, elegant, and clean. Aside from the Easter lilies grouped around the altar, the only adornment in the entire sanctuary was the windows. "This is the oldest church in Oyster Bay," she told Michel. "Think of all the couples that have walked up this aisle. All the music that's been played. How many secret hopes and fears have been whispered into folded hands. This place is redolent with history."

Sinking into a pew, Michel frowned. "I think it's gloomy, but my mother will love it. It speaks of Old World Europe."

"That's not gloom. It's patina." Olivia wandered over to the windows on the east wall and studied the Biblical scenes. Though she'd attended only a handful of church services throughout her life, she recognized most of the scenes. She didn't tarry long before Mary and Joseph, the nativity, or Christ cradling a lamb. After noting more cracked glass and sagging lead in the John the Baptist window, she moved to the west wall. She liked the Daniel in the lion's den window and paused to take in the detailed faces of the slumbering felines. Again, she saw damage to the glass, lead, and putty.

"I'd think these would be more important than the cloakroom renovation," she murmured to herself and walked by a window featuring a young boy holding a harp. In the next scene, she admired how the glass artist had used pieces of green, orange, and red glass to create a burning bush. But she didn't linger, finding that she was inexplicably drawn to the last window.

This one, which was in the worst condition of all, portrayed a woman and child. The child, a girl with an ageless face, gazed forward. Her expression was both hopeful and serene. Most of her body was enfolded in the woman's gown, and as Olivia edged closer, she realized that it wasn't a gown but a feathered wing curving protectively around the girl. The angel was in profile, her eye closed and her cheek pressed against the girl's cheek. Olivia could almost hear her whispering words of comfort into the child's ear. The more she stood and stared, the more the angel looked like her mother.

Hesitantly, Olivia placed her fingers against the glass and traced one of the white flowers hanging near the angel's outstretched hand. The girl's small hand rested in the angel's cupped palm, and Olivia had the urge to lay her own hand on top of theirs. She wanted to go where they were going, to see what lay beyond the curtain of dogwood blossoms.

"She's a guiding angel," Pastor Jeffries said from behind

Olivia, causing her to start. "Sorry. Didn't mean to creep up on you." He flashed her a sheepish smile. "This is my favorite window."

Olivia pointed at the angel. "Her face is completely two-dimensional, and yet she reminds me so much of my mother."

The pastor nodded. "Everyone recognizes a special woman in her. A mother, sister, daughter, wife, nurse, teacher."

"Can the windows be restored?"

"At great cost, yes. We'll have to raise more funds, but I have faith that we'll get the money. The capital campaign has been eaten up by all the problems we've run across with our current project, so it's fortunate that we have a devoted benefactor." Pastor Jeffries didn't seem overly bothered by the setbacks. In fact, he looked quite cheerful. "It seems we were meant to dig deeper than we'd originally intended. The men have just discovered a large lead box buried above the foundation stone."

Olivia was immediately intrigued. "How big is it?"

"About the length of my arm. Let's just hope the first pastor didn't bury his faithful hound inside." With a boyish grin, he waved Michel over and explained what was happening. "The men have asked me to open the box. It could be empty, and I don't want to interrupt the staff unless there's something worth seeing, so I'll grab the digital camera from my office and let them finish Sunday's program. You two are welcome to watch if you'd like."

Michel's eyes were shining. "I'll serve as your photojournalist, but if you unearth a cache of gold, I might have to charge a hefty fee for my services. Weddings are ridiculously expensive."

Pastor Jeffries laughed and then gestured at the stained glass angel and child. "If there's anything of value inside that box, I'll use it to save our real treasures. I'm not supposed to put much stock in worldly goods, but I love these windows. I want to make sure the next generation can enjoy them as much as I do." He rubbed his hands together, looking like a kid on Christmas morning. "Be right back."

Too curious to wait for his return, Olivia and Michel headed for the vestibule. In the cloakroom, two workmen wearing hard hats and gloves stood, hands on hips, staring down at a battered lead box. A third was on his knees, scraping pieces of mortar from the surface of the box with his fingers. The men looked up when Olivia and Michel entered.

"Is it marked anywhere?" Olivia asked the man on the floor.

"I think there's a date stamped into the lid." He turned to one of his coworkers. "Hand me a flathead screwdriver, will you?"

With the tool in hand, he carefully worked its edge under the mortar. It gave way, coming off in large pieces. Brushing a chunk aside, the man maneuvered the screwdriver head until two numbers became clear.

"Looks like a one and a nine so far," the man said. "And the next number looks like a seven. No, it's another one."

At that moment, Pastor Jeffries returned. He crouched down next to the man with the screwdriver and watched, fascinated, as the last digit was revealed. "Nineteen seventeen. Wow."

"The beginning of World War One," another workman said.

"But not the year the church was founded," the pastor said, clearly perplexed. "This box was buried some sixty years after the original church was built." He rubbed his chin, his gaze distant. "There was a fire about that time. A bad one. I wonder if this was placed inside the wall during the reconstruction. I'd have to check with the historical society, but if there are relics of our past inside this box, I'll be calling Bellamy Drummond anyway. Let's open it and find out."

Olivia was thrilled that they wouldn't have to postpone the event for Bellamy Drummond. While she certainly approved of the historical society's president's efforts to preserve Oyster Bay's past, Olivia found Bellamy's punctiliousness a bit overbearing. She was certain to ruin the excitement of the workmen's discovery by lecturing them in her rich, languid drawl on the proper technique of opening an antique lead box.

"May I have the honors?" Pastor Jeffries asked the man with the screwdriver.

The man passed him the crowbar and backed away. "Sure thing. Hold this straight edge under the lid and I'll hit the hooked end with a mallet. You want a pair of gloves? If that bar slips, you could get a nasty slice."

The pastor shook his head with impatience. "I'll be fine." Handing Michel the digital camera, he lowered himself to his knees.

Olivia wondered if he felt less manly in his khakis and dress shirt than the workmen. With their tattooed forearms, dirt-encrusted jeans, and weathered faces, these men seemed a different breed than Pastor Jeffries. Next to them, he looked like a naïve and sheltered academic, though Olivia suspected that was far from the truth. Michel had told her that the pastor had led his flock for over twenty years, and Olivia could only imagine the things he'd seen and heard during that time.

Baptisms. Confirmations. Marriages, she thought as the workman struck the end of the crowbar with his mallet. *Memorial services and funerals.*

The sound of the mallet striking the metal curve of the crowbar reverberated around the empty room. *Clang, clang, clang.*

"Keep going," Pastor Jeffries said, sounding a little winded. "It's moving!"

The man hit the crowbar again. Without warning, the lid gave way and the crowbar shot sideways, causing the pastor to cry out in pain. Olivia could see a jagged line of red appear on his palm. He dropped the crowbar and stared at his hand as the blood flowed over his wrist and dripped onto the floor.

Michel pulled a blue bandanna from his pocket and offered it to the pastor. Having seen dozens of knife wounds over the years, he was unfazed by the injury. Pastor Jeffries fumbled with the cloth until Michel took it from him, wound it tightly around his palm, and tied it into a knot. "You'll have to disinfect that and you may even need stitches. If not stitches, at least a few butterfly bandages."

"I'll take care of it later. After I see what's inside." Pastor Jeffries glanced up at the man with the mallet. "I should have used the gloves. Right, Kenny?"

Kenny gave a noncommittal shrug and picked up the crowbar again. He inserted the bloodied edge under the lid, pushed down on the opposite end, and gave a satisfied grunt when the box top separated from the base with a low groan.

No one spoke as the pastor raised the lid with his good hand. He reached in and pulled out a sheaf of paper. It had yellowed with age, but otherwise, looked to be in perfect shape.

"It's a time capsule," Pastor Jeffries whispered in awe. "This is an inventory of the contents as well as a list of the contributors." He scanned the document. "Here's the pastor—my grandfather, if you can believe it—and a deacon. Also a physician. The head of the local school. And—" Suddenly, he stopped. "I should get Bell—ah, Mrs. Drummond." He hurriedly set the letter back into the box and then glanced at the bright drops of blood on the floor.

Olivia was confused by the pastor's abrupt change of demeanor. He'd lost all traces of youthful anticipation. The pleasure and excitement had completely vanished from his face. It had been replaced by an emotion Olivia recognized all too well.

Pastor Jeffries's eyes had gone glassy. His body was rigid. Olivia didn't know why, but the pastor was suddenly, and very obviously, afraid.

And then he blinked. Pressing his injured hand to his chest, he forced his mouth into a tight smile, apologized to Michel for having to cut their visit short, and left the church.

Chapter 2

Where there is a sea, there are pirates.

—GREEK PROVERB

Kenny was unfazed by the pastor's abrupt departure. Turning to his coworkers, he said, "We might as well grab a smoke."

The men nodded and followed him outside.

The moment they were gone, Olivia took out her phone, retrieved the letter from the time capsule, and took several photos of it.

"What are you doing?" Michel whispered nervously.

Olivia photographed the letter in sections, not wanting to miss a single word. "Didn't you see Pastor Jeffries's face? He was scared, and I want to know why." She glanced into the box, disappointed to find that the contents were covered by a folded piece of fabric. "I doubt he's easily spooked. After witnessing two decades of sicknesses, hospital vigils, loss, and brokenness. All those confessions and last breaths. What's in here that could shake a man who's seen what he's seen?"

Michel peered into the box and frowned. "I'm not sure I want to know."

"Laurel would. This would make a great article. People love time capsules." After darting a look over her shoulder, Olivia handed Michel the letter. "Take this," she commanded and then reached into the box and carefully picked up the piece of fabric. She gently unfolded it and felt a surge of pride when she recognized the horizontal bands of red and discolored white and the vertical field of blue. Embroidered into the wide stripe of blue were a white star, two historic dates commemorating independence from British rule, and the letters *N* and *C*. Olivia was holding the state flag of North Carolina.

"There's nothing frightening about that," Michel said, admiring the flag. "I wonder if the person who added this to the box would be pleased by the fact that the same flag still flies all over town."

Olivia considered the question. "I'm sure they would. After all, it's a symbol of freedom, and our country had just entered a world war to defend that freedom." With the flag gently draped over her left forearm, she leaned forward and gazed at the bundles packed tightly inside the box. "Why did they have to wrap everything in paper and secure it with twine? That's no fun. Now I'm really glad I took a picture of the inventory list."

The only object that hadn't been wrapped in paper was another box. This one was made of copper and was big enough to hold a pair of men's shoes. "A box within a box," Olivia said. "It's been sealed with wax too." She pointed at the blob of green candlewax. "Where have I seen that symbol before?" She frowned, trying to remember, and then slowly pivoted the box so that the seal caught the light. "I think it's some kind of plant."

"Someone's coming," Michel hissed. "Put everything back!"

Hearing voices on the other side of the main doors, Olivia quickly set the cooper box where she'd found it, folded the flag, and returned both the flag and the letter to the time capsule. She quickly shut the heavy lid and retreated several steps.

As Pastor Jeffries entered the vestibule with Bellamy Drummond in tow, Olivia and Michel exchanged guilt-ridden glances.

"Hello, Olivia. Michel." Bellamy smiled regally. "Pastor Jeffries has informed me that a treasure of historical significance has been unearthed." She scanned the room. "Where have the workmen gone?"

"They took a cigarette break," Olivia said.

Bellamy nodded in approval. "Tobacco is the backbone of our agricultural heritage. I wouldn't be surprised if we find a pack of Camels in our time capsule." She clasped her hands together. "This is *very* exciting, isn't it?"

Olivia couldn't detect a trace of concern on Bellamy's face. She was as composed and self-assured as always and had wasted no time laying claim to the discovery. She'd called it "our" time capsule. Olivia studied Pastor Jeffries to see if he seemed bothered by Bellamy's taking charge, but his face was a mask of calm. He was either hiding his true feelings or was no longer frightened.

"I'm sorry I rushed out before," he said to Olivia and Michel. "I decided that we needed an expert on hand before we examined such important artifacts. It was self-centered of me to open the time capsule in the first place." He smiled sheepishly. "Mrs. Drummond and I have agreed that we should gather a quorum of church and historical society trustees before we reveal the contents."

"One of my volunteers is sending a group e-mail as we speak," Bellamy chimed in. "I've asked people to congregate this evening. These items have waited long enough to see that light of day." She studied the box with a proprietary air. "We could create a special display just in time for the Secret Garden Party. Wouldn't that be wonderful?" She directed her question at Olivia.

"It would," Olivia agreed and couldn't help but admire

Bellamy Drummond's shrewdness. The historical society president knew that the time capsule would have curiosity seekers lining up in droves, and if she could capitalize on their interest by making them buy pricey garden party tickets, then the annual fund-raiser would be a smashing success. "It fits right in with the party's scavenger hunt theme. You could have the guests locate clues throughout the house and grounds relating to objects in the time capsule."

"Precisely what I was thinking!" Bellamy beamed at Olivia. Suddenly, the front doors opened, flooding the threshold with afternoon sunshine. "Here comes the cavalry," Bellamy said. "Tread carefully, ladies."

A woman carrying a white tablecloth and a roll of duct tape picked her way over the construction debris, scowling as plaster dust coated her designer heels. A younger, heavyset woman wearing jeans and a loose T-shirt followed behind. She clumsily trod over chunks of mortar and kicked a bent nail aside with the toe of her sneaker. Watching her, Olivia realized that she bore a close resemblance to Bellamy.

"We're going to secure the time capsule until this evening," Bellamy informed the volunteers. "Whenever you're ready, Melinda."

The slim, well-dressed woman hesitated for a moment. She held out her manicured hands and stared at the dusty box in distaste, but finally managed to drape the tablecloth over the box. Stooping awkwardly, she affixed the end of the tape to the tablecloth and began to wind it around the box.

"Jon, could you and Stella lift up one end at a time? Melinda can't get the tape under and over the box unless it's off the ground."

Olivia shot Michel a befuddled glance as the pastor and the younger woman struggled to raise the box high enough for Melinda to pass the duct tape under it three times.

"It looks like you're preparing an Egyptian mummy for burial. Did gold bars or rare diamonds number among the items in the time capsule?" Olivia joked, her gaze fixed on the pastor.

Easing the box down, he flushed. "We're not doing this to protect the contents but to make sure the unveiling is official. Everyone will see what's inside at the same—"

"I'm sure the original trustees would have wanted us to follow proper protocol," Bellamy interjected. "Where should we move it?" she asked Pastor Jeffries. "We need a clean place with a sturdy counter and good lighting."

"The kitchen would be best," the pastor said. "But let me have the workmen carry it. It's too heavy for your daughter."

Bellamy eyed Stella with ill-concealed disapproval. "Very well. Stella, you and Melinda can go back to your office work." She turned to Olivia and Michel. "Since you're here, may I have a look at the proposed garden party menus?"

"Would you like to sit in a pew?" Olivia asked. "We can talk while Michel and the pastor finish discussing wedding details."

"Certainly," Bellamy said, and the two women moved into the sanctuary.

Bellamy quickly became engrossed in the menus, so Olivia watched Pastor Jeffries lead Kenny and his crew slowly up the center aisle. She was hypnotized by the strange procession. Wrapped in its white shroud, the box looked like a small coffin, and the workmen carried it with mute solemnity, their gazes fixed straight ahead. Michel followed behind, his hands clasped like a penitent parishioner. The men passed through a doorway in the back of the chapel and the door closed with a whisper behind them.

Once again, Olivia's eyes were drawn to the stained glass window of the girl being guided by the angel. For no logical reason, Olivia felt a shiver of dread creep up her spine. Annoyed with herself for being fanciful, she returned her attention to Bellamy Drummond. The men hadn't distracted the older woman at all. She'd taken the pencil from the pew's attendance pad and was using it to make notations in the margin of each menu.

"You've made this a difficult choice," Bellamy said. "But I'll pass on the menu with the lamb entrée. Even though Easter will have come and gone by the evening of garden party, I don't want people thinking about church." She waved a hand to indicate their surroundings. "On this particular night, I'd prefer our attendees to forget about being upright, responsible citizens. I want them to give in to more hedonistic whims."

"In other words, while under the influence of champagne cocktails and glazed Cornish hens stuffed with wild rice and apricots, you'd like them to write generous checks to the historical society," Olivia said.

Bellamy grinned. "Precisely."

Olivia gestured at the menu in Bellamy's right hand. "Is this your first choice?"

"Yes, but I have two concerns. The Asiago-stuffed dates wrapped in bacon sound messy." Bellamy spoke the latter word as if it were a capital offense. "And yet men are fond of their bacon. Could we wrap bacon around something other than dates?"

"Shrimp?" Olivia suggested and Bellamy readily agreed.

"My other concern is the butter lettuce salad. It sounds unsophisticated." She touched the menu with a rounded, petal-pink nail. "Especially when compared to these fingerling potatoes with crème fraîche and caviar."

"The salad is refreshing and chic. With fresh slices of avocado and radish, it's elegant in its simplicity." Olivia smiled. She knew how to speak Bellamy's language. "That's why we're finishing the meal with lemon angel food cupcakes. They're light as air and yet bursting with a rich, complex flavor. Just a kiss of lemon and sugar to create a sense of contentment. You want the guests to feel as if they've just had the most incredible dining experience of their lives. Couple that with aperitifs and a scavenger hunt, and you'll have given them a night to remember. The donations will roll in like waves at high tide."

Bellamy's eyes sparkled. "It'll be both mysterious and romantic. Gardens at twilight, a sumptuous meal, and a candlelight dance beneath the stars. I can control every component but the weather." She curled her fist into a tight ball and shook it. "But so help me, if one drop of rain falls the night of the party, God will have to answer to me." She glanced at the altar and, having delivered her threat, dropped the menus on the pew. "Thank you, Olivia. Now I must be off. There's much to do before tonight's reveal."

Olivia dropped Michel at The Boot Top and then headed to the park with Haviland. She felt restless. It was a sensation she experienced more and more as the months passed. Ever since she'd accepted Sawyer Rawlings's marriage proposal, she'd been feeling uneasy. It wasn't that he was pressuring her. He'd suggested only once or twice that they set a date, but with the onset of spring, Olivia knew that Rawlings would start to wonder why she kept avoiding the subject. After all, they'd already come to terms on what kind of ceremony to have and the fact that Olivia wouldn't change her name. And though Olivia's house would be their prime residence, Rawlings would hang on to his house in town for those times he needed to be close to the station. They'd been living like this for nearly a year, and Olivia was perfectly happy with the status quo.

He's sure to ask me to pick a date. It won't be long now, she thought glumly.

It wasn't that Olivia didn't want to marry him. She did. She was deeply in love with him. But because she loved him, she feared that he'd discover the secret she was keeping from him. Secrets had a way of destroying relationships, and Olivia feared she'd lose Rawlings should he discover hers.

"I won't think about that today," she told Haviland. He dropped a tennis ball at her feet and nudged it toward her with his left paw. She tossed the ball into a copse of pine trees and he dashed off after it, a blur of black racing over the brilliant green grass. Haviland scooped the ball into his mouth, juggled it a bit between his teeth to gain purchase, and then trotted back to her. He was several feet away, his tail wagging and his brown eyes smiling with pleasure, when Olivia's phone rang.

"I can see you! You're on a park bench," whispered Laurel Hobbs theatrically.

"I'm sorry. Do I know you?" Olivia teased and scanned the park for her friend. Ever since Laurel had been promoted to assistant editor of the *Oyster Bay Gazette*, she'd been too busy to do much socializing.

"Come on, it hasn't been that long," Laurel protested. "Don't you want to know where I am?"

Olivia looked around the crowded park again. Mothers with strollers gathered near the playground, old men read newspapers or dozed on the benches, couples stretched out on picnic blankets, and dog owners played catch with their companions.

"You're not in the park," Olivia said.

"Nope. I'm sipping coffee and eating a buttered croissant at Bagels 'n' Beans."

Olivia was surprised to hear this. It had been ages since any of the Bayside Book Writers had frequented the café. Ever since the owner, and a good friend of Olivia's, was sent to jail, they'd all lost the taste for bagels. "Why?" Olivia asked.

"Research," was Laurel's cryptic answer. "Care to join me?"

Thinking of the time capsule, Olivia said she'd be right over and whistled for Haviland.

With the poodle at her heel, she crossed the street and

strode over to where six patio tables with striped umbrellas were lined up on the sidewalk.

Laurel sat at the table closest to the front door. A magazine, a notebook, a cell phone, a coffee cup, an empty dessert plate, and crumpled napkins were spread across the metal surface.

"Is this your new office?" Olivia smiled and pulled out a chair.

Casting a furtive glance around, Laurel whispered, "I'm on a stakeout."

Olivia emptied the contents of a water bottle into Haviland's travel bowl and then reached for Laurel's notebook. "Is this where the ring of bagel thieves will strike next?"

Laurel slid the magazine closer to Olivia. "Not exactly."

The cover showed two seamen in royal blue uniforms standing in front of a military cutter named *Diligence*. "Why are you reading a publication written by members of the Coast Guard *for* members of the Coast Guard?"

"Look at page thirty-three. You'll find a fascinating article on drug smuggling and the city of Wilmington."

Complying, Olivia turned to the page. "Wilmington's one of North Carolina's major ports. Is there a connection between the port's illegal drug trade and Oyster Bay?"

Laurel tapped on the magazine. "Just read it."

Though she was eager to tell Laurel about the time capsule, Olivia did as her friend requested. The article focused on the increased smuggling activity along the coastline of North Carolina and outlined how the Coast Guard was partnering with other law enforcement agencies to apprehend the smugglers.

"That must be a major challenge," Olivia mused aloud. "The vessels transporting the drugs range from fishing trawlers to pleasure yachts. It also says that many of the smuggling rings are comprised of young men in their mid to late twenties who—"

"Are college-educated," Laurel interrupted. "We're

talking about kids from good Southern families here. These kids complete a four-year degree with expectations of landing a job with a six-figure salary. When that doesn't happen, a select group of them will move to a small town on the Atlantic coast and go into the drug-trafficking business. North Carolina has over three hundred miles of coastline and hundreds of small towns with harbors and docks, Oyster Bay included."

Olivia turned back to the magazine's cover image. "Our little Coast Guard station could never keep track of all the boats coming in and out of our harbor."

"That's right." Laurel nodded vigorously, her high ponytail bouncing as if to emphasize her excitement. "Tell me something else: What was this place like when Wheeler ran it? Describe his clientele."

Perplexed, Olivia said, "For the most part, they were locals grabbing coffee and a bagel before heading to work. Later in the morning, there'd be some tourist traffic."

Laurel leaned closer, still speaking in a hushed tone. "The locals were a diverse group too. A dockhand might be waiting in line behind a banker. The tourists usually had sunburns or kids in tow. And at this time of the year, spring breakers nursing hangovers would appear shortly after noon."

"Are you here because Bagels 'n' Beans is attracting a different sort of patron these days?" Olivia glanced at her watch. "When Wheeler ran this place, it closed at three every day. Even when the business passed to his son, Ray kept the same hours. It's almost my cocktail time and the open sign is still lit."

"One of several major changes," Laurel said. "Ever since Ray Hatcher sold the place, the décor's changed, the music's gotten louder, and the bagels are shipped in frozen. All of this has happened over the past year."

Olivia tried to remember who'd bought the eatery, but the sale had warranted only a few lines in the *Gazette*. "Go on."

"Bagels 'n' Beans is now open until ten at night. You can have a lackluster sub sandwich and a beer for supper. The manager, Grady, looks like he's twelve and the majority of his customers don't seem much older. Go in and order something. You'll see what I mean. But don't talk to Millay. She's flirting with some of the regulars in hopes of gaining their trust."

Intrigued, Olivia told Haviland to stay and then entered the bagel shop. She got in line behind a lanky kid carrying a skateboard who was in the middle of ordering an Italian sub. While he deliberated over whether to add Doritos or Sun Chips to his meal, Olivia scanned the room.

Everywhere she looked, she saw young men dressed in board shorts, faded T-shirts, and boat shoes. Their sun-kissed hair was pushed back off their foreheads with the help of mirrored aviator glasses. All of these men, who were little more than boys in Olivia's eyes, were tanned and toned. Clean and polished. Theirs was the relaxed, self-assured air of the privileged, and Olivia only had to catch glimpses of their watches, shoes, and perfect dental work to know that these kids were accustomed to the good life. There were a few women in the café too, but for the most part, the men ignored them.

A real boys' club, Olivia thought and then spotted Millay at a corner table. The blunt ends of her short black hair were dyed an electric blue and her fingernails were painted the same color. Her knee-high leather boots were propped on a chair, providing everyone with a clear view of her shapely legs, and her white *Sons of Anarchy* T-shirt was stretched tight over a black bra. Chewing on a straw, she flashed Olivia a nearly imperceptible grin and then turned back to her audience of three men and said something in a bored monotone. Though Olivia knew that Millay was playing a part, she wasn't sure what that part was. But since Millay had spent her school years being bullied and belittled by the rich and preppy crowd, Olivia suspected she'd been given an opportunity to exact revenge on their kind and was enjoying every second of it.

"What can I get you?" the boy behind the counter asked, his eyes flicking over Olivia with disinterest.

Olivia tried not to grimace. She wouldn't feed the deli meat that had gone into the previous customer's Italian sub to a stray dog. The salami was brown, the ham was wilted, and the pepperoni was an odd pinkish hue. "Do you have any croissants?"

The young man shook his head and Olivia leaned forward to examine the remnants of the day's bagels. "A sesame bagel with peanut butter," she said and laid money on the counter. "No need to toast it. And it's to go."

Having slapped a thin layer of peanut butter on the bottom half of the sliced bagel, the young man dropped it into a bag and unceremoniously dumped it on the counter. He handed Olivia her change with a stiff "have a good one" and picked up his cell phone. After a few seconds of scrolling, he glanced up and caught the eye of a boy sitting near the front door. Pointing at his phone, he raised his eyebrows in question and a silent message passed between the two young men. Olivia paused by the condiment bar, but before she could scrutinize the second twentysomething more closely, he abruptly exited the café.

Olivia went outside to rejoin Laurel. Gesturing at the empty plate on the table, she said, "How could you possibly eat anything from this place?"

Laurel laughed. "I told you I was eating a warm, buttery croissant and that was true. I heated it in the microwave and slathered it with butter. I used twenty packets and it still tasted like tire rubber." She nodded at the bag in Olivia's hand. "What did you get?"

"A bagel for the birds." Olivia stroked Haviland's head. "I'm sorry, Captain, but there's nothing edible in there. On the bright side, I'm likely to rid Oyster Bay of its pigeon problem using this single bagel."

Laurel reached across the table and squeezed Olivia's arm. "Oh, I've missed you. We haven't seen nearly enough of each other since Harris left."

"I know. I'm so glad that he's returning home tomorrow. And even gladder that he's coming back to stay."

"Will you tell him what's happened to the Bayside Book Writers since he relocated to Texas?"

Olivia frowned. "You mean, how we've only met two times, or that I haven't added a single word to my horrid historical fiction? Or how Rawlings keeps saying that he needs to conduct more research before proceeding with his book or how you're far too busy writing articles to pen your women's fiction novel?"

"At least Millay makes us look good," Laurel said brightly. "Imagine landing a three-book deal from Penguin Random House! By September, her first YA novel will be published. I wonder if she wakes up every morning and pinches herself."

"That's not her style," Olivia said. "Actually, I think she's a bit worried. She sent me a text a few weeks ago saying she was way behind deadline for the next book in the series."

Laurel sighed. "We talked about that earlier today. She's feeling completely uninspired and I know exactly how she feels. I've felt totally flat for the past few months. That is, until I came across this Coast Guard article. Something about this"—she waved at the café's façade—"has my blood pulsing again. And having Millay involved . . . well, it's like how things used to be when the Bayside Book Writers were together. When we were writing, socializing, and balancing the scales of justice."

Though Olivia understood exactly what Laurel meant, a surge of inexplicable anger swept over her. "Hasn't there been enough drama? Haven't we lost enough? I hate sitting at this café. I hate the fact that the man I cared about isn't behind the counter. I hate that when I visit Through the

Wardrobe to buy books, Flynn isn't offering me a cup of his horrible coffee. This whole damned town is haunted."

Responding to Olivia's agitation, Haviland nudged her leg with his nose. She scratched him behind the ears and whispered soothingly to him.

"I didn't mean to bring up bad memories." Laurel looked stricken. "I just want us to be like we used to be. We haven't healed since Harris left. Instead, we drifted away from one another like boats cut loose from their moorings." Her eyes grew moist. "I don't want us to lose anything else. I really need you guys. I love my family and my job. But you, Millay, Rawlings, and Harris are my friends. I can be myself with all of you. Do you know how rare that is? How wonderful?"

Olivia immediately regretted her outburst. "I do," she said softly. "And I miss the way we were too. I also think you could be on to something here. I don't know if it's drugs or another illegal activity, but the whole café is filled with Abercrombie poster boys. They have a smug, authoritative air about them, like Mafia men hanging out at their favorite Italian restaurant. You'll have to let me know what Millay discovers."

Laurel grinned. "They won't be able to resist her. She's like an exotic bird surrounded by sparrows." Suddenly, her expression turned anxious. "Speaking of men becoming smitten with Millay, how do you think it'll be between her and Harris when they meet again?"

"We'll find out over dinner tomorrow night," Olivia said. "It's difficult to know how much the breakup affected Millay, but Harris Williams is the kind of guy who only falls in love once in his life."

"For his sake, I hope that's not true. In any event, I'm sure the reunion of the Bayside Book Writers will be a happy affair." She checked her watch and frowned. "I need to run. Was there something you wanted to talk about?"

Olivia took out her phone and showed Laurel the photograph of the inventory and contributor list from the time capsule.

"What am I looking at?" Laurel asked.

"The beginning of an interesting article," Olivia said and then recalled the look of fear on Pastor Jeffries's face. "Though I have a strange feeling that it could be much more than that. Today, three workmen found an old box buried in the wall of the First Presbyterian Church. As you can see from the list, this time capsule contains fascinating objects from Oyster Bay's past, but I think something else escaped when the box lid was removed. Something shameful. Or possibly dangerous."

"Like what?"

Olivia stared out across the park to where the tip of the church steeple was just visible over the tree line. It looked like a black spear against the pale horizon, stretching up and up as if intending to pierce the clouds. Olivia glanced back at Laurel and said, "I think a secret got out."

"A secret," Laurel repeated breathlessly.

The women fell silent, and in the silence, the word hung between them like a spider dangling from a long, invisible thread.

Chapter 3

In the ancient recipe, the three antidotes for dullness or boredom are sleep, drink, and travel. It is rather feeble. From sleep you wake up, from drink you become sober, and from travel you come home again. And then where are you?

—D. H. LAWRENCE

Olivia sat in a plastic chair in the waiting area just outside the Delta terminal, her eyes locked on the automatic doors adjacent to the security gate. She watched emotional reunions between soldiers and their families, parents and children, and lovers. The relationship Olivia and Harris shared didn't fall into any of these categories. Harris was a friend and fellow author. She trusted and loved him like a brother.

Of course, that was before he'd gone to work in Texas. When Harris had lived in Oyster Bay, Olivia knew what was happening in his life. But she hadn't seen him since last summer, and aside from the occasional e-mail, he didn't have much to say to the Bayside Book Writers. His lack of communication made Olivia anxious. She didn't know what to expect when Harris walked through those doors. Would their reunion be stiff and uncomfortable, or would they fall back into their old roles? Could she continue treating him like a younger brother and would he still try to make her laugh?

Olivia, who was not a fan of change, hoped so.

It was easy to spot Harris as he stepped through the wide doorway. Tall and thin with a mass of wavy ginger hair, he had intelligent eyes and an impish grin—a grown-up Peter Pan. Olivia smiled when she saw him stop to help an elderly woman who was having trouble expanding the handle of her rollaway bag. Harris gave the handle a forceful tug, and it shot upward with a click. The woman thanked him and patted his bicep, which was more pronounced than Olivia remembered. Harris had always been lanky and lean, but he'd bulked up over the past nine months.

He looks good, Olivia thought. *He was a boy when he left for Texas, but he's come home a man.*

Olivia waved and was relieved to see Harris's face break out into a broad smile. Reaching her in three strides, he lifted her in his arms and swung her around in a tight circle.

"I missed you!" he declared after setting her down.

Olivia laughed. "I think I just flashed all the passengers from the Cleveland flight."

"Then that was probably the highlight of their day." Harris threaded Olivia's arm through his. "Let's fight for a prime spot around the luggage carousel."

Pleased to find that Harris hadn't lost his playfulness, Olivia squeezed beside him on the down escalator. "You've gotten buff," she said.

Harris shrugged. "Some of my coworkers convinced me to join a gym. I was sitting in front of the computer more than ever and my back and shoulders were starting to really bother me. Going back to my apartment every night and flopping on the sofa wasn't helping either. One day, I told this guy on my project team that I felt like an eighty-year-old, and he invited me to work out with him. Because my social calendar was totally blank, I agreed." He gestured around the terminal. "The gym looked like an airplane hangar. Seriously. It had metal walls, rubber flooring, and tons of Olympic weights. There were pipes to hang from, rings to swing from, and all kinds of scary-looking stuff. I wanted to run away, but the other guy drove me there so I was stuck."

"What happened?"

"It was crazy. Everyone does the same workout at the same time. Instead of being on your own, you work with a partner or in a small group. The idea is that you psych each other up." Harris and Olivia stepped off the escalator and joined the crowd clustered around a moving carousel. "People I'd never met before were cheering me on. It was such a rush, and it made me feel like I was capable of anything. I guess I became a bit of an addict after that first workout."

Olivia guessed that there might have been other motivational factors. "Were most of the fitness junkies your age?"

"Yeah, but not all. Seriously, Olivia, there was this one woman in her mid-forties who could kick my ass any day of the week. She reminded me of you." Harris gazed at the pieces of luggage drifting by. "She was tough as nails, but she never let me quit. She was a great partner."

Olivia knew Harris was paying her a compliment, but she didn't like the idea of being replaced, no matter how temporarily. "Did your social calendar fill up after you joined the gym?"

"Definitely. A group of us had work and the gym in common, and we eventually got together for pizza and Xbox marathons too. We went to clubs a few times, but most of us are nerds. We prefer our excitement to be in pixelated form. There's my bag!" Harris gently inserted himself between a pair of businessmen studying their cell phone screens and grabbed a behemoth of a suitcase from the carousel.

"I thought you shipped most of your stuff to your house," Olivia said when he'd set the bag down with a heavy thud.

"I did. But these are very important souvenirs. No peeking either," he warned.

Olivia picked up Harris's backpack and the two of them chatted amiably on the way to the Range Rover. As soon as Olivia unlocked the doors, Harris jumped into the backseat to say hello to Haviland. After shaking his paw, ruffling his fur, and accepting several poodle kisses, Harris said, "I brought you some Texas taffy, Captain. If Olivia says it's okay, you can chew on this strip of beef jerky all the way to Oyster Bay." Reaching into the outer pocket of his suitcase, he pulled out a shrink-wrapped package and showed it to Olivia. "It's all-natural. Can he have it?"

Olivia gave Haviland an indulgent smile. "Be my guest. It's not like I mind having the seat covered in drool."

"I know you don't," Harris said. He gave Haviland his treat and then loaded his suitcase into the car. It wasn't until Olivia had exited the airport and was heading east on the interstate that he spoke again. "How is everybody?" he asked. "Have you guys been writing up a storm?" Though his tone was casual, Olivia couldn't help but wonder if Harris was nervous about returning to where his heart had been broken.

"Yesterday, Laurel compared us to boats cut loose from their moorings," she said. "It's an apt description for our group. We stopped meeting, Harris. And because we stopped meeting, we stopped writing."

Harris looked out the window, and Olivia noticed that he was clenching his jaw. "Is it my fault?" he asked in a low voice. "Did I ruin things for everyone?"

Olivia punched him in the arm. It was like hitting a chunk of stone. "Don't be such an egomaniac. We screwed up all by ourselves." She paused, searching for the right words. "At first, it just felt weird not having you at our weekly meeting. We tried to address our sense of discomfort by getting together at the library or at various restaurants. Anywhere but the lighthouse keeper's cottage. However, when we changed venues, we started coming up with reasons why we couldn't attend. Millay would have to be at Fish Nets earlier than usual or Laurel's sitter would cancel. Rawlings was needed at the station and I had my own array of excuses. I'd rather stay home and clip Haviland's nails than admit that not only had I made zero progress on my book, but that I hated the drivel I'd written over the past two years so much that I wanted to toss the entire manuscript in the ocean."

Harris gaped. "But you wrote over two hundred pages . . ." He let his protest die away and passed his hands slowly over his face. "Confession time. I looked at my sci-fi novel exactly once. I don't know if it was because I was in a different environment, but it sounded juvenile. I decided I wasn't a real writer. I was just pretending to be one."

"We're all writers, Harris. We lack discipline, not talent. Our problem is that none of us has the drive to finish and polish a manuscript and submit it to a literary agent."

"Except Millay."

Olivia nodded. "True. But she has her own set of challenges. I'm sure she'll tell you about them tonight."

Brightening, Harris said, "I can't wait to eat at The Bayside Crab House again. Is it warm enough to sit outside?"

"We have heat lamps on the upper deck. Do you want me to reserve a table?"

"That would be great." Harris's gaze turned distant. "I miss the sight of the harbor. You can see billions of stars in Texas, but there's something magical about the stars reflecting in the water. It feels like the tide will bring them right to your feet if you stand still long enough." He shook his head. "Listen to me. Do I sound like one of the chief's favorite poets or what?"

"You sound like a man talking about his home, and that's poetry to my ears." Olivia stared out at the stretch of flat highway before her. After several minutes of silence, she added, "I've learned that people define our sense of home too. The ocean and the lighthouse, the beach and the shops downtown are how we picture Oyster Bay, but it wouldn't really be my home without Hudson and his family, Dixie and Grumpy, Michel and Shelley, and Rawlings, you, Millay, and Laurel. It would just be another dot on a map."

"But people say you can never come home again—that even if the place doesn't change, you do." Harris's voice was even, but his eyes betrayed his anxiety.

"They're wrong," Olivia said. "Even if you change, you can still belong. I left for decades, but the moment I walked on the sand in front of the lighthouse, I knew I'd never leave again." She glanced at Harris, willing him to believe her. "I traveled all over the world looking for home when it was here all along. Home was waiting inside a handful of precious people, some of whom are now waiting for you."

Harris released a pent-up breath and smiled. "Maybe you should forget about Egypt and write about Oyster Bay. Your past, present, and future are all tied to the town and its people. They always say to write what you know."

The truth of Harris's suggestion hit Olivia full force. No wonder she'd never felt truly connected to a concubine from nineteenth-dynasty Egypt. Kamila was and would always be a cardboard character. Meanwhile, Olivia was surrounded by fascinating characters. Rich and complex characters. A montage of faces paraded through her mind. Shrimpers with weathered skin and sea-sharp eyes, farmers in denim overalls and dust-covered baseball caps, soft-voiced librarians, fast-talking waitresses, sunburnt tourists—all of them made up the story she'd been born to tell.

You're already inspiring us, already stitching us back together, Olivia thought and shot Harris a tender glance.

And then she pressed down on the gas pedal, eager to leave the highway and hit the two-lane road winding northeast along the coast. She could sense Harris drinking in the scenery—the swamps and fields, gated subdivisions and dilapidated tobacco barns, roadside fruit stands and souvenir shops. And when he cracked his window and leaned forward with his eyes closed, she knew he was breathing the first hints of salt-tinged air. Smiling, Olivia took the exit for Oyster Bay and then put down her own window.

* * *

That evening, the Bayside Book Writers shared platters of crab legs and pitchers of cold beer. It was as if they'd never been apart. They laughed, swapped anecdotes, and made a mess with their claw crackers and bowls of melted butter. Being the only party dining al fresco, they had the stars and the twinkling mast lights of the boats moored in the harbor to themselves.

Olivia was relieved to see that there was no tension between Harris and Millay. She teased him and he teased her back, and they seemed comfortable with each other. In fact, the entire group was reinvigorated by Harris's presence. They all talked too loudly and overindulged on food and drink. Olivia felt ridiculously giddy, as if she'd had too much champagne and was so filled with bubbles that she might rise out of her chair and float to the moon.

"You look beautiful tonight," Rawlings whispered in her ear as the waitstaff cleared their table.

She touched his knee under the table. "Harris gave me an incredible idea in the car. I'm going to ditch my novel and start a new one." When he frowned in concern, she said, "No, it's a good thing. I know exactly what to write. The words are practically singing in my head."

Rawlings raised his bottle of beer and toasted Harris. "Well, Clark Kent, you've truly turned into Superman."

Millay raised the edge of the checkered tablecloth. "I don't see any red rubber boots under here."

"I'll wear them to our next writers' club meeting. I take it the rest of you will be there." Harris raised his brows in a question.

"We'll be there," Olivia said, and Laurel whooped and clapped, her ponytail bouncing.

"You can take the pompoms away from the cheerleader . . ." Millay began and everyone laughed.

"Mock me and I won't tell you about last night's time

capsule reveal," Laurel said. Her eyes shone with bright pinpoints of light, and Olivia sensed that her friend was a little tipsy.

Rawlings raised his hands in surrender. "You win. I want to know everything."

"How did you get invited to the unveiling?" Olivia asked, incredulous.

"Believe it or not, Steve's a trustee. They needed him or they wouldn't have a quorum. Naturally, I insisted on going along. I think Bellamy Drummond had half a mind to kick me out until I promised her free press on the Secret Garden Party in exchange for letting me stay."

Millay flicked her napkin at Laurel. "Smooth move, Brenda Starr."

Laurel went on to describe the contents of the box. "My favorites were household items like the canned goods," she said. "The lady who donated them, a Mrs. Margaret Wilson, included a note detailing her involvement with Uncle Sam's Saturday Service League." In her state of tipsiness, Laurel slurred the *S*'s together. "This group was established to inspire people across the state to grow and preserve more food. It was something women could do to assist in the war effort. Mrs. Wilson enclosed a photo that showed African-American women working alongside white women. How cool is that? I mean, agricultural clubs like this used to be an all-boys outfit until women of all colors and creeds were allowed to join. Thanks to their efforts, American troops were fed throughout the conflict, and these groups continued to send food to the people of postwar Europe. I already have several article ideas from Mrs. Wilson's contribution alone."

"Fascinating." Millay stretched her mouth into a mock yawn.

Harris tried to toss an ice cube into her open maw but missed.

Ignoring them both, Laurel went on to describe other objects in the time capsule. From a cloche hat to a vintage telephone, there were plenty of everyday items, but there were also genuine treasures. "Someone bequeathed a set of valuable Shakespeare plays to the Drama Society of Oyster Bay."

"Does that still exist?" Rawlings asked.

"No, it folded ten years after the capsule was buried," Laurel said. "Pastor Jeffries wants to sell the books to fund the repair of the church's stained glass windows, but one of the trustees happens to be a descendant of Willard Campbell, the man who put the books in the time capsule. The contemporary Mr. Campbell believes that the books should be returned to his family."

Olivia released an exasperated sigh. "When the original trustees packed that box, I doubt they pictured future generations squabbling over its contents."

"Unfortunately, tensions continued to rise as the evening progressed," Laurel said. "A portrait of a girl named Eleanor Scott was another item of value. The painting was donated by Eleanor's son and daughter-in-law, Oliver and Mary Scott. The Scotts wished to have the portrait hung in the Oyster Bay Art Museum. Unfortunately, the art museum became the Maritime Museum in the forties, and any works lacking a nautical theme were sold to the North Carolina Museum of Art in 1947. As a result, the current Mr. and Mrs. Scott want to keep the portrait, but Bellamy Drummond argued that it should be exhibited in the historical society."

"What did the Scotts say to that?" Harris asked.

Pressing her fingertips to her temples, Laurel groaned. "I think they agreed to a long-term loan, but I really can't remember. There was so much to take in. The trustees took turns unwrapping a time capsule object, and everyone was shouting and craning their necks for a look. It was like a Christmas morning. But I'm sure Bellamy Drummond got her way. She's a bit of a dragon lady."

"But she'll be your best friend after you pimp the garden party," Olivia said. "Did she dictate the article for you?"

"Pretty much. She also suggested I do a piece on how the Drummond family has impacted Oyster Bay history. I was glad to oblige. It'll give me an excuse to see the inside of their house, the famed White Columns." Laurel did a little dance in her chair. "I can't wait for the party! It's not often that we get all dolled up and are invited to wander through people's gardens, enjoy a sit-down dinner, and then dance by candlelight. It sounds incredibly romantic."

Rawlings turned to Olivia. "The Boot Top's catering this event, right? This is the reason I'll have to finally pick up my suit from the dry cleaners."

Olivia plucked at the sleeve of his Hawaiian shirt, which featured a pattern of hibiscus flowers and pineapples, and frowned. "You can't come in this, that's for sure. Maybe you should buy a tux. It could serve double duty."

Understanding her meaning, Rawlings smiled. "I'd wear it the first time as your date and the second time as your husband."

Olivia's heart fluttered at the word "husband." It seemed such a foreign concept that Olivia Limoges, longtime bachelorette and headstrong entrepreneur, was on the verge of taking a husband. A spouse. A mate for life. Feeling uncomfortably warm all of a sudden, she focused her attention on Laurel again. "What was in the copper box? It's the only thing I could see when I peeked under the state flag. Everything else was wrapped in brown paper and tied with twine."

Laurel stared at her beer bottle in confusion. "I have no clue what you're talking about. There was no copper box in the time capsule."

Olivia dug out her phone. "Of course there was. It must be on this inventory list." She began to scroll through the items, recognizing most of them from Laurel's descriptions.

"Don't strain your eyes," Laurel said. "I have printouts in my bag. I figured you'd all be curious about what I saw." She distributed a typed sheet to everyone at the table.

"It's crazy to think that the phrase 'set of eight volumes' ended up being a rare collection of Shakespeare plays," Harris said, studying his paper. "I'd love to know what they're worth."

"No need. Mr. Campbell did a Google search on the spot," Laurel said. "The last set sold at auction for over twenty grand."

Millay whistled. "The gloves are off. What's this Mr. Campbell look like? Could he take Pastor Jeffries if it came down to a duel?"

Harris laughed. "That would give the term 'Bible thumper' a whole new meaning."

Olivia felt compelled to defend the pastor's cause. "I'd be in the pastor's corner. Those stained glass windows are worth saving."

Rawlings arched a brow. "What brought you to the church? Are you making plans for us?"

Olivia squirmed. "Michel and Shelley will marry there. Michel had to drop off the wedding program and I needed to meet with Bellamy, who was just next door, so we drove together. That's why we were around when the time capsule was first discovered."

"I hope I'm invited. A wedding of two chefs? Yum." Harris rubbed his flat stomach. "Imagine the feasting!"

"Aren't you worried about polluting the temple that your body has become?" Millay scoffed.

Harris shook his head. "Nah. I can eat whatever I want. I just have to put more effort into my next workout, which is cool with me. Strength training has become a good way for me to burn off stress."

"That's why I paint," Rawlings said.

Over the past year, he'd been experimenting with watercolor, producing what Olivia believed to be his best work yet. For years, he'd hung his finished landscapes on the walls of Bagels 'n' Beans and had given Wheeler a commission for each sale, but after the café changed hands, the paintings had slowly been piling up in the chief's garage. When Olivia asked what he meant to do with them, Rawlings would mumble something about selling them online. However, Olivia knew that the act of creation was more important to Rawlings than making a profit off the finished product. And she was relieved that, although he'd lost the desire to work on his novel, his artistic muse hadn't completely abandoned him.

While Rawlings and Harris discussed their hobbies, Olivia reviewed the time capsule inventory. The copper box wasn't listed, and its absence only increased her curiosity.

"I wish I'd taken a picture of that box," she grumbled to herself.

Millay caught her words. "Do you think someone took it?"

"I don't know," Olivia said. "It was big enough to hold a pair of Harris's shoes." She returned to the moment when Bellamy first saw the time capsule. She hadn't even peeked inside. "Bellamy Drummond spoke with such conviction about doing things properly, and yet that copper box was obviously removed *before* the trustees were gathered for the official time capsule reveal. But why?"

Laurel, who'd been listening to the conversation between Rawlings and Harris, suddenly realized that a more interesting topic had been raised at the other end of the table. Scooting her chair closer, she whispered, "Do you think the box has something to do with the feeling you had when the time capsule was discovered? Or with the fear you saw on Pastor Jeffries's face?"

"He only saw the inventory list and the names of the people who'd contributed items, so if he was scared, it had nothing to do with the copper box," Olivia said. "Maybe he wasn't frightened. Maybe the light was just playing tricks on me."

Millay snorted. "I don't buy that for a second. After all we've been through, we can recognize fear. A shift happens. It's like a cold eddy of air swirls around the person. A shadow. It darkens their eyes for a second, and then it's gone again."

Olivia stared at her. "That's exactly what it was like. And

it happened so quickly that, in hindsight, it's easy to doubt what I saw. But now that I know an item has been taken from the time capsule, I have to wonder what happened to it. And what was placed inside for someone in the future to find."

Olivia fell silent. She watched the boats bob in the gentle current and heard the water lap against the dock pilings. The town was already filling with tourists, but the locals still had a few more weeks before the rush began, and it was pleasant to be the only people on the restaurant's deck. Olivia didn't want to ruin their jovial party by fixating on another man's fears or a missing box. She was about to change the subject when Laurel put a hand on her arm.

"That time capsule belongs to everyone. It's our history," she said very softly. "No one has the right to edit what the people from the past wanted us to see. We should pay a visit to the historical society. Since the contents are going on display in two weeks, Bellamy Drummond and her staff will be working round the clock conducting research, writing exhibit cards, and preparing special cases in time for the garden party. I can be there to document their labor and you—"

"Can offer to help," Olivia said. "Not only would I be glad to lend a hand, but I know of someone else who's particularly adept at research."

All three women turned to look at Harris.

He paused mid-sentence. "Okay, something's up at the female end of the table. I can tell because your eyes are boring holes into my cranium. What kind of diabolical scheme are you ladies cooking up?"

"The kind that involves the Internet, a few white lies, and the two of us poking around where we don't belong," Olivia said.

Harris leaned back in his chair and cradled his neck in his hands. Lifting his face to the star-pocked sky, he smiled in contentment. "It's so good to be home."

Chapter 4

One cannot collect all the beautiful shells on the beach. One can collect only a few, and they are more beautiful if they are few.

—ANNE MORROW LINDBERGH

Olivia intended to volunteer at the historical society, but not immediately. She already had plans for the following day, and they were more important than a missing copper box or a curious feeling that the time capsule wasn't all that it seemed.

"Are you ready?" Rawlings asked the next morning. Dressed in an old UNC sweatshirt and shorts, he stood in the kitchen, eating a piece of toast over the sink.

Olivia examined the items on the counter. There were water bottles, tubes of sunscreen, towels, juice boxes, a travel-sized first-aid kit, and four tangerines. "Looks good."

"The blanket, umbrella, and chairs are in the car." Rawlings chewed his toast and frowned. "Do we need more food? Maybe we should bring those Goldfish crackers Anders loves. What's Caitlyn into these days?"

"Something called fruit tape," Olivia said. "I'm not exactly sure what it's made of, but she said it's sweet." Stepping up to Rawlings, she wrapped her arms around his neck. Instead of kissing him, she took a bite of his toast.

"Thief," he said, pushing her away. "Make your own."

She smiled and grabbed the rest of his piece. "Yours always tastes better."

"That's because I use enough butter to clog every artery in my body. I'll have to chase the kids up and down the beach to work off the bacon I just ate." He gestured at the empty plate on the table. "I suspect Haviland stole a strip while I wasn't looking. He swallowed it whole and then gave me this blank look of mock innocence. I've seen that expression on my fair share of criminals, but never on a dog."

Laughing, Olivia looked around for her poodle. "Where is he?"

"Waiting by the car. The second he saw the beach chairs, he started dancing in excitement. I was trying to read the *Gazette*, but all I heard was the click, click, click of his nails on the hardwood."

Olivia grinned. Haviland loved the beach, and he liked it even better with children to play with and gulls to chase. "I can see that I won't be lingering over my coffee this morning," she said. "Let me fill a travel mug and then we'll pick up the kids." After polishing off Rawlings's toast, she leaned into him, her lips brushing his rough cheek. "Thanks for coming with me. I can handle one pint-sized troll at a time, but two?" She shivered. "Unthinkable."

"You're crazy about those kids." Rawlings brushed a strand of hair off her forehead.

"Yes, I adore them, but I don't enjoy being responsible for their safety and well-being. I prefer to swoop in with gifts, ooh and aah over the latest artwork on the fridge, and then leave. It's easy to be the doting aunt."

Rawlings grunted. "You're so full of it. You'd lay down your life for them and we both know it. Now fill your thermos and pack a bag. It's time to go."

"Yes, Chief!" Olivia saluted him, grabbed a banana from the fruit bowl, shoved the supplies into a beach tote, and hurried outside to cover Haviland's black nose with good morning kisses. Rawlings finished loading the car and the trio set off.

This is what I always wanted, Olivia thought as they headed into town. *This quiet happiness. Morning after morning of breakfasts, cups of coffee, and making plans for the day. So why can't I just set a date and speak a vow?*

But when she pulled into her half brother's driveway, a knot formed in her throat. Hudson, the taciturn and loyal man she'd met for the first time a few years ago, was her only family. Hudson, his wife, Kim, and their two children, Caitlyn and Anders, had given Olivia something she'd never had before. And though Olivia loved them, she didn't share their blood. Olivia knew this for sure because over the summer, she'd met her real father. Charles Wade, the twin brother of the man who'd raised her, had shown up in Oyster Bay and shattered everything Olivia had believed to be true about her past.

Olivia told no one what she'd learned. Charles Wade flew back to New York, and Olivia did her best to forget him. She didn't want to lose the family she'd longed for her entire life. She loved being asked to holiday dinners and school plays. She loved belonging to them. The person she didn't want to belong to was Charles Wade. He was an ambitious egomaniac who'd mistreated Olivia's mother and despised Oyster Bay. Considering his feelings about the town, Olivia was stunned to learn that he'd bought Flynn McNulty's bookstore, Through the Wardrobe. Though Olivia couldn't understand why her father purchased a business in a town he hated, she didn't pursue the subject with him. She wanted to deny their connection by pretending he didn't exist.

At the sound of a child's squeal, Olivia cut the engine and got out of the car. Her niece and nephew were on the front porch, plastic pails and shovels in their hands. Their faces were glowing with anticipation.

Looking up at them from the bottom of the steps, Olivia cried, "Who's ready for the beach?"

The children bounced up and down. "Me! Me!"

"The water's a bit chilly, but Anders can play in the shallows," Olivia told Kim, who'd just finished braiding Caitlyn's hair. Olivia glanced at her niece. "I bet some amazing seashells washed ashore during last night's storm."

Caitlyn's eyes widened. "Really? Because I need lots of unbroken ones."

"Caitlyn used her allowance to buy a frame kit," Kim explained. "I told her the shells for the frame don't have to be perfect, but she doesn't want them to be cracked or chipped."

Olivia put a hand on Caitlyn's head. Her silky brown hair smelled of oranges. "I'm sure we'll find some beauties," Olivia told her niece. "But the imperfect ones you find are still better than the shells for sale in the souvenir shops. Those aren't even from North Carolina. They're shipped in from another country."

"I don't want those," Caitlyn said firmly. "If I use them to listen to the ocean, it might not be *my* ocean."

Olivia grinned. "That's right. Seeing as you were born on Ocracoke Island, the Atlantic is a part of you. You have salt water running through your veins."

"Mom says I swim like a fish too." Caitlyn skipped to the Range Rover, climbed in with Haviland, and gave him a hug.

"Poodle!" Anders cried, spying Haviland through the open door. He toddled to the car, his chubby legs moving as fast as they could, his bright yellow pail swinging back and forth like a conductor's lantern.

Rawlings made sure Caitlyn was in her booster seat before deftly buckling Anders into his car seat. Kim handed her son his plastic shovel, closed the car door, and smiled at Olivia. "I can't tell you how much I appreciate this. Hudson and I haven't had a breakfast date since before Caitlyn was born. After we eat, we're going car shopping. My minivan is about to breathe its last."

"Can I take the kids to Grumpy's for lunch?" Olivia asked. "Caitlyn loves Grumpy's cheeseburger sliders."

"Keep them for lunch *and* dinner. The rest of the month if you want." Kim laughed. "I might actually be able to put a dent in Mount Laundry."

"You and Hudson work too hard," Olivia admonished gently. "You don't have any time to yourselves."

Kim gestured at the house behind her. "This isn't work. This is us building a life together. I never dreamed we'd have it this good so don't pay me a lick of attention when I complain about dust bunnies or the fact that my garage is a fire hazard. Hudson and I wake up every day with money in the bank, jobs we love, great schools for our kids, and you. All this, and we're near the water. What you said about Caitlyn is true for all of us. If I can't look out over a big stretch of ocean once a day, I feel claustrophobic."

"Me too," Olivia agreed. "Let's just hope that the tourists won't feel the need to borrow our stretch of sand this morning. I want Caitlyn to have first dibs on the best shells."

Kim thanked Olivia and Rawlings again, told her children to behave, and went back inside.

Olivia drove to an area of public beach known mostly to locals. It was closer to the fishing docks than to the rental houses and boutique hotels, and there were no chairs or umbrellas for rent. However, the lifeguard stand was staffed year-round, and weather permitting, the sand was raked every morning.

Olivia parked and put a collar on Haviland. Over the past year, she'd trained him to act as a guide for Anders. The toddler would wrap his plump fingers around the collar and walk at Haviland's side, willingly going wherever the poodle led him. Anders would do anything to be near Haviland. Boy and poodle had taken to each other from the moment Anders was born. As soon as Anders became mobile, he'd ignore every person or toy in the room and crawl to wherever Haviland was sitting. Then he'd curl up beside him and coo until he eventually fell asleep. Olivia had dozens of pictures of them napping together.

"While you and Caitlyn hunt for shells, Haviland and I will help Anders make a sand castle," Rawlings said.

The group made their way to a patch of sand near the lifeguard stand. Rawlings said hello to the young man on duty, who immediately stopped twirling his whistle and jumped down from his perch. He insisted on setting up their umbrella and, because no one else was on the beach, gave Rawlings a hand carrying the cooler and chairs from the car.

"Are you abusing your position of power?" Olivia teased Rawlings while applying sunscreen to Anders's face.

"That's Jake Truman. His older brother, Matt, is one of my newest officers, and I think Jake plans to follow in his footsteps," Rawlings explained. "I have to admit that I don't mind having an extra set of eyes on the kids. I don't move as quickly as I used to."

Olivia grinned. "I'd remind you about how you moved last night, but there are young children present."

Caitlyn, who'd already wandered several feet away from the beach blanket, bent over to examine a clamshell. Frowning, she tossed it back onto the sand and then gave Olivia an expectant look.

"I'm coming." Olivia dabbed a final blob of sunscreen on Anders's nose, grabbed a blue plastic pail and her backpack, and joined her niece.

They moved slowly, heading toward the distant pier, where old men liked to gather to fish and smoke in the early morning hours. Caitlyn was very particular about the shells she chose to keep. "The lightning whelks always have holes," she complained. "I want to put one on every corner of the frame, but it'll take forever to find four good ones."

"Maybe," Olivia said, discarding a chipped moon snail shell in favor of an undamaged calico scallop. The shell was a lovely pale pink with ribbons of deep red running across the ridges. "Imagine the journey this shell took to make it here. The way it's been pushed by the current, somersaulting over the ocean floor, never sitting still. Eventually, it ended up in the shallows. And when a big wave crashed during last night's storm, this fragile, beautiful thing was deposited onto the sand. The water retreated, inch by inch, and left it here. A gift for you."

Caitlyn glanced over to where Anders and Rawlings sat just out of reach of the incoming waves. Rawlings was digging a moat while Anders buried his shovel in the sand and waited for Haviland to uncover it with his front paws. She ran her fingertip along the glassy surface of a coquina and said, "Animals used to live in all these shells. It's like we're walking over a million skeletons."

Olivia wasn't surprised by her niece's unusual comment. Caitlyn had always been a sensitive child—a fact her parents attributed to her artistic nature. When Caitlyn wasn't reading, she was painting, drawing, or sculpting clay. Though reserved and pensive, she possessed a quiet confidence that Olivia admired. "If only our bones were this pretty," Olivia said, offering Caitlyn the scallop.

Caitlyn pinched it between her fingers and raised it so that the sun's rays highlighted the pinks and reds. "It looks like an Atomic Fireball mixed with cotton candy."

"Two of my favorites," Olivia said.

They spent the next hour combing the beach for conch shells, shark's eyes, augers, and angelwings. Caitlyn was pleased with what the storm had left behind and was humming by the time they drew close to the pier. "I wish I could find a Scotch Bonnet. I've never found one."

"They're pretty scarce, but we can try again after the next storm. The plaid pattern on the shell would look really nice on your mirror." Olivia unslung her backpack and pointed at the shady sand beneath the pier. "Water break?"

Caitlyn nodded. "I'm hungry too."

"I figured you would be," Olivia said as they stepped out of the sun and under the shelter of the pier. "Fruit roll or cheese crackers?"

"Both," Caitlyn said. Accepting a bottle of water, she

drank half of it in three swallows and then started to unwrap her fruit snack. And then suddenly, she froze.

Olivia, who'd been gazing in the direction from which they'd come and wondering how the castle building was going, sensed a ripple of unease in the air. When she turned and saw the anxiety on Caitlyn's face, she took a step forward, searching for what had alarmed her niece.

"Is she asleep?" Caitlyn whispered, pointing into the shadows.

It took a moment for Olivia's eyes to adjust to the gloom deeper beneath the pier, but slowly, she could make out a body near the base of a pylon.

Someone had one too many last night, Olivia thought. The person was on their side, shoulders and legs curled in toward their stomach. It was hard to tell if the stranger was male or female. He or she wore a baseball cap, a long-sleeved T-shirt, and a pair of sweatpants. A backpack not unlike Olivia's lay nearby, and Olivia wondered if it contained booze, drugs, or both.

"We should go back to our blanket," Olivia whispered. She didn't want the drunkard to wake and scare her niece.

However, Caitlyn was clearly in no rush to leave. She finished her water and screwed the cap back on, her gaze fixed on the inert form. "Maybe she's sick. We can't just leave her like that." Now she looked at Olivia, her eyes wide and questioning. "Right?"

Staring at her niece, Olivia felt a rush of conflicting emotions. She was relieved that Caitlyn didn't know what someone in a drunken stupor looked like, but the sight brought back plenty of bad memories for Olivia. After all, she'd grown up with Willie Wade, a man who'd always enjoyed his liquor. That enjoyment turned to a terrible addiction following the tragic death of Olivia's mother. In the months leading up to the night Willie abandoned his ten-year-old daughter by setting her adrift in a dinghy, he'd had a whiskey bottle on his person around the clock.

Everyone in Oyster Bay believed Willie had been lost at sea, but he'd made his way to Okracoke Island, where he started a new life. He'd changed his surname to Salter, remarried, had a son, and never looked back. And from what Hudson had told her, Willie had continued his love affair with whiskey until the day he died.

Olivia thought of how often she'd seen her father slip into unconsciousness, how she'd smelled his putrid odor of sweat, unwashed clothes, and fish, and how he used to snore with his mouth open, the sawing noises gathering deep in his chest and rumbling up his throat like thunder. Shoving the memories aside, Olivia focused on Caitlyn again. "What makes you think that person's a woman?"

"She's wearing an ankle bracelet."

Squinting, Olivia was able to see a thread of silver encircling the woman's right calf. "You have an owl's vision," she told Caitlyn. The longer Olivia studied the woman, the more concerned she became. The woman was too still. Too silent.

She sleeps like the dead, Olivia thought and then started.

"Caitlyn, I want you to go back to the lifeguard stand." Olivia kept her voice calm and even. "I'm going to check on this lady, but I don't know how she's going to react when I wake her. She might be scared or confused or, like you said, sick. I need to make sure that you're safely on your way to the chief before I talk to her, okay?"

Caitlyn hesitated. "Can't I help?"

"Yes, you can get the chief's phone from his bag and bring it to him. If this lady needs a doctor, I can call an ambulance on my phone first, but after that, I'll need to be able to call the chief and tell him what's going on. Can you do that for me?"

Nodding, Caitlyn picked up her bucket and hurried away, casting a last glance over her shoulder at the sleeping woman.

Olivia waited until her niece was halfway to their umbrella

before moving toward the shape in the shadows. "Hello?" she whispered and then raised her voice. "Hello? Ma'am?"

When there was no response, Olivia walked in a wide arc around the woman's feet, hoping to catch a glimpse of her face while keeping a body's length between them. Unfortunately, there was no way to tell if her eyes were open or shut because the gloom around the pylons was too thick. "Ma'am?" Olivia was speaking loudly now. "Hello!"

Nothing happened.

Olivia inched closer, bending over and moving slowly, carefully. The woman was curled in the fetal position with her chin tucked into her chest. Her chest wasn't rising and falling.

"Please be sleeping," Olivia murmured, but she already knew that the woman wasn't asleep. There were no sounds of open-mouthed breathing. No ripe odor of alcohol-infused sweat.

A different aroma clung to the woman—the sickening scent of rot—and Olivia held her breath as she stretched out her hand to touch the stranger's shoulder. At first, Olivia settled for a tentative pat, but then she pressed her fingers into the woman's soft flesh and shook. The body felt wooden. Lifeless.

Gingerly, Olivia cupped the woman's chin and lifted it away from her chest. A pair of unseeing eyes stared at her and she nearly jumped back, but her fear dissipated as quickly as it had formed, replaced by a heavy sadness.

The woman was very young. Her dark hair and smooth skin were similar to Millay's, but her eyes were light. Olivia's instinct was to brush the sand from the woman's nose, cheek, and eyelids, but she refrained. Instead, she retreated several steps. Leaning against the pylon, she called Rawlings.

He answered after a single ring. "Is everything okay?" he asked. "Caitlyn told me that she found a sick woman under the pier."

"I'm okay," Olivia said in a hushed tone, as if trying not

to wake a slumbering child. "I'm with the woman. But she isn't sick. She's dead. I didn't call 911 yet because I figured they'd respond more quickly if the call came from you."

"Did you touch her?"

Olivia looked down at her left hand. "On the shoulder and the chin. I had to make sure she was gone, though I can't tell what happened to her." She glanced at the shape in the gloom and added, "She's very young, Rawlings. Younger than Millay."

"Come to me," Rawlings ordered gently. "We need to trade places now."

"All right," Olivia said, and hung up. She stood quietly for several seconds listening to the distant cry of the gulls and the waves curling onto the beach. The late April wind swept under the pier and stirred up small dervishes of sand.

Olivia was reluctant to leave the young woman alone. After a moment's hesitation, she closed the distance between herself and the dead woman again. Her eyes traveled down the stranger's body and came to rest on the silver anklet. It was a plain chain with a tiny sand dollar pendant. Other than a cheap digital watch and a pair of hoop earrings, she wore no other accessories. Her baseball cap was embroidered with the letters *OB* for Oyster Bay and looked well worn. "Why are you here?" Olivia whispered, and then, despite the fact that Rawlings would be furious with her, picked the woman's backpack off the ground and opened it.

Olivia found little inside. There was a reusable water bottle—teal with a black flip top—and a plastic bag lined with paper towels. The bag was filled with shells. Like Caitlyn's, they were all perfect specimens. Each shell was flawless—lacking chips, cracks, or holes.

"Another collector," Olivia mused softly. "That explains why you hit the beach so early. But why are you under the pier if you were looking for shells?"

Olivia didn't dare search the woman's pockets or check

her body for injuries. She'd already gone too far in digging through the backpack. Besides, she didn't think she could touch the woman again. Not in such an invasive manner.

"I'm sorry," Olivia said, placing the backpack exactly where she'd found it. "I have to go now, but you'll only be alone for a few minutes. The chief is coming. He'll watch over you. He won't leave you."

A lump formed in Olivia's throat. She didn't know this woman at all, but she looked so childlike and vulnerable that Olivia couldn't help but feel a stab of grief. In an hour or so, the woman would be laid out on a steel table with a crisp white sheet pulled taut over her naked body. People wearing latex gloves would have methodically poked and prodded her dead flesh, written notes about her, and thoroughly examined her belongings. Finally, these unfazed professionals would call in a family member to identify the woman. And while her loved ones stood in mute terror, someone in green scrubs would fold back the white shroud and wait for a mother or a father to cry out in anguish. The sound of raw loss, high and shrill and earth-shattering.

With a last glance at the woman, Olivia turned away and headed for the children and Rawlings. When she reached him, he took her hand and squeezed it, his eyes imploring. She assured him that she was well enough to take care of the kids.

After searching her face for a long moment, he pointed at the lifeguard. "Jake loaded the car. I'll meet up with you when I can."

Olivia scooped Anders from his perch on a mound of damp sand and called Haviland. He trotted away from the water's edge, shook himself several times, and then gave Olivia a toothy grin as if to say that he was glad to see her.

"Poodle," Anders said and smiled.

Caitlyn, who was still holding the handle of her bucket with both hands, watched Rawlings walk away. "Will she be okay?"

Olivia didn't know if she should be honest and admit that the woman was beyond help or reassure her niece that all would be well.

"I don't know, honey," she said eventually. "But the chief will take good care of her. You don't have to worry."

It was a cryptic answer, but it seemed to comfort Caitlyn.

"What are we going to do now?" she asked.

"First, I'm going to get your brother out of these wet clothes. I think he has enough sand in his shorts to refill the sandbox at the park," Olivia said with forced levity. "After that, why don't we all go to the bookstore?"

Caitlyn's face lit up. "Yes, please. Mom said that the whole front window is full of mermaid books."

Olivia carried Anders to the back of the Range Rover, where she stripped him, toweled him off, and dressed him in cotton pants and a dolphin-gray shirt that matched his eyes. "Books," he said. And then, "Crackers."

On the way to Through the Wardrobe, Olivia and Caitlyn talked about mermaids while Anders gorged on Goldfish.

"I know they're just stories," Caitlyn said, looking at the shells she'd found that morning. "But I think mermaids are cool. I like drawing them riding sea turtles. And when I paint their castles on the bottom of the ocean, I use lots of glitter." She tilted a shell this way and that. "I guess that sick lady likes mermaids too."

Olivia shot her niece a curious glance. "What makes you say that?"

"Her anklet had a sand dollar on it. They're mermaid coins, you know." Caitlyn spoke with authority. "Sometimes the mermaids drop the coins and they wash onto the shore. And if you break one open, there are seven birds inside. I read a story that said they were supposed to be doves, but in this other book I got from the library, it said that they were white butterflies from the mermaid kingdom."

"Underwater butterflies," Olivia said. "I like that."

"Sand dollars are purple in the water," Caitlyn continued.

"When they're alive. They only turn white after they've been on the beach for a while. I wonder if that lady ever found one. They're supposed to be really lucky."

"Then I hope she did," Olivia said and pulled into the bookstore's parking lot. She opened the back door and unbuckled Anders, who stretched out his arms, wordlessly asking to be lifted. Olivia gathered him close and pressed her nose against his neck, inhaling his scent of salt water and sunshine. He squirmed as if she'd tickled him, prompting her to blow raspberries against his skin until he squealed in merriment.

Straightening, Olivia traced her nephew's ear—a perfectly smooth spiral-shaped shell—and her thoughts returned to the dead woman and her backpack of treasures.

Joining Caitlyn and Haviland in front of the bookshop's display window, Olivia slipped her free arm around her niece's shoulders and said, "I should read some of those mermaid stories. I like to think that there are wondrous things below the surface that we'll never see. Beautiful, magical things. Places full of light at the bottom of the deepest, darkest parts of the ocean."

"Secret places," Caitlyn said in a conspiratorial whisper. "And maybe sometimes, when no one's looking, the people from those places come ashore."

As Olivia pictured the woman lying in the gloom beneath the pier, the idea of strange creatures moving about in the predawn shadows was suddenly unnerving.

Taking a brief glance at the colorful window display of undersea creatures, Olivia squeezed Anders a little tighter and ushered Caitlyn into the store.

Chapter 5

We have lingered in the chambers
of the sea
By sea-girls wreathed with seaweed red and
brown
Till human voices wake us, and we drown.

—T. S. ELIOT

Their little party had barely gotten inside when Jenna, the store manager, rushed out from behind the checkout desk to greet them.

"It's been ages since I've seen you, Ms. Limoges," she said and then turned to Haviland. "While your two-legged companions were admiring the window display, I put something special in my pocket for the world's most handsome poodle."

Haviland sat on his haunches and offered Jenna his paw.

"Treat," Anders said and held out his small hand.

Jenna laughed and looked at Olivia. "I made chocolate chip cookies this morning. Could I give one to the kids?"

"That's really sweet of you. Thanks, Jenna." Olivia put Anders down and he immediately stood next to Haviland, grabbed a hunk of fur in his fist, and waited for his treat.

"Why don't we have snacks in the kids' area?" Jenna said to the kids. "You can get comfy in a beanbag with a pile of books."

Jenna led Caitlyn, Anders, and Haviland deeper into the store. Knowing the kids wouldn't move from their beanbags once plied with cookies and books, Olivia lingered behind for a moment. She hadn't stepped foot in the bookstore for far too long, and she suddenly realized how much she'd missed it. She missed the lazy Saturday afternoons browsing the shelves and gathering stacks of books to purchase. And she missed Flynn McNulty.

Pivoting around the front room, she looked at all the antique wooden wardrobes he'd bought and refinished. Each one was different. There were wardrobes of pine, walnut, oak, and mahogany. Some had carved aprons, delicate inlay, and cabriole legs, while others were unadorned. They were all beautiful. Their deep shelves, which glowed with the warm patina of time, were the perfect repositories for books. Olivia touched the colorful spines in the section devoted to coastal gardening, half expecting Flynn to enter the room with a loaded reshelving cart. Olivia's hand closed around a group of books and she stood very still, inhaling the store's familiar scent of lavender beeswax and coffee, and remembering.

"I know you never liked Mr. McNulty's bookstore blend," Jenna said, rounding the corner of a wardrobe featuring books on sport fishing. "But we're about to offer a whole menu of coffees and espresso drinks. Would you like to try a sample?"

Olivia gave the pretty manager a quizzical look. "Did you buy a commercial machine?"

Jenna shook her head. "It's way bigger than that. The man who owns this building just bought the warehouse next door. He plans to expand this space and open a café. We're going to be Oyster Bay's first Starbucks."

Olivia could only manage a weak, "No."

Mistaking her stricken expression for disappointment, Jenna hurriedly added, "Don't worry, it won't actually be a Starbucks. We're going to be an independent bookstore and eatery. No franchises here." She smiled. "But major changes *are* coming. The second warehouse will house the café and a small stage. It'll be a place where local bands and poets can perform while our customers dine at our hip café. It's not going to just be a place for coffee lovers, but a new hot spot for art lovers of all kinds. It'll be familiar and cozy and yet chic and urban too. I am *so* excited."

Stunned, Olivia was about to question Jenna more about the bookstore's new owner when Caitlyn came rushing to the front. Her eyes were wide with fear, and she immediately crashed against Olivia and buried her face in her shirt.

Olivia wrapped her arms around her trembling niece. She could feel moisture soaking through her T-shirt. Caitlyn was crying, silently and fiercely. "What is it, sweetheart?" When Caitlyn didn't answer, Olivia turned to Jenna. "Would you do me a huge favor and check on Anders?"

Jenna hurried off and Olivia dropped to her knees. She then pushed Caitlyn away just far enough to examine her tear-streaked face. "Talk to me," she urged. "What scared you?"

"I saw . . ." Caitlyn sent a wild glance in the direction of the children's section. The words died in her throat, but she swallowed and tried again. "I saw Grandpa."

For a second, Olivia paled. Caitlyn's grandfather was Willie Wade, the man who'd raised Olivia, and he'd been dead for over two years. But Olivia knew why Caitlyn believed she'd seen her grandfather's ghost. There was only one explanation. Willie's twin, Charles Wade, was in the bookstore.

"It's all right." It was difficult for Olivia to keep her voice steady when anger was coursing through her, heating her from the inside out. "Your grandpa had a brother. They were identical twins, so the man you saw looks just like your grandpa. But it wasn't him, honey. And it wasn't his ghost. Grandpa Willie is gone. Look at me. Please, honey. Look at me."

Sniffling, Caitlyn met her eyes. "But I saw him."

"I know, and it must have been really spooky. But the man you saw is Charles Wade and he owns this bookstore now. He must be visiting from New York." She wiped a tear from Caitlyn's cheek. "I thought he was a ghost when I first saw him too. So did your dad. I had no idea he was here today or I would have warned you."

"Warned her?" a male voice from behind Olivia asked. "About me?"

Olivia swung around to find her biological father leaning against a Victorian wardrobe, his fingers idly tracing the swag carving on the door panel. "Yes," she said through a clenched jaw. "I would have told her not to be afraid." Keeping a protective arm around her niece, she used her free hand to gesture at the man standing before her. "Caitlyn, this is your great-uncle, Charles."

Olivia's father was taken aback. "Willie had a granddaughter?"

"He did, and the little boy in the children's section is his grandson, Anders." Olivia's tone was icicle-cold. "I'm going back there to make sure he's okay. Come on, Caitlyn."

Breezing past the tall, handsome man in immaculate chinos and a pink button-down, Olivia walked deeper into the store. She found Anders stretched out on the colorful alphabet rug, his head resting on Haviland's belly, and a board book of moving optical illusions in his hands. Jenna, who was sitting in a child-sized throne behind boy and dog, pressed her finger to her lips. Olivia slowed, watching as Anders flipped a page back and forth and then gasped in delight as a horse galloped in a window of black and white.

"Cute kid," Charles said, shooting Anders a disinterested glance. He skirted around Haviland and touched Jenna on the shoulder. "I'd love a chance to visit with our customers, Jenna." He flashed her a winsome smile. "I'm sure you have tons of things to do. Aren't you hosting your weekly book club today?"

Jenna sprung to her feet. "I am." She gave Haviland a pat on the neck. "Just holler if you need me. Oh, and Caitlyn?" She spoke the little girl's name quietly, as if sharing a secret. "I'll hold that book you wanted at the register. It's my last one and I believe it was meant to go home with you."

Caitlyn, whose initial shock had morphed into embarrassment, nodded and hid her face behind a copy Hans Christian Andersen's *The Little Mermaid*.

"I'd like to speak with you," Olivia said to her father. "Let's move to the puppet theater. It'll give us a little privacy while allowing me to watch the children."

Charles joined her on the narrow bench in front of the puppet theater. "She's into princess stuff, eh?" He jerked a thumb at Caitlyn. "My daughter was like that at her age." He stopped abruptly. "My other daughter, I mean. I—"

"You don't need to add the qualifier. As far as I'm concerned, you're not my father," Olivia said curtly. "And Caitlyn *isn't* interested in princesses. Not all fairy tales are about dressing in fancy gowns and marrying handsome princes."

Charles Wade arched his brows in disbelief. "Aren't they?"

Olivia fought to control her annoyance. "No. In fact, Andersen's mermaid wants to acquire an eternal soul. In his version of the story, she fails. And when she dies, she turns into sea foam. Hardly a fairy tale ending. But Caitlyn is mature for her age, so I know she can handle it." Picking a yellow spotted octopus puppet off the floor, Olivia studied the stranger beside her. "Why did you buy this business and the building next door? When we met that first time, you claimed to hate Oyster Bay."

"I do hate this place, but I'm rather fond of money. And success. This town is an untapped haven of opportunity." He prodded a crab puppet with the toe of his Italian loafer. "You should be pleased. This project will boost the local economy, especially during the off-season. There's not much to do in this charming berg when the sea and air turn cold."

There was a haughty sneer to his tone that set Olivia's teeth on edge. "So you're going to take one of our quaintest businesses—this bookshop—and turn it into another giant box store? There won't be much charm left to our little hamlet if you continue to invest in local real estate."

Charles put a hand over his heart, feigning offense. "You're not worried about a little friendly competition, are you? I know that you own quite a few properties yourself. A chip off the old block."

"Let me make something clear." Olivia's voice was low and threatening. "I don't know you. I don't want to know you. If I could, I'd deny your existence. So don't go around introducing yourself as my father. Your brother was my father. This was his town."

Charles snorted. "Until he left it. And you. Without looking back, I might add. No wonder you're all sharp edges and harsh words. You spent half of your childhood as an orphan."

Olivia's anger bubbled over. "My life, past or present, is none of your business. It's not like you swooped in to save me when Willie took off. Abandoning ladies in distress seems to be a character trait among the Wade boys. You ditched my mother and Willie ditched me."

"I told you that I had no idea your mother was pregnant. And even if I knew . . ." He gave a callous shrug. "I was already married. My wife's dad was my boss. I wasn't going to throw away my career for a love affair that was doomed from the start. Besides, being with Camille meant living in Oyster Bay. No way would I get trapped here. Being raised in this dump was punishment enough."

Olivia wanted to slap his smug face, but she took out her fury on the octopus, twisting its plush legs into tight knots. "So why invest in a place you despise? Your life is in Manhattan."

Charles shrugged again. "My kids are grown, my wife only cares about tennis and shopping, and my company is in the hands of a capable manager. In short, I'm bored." He grinned at Olivia. "I thought I'd come down, start a new enterprise, and get to know you better. You seem to take

after me more than my other kids. You're smart, s
and you don't mince words. I figured we could spend s
quality time together."

Olivia got to her feet. "I hope your warehouse restoration project is a success because preserving Oyster Bay's history is important to me. But unlike the dilapidated structure next door, you and I have no foundation upon which to build. I had a father. He had his faults, but he did his best to raise another man's daughter. *Your* daughter. And he loved the woman who loved you with all of her heart." Shoving the octopus puppet in his lap, she said, "Go back to New York. You don't belong here."

Unfazed, Charles picked up the puppet. Staring at it, he whispered, "Do you think she'll invite me to her wedding? I could give her away. That's what fathers do."

"Keep talking," Olivia muttered. "You stand a better chance of having a relationship with that toy than you do with me." Turning her back on Charles, she scooped Anders off the floor, told Caitlyn it was time to go, and ordered Haviland to heel.

"Come back soon!" Charles called as if they'd just shared a congenial chat. "I'd love to show you the blueprints for the café."

Olivia bought the kids two books each and ushered them out of the store. She didn't think she could stand listening to Jenna gush over the wonderful Mr. Wade for another second.

"I think we need one of Grumpy's cheeseburgers, a big pile of fries, and a chocolate shake," Olivia told Caitlyn when they were all back in the car.

Caitlyn, who had already cracked open one of her new books, said, "Yes, please!"

At the diner, Olivia was relieved that her niece seemed to have fully recovered from the morning's unsettling events. She ordered her food and then helped Anders cover his paper placemat with crayon squiggles. As the children waited for their lunch, Olivia wished she hadn't ordered anything for herself. She had no appetite at all. Her stomach felt twisted and thorny, like a blackberry bush. How would she tell Kim and Hudson that after Caitlyn had stumbled upon a dead woman, she'd been shocked into tears by the sight of her grandfather's twin brother?

"I have the world's bestest mac and cheese for my favorite boy," Dixie said several minutes later. After placing a bowl of steaming noodles in front of Anders, she wagged her finger at him. "It's too hot." She put a lidded cup with a bendy straw in his hand. "Drink some milk first."

She then skated off to collect the cheeseburger platters from the kitchen. Her tiered, ruffled skirt, a diaphanous pink trimmed with silver sequins, expanded and deflated as she moved, reminding Olivia of a jellyfish moving through water.

When Dixie returned, she served Caitlyn first. "Grumpy wanted me to tell you that he's given you so many pickles that you might actually turn green."

Caitlyn laughed and Olivia shot Dixie a grateful smile.

"Sorry, 'Livia. There wasn't a single pickle left for your burger. But you already look a bit green about the gills. Everythin' all right?"

Olivia said that it had been an eventful morning but then jerked her head in Caitlyn's direction and gave a little shake of the head as if to say, "Not now." Dixie picked up on Olivia's unspoken message and nodded. Luckily, Caitlyn was too busy covering her fries with rivulets of ketchup to notice the exchange.

Dixie skated off to deliver a check to a couple in the *Cats* booth and to clear plates from the *Evita* booth. As Olivia bit into a crisp, salty French fry, she was happy to note that every table in the Andrew Lloyd Webber–themed diner was occupied.

The season is starting early this year, she thought.

Anders was making a mess of his macaroni. It was on

the table, the booster seat, and his lap, but Olivia knew he wanted to manage his lunch on his own so she let him be. Haviland sat by the little boy's elbow, catching cheese-covered noodles midair before they had the chance to hit the floor. Every now and then, he'd lick cheese from his nose and flash Olivia a toothy smile.

When lunch was finished, Dixie invited the kids to join Grumpy in the kitchen. "He's got a special ice cream bar lined up for you two."

The children clapped in delight and Olivia released Anders from his booster seat and did her best to wipe his face before Caitlyn took his hand and led him to the back of the diner.

"Are you sure Grumpy wants them underfoot?" Olivia asked. "The diner's pretty full."

"Everyone's been served except for the folks at the *Starlight Express* and *Phantom* booths," Dixie said. "Besides, I can tell somethin's up with you and I want to know what it is."

Caitlyn pushed open the swing door to the kitchen and helped her brother through. Olivia held back, keeping Haviland at her side. She didn't think Dixie's patrons would appreciate seeing a poodle entering the room where their food had been prepared, but this was also her only chance to talk with Dixie privately. Bending low, because Dixie was a dwarf and only reached the five-foot marker in her roller skates, Olivia whispered, "We found a dead woman on the beach this morning. Caitlyn saw her first. She still believes the woman was sick, but she's a sensitive girl and I'm worried about her."

"The poor lambs!" Dixie exclaimed. "Both Caitlyn and the woman. Why'd she die right there on the beach? Heart attack?"

"She looked like she'd gone to sleep, but I think she was too young to have had a heart attack," Olivia said. "I don't know what happened to her, Dixie. It's sad and senseless." She suddenly realized that several patrons were gawking at her. It was one thing to have Haviland politely seated at a booth, but he was now standing the middle of the diner. It was time to take him outside. "Let me take Haviland around back. I'll meet you and the kids on the patio. I don't dare leave Anders unsupervised when dessert's involved. Caitlyn's an attentive sister, but I think she's been through enough today."

The women moved in opposite directions. Dixie delivered two more checks, picked up a credit card receipt, and then zipped into the kitchen.

Olivia headed to the exit, but had to scoot behind the unmanned hostess podium to allow a family of four to claim seats at the counter.

"Maybe we should wait for a booth," the mother said. "If that little, ah, woman is our waitress, she might not be able to reach this high."

"A dwarf on roller skates." The father shook his head in disgust. "What's next? A bearded lady? A kid with three arms? What a freak show."

The mother laughed and balanced her generous rump on one of the stools. "We were looking for local color, right? Looks like we found it."

"Maybe Snow White is back in the kitchen," the teenage girl chimed in, clearly hoping to inject some levity to the conversation.

"Yeah, totally naked except for an apron." Her older brother sniggered. "And when she's not frying bacon, she's getting down with the other six dwarves. A midget gang-bang."

The mother made a weak attempt to shush her son, but she was smiling behind her hand.

"You're such a perv." The girl frowned at her brother. "The dwarf waitress is a girl, so she doesn't even fit with your revolting picture."

"That's because *somebody* has to do the dishes and wait on customers," the boy scoffed. "Hot chicks and princesses get other people to do that stuff. Maybe you should buy a pair of skates and apply for a job here, Icky Vicky. I bet one of those rednecks we saw by the docks would be willing to take you home."

The girl muttered a curse under her breath and swiveled her stool, turning her back to her family. Olivia couldn't blame her. The girl's father, who'd undoubtedly overheard the entire conversation, didn't even admonish his son.

After shooting him a venomous glance, Olivia strode through the doorway and out into the spring sunshine. Temporarily blinded by the light, she closed her eyes. Images came rushing into her mind. She saw the dead woman under the pier and the backpack of seashells. She and the woman had early morning treasure walks in common. At least once a week, Olivia would sling her metal detector on her shoulder and head east, past the lighthouse, to the long stretches of deserted beach. Haviland would prance along the waterline while Olivia lost herself in the blips and beeps of her machine. Her searches rarely amounted to anything, but she was always at peace during the solitary hour she spent collecting coins, pieces of jewelry, or whatever else the ocean decided to leave for her.

Entering the alley behind the diner, Olivia was so caught up in thoughts of the dead stranger that she was startled by the sound of laughter. Caitlyn and Anders were sitting at a picnic table on the patio outside the kitchen door. Colorful bowls containing Maraschino cherry bits, rainbow sprinkles, chopped strawberries, and sliced bananas were clustered in the middle of the table along with a tub of whipped topping and a bottle of Hershey's chocolate syrup. Anders had chocolate sauce all over his mouth, on both hands, and in his hair. Caitlyn had whipped cream on her nose and was balancing a banana slice on the tip of her tongue.

"We'll have to hose Anders off before we bring him home," Olivia said, joining her niece and nephew at the table.

"Poodle bath!" Anders cried and held out his chubby fist for Haviland to lick.

Caitlyn grinned. "Or we could just cover him with whipped cream and let Haviland clean him."

Dixie appeared a few minutes later with a pair of damp dish towels. "Lord have mercy!" she cried. "Anders, my sweet angel baby, I should've given you a lobster bib."

Anders gave her a fierce scowl. "I'm a big boy."

Hesitating, Dixie looked at Anders. "Was it somethin' I said?"

"He doesn't like anything that he thinks is for babies," Caitlyn explained. "It's because he started potty training."

"You *are* a big boy," Dixie told Anders. "You'll be taller than me in no time. Why, you might even be bigger than Grumpy."

At the mention of Grumpy's name, Olivia slipped into the kitchen to say hello to Dixie's husband. Grumpy, who was over six feet and tattooed from neck to ankle, took his job very seriously. He'd never had professional training in the culinary arts, but had been preparing belly-warming meals for decades. Olivia told him time and time again that he was a natural-born cook. He instinctively knew which flavors to pair and could make everything from a gourmet frittata to a mammoth bacon cheeseburger. Therefore, it was no surprise that he balked at Olivia's suggestion to serve the tourists at the counter subpar food.

"Except for the girl. Make hers extra special," Olivia said and quickly repeated the conversation that had taken place among the family.

Grumpy glared at their ticket. "Let's see. She wants a turkey club on rye, but the rest of them ordered BLTs with extra crispy bacon. I reckon I can handle that. You'd better get the fire extinguisher ready." He turned to the kitchen door. "Dixie! Come on in here and fix a root beer float for the young lady at the counter."

"She didn't order one," Dixie called back.

"Maybe not," Grumpy said with unusual firmness. "But she's getting one all the same."

While a befuddled Dixie retrieved the vanilla ice cream from the freezer, Olivia went back outside and sat with the kids until they finished their desserts. She then used the dish towels to clean Anders, but Caitlyn preferred to wash up in the ladies' room. Olivia wiped off the table and gave Anders his book of moving pictures. He immediately became fascinated, giving her the chance to carry the ice cream fixings into the kitchen. When Dixie skated back into the room, Olivia waved for her to follow her to the patio.

"So tell me more about the lady you found," Dixie said in a hurried whisper. "I've got about five minutes until my next order is up."

Olivia gestured at the open door. "Okay, but when Caitlyn comes out, the subject is closed. I'm hoping you can identify this woman, especially since I haven't heard a word from Rawlings since I left him at the beach. Anyway, the young woman was in her mid twenties. Plain face. Dark hair. I'd guess that her eyes were light blue. She was in shadow so I couldn't tell. Her clothes were unremarkable. Cheap sweats, a plain T-shirt, and a well-worn OBX baseball cap. She had a digital watch and hoop earrings. And an anklet with a sand dollar."

"Was it silver?" Dixie asked in a small voice.

Olivia stared at her friend. "Did you know her?"

Dixie took a moment to recover. "She came in for our special breakfast now and then. The one we serve the guys and gals coming off the third shift or just getting ready to go to work."

"Fried eggs, sausage, toast, and tomatoes." Olivia recited the meal Grumpy's Diner offered at a discounted price to the town's laborers, barmaids, fishermen, farmers, and housecleaners—the people with calloused hands, weathered skin, and sore backs.

Dixie nodded. "Her name's Ruthie. She was real quiet. Would always sit at the counter and read a library book while she ate. She paid me in change. I could tell she was just scraping by, so I told her the only tip I ever wanted from her was a pretty shell every now and then."

"You knew she was a collector?"

"It took months before she'd talk to me. I asked why she was up so early and she told me she was a shell artist. She made picture frames, wreaths, boxes, jewelry—that sort of thing. Sold them at the farmer's market and on the Internet." Dixie sighed. "She seemed so lonely, 'Livia. I hate to think she died alone too."

Both women fell silent.

Olivia watched Anders tilt the pages of his book, his eyes wide with wonder. Haviland finished sniffing around the base of the table and settled down by the little boy's feet. His nose was still alert, his caramel-colored eyes roaming around the patio and the alley. Eventually, his gaze came to rest on Olivia's face. He looked at her intently, as if he knew she needed comfort. She felt a rush of love for her devoted companion.

"Ruthie." Olivia tried out the young woman's name. It somehow sounded Biblical and antiquated and yet fresh and youthful too. "Did she have any family that you know of?"

"That girl acted like an old maid and she couldn't have been a day over twenty-two," Dixie said forlornly. "Once, she had breakfast with a woman who had to be her mama, but that was years ago. The only other person I saw her with was a girlfriend. Her best friend, I'd say. Ruthie used to act like this other girl walked on water. And that's okay, I suppose, because the girl was real nice to her. She made Ruthie smile."

"Who was this other girl?" Olivia asked.

Dixie furrowed her brow. "A rich kid. I saw her last name in the paper the other day. Oh, I can almost feel it floatin' around in my gray cells."

As Dixie rubbed her temples in frustration, Caitlyn reappeared on the patio.

"I am *so* full," she said. "But I'm not sticky anymore."

Dixie gave her a one-armed hug. "You're just perfect,

sticky or not. I bet Grumpy told you to send me back inside, didn't he?"

Caitlyn gave her a shy grin. "He said something about you quitting your yammering and I think he burned a whole bunch of bacon. It's totally black and he's *still* using it!"

"What's gotten into that man?" Dixie threw her hands in the air and then gave Anders a peck on the cheek. "Bye, big boy. Dixie's gotta go. Uncle Grumpy's lost his marbles." She skated for the door and then paused and snapped her fingers. Turning back to Olivia, she said, "Drummond! That was her friend's name. Stella Drummond. Another lonely, quiet girl. But at least she and Ruthie had each other."

Not anymore, Olivia thought sorrowfully and bent down to accept a nuzzle from Haviland.

Chapter 6

The pieces I am, she gather them and give them back to me in all the right order. It's good, you know, when you got a woman who is a friend of your mind.

—TONI MORRISON

When Olivia pulled into her brother's driveway, she saw a shiny red minivan parked in front of the garage. Caitlyn scrambled out of the Range Rover and ran to the unfamiliar car.

"Is this ours?" she cried, tugging on the rear door handle.

A beep sounded from somewhere close by and the door slid open as if by magic. Caitlyn jumped into the back of the van while Olivia unbuckled Anders from his car seat and watched as he trotted off to join his sister.

"Wow!" Caitlyn shouted. "There's a TV in here! Can we go for a ride?"

Kim popped up from behind a butterfly bush and waved a pair of car keys in the air. "Each and every day! Your daddy finally traded in Big Bertha."

Hudson came out of the garage, smiling widely. He walked over to Olivia with the self-satisfied gait of a man who's brought contentment to his family.

"Thanks for keeping the kids," he said. "As you can see, Kim's walking on air. And I got a great deal on the van."

He looked at Olivia and his smile wavered. "Are you okay? The kids give you any trouble?"

"Not at all." Olivia waved her brother away from Kim and the children. "Hudson, there was a dead woman under the pier this morning. Caitlyn found her."

Hudson drew back. "Jesus."

"She thinks the woman was sick—not dead—and I didn't say anything to dissuade her. I thought it best if Caitlyn believed she could be saved. I'm sorry, Hudson. I never imagined something like this would happen."

"It's part of life. Sooner or later, we all have to see death close-up." Hudson cast a glance toward the minivan. "Caitlyn will be okay. She's a tough kid. Kim will know what to say to her. She's better at talking than I am."

Olivia nodded. To have a partner who complemented one's strengths and weaknesses was a true gift. Olivia thought of Rawlings and of how they worked as a unit. She pictured him as he'd been this morning—in the kitchen, organizing items for their trip to the beach—and felt a powerful surge of love for him. She wanted to hear his voice.

Touching the engagement ring he'd given her, Olivia said, "I wish that was the end of my bad news . . ." She reached down to pat Haviland's head, but her hand met with empty air. She heard a bark and realized that Haviland was exploring the new minivan too.

"Tell me," Hudson said.

"Remember that day at the Coastal Carolina Food Festival when you saw Dad's twin brother?"

Hudson groaned. "Of course I do. Christ, I nearly went out of my mind. I thought I was seeing a ghost, and I don't believe in that supernatural crap."

"It's been over a year and a half since then and I didn't expect to lay eyes on him again, but he's here. He's in Oyster Bay. After leaving the beach, I took the kids to the bookstore and he was there. Caitlyn reacted just as we had. She was really scared, Hudson." Olivia sighed. "I explained who he was and introduced them. Caitlyn calmed down pretty quickly, and by lunchtime, she seemed completely fine, but it wasn't exactly the pleasant morning I wanted to share with her. It was pretty much a disaster."

Hudson shook his head. "Ah, it's not all that bad. And at least she was with you when this stuff happened. You're family."

Olivia felt a knife twist in her belly and averted her eyes.

"Dad's twin," Hudson said, shaking his head in disbelief. "I forgot his name."

"It's Charles."

"*Charles.*" Hudson puckered his lips as if he'd tasted something sour. "What does he want with a bookstore? I thought he was some Donald Trump type from New York."

Olivia frowned. "Apparently, he's renovating Through the Wardrobe and opening some kind of cybercafé. I don't like it. And I don't like him."

Hudson, who was as loyal as an old hound, murmured something about doing his best to make Charles Wade feel unwelcome. "Who wants his type here anyway?" he asked, growing angry. "I don't mind the tourists. They eat, pay their bill, and leave. But I didn't like it when those TV people were in town for that Foodie Network show. They acted like they owned the place and treated us like second-class citizens. If our uncle has an entourage of jackasses like them, I'm going to leave the bones in their fish filets."

Olivia grinned. She and Hudson might not share an ounce of blood, but they were alike in many ways. They both viewed change with a heavy dose of distrust.

"I keep trying to tell myself that anything is better than the bookstore going bankrupt," Olivia said.

"Well, Chuck had better watch his step," Hudson grumbled and then brightened at the sight of his son toddling toward him, his plump arms outstretched and a radiant smile on his little face. Olivia watched her brother scoop up his son, said good-bye to the entire Salter clan, and called for Haviland.

Back at home, she brewed coffee and took a cup out to the deck. She tried to relax, hoping that by listening to the waves tumble into the shore, she might still her mind. Once she felt calmer, she called Rawlings.

"How's Caitlyn?" was his first question.

"I think she's okay. Do you find out what happened to the girl?"

Rawlings paused. "No. I'm still trying to ID her. She wasn't carrying a purse and we've yet to get a hit on her prints. I'm not sure if she ever saw a dentist, so dental records won't help. According to the ME, her teeth are in pretty bad shape."

"Her first name is Ruthie," Olivia told him and then repeated her conversation with Dixie. "Dixie said that Ruthie knew Stella Drummond. Apparently, the girls were very close."

"Millay's close to the same age," Rawlings said. "She'd scratch your eyes out for calling her a girl."

But Millay wasn't a typical twentysomething. "Millay knows who she is and what she wants. She rules her own life," Olivia said. "According to Dixie, Ruthie was painfully withdrawn and very unsure of herself." Olivia thought back to the day the time capsule had been discovered. "As for Stella, I only met her once, but she's clearly under her mother's thumb. She neither spoke nor made eye contact with Michel or me. She did what her mother commanded and then left. I get the impression that both of these young women move or moved through life attracting as little notice as possible, which is why I see them as girls."

"In other words, their inner age hasn't caught up to their actual years?" Rawlings asked.

Olivia loved that he always gave weight to her ideas, no

matter how absurd. "Exactly," she said. "What does the ME think? Has he shared any initial theories?"

"Only that the cause of death was probably drug related. Someone Ruthie's age with no evident sign of injury or trauma is most often a suicide or victim of accidental death by drug overdose. He didn't find any needle marks, but there was cyanosis of her right index finger. That means that the skin had a bluish cast due to decreased blood flow. I have no idea if that's relevant, and at this point, neither does the ME. There are so many ways to get drugs into the body that we won't have a clearer picture of what happened until the tox screen results come back."

"Which could take weeks," Olivia sighed. "What will you do next? Call Stella Drummond?"

"Yes."

"Be gentle with her," Olivia said, though she knew it wasn't necessary. Rawlings showed courtesy and consideration to everyone who entered the station, whether they came of their own volition or wearing handcuffs. "Ruthie may have been the only person in the world who understood Stella Drummond, who loved her exactly as she was. The loss will undoubtedly crush her. And having to identify her best friend's body? It'll take everything she's got just to survive today."

Rawlings made a noise of assent. "I'll make sure Ms. Drummond has a family member present. And Olivia?"

"Yes?"

"This is one of the many reasons why I want to marry you. You're genuinely concerned about a young woman you saw once—a young woman who didn't even speak to you. And yet, you're already acting as her champion."

"She could use one," Olivia said. She heard voices in the background, and Rawlings covered the speaker, spoke to someone in the room, and then came back on the line.

"I have to go," he said. "I'll see you tonight."

Olivia remained on the deck listening to the cry of gulls

and watching the sea oats sway back and forth in the salt-tinged air. Her gaze drifted to the lighthouse, and she suddenly pictured the keeper's face—the one who'd maintained the historic beacon his whole life. He'd seemed ancient to her when she was a girl. She'd never met someone whose skin was etched with so many deep lines and creases. It was if the waves had washed over him and then retreated, leaving behind permanent ripples in his flesh. His eyes were watery, and his voice was hoarse. Olivia remembered her mother saying that the man had lost his only child in a boating accident and that the townsfolk believed he worked in the lighthouse so he could be close to the ocean day and night.

Olivia knew this was true because the old keeper told her as much. He said that he waited and waited for a storm to move across the open water because during a storm, he could hear his son calling to him over the crashing waves and claps of thunder.

Words swirled in Olivia's mind. They stuck together and became vibrant, colorful phrases filled with such frenetic energy that she was almost afraid she wouldn't be able to capture them in time—that they'd fly away like frightened birds. But they didn't fly away. They grew and multiplied until she felt compelled to release them.

Olivia went inside, turned on her laptop, and opened a blank Word document. As she began to write the lighthouse keeper's story, she realized that she was writing her own story at the same time. It felt good. It felt as if she'd finally found the voice she'd been looking for. This was her voice, and it was strong and true.

An hour passed. And then another. Olivia didn't notice. She was inside the lighthouse keeper's small room at the base of the spiral stairs. She was staring at his cot, the stack of books on an overturned produce crate, and the faded photographs tacked to his bulletin board along with a list of sunrises and sunsets and yellowing nautical charts. She saw his supply of canned goods, his hot plate, and coffeemaker. She opened his tattered copy of *Old Man and the Sea* and knew he'd read it over and over again, recognizing a fellow sufferer in Santiago, the fisherman.

Eventually, Haviland tried to get her attention by resting his head on her lap. She gave him an absent pat. Dissatisfied, he nudged her arm with his nose, making it impossible for her to type. Olivia didn't want to be wrenched from the story. She was submerged in another world and wasn't ready to float to the surface.

Haviland trotted into the kitchen, tipped over his empty food bowl, and batted it across the floor. The clanging noises broke the spell Olivia was under. She blinked for what seemed like the first time in hours, stretched, and pushed back her chair.

"Sorry, Captain," she said as he reentered the room. "I had no idea it was so late."

Glancing out the nearest window, she saw the light ebbing from the sky. Broad swaths of orange and yellow sank into the sea and the clouds had gone from egret white to heron gray. Olivia fed Haviland and made herself a tuna sandwich for supper. She filled a cereal bowl with fresh strawberries and carried them to the deck to watch the day turn into night. As the first stars appeared in the dusky sky, Olivia tried to return to the lighthouse keeper's story, but she was too tired to write any more.

Instead, she ate strawberries and thought about Ruthie. The ME expected to find an overdose, but Olivia struggled with the idea. In her mind, she imagined a person who was acutely shy and lonely—someone who used her art to survive; who took the gifts the sea freely offered and carefully arranged them into decorative objects. Olivia knew this was a fantasy of her own creation, and one that was completely spoiled by the thought of Ruthie spending her money on drugs.

"Stella was her best friend," Olivia said to Haviland,

who now had a full belly and was ready for some exercise. "She could afford drugs far more easily than Ruthie."

A bat flew across the darkening sky and Haviland followed its zigzagging trail with his eyes before jogging down the steps to the path between the dunes. Olivia watched him for a while before focusing her gaze on the water. The line on the horizon where sea met sky was a shadowy smudge, and Olivia could just make out a few twinkling navigation lights on ships anchored far offshore.

When Olivia was little, she liked to pretend that the lights were stars that had drifted too low and had been caught in a mermaid's net. The mermaids would use the stars to illuminate their cold underwater world. Now Olivia saw the mast lights and didn't think of mermaids, but of how many of the boats moving across her vision were carrying contraband into harbors like hers. She wondered how many gullible souls like Ruthie, and possibly Stella Drummond, had purchased merchandise from these modern-day pirates.

Finally, submitting to her exhaustion, Olivia went inside, cleaned the kitchen, and put on HGTV to keep her company while she enjoyed a nightcap of Chivas Regal over ice. The twenty-five-year-old blended Scotch whiskey helped calm her agitated mind. During a particularly long commercial break, her conversation with Charles Wade came back to her and she ended up pouring a second cocktail to banish the memory of their meeting.

The booze, combined with the strange events of the day, had her ready to turn in unusually early. After calling Haviland away from a nighttime world filled with tantalizing scents and whirring insects, she climbed the stairs to the second floor.

Much later, she heard the sound of water running in the bathroom. The part of her that was awake enough to register that Rawlings was home waited until he was in bed before turning to him. Without opening her eyes, she curled her arm around his back.

He released a long, weary sigh into his pillow and drew her closer.

"Was it bad?" she whispered, moving her hand to his face.

He nodded, his stubble rough against the skin of her palm. "Stella . . . her heart broke. Right then and there. I've seen it happen more than I'd care to, but rarely to one so young. When the ME pulled back the sheet, that poor girl shrank inside herself so deeply that I'm not sure she'll ever come out."

She moved her hand over his hair, trying to soothe him. "It must be a terrible thing to witness."

"Yes, it is." His voice was leaden with sorrow and fatigue. "I'll never get used to it. God, Olivia. If I ever do, then I'll know I've done this job for too long."

Olivia kept quiet, waiting for Rawlings to say what he needed to say.

"You were right to call Stella a girl," he continued. "Her mother told her where to sit, how to stand, when to speak. And when her daughter's world fell apart, she handed her a tissue and waited for her to compose herself. That is, until she saw me staring. Then she managed to pat her child's heaving shoulder. It was like watching someone pet an unfamiliar dog."

Olivia had no difficulty believing that Bellamy Drummond would fall short when it came to comforting Stella. She'd probably disapproved of the friendship between her daughter and Ruthie. The young women were from very different worlds and Bellamy wouldn't hesitate to chastise Stella for befriending someone who lacked an acceptable pedigree. And yet Olivia felt she had to defend Bellamy. Perhaps she wasn't as cold as she seemed. After all, the townsfolk had called Olivia "Ice Queen" for over a year before realizing that there was more to her than met the eye.

"Maybe Bellamy didn't know what to say. I don't know that I would."

Rawlings sighed again. "Jesus, Olivia. Her daughter just

lost someone she loved. Even if Mrs. Drummond couldn't find the right words, she could have hugged her kid. She could have showed a shred of compassion. Instead, she could barely conceal her relief. I saw it in her eyes." His words were punctuated with anger. "I pulled her aside to ask her if Ruthie had any other family. She told me that she had no idea who Ruthie's people were. Her voice was full of scorn."

"Maybe she suspected Ruthie was using drugs and was worried that Stella might be tempted to try them too." Olivia massaged the base of Rawlings's neck, trying to ease some of his tension. "That would send any parent's protective instincts into overdrive."

Rawlings relaxed a bit beneath her touch. "I asked her about that. She said Stella wasn't the sort of young lady who'd abuse drugs. Apparently, Mrs. Drummond believes only the poor and uneducated turn to illegal drugs for their 'entertainment.' She refused to let me speak to her daughter about the subject, and with the state Stella was in, I didn't press the issue. I just told Mrs. Drummond to take Stella home and treat her kindly."

Olivia could tell that Rawlings didn't expect Stella to receive much of the tender loving care she'd so desperately need in the upcoming days.

"I'd planned on stopping by the historical society tomorrow to offer my help with the time capsule display. When I'm there, I can at least ask after Stella. If she's up to seeing visitors, perhaps Bellamy will let me speak with her. I have no bedside manner, but maybe I can make Stella feel a little bit better by telling her that I found Ruthie and that her friend didn't suffer."

"That might not be the truth," Rawlings said. "We don't know how she died, Olivia."

"Sometimes people need a different version of the truth," Olivia said softly. "I can tell Stella what I saw—that Ruthie looked like she'd just stopped for a rest while hunting for shells."

"That is a peaceful picture." Rawlings kissed her lightly. "And for the record, I love every version of you."

Olivia continued to rub his head until his breathing became slow and regular. Then, despite being very tired, she stayed awake a little longer, wondering if Rawlings would like the part of her that failed to mention that she'd met a man named Charles Wade over a year ago. And that he was her father.

Why haven't I told Rawlings? I know that if I ask him to keep my secret, he will.

And she desperately wanted her connection to Charles Wade to remain secret. If it came out that she was the daughter of a wealthy egomaniac who hated every stone, brick, and grain of sand that made up Oyster Bay, people might see her differently. She didn't want that. She wanted to be Willie's daughter. The skinny, towheaded child with the sea-blue eyes who'd grown up in the lighthouse keeper's cottage. She wanted to continue belonging to the town and its people. It was all she'd ever wanted.

Olivia flashed on an image of Charles in the bookstore. Recalling his smug smile, she felt a surge of anger. Dark, dangerous words swam through her head like a school of carnivorous fish.

If you try to take away what I hold most dear, her mind whispered to the image of her biological father, *I will kill you.*

Rawlings was up early the next morning. He told Olivia that he hoped to hear back from the ME by day's end, but she guessed that he wanted to review all the preliminary findings while the station was quiet. Olivia knew that something about Ruthie's death bothered him. If she had died from an overdose, Rawlings would hunt down the dealer who sold her the drugs. He'd make someone pay for helping her die so young. Olivia could almost see him at his desk searching vital records and other databases to form a picture of Ruthie's past. The ruling on her case might be accidental overdose or even suicide, but Rawlings wouldn't close her file and forget about her. He would keep gathering information until he felt he'd done his best by the girl who'd died under the pier.

"Suicide," Olivia murmured as she stood in her closet. "Why would she kill herself? She had Stella. She had someone who loved her."

Olivia ran her eyes over her clothes. She had to dress to impress today. Her outfit had to remind Bellamy that even though Olivia didn't descend from one of North Carolina's first families, she was just as influential as the Drummonds.

After selecting a navy shirtdress, she draped a silk scarf around her neck, slid on several gold bracelets, and put on a pair of diamond earrings. Because Olivia was so tall, she rarely wore heels, but Bellamy wouldn't be caught dead without them, so Olivia reluctantly wriggled her feet into a pair of Manolo Blahnik pumps.

Haviland sniffed the shoes and raised his ears in question.

"I know, I know, but I'm on a mission. And you, my sweet, are having a spa day. A swim in the canine pool followed by a complete shampoo, brushing, and nail trimming session. You'll probably be more relaxed than I've been in months," she said, smiling indulgently at the poodle.

After dropping Haviland at the groomer's, Olivia walked two blocks to the historical society and ascended the front steps to a polished oak door flanked by a pair of ornate jardinières. One of several house museums in town, this was the largest and most luxurious. Named Hanover House after the merchant who built it in the mid eighteen hundreds, the Italianate-style home boasted sixteen spacious rooms, an impressive collection of antiques, photographs, and documents, and a magnificent walled garden.

Because Hanover House was open to the public, Olivia entered without knocking and closed the door gently behind her. The crimson runner in the front hall muted her footfalls, and she called out a soft hello. Receiving no reply, she moved to the left. Bellamy's office was situated off the original kitchen in what was probably once a pantry, and as Olivia drew closer, she caught Bellamy's voice. The historical society president was clearly annoyed with someone.

"You can't spend the rest of your life in your room," Olivia heard Bellamy say, and when no one answered, she assumed she was hearing one side of a phone conversation.

"I *am* trying to understand. But I really can't, Stella. I never could. Why you, a girl raised with every advantage, ever took up with a creature like that is beyond me. Look at Hunter. His friends are from the right circles and he doesn't spend his time with people who use *drugs*." There was a pause and then Bellamy's voice grew sharp. "Stop deceiving yourself, Stella! You obviously you didn't know Ruthie like you thought you did." Another pause. "Please. No more of that. You're a Drummond. Blow your nose, wash your face, and get out of the house. If you refuse to come to work, even though I'm up to my neck with the time capsule exhibit, then do something else. Take a walk. Physical activity would do you good. I know what's best for you. I always have."

Olivia heard a thud as Bellamy put the phone down. "I've gone gray worrying about that girl. And now she's tearing her hair out over Ruthie Holcomb. Ridiculous."

Realizing that Bellamy was either talking to herself or to someone else in the office, Olivia backed out of the kitchen. She didn't want to be caught eavesdropping, so she returned to the foyer, opened and closed the door, and called out a much louder hello.

"Bellamy?" she repeated, heading deeper into the house as if she expected to find the historical society president straightening the embroidery hoop in the sitting room or polishing the silver in the dining room.

"Here I am!" Bellamy trilled in her best hostess voice. "Why, Olivia. What a lovely surprise. Were we scheduled to meet today?"

"No. I'm here because I have some free time and thought I might be able to help set up the time capsule exhibit. I could create placards or research the objects. And if you need additional display cases, I happen to know a vendor who could deliver whatever we need within the next three days." Olivia smiled. "I'd be happy to cover the cost. It's the least I can do, seeing how much time and energy you devote to Hanover House."

Preening, Bellamy accepted Olivia's offer and invited her to the kitchen for a cup of coffee. "I brewed a second pot less than fifteen minutes ago. My son volunteered to help this morning but only in exchange for fresh coffee." She laughed merrily. "He's been gone for weeks and I've missed him terribly, so he knows I'll indulge his every whim." She gestured at a young man sitting at a café table in the kitchen. "Hunter, this is Olivia Limoges."

Hunter jumped out of his chair and held out his hand. Smiling, he said, "It's a pleasure to meet you," as if being introduced to one of his mother's colleagues was the highlight of his day. He was incredibly good-looking with a tall, athletic frame, bronzed skin, shiny blond hair, brilliant blue eyes, and dimpled cheeks. He wore a faded T-shirt and madras shorts and exuded an aura of self-confidence bordering on arrogance.

"Excuse me for a sec." Releasing Olivia's hand, he reached into his pocket and pulled out his phone. Pivoting his shoulders slightly as if to protect his privacy, he glanced at the screen.

"Hunter," his mother said in an admonishing tone. "Must you check that thing every ten seconds?"

Still focused on the screen, Hunter nodded. "I have to let the ladies down gently, Mom. No one can compare to you."

Head bent, he began to type a text message. His thumbs moved swiftly over the touch screen keys and a grin tugged the corners of his mouth upward.

Watching him, Olivia was struck by a feeling of déjà vu.

And then she realized that she recognized Hunter Drummond. He was one of the golden boys she'd seen in Bagels 'n' Beans, the place where the new wave of drug dealers purportedly gathered. He'd recently returned from a trip, and following his return, his sister's best friend had been found dead on the beach, allegedly of a drug overdose. Olivia knew what Rawlings would say about such a string of coincidences. He would say that there was more to this story.

Olivia felt a quiver of dread. She'd come to Hanover House to search for the missing copper box and to see how Stella was doing, but she had a sense she'd just encountered another collection of secrets.

Chapter 7

Dolls with no little girls around to mind them [are] sort of creepy under any conditions.

—Stephen King

Hunter didn't notice Olivia's unease. Pocketing his phone, he slid an arm around his mother's waist and said, "Looks like you're not going to need me after all. I'm sure Mrs. Limoges is way better at this museum stuff than I am."

"It's *Ms.* Limoges, dear," Bellamy corrected. "She's not married. Not yet anyway. But she's engaged to the chief of police. How's that for home security?" She chuckled at her own joke.

Hunter surveyed Olivia with new interest. "Cool." He then glanced at his watch, clearly eager to be on his way. "Listen, Mom. I'm going to drop by the bagel store and get Stella one of those breakfast sandwiches she likes. Maybe a mocha latte too. She's really upset and I don't think she should be alone. I'll hang out with her for a bit."

Bellamy beamed at him. "You're such a sweet brother. Stella's lucky to have you." Then her smile vanished. "But I left her a protein shake. That's what she should be having instead of all those fattening carbs."

"Stella needs comfort food, Mom. I'll try to talk her into a bike ride later this afternoon. Deal?"

Bellamy turned to Olivia. "He's forever negotiating." She feigned an exasperated sigh and patted Hunter on the arm. "Oh, all right. Spoil your sister. I know she could use the company, and I'm afraid I only make her feel worse even though all I've ever wanted is for her to be happy."

"Stella will be okay," Hunter said. "We just need to be patient with her."

"Would you let me know if she's up to having a visitor?" Olivia directed her question at Hunter. "I feel somewhat invested in this affair because I found her friend." She deliberately avoided using Ruthie's name, knowing it would trigger a negative response from Bellamy. "Actually, my niece found her. We were walking the beach in search of seashells, and when we reached the pier, we saw her body."

Bellamy put a hand over her heart in shock. "I had no idea! How awful for you and your poor niece."

Olivia was stunned that Bellamy could express sympathy to an acquaintance but not her own daughter. "I didn't mean to be theatrical," Olivia said hastily. "In fact, Stella's friend looked so peaceful that my niece didn't realize she was beyond our help. If I could describe the scene to Stella, she might be comforted by it."

Bellamy hesitated, but Hunter immediately nodded. "Yeah, I think that would be good. Should I call here if Stella agrees to see you?"

"Yes," Bellamy said.

Olivia handed Hunter a business card. "Just in case." She smiled at Bellamy.

Hunter slipped the card in his wallet, kissed his mother on the cheek, and left. Olivia wondered if her initial judgment of the young man had been too harsh. At least he showed compassion for his sister.

"How about that coffee?" Bellamy asked. Her lips were

pulled into a thin line and it was clear that she was displeased that Olivia had offered to speak with Stella.

Olivia knew that she needed to change the subject or she'd be spending an unpleasant day with Bellamy Drummond.

"Hunter's so courteous," she began. "And handsome. Is he your only son?"

"He is." Bellamy's eyes shone with pride. She offered Olivia a porcelain pitcher of cream. "I have one of each. A boy and a girl. Hunter is our firstborn, and even though he was named after my husband's father, he favors my side of the family. Like me, he loves history and tradition, but his real passion is science. Everyone expected him to work at Drummond Properties, but he insisted on making his own way in the world."

Olivia took a sip of coffee. It was piping hot and very bold. "This is excellent coffee," she said and then, "So he followed his calling. I admire that. What does he do?"

"I know he barely looks old enough to be out of college, but he's a marine biologist. He majored in marine biotechnology. I don't quite understand the term myself, but I know he sails up and down the southeastern coast as far as the Caribbean to collect samples and specimens for his company."

What kinds of samples? Olivia wondered while she drank her coffee. "Is he based out of Oyster Bay?"

"I wish!" Bellamy exclaimed. "He spends most of his time in Florida, but I shouldn't complain because he makes regular trips north to see his family. So many of my friends have children who fly out of the nest and are hardly ever seen again. They're too busy to visit their own parents. Not my Hunter. He's a very thoughtful boy."

"And so independent," Olivia added, hoping Bellamy would continue to let her guard down. "What kind of boat is he operating? I'm picturing him out in the Atlantic in a little pontoon, filling test tubes with salt water, so that shows you how clueless I am."

"Thankfully, that's not the case," Bellamy said. "Hunter's in charge of an entire crew. He's the captain of an eighty-foot research ship. A motorized behemoth with state-of-the-art equipment. I know more than I care to about that boat. Hunter made me tour the thing a dozen times before coercing his father and me into covering the first loan payment."

Olivia looked impressed, but she was silently wondering why Hunter's company hadn't purchased the ship. "That's a large vessel. Sounds expensive too. Did Hunter somehow convince his boss to pay the remainder of the balance?"

"He must have, because we were remunerated in less than three months. With interest." She raised her brows as if to say that she and her husband had benefited from the experience. "Hunter told me that the company ships were too slow and too old for him to successfully carry out his experiments, and he must have convinced his employer that a new ship would increase profits. He'd never say as much because he's so modest, but I think his floating lab must be getting results because he's making an excellent salary. I mean, he's only twenty-seven and he's driving a Porsche."

"Good for him," Olivia said. "If your son is smart and ambitious, why shouldn't he be appropriately compensated? In today's world, you don't always have to climb the ladder to make it big. Twenty-year-olds are the new millionaires. They have the edge in our high-tech society." However, Olivia didn't think that marine biologists made the kind of money that the crop of young cyber entrepreneurs did. Frowning in thought, she said, "I guess I'm terribly uninformed, but I have no idea what a marine biotechnologist does."

Bellamy laughed. "That makes two of us. Let's talk about our time capsule now, shall we? I have another volunteer coming at ten, but I'll have her man the office. Since I have your vast array of talents at my disposal, I want to put them to good use. Why don't I show you the objects I've researched and cataloged so far? I haven't done many and I'm growing very anxious about having this display ready for next week's benefit, but if I have to work into the night, I will."

"Let's hope it doesn't come to that," Olivia said. She didn't want to spend any more time with Bellamy Drummond than necessary. "I wouldn't want to miss my cocktail hour."

"I know you're teasing, but if I don't have my gin and tonic by six, I turn into Medusa." Bellamy smiled at Olivia. "You and I must be cut from the same cloth."

Definitely not, Olivia thought. *I treat Haviland with more love and respect than you show your daughter.*

Despite her growing dislike for the historical society president, Olivia didn't object when Bellamy hooked her arm through hers and led her toward the stairs. She'd pretend to be Bellamy's best friend if it meant finding the copper box and helping Rawlings piece together Ruthie Holcomb's story.

Upstairs, Bellamy had cordoned off the study adjacent to the master bedroom and attached a NO ADMITTANCE sign to the velvet rope. Except for the clothes, which were hanging from a modern clothes tree in the corner of the room, the time capsule objects were neatly arranged on top of a library table. "I'm finished with the canned food and the clothing, but the art, photographs, books, and letters still need to be researched and cataloged," Bellamy said. "Where would you like to begin?"

Olivia offered to handle the leather-bound volumes of Shakespeare plays, the watercolor painting, and the collection of black-and-white photographs of men and women posing in front of homes and public buildings throughout Oyster Bay.

"We should have these made into posters," Olivia said, showing Bellamy the topmost image of a young couple standing in the doorway of a general store. "They're wonderful."

Bellamy's eyes glittered. "Yes! We could sell them in the gift shop. They'd make charming notecards."

"And postcards. You could give a packet of cards to the

people who donate during the Secret Garden Party. As a little thank-you."

"I love that idea. Let me run downstairs and call the print shop. Help yourself to the laptop. The password is 'preserve.' Be back in a moment."

Olivia waited two full minutes before she initiated her search for the missing copper box. She checked inside the bookcase, looked in the drawers of the antique desk, and even opened the door of the grandfather clock and peered into the space below the brass pendulum bob. The copper box was nowhere in sight.

"Damn it," Olivia muttered. The only other pieces of furniture in the room were two metal folding chairs, an antique wing chair, and a mahogany side table. The side table held a single object: a cast iron book press. Olivia recognized the utilitarian piece from a time when the public library had put on an exhibit of antique bookmaking tools.

Those items had been under glass, however, and there was something irresistible about the wheel on the top of the book press. Glancing over her shoulder to make sure she was still alone, Olivia put her hands on the cool metal and turned, raising the iron plate by a few inches. Underneath the plate was a folded piece of lined paper and inside the paper was a photograph similar to those found in the time capsule.

"What have we here?" Olivia whispered and moved closer to the window to take advantage of the morning light.

The image showed three people posing for a formal family portrait. The father was a stern-looking man in a dark suit. He sat rigidly in a leather chair. His legs were crossed and he held a pipe in one hand. Standing to his right was an unsmiling woman in a white dress with a high neck and ruffled sleeves. Her hair was piled high on her head, and there was a haughty tilt to her chin. Beside the woman stood a girl, also in white, who'd been captured in the middle of a sulk. Her brows were furrowed and her lips were pursed in a full-on pout. She held her china doll by one arm and carelessly brushing the floor with the hem of its dress. It was as if the girl wanted to convey the message that she was too mature for such a toy. Olivia guessed she was probably ten years old or thereabouts.

"A happy lot, aren't you?" she said, addressing the family, though she knew she was being unfair because family portraits from the Victorian era and beyond often showed solemn faces. Turning the photo over, Olivia saw words written on the back in thick black ink.

Nathaniel, Martha, and Josephine Drummond. White Columns, 1910.

Olivia sucked in a breath. What was this picture doing in the book press? Other than a pair of nearly imperceptible indentations on either side, it was in perfect condition. Olivia crossed the room and examined the photographs from the time capsule. They all had the same indentations as the Drummond family portrait, indicating that the entire stack had been snugly tied with the piece of twine lying on the table. But why had this photo been removed? Was Bellamy trying to hide it?

Olivia studied the image of the Drummonds more carefully. And that's when she noticed the wallpaper behind them. The repeating floral design was an exact match to the flower impressed into the green wax on the copper box.

"A family seal," she mused aloud, feeling her heartbeat quicken. She didn't know exactly what she'd stumbled upon, but she was now certain that there was a connection between Bellamy Drummond and the missing box.

Hurriedly replacing the photograph and returning the book press to its original position, Olivia used the laptop Bellamy had given her to find the value of the Shakespeare volumes. Even when her research confirmed Harris's theory that the books were worth tens of thousands of dollars, she couldn't stop thinking about the floral stamp in the green wax seal.

"I'm sorry to have left you alone for so long," Bellamy

said when she reappeared. "After I talked to the printers, I had to field two other phone calls. Luckily, the other volunteer I mentioned is here now. Have you found anything of interest?"

Olivia put her hand on the top of the leather-bound volumes. "Only that these are worth over thirty thousand dollars."

Bellamy sighed. "I know they're valuable, but I wish they weren't. When I first heard about the time capsule, I envisioned it bringing the people of this town together, but items like this are causing rifts instead."

"My friend Laurel Hobbs told me that there was a bit of squabbling during the reveal," Olivia said. "It's a shame. These are relics of our past and should be made available to the public. Even as a permanent loan." She waved her hand around the room. "Did your distant relatives contribute an item? I know they were one of Oyster Bay's most prominent families when this capsule was being filled."

"And still are," Bellamy said. She reached inside a cardboard box stuffed with Bubble Wrap. "I put the fragile things in here until we could place them in a velvet-lined display case. Here's what my family contributed. Isn't she exquisite?"

Bellamy handed Olivia a bundle swaddled in tissue paper. After peeling back the layers, Olivia saw a familiar face. It was the doll young Josephine Drummond had been holding in her portrait.

"Look at the lacework on her dress," Bellamy said as if she'd made it herself. "And these ringlets in her hair. What girl wouldn't adore such a beautiful thing? Unfortunately, my daughter never cared for dolls. I bought her several antique bisque dolls like this, but she never took to any of them. She said their eyes were creepy."

Olivia lifted the doll upright. The moment she did so, the doll's eyes opened and it stared at Olivia with a guileless brown gaze. Though pretty, it felt too fragile to have ever been hugged or coddled by a young girl. To Olivia, it seemed as cold and unapproachable as the people in the portrait. "Would Stella enjoy seeing something that once belonged to an ancestor?"

"Not her," Bellamy said scornfully. "She isn't interested in our family's history."

Touching a silky ringlet on the doll's head, Olivia wondered if life would have been easier for Stella if she'd been born with the same creamy skin, rosebud mouth, and delicate beauty as the antique toy her mother so admired. "Who owned this lovely doll?"

"Josephine Drummond. Sole heiress to the Drummond fortune."

"I'm surprised she'd give up such a treasure."

Bellamy shrugged. "She probably had dozens just like her. Her father was a very wealthy man."

"Oh? What was his field?" Olivia asked.

"In his younger days, he was one of the most successful cotton merchants around," Bellamy boasted. "Eventually, he started buying land both in town and near his cotton plantation. Not a bad inheritance for Josephine Drummond, and we still manage most of those properties today."

Touching the doll's delicate hand, she compared it to her own freckled, middle-aged hand. "I've reaped the benefits of another's labors as well," she said. "My French ancestor made his fortune making oak barrels. I doubt I would have become a restaurateur without his money, so I'm grateful for his hard work and the sacrifices he must have made to achieve such success." She passed Bellamy the doll.

Bellamy cradled it in her arms as if it were a newborn infant. She stroked its hair and murmured wistfully, "There is always a price, isn't there?"

At that moment, they heard the sound of footsteps on the stairs. "Mrs. Drummond?" a woman's voice called.

"In the study," Bellamy replied. She rewrapped the doll and gently set it in the box.

A woman wearing too much makeup and jewelry appeared in the doorway. "Your son called. He said that Ms. Limoges could head over to your house anytime, and that he'd consider it a favor if she could be there sooner rather than later."

"Thank you, Deidre."

"I've barely made a dent here," Olivia said, pretending to be torn. "Still, I hate to let Hunter down." She sensed that Bellamy gave in to her son's every whim and would therefore encourage Olivia to abandon her volunteer work and head to White Columns, the Drummonds' historic home.

"I'd be grateful if you could try to talk with Stella," Bellamy said, confirming Olivia's theory. "It sounds like Hunter wasn't able to get through to her."

Getting to her feet, Olivia nodded. "I'll do my best."

Olivia had never been inside White Columns before. The grounds were always included in the annual garden tour, but only members of Oyster Bay's high society were invited to the Drummonds' dinner parties or wine tastings. Olivia had received several invitations over the years, but she'd always politely declined. As much as she'd enjoy a tour of the antebellum mansion, Olivia had no interest in spending an evening with a bunch of socialites and sycophants.

White Columns was one of Oyster Bay's architectural jewels. Because of its bright white paint, rows of Corinthian columns, oversized windows, and elaborate friezes, Olivia's mother used to refer to it as The Bridal House.

Now, as Olivia approached the mansion, she saw exactly what her mother had meant. In the midday light, White Columns drew the eye of every passerby with her elegance and beauty; a bride prepared for her wedding day.

After parking on a side street, Olivia walked around the wrought iron fence enclosing the grounds and pushed open the low gate separating the front garden from the sidewalk.

The house seemed to be watching her approach. Drawing closer, she noticed a note taped to the front door. It fluttered slightly in the breeze, as if trying to get her attention. Olivia was surprised to discover that it was addressed to her.

Ms. L—

Please let yourself in. Stella's room is upstairs, second door to the left. She didn't want to talk to me and I had to roll. Thanks so much for coming. Hunter

Feeling like an intruder, Olivia glanced around. The yard felt quiet, and the only sound was a gentle whisper from the rustling fronds of the potted ferns. Raising her eyes to the frieze over the front door, Olivia sucked in a sharp breath. The floral design carved into the plaster was the same design she'd seen in two places: the mantel in the old photo of the Drummond family and pressed into the wax seal of the copper box.

Olivia used her cell phone camera to photograph the frieze. She then composed a quick e-mail to Harris asking him to identify the flower and sent an attachment of the image.

Finally, she entered the house.

Inside, Olivia peered into the first two rooms off the main hallway. She saw expensive antique tables and bookcases, plush upholstered chairs, custom draperies, Oriental rugs, polished brass, and the wink of crystal. To Olivia, White Columns looked like another house museum. It was beautiful but cold. It did not feel at all like a home.

"Stella?" Olivia called softly from the foot of the wide, curved staircase. She waited for a moment and then ascended to the second floor. She heard music coming from Stella's room, but the volume was low enough that Olivia knew Stella could hear her voice. Knocking twice on the door, she said, "Stella? My name's Olivia Limoges. I don't know what your brother told you about me, but I wanted to talk to you about Ruthie. First, I want to say how sorry I am for your loss. I know it's an empty phrase, but I'm sorry."

There was no answer. Olivia couldn't even be certain that Stella was inside, but she had a feeling that she was listening.

"My niece and I found Ruthie yesterday. We were collecting shells because my niece, Caitlyn, wanted to use them to decorate a mirror frame. She and Ruthie were probably alike when it came to collecting. Caitlyn was very particular about which shells were good enough for her art projects." Olivia paused, but there was still no sound from within the room. "I saw the ones Ruthie found that morning. Every one was perfect. She had a really good eye."

Olivia heard the tiniest movement on the other side of the door, and she sensed that Stella had inched closer.

"Ruthie looked like she was resting. It was quiet and cool where she was, Stella. She had the beach to herself, but she wasn't alone. There were birds scurrying along the waterline and the waves were rolling gently into the shore. Almost like a whisper."

Olivia felt a little foolish. She wasn't given to flowery language, but she really wanted to paint a positive picture for Stella.

"People will tell you to move on with life," she continued. "They'll be full of advice and stupid clichés about time healing your wounds and how you can't stop living because someone you love has died. Most of those people have no idea what they're talking about." Olivia leaned against the wall next to the door and closed her eyes. "That hole you feel in the center of your heart? I know how deep it is, Stella. My mother died when I was seven, and that hole is still there. For years, I felt like everything good leaked out of it. My laughter. My hopes and dreams. Eventually, it closed a little. And then a little more. I found things to smile about again. But it'll never go away, Stella. I can't say my mother's name or picture her face without feeling a dull pain. Your pain is sharp as barbed wire right now, I know. And no amount of fresh air or exercise is going to make it disappear. But I just wanted to tell you how Ruthie looked. I wanted to give you a tiny bit of comfort, though I wish I had more to give."

From inside the room, Olivia heard a muffled sob. The sound was so raw with anguish that Olivia's eyes grew moist.

"I'll go now, Stella," she whispered. "But if ever need to talk to someone about this, you can talk to me. I won't judge you or give you advice. I'll just listen and try to be a friend to you."

Olivia waited for another long minute and then headed back down the hall. Her hand was on the banister when she heard the click of a lock.

Stella slowly opened her door and stepped onto the Persian runner. Curling her bare toes into the wool, she kept her gaze fixed on the rug. "They think she did this to herself." Her voice was so soft and ragged that Olivia had to strain to hear her. "But she didn't. I knew everything about her and she knew everything about me. Ruthie didn't do drugs. Not ever."

Olivia nodded. "Everyone will realize that when her tox screen comes back clean."

Stella shook her head. "It won't matter. By then, my mother will have told all her friends that Ruthie OD'd—that she committed suicide because she was fatherless, poor, and didn't have a college education."

Olivia saw how Stella's hands trembled. She wanted to cup them tenderly, to hold them like she'd hold a wounded bird, but she was afraid the attempt would startle Stella.

"I know she didn't kill herself," Stella said. "I saw her the night before. She was fine. She was working on a bunch of new pieces for the farmer's market next week."

"I believe you," Olivia said. "And if that's the case, we have to figure out what really happened to her. Was there anything, anything at all, that seemed different about her that last night?"

Stella looked up and glared at Olivia.

"Hey, I believe you," Olivia repeated, raising her hands with her palms out to emphasize her point. "But if Ruthie wasn't sad, was there something else off about her? Was she especially quiet? Or scared? Did you feel like she was keeping a secret?"

Stella wiped a tear from her left cheek. Her hair was a tangle of knots and the skin beneath her eyes was puffy and blue-tinged. She wore pajama pants and a baggy T-shirt, but her toes had been recently painted in a rainbow of colors.

Olivia pointed at her feet. "Did Ruthie give you that pretty pedicure?"

"Yeah." Stella stared at her toes, her shoulders shaking as she cried.

Olivia crept forward and held out a tissue. Stella took it and turned away to blow her nose.

"We didn't keep secrets from each other," Stella whispered, squeezing the tissue until it was a tight ball. "I knew that she didn't have enough money to pay the power bill this month and she knew that I applied for a job as a live-in nanny because I want to get out of this house. She knows how much I hate my family." Suddenly, Stella raised her head and looked Olivia in the eye. "They never wanted us to be friends. I hate them for being happy that she's dead. I hate them more than ever!" Stella's eyes filled with tears again, but Olivia saw rage behind the sorrow.

"So if Ruthie never used drugs and wasn't sad, then—"

"Someone killed her. Isn't that obvious to anyone but me?" Stella's voice was a thin, furious hiss. "But why. *Why?* After I saw her . . . on that table—" She broke off, sucked in a fortifying breath, and went on—"all I wanted to do was come home and swallow a bunch of sleeping pills. But I didn't. I'm standing here going through hell for one reason: I'm going to find out who did this to her, and when I do, I will make them pay for murdering the only person who ever really loved me. Without Ruthie, all I have left is hate." Her gaze drifted to her feet again. "Lots and lots of hate. A whole lifetime of hate."

And with that, she went back into her room and closed the door.

Chapter 8

The great events of life often leave one unmoved; they pass out of consciousness, and, when one thinks of them, become unreal. Even the scarlet flowers of passion seem to grow in the same meadow as the poppies of oblivion.

—OSCAR WILDE

Olivia didn't linger at White Columns, but drove straight to the groomer's. Even though Haviland wasn't due to be picked up yet, Olivia wanted to sit in the familiar waiting room and think. While other pet owners flipped through magazines and exchanged anecdotes about their dogs, she stared out the window and replayed her conversation with Stella.

Olivia had been unsurprised by Stella's tears and anger. She'd expected both. But Stella's declaration that her best friend had been murdered was unnerving. The cold fury in her eyes was also cause for concern, as was her mentioning sleeping pills. Would Stella try to hurt herself or to strike out at someone else in despair and anger?

As she watched the passersby on the sidewalk, Olivia recalled her first impression of Stella. It had been formed quickly the day the time capsule was found. Maybe too quickly. Was Stella that meek and malleable? Or was she someone else entirely away from her mother's domineering presence?

Stella said that Ruthie was the only person who'd ever loved her. If that was true, then her loneliness would be unimaginable. Maybe even unbearable.

"Haviland's all set!" A cheerful voice interrupted Olivia's grim reflections. Trisha, Haviland's favorite tech, appeared in the waiting area. "He sure loves our Best in Show package." Trisha scratched Haviland's head and he glanced up at her in adoration. "Whenever I stopped massaging him, he'd give me this over-the-shoulder look like he was telling me to keep going."

"This is the downside of spoiling him," Olivia said. "He'll put on airs for the rest of the day."

Trisha wagged a finger at Haviland. "Be nice to your mama or there'll be no special treats, you hear?" She handed Olivia a paper bag. "I made these last night. Peanut butter and banana with a little parsley to keep his breath smelling nice. And here comes my next customer." Trisha gave Haviland a final pat and moved off to greet a bulldog and his owner.

Olivia paid for Haviland's service, got him settled in the Range Rover, and then called Rawlings. "Can you meet for lunch?" she asked.

"If it's a quick one," Rawlings said.

"How about a cup of soup and half a sandwich at The Boot Top? We can eat in the bar."

"Soup's fine, but I need the whole sandwich. It's been a long day already."

After giving Haviland a few minutes to explore the grassy area around the restaurant's parking lot, Olivia walked him through the kitchen and into her office. She'd just started answering e-mails when her cell phone buzzed. It was Harris.

"Thanks for the text," he said. "I was stuck in the world's dullest meeting. Seriously, the guy to my left was playing Candy Crush on his phone and the woman to my right was picking all the polish off her fingernails. My boss just droned on and on. The guy is wicked smart, but he can be totally oblivious."

"Any luck identifying the flower?"

Harris snorted derisively. "I'm a master of cyber research. Luck has nothing to do with it. This was a tough one, though. Care to guess?"

"No."

"You're no fun," Harris said, amiable as ever. "It's an old design of a cotton flower. Turn-of-the-twentieth-century or older. Where did you take that pic?"

Olivia told him about her visit to White Columns.

"Man, that must have been rough. I'm not sure who had it worse, you or me. But I think I'd rather talk to Stella than look at another quarterly projection."

"I thought you were focused on moving up the corporate ladder. Have you changed your mind?"

"Yeah, ever since I realized that being on the higher rungs means sitting through torturously boring meetings. What I love is writing code. Building amazing worlds. Turning fantasy into something three-dimensional." Harris sounded deflated. "The money's a plus. I bought my first new car and a bunch of cool stuff for my house, but the killer paycheck isn't making me happy. I miss creating. I miss hanging out with the other software geeks. This suit and tie stuff sucks. I'm too young to feel this old."

Olivia laughed. "Sounds like you're having a midlife crisis in your late twenties. Maybe that's a good thing. Now you can turn fifty without buying a red convertible and dating a woman young enough to be your daughter."

Harris was silent for a long moment. "Er, speaking of women, I met one in Texas. Well, I met lots of women, but this one's special."

"I had a feeling there was more to the gym you joined than a grueling workout."

"Yeah. Her name's Emily and she's really cool. You'd like her." Harris hesitated. "But she's in Texas and—"

"Millay is here," Olivia said.

She heard a thwack in the background and pictured Harris striking the surface of his desk with a book. "That's just it. Millay is here. And she's every bit as awesome as she was when I left." He groaned. "How can I ask Emily to visit when I'm still hung up on Millay?"

"You didn't seem hung up on her during your home-coming dinner."

"I can fool everyone but myself." Harris sounded glum. "Let's face it. I'll never get over Millay. There's no one like her."

Olivia felt sorry for her friend. "We can fall for people who aren't good for us, Harris. It happens all the time. She's an incredible person and so are you, but you're not incredible together."

"So I should keep seeing Emily? Even though I'll never love her the way I love Millay?"

"You and Millay share a colorful history," Olivia said carefully. "No one will ever compare to her. You rescued her, Harris. You took a bullet protecting her. The two of you will always be tied together, but that part of your life is over now. It's time to turn the page."

"I tried," Harris protested. "Being in Texas was fine, but it was nothing like Oyster Bay. Coming back here made me realize that even though all of us have been through several circles of hell, I've never felt so alive as when I'm with Millay and the rest of you."

Olivia understood exactly what he meant. "Maybe this isn't about Millay at all. Maybe it was chasing after bad guys that you found so fulfilling. You should quit your job and go work for Rawlings."

Harris didn't reply and Olivia began to worry that he hadn't found her jest funny. "Harris—"

"You've totally nailed it!" Harris exclaimed. "Whenever the chief asked me to do research for one of his cases, I'd get this zing. There's nothing I'd rather do than peer into the far corners of cyberspace for a clue. And when the info that I find helps the chief catch the villain?" He gave a soft cry of triumph. "It's the best buzz. *That's* what I want. I want that buzz over and over again."

Olivia was confused. "I thought you loved creating software."

"I do, and I can keep doing my part to design the world's most awesome games on my own time. Lots of guys work from home. As long as you meet your deadline, you can work from the surface of the moon. Shoot, I could write code at night while I'm watching TV." He chuckled. "I'm going to call the chief right now and see if he can get together for a beer after work."

Pleased to hear the renewed energy in Harris's voice, Olivia asked him to poke around the Internet for any information he could find on both Hunter Drummond and Ruthie Holcomb. "I want to know what the favored child of the Drummond family looks like on paper. And I don't know if you'll find anything on Ruthie, but it would be nice to have a better sense of her and her family, if she has any. But maybe not in the middle of a meeting. I don't want you to get fired, even if you find the idea appealing."

"No problem," Harris assured her. "I'm already done with this week's tasks, so I have all afternoon to read up on these two." He paused. "Hey, I'm sorry that I never asked if you were okay. Laurel told me that you and Caitlyn found the dead girl."

"I'm fine, but the people who loved her aren't." Olivia flashed on an image of Stella's anguished face. "Ruthie Holcomb shouldn't have died. Her life was just beginning."

"Laurel said the same thing. She's really angry. She hardly ever curses, but when we started talking about those purported drug dealers, she started swearing like a sailor."

Olivia realized that she needed to touch base with Laurel. Perhaps she'd seen Hunter Drummond during her recent stakeouts of Bagels 'n' Beans. "We might have to call an unscheduled meeting of the Bayside Book Writers," Olivia said. "Something suspicious is going on and we need to find out what it is. Even if Ruthie Holcomb's death was an accident, I don't want to discover another young woman lying dead on the sand. We have to stop these drugs from coming into our town."

"Maybe I should try to get close to these yuppie bastards," Harris suggested. "Do some undercover work."

"Not without Rawlings's approval," Olivia said. "He might have a plan in place and we don't want to jeopardize it." Then, she got off the phone before she was forced to admit to herself that she had no idea what that plan was.

An hour later, Rawlings entered The Boot Top's bar to find Olivia and his lunch waiting for him.

Olivia, who rarely demonstrated physical affection in public, surprised the chief by giving him a long and tender kiss.

"Did you miss me that much?" Rawlings asked several moments later.

"I'm just counting my blessings," Olivia said, a little embarrassed over her choice of words. She'd always felt that such phrases should be restricted to embroidered throw pillows or stenciled plaques.

Rawlings pulled her closer to him. "Oh, really? Would you like to count some more?"

Olivia laughed, and the black cloud that had followed her from the Drummonds' house lifted. One of Rawlings's greatest gifts was his ability to put people at ease.

"Sit down," she said. "Your sandwich is getting cold."

Rawlings took a seat in a leather club chair and eyed his lunch. "What, no radish flower? No pommes frites?" His eyes glittered with humor. "Is the kitchen staff on strike?"

Olivia tossed a napkin at him. "They're busy working on the menu for Michel's wedding, so I made your lunch."

"What a woman I'll be marrying," Rawlings said and shook his head in wonder. "I'm a lucky man."

"Speaking of weddings, we should apply for our license." Olivia squeezed a lemon wedge into her iced tea and glanced shyly at Rawlings. "The end of May would be lovely. On the beach. Around sunset. With champagne and cake. Maybe a little dancing. How does that sound?"

"I couldn't imagine a more perfect evening." Smiling, Rawlings put down his sandwich and took her hand. "It suits you and me." He squeezed her hand excitedly. "Does this mean I can skip the tux?"

"As long as you don't wear a Hawaiian shirt, you can say your vows naked if you'd like."

"That might shock the flower girl, and Caitlyn's already applied for the job."

At the mention of her niece's name, Olivia's thoughts returned to Stella and she no longer felt like discussing weddings. It was too difficult to focus on her own happiness in the face of what she'd seen and heard at White Columns.

While Rawlings ate, she told him everything that had happened from the time she'd arrived at the historical society to the moment Stella had ended their conversation by shutting her bedroom door.

"Do you believe she'll harm herself?" Rawlings asked when Olivia was done.

"I think she's raging inside," Olivia said. "And there's no telling what she'll do with all of that pain and anger. I don't know her, so I can't predict her next move, but she needs help. She's standing on the edge of an abyss." She lowered her voice. "I'm afraid Stella may want to follow Ruthie into the dark. I think those girls were everything to each other."

Rawlings wiped his mouth and then carefully folded his napkin. "Were they lovers?"

Olivia shrugged. "I don't know. If they were, it might explain Bellamy's overt disapproval of Ruthie."

"Then again, the Drummonds may just be terrible

snobs." Rawlings sighed. "I'm sorry, Olivia, but I have no cause to get involved. My heart hurts for Stella. You know that. I can suggest counseling, but that's about it. Until I have the lab results, I can't draw conclusions about Miss Holcomb's death. And yet Stella is the second person claiming that Ruthie Holcomb wouldn't abuse drugs."

"Who's the first?"

"Cheryl Holcomb, Ruthie's mother. We met for the first time yesterday and spoke again today. She vehemently denies the possibility of an overdose and begged me to search their home—her daughter's room in particular—for proof of what really happened to her." Rawlings leaned back in his chair as if the weight of Cheryl Holcomb's grief was pressing down on him.

Olivia fixed him with an intent gaze. "What if she's right? Maybe Ruthie didn't take the drugs voluntarily. What if someone forced her? Or what if she didn't OD at all?"

Rawlings shook his head impatiently. "There's no use speculating. I can't launch a full investigation without those lab results."

"And what of Mrs. Holcomb's request?"

Rawlings pushed a strawberry around on his plate. "I've agreed to it. It won't be an official visit, but I couldn't refuse her. She was so fragile, and much to my surprise, she and I are about the same age. Apparently, she's been struggling with health issues for years, but she seemed much older than her years. She can't even drive. A neighbor had to bring her to the station."

"Is she married? Was Ruthie her only child?"

"There's a son. Ruthie's older brother. Luke Holcomb works on an offshore drilling rig somewhere in the Gulf of Mexico. Not much chance of him showing up to help." Rawlings's eyes were full of sympathy. "Her husband's dead. He had a stroke about the same time Mrs. Holcomb's medical problems forced her to go on disability."

"Good Lord," Olivia muttered. "I bet she needs

groceries. I could load up on sundries at Food Lion and then stop at the farmer's market for fresh produce."

Rawlings folded his arms over his chest. "I can see that you plan on accompanying me whether I okay it or not." His amused smile dimmed and he studied Olivia. "Before you charge ahead, you should know that she's in a mobile home in Seaside Estates. I have no idea what we'll find there."

Olivia bristled. "I can handle trailer parks, Chief. I didn't grow up living in the Ritz-Carlton. I know what the home of a broken family looks like too. I want to offer Mrs. Holcomb my assistance and I won't shrink from the sight of dirty dishes or the smell of unwashed clothes."

"I never imagined you would." Rawlings made a placating gesture with his hands. "What I meant was that we might encounter more problems than we can handle in one visit. I'm also treading a fine line. If this becomes an official investigation later on, my traipsing around the Holcomb residence at the request of Mrs. Holcomb could create legal complications. Bringing you along increases those complications."

"Not if you don't go into Ruthie's room," Olivia said. "Tell Mrs. Holcomb exactly what you just told me, and explain that I volunteered to search in your stead."

Rawlings considered the idea. Eventually, he gave a slow nod. "All right. We'll go tomorrow morning." He picked up his plate and moved to carry it to the kitchen, but Olivia blocked his path.

"I'll take care of this. You can clean up after dinner tonight." She hesitated. "Unless you don't make it home in time."

"I'll be there. It's my turn to cook, and I'm going to grill some caveman-sized ribeyes." His expression turned dreamy. "Steak and wine on the deck with my girl. Ah, that's something I'll look forward to this afternoon while I'm dealing with staff meetings, case log reviews, and equipment inspections."

"If Harris has his way, you'll be having beer and burgers tonight." When Rawlings opened his mouth to question her, Olivia put her finger to her lips. "I'm not saying another word, but I think the two of you should get together. He has an idea that might be good for both of you."

"You've certainly aroused my curiosity," Rawlings said and kissed Olivia on the cheek on his way out.

Olivia washed their lunch plates and then spent the next hour finalizing Michel's wedding menu with the kitchen staff.

"He'll be delighted," she told them. "It's very generous of you to come in on your day off and cook while the rest of us are in the church witnessing Shelley and Michel exchange vows."

One of the sous chefs rolled his eyes. "You'd better hope he didn't write his own. You'll be there all night."

"That's so true." Olivia laughed. "Just be sure to bring a change of clothes. Once the food is served, I want you to kick back and enjoy yourselves. Did I mention that I'm sponsoring the open bar?"

"You're going to have a troupe of zombies with hangovers working this kitchen on Tuesday," someone said and the chefs chuckled.

Olivia shrugged. "I'll buy a big bottle of Advil and we'll serve a simplified menu. No Beef Wellington or soufflés the next day. And definitely no calf's brain fritters. I don't want to tempt the zombies."

Having finished the impromptu meeting, Olivia returned to her office to place orders with suppliers. When she was done, she checked with the florist to make sure there were no hang-ups with the reception flowers. After that, she spent an hour reviewing the wine, champagne, and hard liquor inventory with Gabe.

When they were done, Olivia suggested they might need more cases of champagne.

"It's going to be a helluva party," Gabe said cheerfully.

Olivia turned to her bartender. "You don't have to work

Michel's wedding, you know. I could borrow a tender from The Bayside Crab House."

"Please don't," Gabe protested. "As long as I have a barback, I'll be fine. Besides, I want to serve Michel's guests their drinks. It'll be my gift to him and Shelley. I figure keeping their friends and family happy beats a waffle iron."

Olivia smiled. "You're right about that. Plus, this is a wedding for two chefs. They probably own every kitchen gadget known to man."

By the time Michel arrived for his shift and began shouting at everyone within hearing distance, Olivia had caught up on her paperwork and felt confident that she'd done all she could to prepare for his upcoming reception.

"There's the congenial groom-to-be," she teased him upon entering the kitchen. Michel was in the midst of threatening one of the sous chefs with a raised spatula, but he stopped mid-yell and turned to Olivia. "Everything's set," she said. "As long as you drop off your wedding cake and get to the church on time, yours should be the most magical Monday in Oyster Bay history."

Michel tossed the spatula in the sink, came around the counter, and enfolded Olivia in a crushing hug. "*Merci, ma chère*. I cannot wait. And when it's your turn—"

"You won't lift a finger. The chief and I are having a casual gathering on the beach in late May. Just dessert and drinks."

"On the beach? Can I wear my Speedo?"

Olivia swatted him with a dish towel. "It's not *that* casual."

She returned to her office, collected Haviland, and headed home. As predicted, Rawlings called to say that he couldn't make it for dinner.

"Since we're going to the microbrewery, I'd better stay in town tonight," he said. "Meet me at the station at ten and we'll drive to Mrs. Holcomb's together."

"Haviland will be delighted. He loves sleeping on your side of the bed when you don't make it home."

Rawlings issued a low growl. "Tell that poodle that he's only welcome to my spot on a temporary basis. I like my side of the bed. I'm very fond of the view across the pillow."

Olivia smiled on the other end of the phone and wished him a good night.

The next day, Olivia dressed in jeans and an old UNC basketball T-shirt and headed to the grocery store. Leaving Haviland in the car with the window cracked, she filled a cart with bread, peanut butter, toilet paper, soap, shampoo, dairy products, and healthy snacks. Afterward, she and Haviland strolled through the farmer's market, where Olivia bought a cornucopia of fruit and, on impulse, a bouquet of orange poppies. It wasn't until she was driving to the police station that she started to question her choice of flowers. Staring at the bright blooms, she recalled the scene from *The Wizard of Oz* where Dorothy falls asleep in the middle of a poppy field.

"The flower of slumber," Olivia murmured. She wondered if Mrs. Holcomb would see the bouquet and be reminded that her daughter had gone to sleep for the last time on the cool sand beneath the pier. Unlike Dorothy, no one had discovered Ruthie until it was too late.

Grabbing the flowers, Olivia walked into the station and presented them to the desk sergeant.

"How nice!" the woman cried. "Orange is my favorite color. Did you know that poppies are symbols of Morpheus, the Greek god of dreams? Maybe I'll dream of the gorgeous fireman I met at the gym yesterday."

Olivia didn't think the pretty young officer would have much trouble catching any man's eye. Haviland trotted around the desk, sniffed the carpet, and whined.

"He's looking for Officer Greta," Olivia said, referring to the German Shepherd K9 officer. Haviland was very fond of the police dog and searched for her whenever they came to the station.

"Officer Cook is Greta's new handler," the desk sergeant said. "He's in the break room if you want to say hi."

Haviland didn't need further encouragement. He knew exactly where the break room was located and hurried down the hall, glancing over his shoulder to make sure Olivia was following. She waved him on. "I'm right behind you."

Upon entering the room, Olivia found Officer Cook seated at a table across from a gorgeous blonde. They both had notepads, file folders, and coffee cups set in front of them.

"Sorry to interrupt," Olivia said. "When he heard Greta was here, he just took off." Olivia gestured at Haviland, who was exchanging nose rubs with Greta. Their tails were waving so furiously that Olivia was afraid they'd knock over the trash can.

"They're like two friends who haven't seen each other in a while," the woman said, clearly delighted by both dogs. "Aren't they sweet?"

"Olivia, this is Petty Officer Second Class Lindsay Parker of the United States Coast Guard," Cook said, standing to perform the introduction.

"Just Lindsay is fine, though most of my coworkers call me Parker," the young woman said and shook Olivia's hand.

Cook stepped away from his chair and offered it to Olivia. "The chief said that you'd be in this morning. I was hoping you could put Petty Officer Parker in touch with your reporter friend."

"Laurel Hobbs?" Olivia asked Cook and then turned to Lindsay. "Does this have anything to do with Laurel's investigation into drug smuggling?"

Lindsay's brown eyes widened in surprise, and she looked to Cook for guidance.

"It's okay. Ms. Limoges is the chief's fiancée. She's often in the know about our high-profile cases."

Olivia was stunned that Cook had managed to utter this statement without a trace of scorn. She and Cook had had their differences, but over the past year, they'd arrived at an unspoken truce. Cook had started treating Olivia with more courtesy, and she'd gone out of her way to praise his police work. He was one of Rawlings's sharpest young officers and had been showing more maturity and initiative of late. Olivia smiled at him, relieved that she and Cook could now be civil to each other.

"We're teaming up with the Coast Guard in an attempt to apprehend the dealers," Cook went on.

"Have you been to Bagels 'n' Beans lately?" Olivia asked.

It was Lindsay who answered. "Yes, and we didn't blend in well. We're too old to fool those kids and neither of us speak their lingo."

"Parker did better than me," Cook said. "Most of the locals know I'm a cop and one of the kids called me out right away. Guess it's my bearing," he added with a hint of pride.

"You do have excellent posture," Olivia agreed. "And though you could double as a supermodel, Ms. Parker, you have an authoritative air too. However, I happen to know someone who's already begun making inroads with the Golden Boy crowd."

"The Golden Boys." Cook cocked his head and then grinned. "I like that title. It suits those little punks. Who's your friend?"

"Her name's Millay, and she's a bartender at Fish Nets. Her exotic looks and bad-girl attitude intrigue the young men at the bagel shop, but my sense is that they don't quite trust her. However, you could easily remedy that problem, Officer Cook."

Cook frowned. "Me? How?"

Olivia took the seat he'd offered and wrote Millay's number on a napkin. "It's simple. All you have to do is arrest her."

Chapter 9

Grief fills the room up of my absent child, lies in his bed, walks up and down with me, puts on his pretty looks, repeats his words.

—WILLIAM SHAKESPEARE

While Rawlings put his car in park in front of the road leading to the Seaside Mobile Home Park and double-checked the Holcombs' house number, Olivia stared at the entrance sign. The bubbly seventies lettering—bright yellow outlined in orange—had been painted on a slab of wood wedged between two dock pylons. Despite the sign's nautical theme, the mobile home park was nowhere near the water. It was tucked away in a pine forest as if it were a secret that needed to be kept.

As Rawlings drove into the park, the warm spring morning did its best to dress the place in a good light. Sunbeams filtered through the trees and the air was redolent with wild honeysuckle. However, neither the sweet smell nor the russet carpet of pine needles could mask the evidence of slow and irreversible decay around the row of squat homes.

With their peeling paint, sagging steps, and holes in the window screens, the houses looked much the same. The yards were patches of sparse grass, tenacious weeds, and a hodgepodge of plastic lawn furniture. Many of the residents had attempted to brighten their plots with garden sculptures or wind socks on stakes, but most of these were so cracked, chipped, or faded that they only added to the overall feeling of dilapidation.

"Here it is," Rawlings said, easing the car behind a dust-covered SUV.

Olivia squinted at the other vehicle. "Looks like Laurel beat us to the punch."

Rawlings frowned. "Did you know she would be here?"

"No, but I'm not surprised. She's determined to follow every lead relating to the Bagels 'n' Beans crew."

Rawlings took hold of Olivia's wrist to stay her. "We've been shadowing those young men as well. The Coast Guard has searched several of their boats over the past week, but other than being short a life vest or two, they haven't broken any laws." He raised a hand to stave off Olivia's protest. "That doesn't mean I think they're innocent. I don't. Many of them are from middle-class or low-income homes and have no steady employment. However, this hasn't stopped these kids from throwing cash around like there's an endless supply. The so-called captains own fishing yachts most sportsmen can only dream about, and yet no one sees fish being unloaded from their hulls. These kids are smart. Wily. They know they're being watched. And we know they're giving us the runaround."

"That's why you should use Millay," Olivia said. "They won't be able to play her. She's too sharp. Just arrest her for a trumped-up misdemeanor, and when she returns to the bagel shop a few days later, grumbling about cops and acting blasé about the whole experience, they'll see her as one of them."

Rawlings sighed and released Olivia's wrist. "I know Officer Cook and Petty Officer Parker were quite taken with your idea, but I want to consider it carefully. In the meantime, let's not keep Mrs. Holcomb waiting."

Laurel was just leaving when they reached the base of Mrs. Holcomb's front steps.

Looking down at them, she smiled warmly. "Hey, strangers."

Rawlings motioned for her to descend the stairs. "Were you interviewing Mrs. Holcomb?" he asked sotto voce.

Laurel nodded. "She called the *Gazette* in the middle of the night and left a message on my editor's voice mail. I just happened to be standing in his office when he played his messages." She lowered her voice. "At first, I thought Cheryl Holcomb had been drinking. I mean, who could blame her? But she swore over and over that her daughter's death was neither an accidental overdose nor suicide. Her desperation spoke to me. And if Ruthie Holcomb's death did have anything to do with drugs, I wanted to know what kind of drug killed her and how she acquired it."

"Did Mrs. Holcomb supply you with answers?" Rawlings wanted to know.

Laurel shook her head. "Not really. For the most part, she wanted to talk about Ruthie—to paint a picture of who her daughter was. Most people tend to turn their loved ones into saints, but Cheryl didn't do that. She was incredibly honest in describing Ruthie. She went into great detail about how her daughter was quiet, gentle, and worked hard without complaining about all the things she didn't have, but Cheryl also told me the things Ruthie did to infuriate her. She knew her daughter well, Chief. And she swears that Ruthie would never do drugs."

Olivia touched Laurel's arm. "Did she mention Hunter Drummond or any of the other boys at the bagel shop?"

"The only Drummond she talked about was Stella. Apparently, Ruthie loved Stella like a sister from the moment they met. Ever since they ran into each other on the beach the summer they both turned eight, they've been finding ways to be together."

"As friends? Nothing more?"

Laurel looked confused for a moment. "What? Oh! No, I don't think they were lovers. They loved each other the way only best girlfriends can. I get the impression there wasn't much room in their hearts for anyone else. Cheryl didn't like that. She wanted Ruthie to make other friends and urged her daughter to pay more attention to her appearance so she could 'get herself a boyfriend.'" Laurel shrugged. "But Ruthie said she didn't need anyone but Stella. With Stella, she didn't have to pretend to be anything other than who she was."

"Isn't that what we all want?" Olivia murmured softly.

"Yes," Laurel said. "That's why Ruthie and Stella wore the same anklet—it was a symbol that they were linked for life. But the life they dreamed of was mostly fantastical. Cheryl said the two girls also made up names for each other." She opened the small notepad in her right hand. "Sea sister. Siren. Undine. Cheryl had no idea what they meant."

"Mermaids," Olivia said. "Maybe the girls were both fond of mermaids."

Laurel's smile was pained. "That makes sense. Mermaids are beautiful, mysterious, and independent."

"Caitlyn likes them too, but she's in grade school. Ruthie and Stella are in their twenties. I wonder—" Seeing a face appear in the window by the front door, Olivia abruptly stopped.

"We should go up," Rawlings said. He mounted the first step and then turned back to Laurel. "Would you share your findings with me later?"

Laurel nodded agreeably. "Maybe the Bayside Book Writers should get together before Saturday. We have lots to talk about and I don't want to take time away from Olivia's story. Which I loved, by the way. Steve's parents have offered to babysit this week, so I can get together tonight. Call me," Laurel said and hurried off.

Cheryl opened her door before Rawlings had a chance to knock. He quickly introduced himself and Olivia.

"You're the lady who found my Ruthie," Cheryl said, pulling Olivia into her home with a sense of urgency. She was a big woman with a doughy face and bloodshot eyes. She wore a shapeless floral housedress and a pair of dollar store flip-flops. Two pink rollers perched above each ear and a rose vine tattoo curled above the swell of her left breast. She sank down on the banquette bench in the kitchen and gestured for Olivia to take a seat across from her.

In describing how she found Ruthie, Olivia tried to give Cheryl Holcomb whatever comfort she could. By the time she was done, Ruthie's mother had used up half a box of tissues.

"Thank you for comin'," she said when she had command of her voice again. For the first time since Olivia and Rawlings had arrived, she addressed Rawlings. "You gonna look at her room now?"

Rawlings explained why he didn't feel comfortable doing so and asked if Olivia could conduct a preliminary search while he put away groceries.

"What groceries?" Mrs. Holcomb was clearly puzzled. She pointed at the orange countertop, which was covered with dishes and stacks of catalogs and takeout fliers. "All I've got is cereal, a box of crackers, and a bottle of grape soda in the fridge."

"Ms. Limoges wanted to stock your pantry, so I'll be unloading the car and filling your shelves while she's in your daughter's room." Rawlings gave the grieving mother a humble smile. "Would it be all right if I washed a few things? Made some room for you in here?"

Cheryl was clearly stunned that the chief of police planned to tidy her kitchen. "Um . . . all right then. Thank you."

Watching Rawlings slip on a pair of yellow rubber gloves, Olivia had the urge to kiss him.

That man is one in a million, she thought.

"With your permission, I'll take notes and photos of

anything I find," Olivia said while Rawlings started scrubbing a grease-encrusted frying pan.

Cheryl Holcomb bit her lip and waved to her left. "Go on back. I haven't been inside since . . . My room's at the other end." She fixed her eyes on the closed door dividing the kitchen from the rest of the home as if it she were tempted to bolt into her private domain and never emerge again.

Olivia put a hand on the woman's shoulder. "I'll be very careful with Ruthie's things. I promise."

Olivia stepped onto the living room's puce shag carpet and felt a wave of sorrow over the sad state of the room where Cheryl and Ruthie probably spent most of their time. A beige sofa with deep depressions in its cushions faced a twenty-year-old television in a wood console frame. The rest of the furniture consisted of a coffee table piled with catalogs and empty potato chip bags and an upholstered chair. Duct tape kept the springs from popping through the thin plaid fabric and the entire room smelled of low tide.

Mold, Olivia thought and wondered if the home's decrepitude exacerbated Cheryl's health issues.

Ruthie's room was a completely different world from the rest of the house. In an attempt to brighten her sanctum sanctorum, she'd painted two walls kelp green and the other two a bright Mediterranean blue. Shell wind chimes dangled from the ceiling and Ruthie had draped blue and purple scarves over the window. A framed poster of a mermaid took pride of place on the longest wall. Drawing closer to the image of the beautiful woman with auburn hair and a fish tail, Olivia saw that the print was of a John William Waterhouse painting. Ruthie had hung necklaces of tiny shells from the top corners and there were dozens more glued to her lampshade and bed frame.

Above the bed, close enough to touch, was a corkboard covered with glossy magazine ads and photographs of Stella and Ruthie. All the clippings featured women with blue makeup, fish tails, or some kind of otherworldly appearance. The photos were of the two best friends throughout the years. They were always taken on the beach and showed the girls dressed in flowing skirts and bikini tops or mimicking the makeup and hairstyles of the magazine ads.

"The little mermaids," Olivia whispered, thinking how pretty both girls looked in the pictures. It wasn't the shell necklaces or the blue-silver eye shadow they wore, but the joy in their faces that transformed them. Tiny stars glittered in their eyes and Olivia imagined the two friends weaving stories of another reality as they danced barefoot in the sand.

"You were so happy together," she said, addressing the carefree girls. She saw them age in the photographs, growing from flat-chested ten-year-olds to heavyset young women. "Your friendship made you beautiful. It also allowed you to dream—gave you the freedom to believe that a wondrous future was possible."

Olivia methodically photographed the room. Then, after saying a silent apology to Ruthie's smiling face on the bulletin board, Olivia searched through drawers, inside the closet, and peered into the boxes under her bed.

Though Ruthie's room was cluttered, it was oddly organized too. Her desk was devoted to her art projects and contained shells, glue, tweezers, paint, glitter, and wire. The shelves above the desk held cheap picture frames, Ruthie's completed projects, and a digital camera. Making a mental note to check the camera's memory, Olivia turned to search elsewhere.

Ruthie kept her mermaid items in a plastic bin beneath her bed. Another bin was filled with an assortment of keepsakes. There were friendship bracelets of multicolored string, fortune cookie papers, movie ticket stubs, gumball machine rings, horoscopes, and postcards. The postcards were from Stella and showed famous monuments throughout the United

States and Europe. On the back of every card Stella complained of boredom and said that she missed Ruthie and couldn't wait to see her again. There was also a stack of blank postcards showing tropical islands from around the world. These were tied with a pale blue ribbon.

Olivia studied an image of one of Fiji's smaller islands. "A perfect place for two mermaids."

Ruthie didn't keep a diary. Olivia reasoned that she had no need of one because she shared her every thought with Stella. In fact, the blue-and-green room didn't seem to hold any secrets. Olivia didn't even find an empty beer can or liquor bottle, let alone drug paraphernalia. The only thing she discovered that might possibly contain a clue about Ruthie's thoughts prior to her death was a thick bundle of note cards and letters wedged into the very bottom of the wicker laundry basket in the closet.

Olivia carried the bundle back to the kitchen, where Cheryl Holcomb stared at her with anxious eyes. "I didn't find anything suspicious," Olivia said. "Your daughter seemed more interested in creating art than getting into trouble. She made so many pretty things. Where did she sell her work?"

"Online mostly. She took pictures of the stuff and brought the camera to the library. She'd go back every few days to see if she'd sold anything." Mrs. Holcomb's gaze grew distant. "She'd buy food with the money she made. Or pay the water bill. Never spent it on herself."

"That's very admirable," Olivia said and couldn't help but wonder if Ruthie had had a choice in the matter. "And your son? Is he coming home to help you?"

Cheryl looked stricken. "He's tryin' to get leave, but it ain't easy when you're on a rig. He sends money home when he can. They're both good kids, and I wanted to give them a better life. But then their daddy died and I hurt my back. There went my job and any chance of that better life." Tears flowed down her cheeks.

Rawlings, who'd been wiping out the refrigerator, shut the door and carefully folded the dish towel he was holding. "Were you injured at work?"

"Yep. It was my own damn fault. I was standin' on a stool dustin' curtain rods and lost my balance. Messed up my back. Been livin' on disability ever since."

"Do you still take medicine for your back?" Rawlings spoke very quietly. "It must cause you a great deal of discomfort."

"Course it does." Cheryl scowled. "I've got pills that help some."

Rawlings gazed at her without blinking. "What pills, ma'am? What's the name of your medication?"

"The pills are in my bathroom," she said tersely. "Go look if you want."

With a nod, Rawlings slipped from the room.

Sensing that Cheryl was offended by Rawlings's line of questioning, Olivia gently placed the letters on the table. "Mrs. Holcomb, I found these in Ruthie's closet. It looks like she saved every note or letter Stella ever gave her. I thought that by reading the recent ones, we might get a glimpse into what was going on in their lives. Maybe it'll help us figure out what happened to your daughter." She put her hand protectively over the bundle. "Would you like them?"

Cheryl shook her head. "No, I can't. I don't want to know anythin' about those Drummonds. I already hate their guts. Not Stella. She loved my Ruthie. But the rest of those—" A low snarl rose in her throat. "The way they put on airs. They wouldn't let Ruthie come to their house. Not ever. Didn't want Stella meetin' her where anybody might see them together either. Stella had to tell a pack of lies whenever she wanted to come here too."

"How strange," Olivia said. "It must have been hard for them to be friends with such obstacles in their way. Did they talk on the phone often?"

Cheryl scrunched up her lips. "Depends. Sometimes we have one and sometimes we don't. The bills, you see."

Olivia nodded.

"Anyhow, my girl was every bit as good as Stella Drummond. In some ways, she was better. She was quiet, my Ruthie, but she dreamed big. She was makin' plans . . ." A shadow crossed her face and Olivia wanted to ask what the plans were, but decided not to press Cheryl. Not today, in any case.

"Would you like me to read the letters?" Olivia asked. "If I find anything unusual, I can call you right away." She glanced around the clean kitchen. "We also want to make sure you have people to look in on you. Bringing you food is one thing, but are you able to get into town?"

Cheryl shrugged. "I don't go out much. Mostly, I look at TV and my catalogs. I've got a few neighbors who visit. We might not have much in these parts, but we take care of each other."

Olivia smiled. "I'm glad to hear that. And I want you to include me as someone who'll be there for you in a pinch. Here are my numbers. Call me anytime."

Reaching out to squeeze Olivia's hand, Cheryl's eyes filled with tears again. "Bless you, honey."

Rawlings returned from the bathroom, his face unreadable. "Ma'am, I found your prescription of Oxycontin. Thirty pills per month, is that right?"

Cheryl grunted in assent.

"Do you ever take more than one per day?" he asked casually. "Maybe if the pain is really bad?"

"No, I do not," Cheryl snapped. "I wish I didn't have to take them at all. Do you think I like bein' this way?" She took a moment to calm herself. "Some days I just deal with the pain and skip the pill altogether. And there's been times when Ruthie needed—" She dropped her gaze to her lap.

Rawlings didn't move. "Go on, Mrs. Holcomb. What did

Ruthie need?" His voice was gentle, but there was no mistaking his tone. He'd given her a command.

"Ruthie's teeth hurt real bad. One of her molars or somethin'. We were gonna have it looked at when we'd caught up on the bills."

Olivia felt another surge of pity for the Holcombs. Her childhood had been hard at times, but she'd always had regular dental and medical checkups. Her parents had never been so financially strained that they had to choose between her health and the power bill.

"So she took your pills for relief," Olivia said. "Was her discomfort getting worse?"

Cheryl's glance was filled with misery. She nodded once and then seemed to retreat deep inside herself. Her eyes turned glassy and Rawlings touched Olivia on the arm and jerked his head toward the door. It was time to go.

"I'll be in touch," Olivia whispered to Cheryl. "Remember, call me if you need anything at all."

There was no response from Cheryl. She sat like a stone, tears dripping from her chin onto her clasped hands.

Outside, Olivia expelled a breath tinged with sorrow. Without speaking, she and Rawlings got in the car and slowly drove away. As they headed back to town, Olivia gazed out the window, taking in the overgrown grass pocked with buttercups on the side of the road and, beyond that, the woods with its carpet of burnished pine needles.

"How many pills were missing?" she finally asked Rawlings.

"I don't know," he said. "It's one thing for me to enter the bathroom and read a label, but I had no right to count Mrs. Holcomb's pills."

Olivia shot a sidelong look at him. "But you're thinking that Ruthie may have overdosed on her mother's pain meds."

"It's a possibility. I'll have to tell the ME and I'd like to review his report and see why Ruthie's jaw hurt so much. She could have had an abscess or an impacted wisdom tooth." Rawlings sighed. "I'm sorry. I know this isn't what you expected to find."

Clutching the bundle of letters in her lap, Olivia shook her head. "No, it isn't. Still, I made a promise to Cheryl and I'm going to read every one of these. Who knows? I might find something of meaning."

"Yes," Rawlings agreed.

The two remained lost in their own thoughts until they reached the station. The desk sergeant told them that Officer Cook had Haviland and Greta in the K9 training area.

"Your dog is smart as a whip," Cook said when Olivia bent down to greet Haviland.

She smiled. "You know how to make a friend of me, Officer Cook."

"Speaking of friends, can we talk about calling yours?" Cook addressed Olivia, but his eyes slid to Rawlings. "What do you think, sir?"

Rawlings put his hand on Greta's head and smoothed the fur between her ears. "Our marijuana and cocaine busts have tripled over the past two months. We've had a significant increase in motor vehicle accidents, B and E's, vandalism, and petty crimes. The majority of the individuals apprehended were high." He stared out into the middle distance. "The influx of drugs is changing Oyster Bay, and if we don't figure out where they're coming from, we'll lose this town."

Cook was watching the chief with a mixture of admiration and excitement. "Would you like me to call Miss Hallowell in for a debriefing?"

Rawlings managed a small, crooked smile. "No. If I'm going to ask Millay to let us arrest her for a crime she didn't commit and then ingratiate herself with a gang of potential drug smugglers, I should at least treat her to pizza." He turned to Olivia. "Can we call that emergency meeting of the Bayside Book Writers?"

She pulled out her phone. "I'm on it."

* * *

That evening, the Bayside Book Writers gathered in the lighthouse keeper's cottage. Laurel started the meeting by presenting them with statistics about the rise of the distribution of both marijuana and cocaine along the North Carolina coast.

"For the most part, the drugs are coming from Mexico," she said. "The contraband is transported by tractor trailer, car, and boat, with coastal drug traffic rising the fastest of all."

"That's where the Golden Boys come in," Millay sneered. "Their parents must be so proud."

When Laurel was done, Harris opened his messenger bag and withdrew a packet of papers. "I present you with the Hunter Drummond file."

Rawlings raised an eyebrow. "Oh?"

"Olivia told me that she saw Hunter hanging with the rest of the Bagels 'n' Beans crew, and since the ME said that Ruthie probably died of a drug overdose, I decided to see if there was a connection between drugs and Hunter Drummond." Looking very pleased with himself, Harris continued. "Hunter owns a very expensive boat, but works a job that pays just over minimum wage. On paper anyway." Harris paused to put two slices of goat cheese and caramelized onion pizza on his plate. "I called the company he works for, MarineBioPharm, and pretended to be interested in a job they're advertising online. MarineBioPharm specializes in creating medicine from marine specimens. They're a subsidiary of a huge pharmaceutical firm. However, Hunter's boat isn't registered to either company. Not only does Hunter own it, but he paid for it in cash."

Olivia handed Harris a beer. "Bellamy said that she and her husband gave him the down payment and that their money was returned quickly and with interest."

Millay gestured at Harris's papers. "Do you have a photo of this Hunter chump? I want to see if I've met him."

Harris handed her a printout.

"*Him!*" Millay's mouth turned down in distaste. "He's only been in town for a few weeks, but you'd think he could turn water into wine. Even when Bagels 'n' Beans is packed, the other Abercrombie models go out of their way to find a seat for this punk. They listen to his stupid stories about collecting sea urchins and snails and laugh at his lame jokes. And he sits there, checking out his cell phone, like people should line up to kiss his ring."

Laurel twisted a piece of pizza crust. "Are you sure you want to get involved with these people, Millay? It's one thing to hang out with them during the day. But what happens when you end up at a party on one of their boats or in some club parking lot at two in the morning?"

"Have you forgotten where I work?" Millay laughed. "I can take care of myself." She elbowed Rawlings. "Okay, Chief. What are you arresting me for? Shoplifting? Possession? Prostitution?"

Harris nearly choked on his pizza.

Rawlings gave everyone a stern look. "We have no evidence that Hunter Drummond or any of his companions have committed a crime, so we must tread carefully. Like it or not, the Drummonds are a powerful family. They have influential friends."

"The mayor, for example," Harris said gruffly.

Laurel put a hand over his. "The chief's right. I've been watching the Golden Boys for weeks, and I can't prove a thing. My gut says they're up to no good, but I have no evidence."

Olivia looked at Harris. "Did you only research Hunter or did you check out everyone in the Drummond family?"

"I poked around a bit." He glanced down at his notes. "Way back when, the Drummonds were cotton farmers turned plantation owners turned merchants. Their import-export business took off, they bought a ton of land downtown, and have been collecting rent ever since. They own half the waterfront." He pointed at Olivia with his beer bottle. "The half you don't own, that is."

Laurel pointed at Olivia with her pizza crust. "Olivia has three properties. The Drummonds have sixteen. Hunter could have bought his boat with trust fund money, for all we know."

"Maybe," Harris said doubtfully. "But the chief always told us to pay attention to coincidence. So is it coincidence that Hunter has a bunch of pics on his Facebook page showing his favorite watering holes around the Caribbean?" He gave a theatrical pause. "And Mexico?" He turned to the chief. "Aren't the illegal drugs flooding into Oyster Bay being imported from Mexico?"

At that, the entire group started talking at once, until Rawlings raised his hands to shush them. "Before we form a lynch mob, let's pool our facts and try to get a clearer picture of what we know and what we don't know."

"But that's so logical," Harris complained. "I've always wanted an excuse to carry a pitchfork and a torch. If we went back in time—"

"Yes." Olivia interrupted. "Back in time. It seems like everything started with the discovery of that time capsule. Maybe it was like a Pandora's Box, letting evil loose into the world."

Laurel pulled a face. "Don't forget about hope. Pandora shut the lid before it could escape. Hope remains."

"Not for Ruthie Holcomb," Olivia said and got up to pour herself another drink.

Chapter 10

A public library is the most enduring of memorials, the trustiest monument for the preservation of an event or a name or an affection.

—MARK TWAIN

According to Laurel, the bagel shop was packed late in the afternoon on Fridays. The Golden Boys gathered to share a beer or two before heading out to the area's trendier eateries and clubs. They seemed to disappear every Saturday, and Laurel postulated that the entire group was engaged in offshore rendezvous. Petty Officer Lindsay Parker confirmed this theory. She told Cook that many of the young men took daylong fishing trips on Saturday, and while the Coast Guard fined several of the captains for minor infractions, none of the officers had discovered proof of illicit activities.

Their attempts to thwart the traffickers failing, Rawlings and Officer Cook strolled into Bagels 'n' Beans on Friday evening and arrested Millay just as she was starting in on her second beer.

"She put up quite a fight," Rawlings told Olivia over dinner later that night. "Gave Cook a solid kick in the shin, elbowed me in the gut, and called us some very colorful names."

Olivia smiled, picturing Millay squirming like a cat in a child's arms. "She didn't inflict any serious damage, I hope."

Rawlings laughed. "No. I think she rather enjoyed acting the part of a delinquent. She was still cursing when we dragged her to the booking area. Afterward, she and I chatted in my office and then she went out through the back door and headed to work."

"How did the Golden Boys react to the scene?"

Rawlings squeezed a lemon wedge over his filet of baked flounder. "They watched us intently, but with a curious sort of detachment. Not one of them seemed bothered by her arrest." He ate a mouthful of fish and shook his head. "There was a communal stiffening when we arrived, like the crowd was half expecting us. Yet they weren't nervous. For some reason, those young men believe they're untouchable."

"Maybe they've been taught what to say and do if questioned by the police. Someone with clout and a ton of money could be running this group from a safe distance," Olivia said.

Rawlings nodded. "I spoke with a buddy of mine in the DEA, and he confirmed what Harris told us the other night. Mexico has become the South's biggest supplier of cocaine and marijuana. The drugs are distributed off the coast of Florida and are then taken north."

Olivia stared at him. "I never thought this would happen here. Not to this extent."

"That's why we need to send a message. If we chop off an arm—"

"Another will grow back."

Rawlings gave her that determined look she knew so well. "Most creatures retreat after being seriously wounded. If the arm grows back, we chop it off again. That's what I do, Olivia. That's what it means to serve and protect. And partnering with the Coast Guard gives my officers the necessary clout to stop the flow of drugs into our town. But we can't just shoo these delivery boys away. We need to catch them with their holds full of illegal drugs."

Olivia considered how the Golden Boys appeared to work in synch. "Maybe some of the boats are decoys. If they all go out at once and return at roughly the same time, only a few of them are likely to have an encounter with the Coast Guard."

"Officer Parker made a similar remark."

"Is she focusing on Hunter Drummond's maritime activities? Remember the photos on his Facebook page? He's been to Mexico. He has a big, expensive boat, and he doesn't make much money at his day job."

"We have nothing on the guy. Nothing solid. I hope Millay has better luck than we've had." Rawlings put down his fork. "So. How was your day?"

"Fine. I got work done at both restaurants, spent time playing with Caitlyn and Anders, and ran errands. While the flounder was cooking, I read more letters. Ruthie must have saved everything Stella ever wrote. There are hundreds of notes and cards." She thought of the first letters that Stella had written on lavender stationary bearing her monogram in a florid script. "They were just little girls when their friendship started, and from what I can tell, their bond grew stronger with each passing year. Because Stella was discouraged from seeing Ruthie and Ruthie didn't always have a working phone, I think they communicated by letter. It's old-fashioned and very sweet."

"What did Stella write about?"

"She fantasized about living in an underwater palace. Or a secluded cove. She wanted to be a mermaid or a selkie—a mythical woman who could turn into a seal—or a siren. It changed from month to month. When Stella was particularly unhappy at home, she'd write about using magic to conjure a tidal wave that would obliterate White Columns and everyone in it. From an early age, she felt alone and unloved. Her fantasies mature over time, but the themes stay the same. Ruthie seemed to be the only light in Stella's life."

"And now . . ." Rawlings trailed off and Olivia nodded sadly.

Leaving Rawlings to do the dishes, she went upstairs to continue reading. She read Stella's letters until late that night and began again on Saturday morning, jotting observations in a little notebook. Before starting in on what looked to be the last year of letters, she reviewed her notes over a cup of strong coffee.

"The girls talked about escaping after Stella graduated from college, and Stella seemed to be trying to convince Ruthie that it was okay to leave her mother," Olivia muttered to herself. "Stella isn't allowed to sneeze without her parents' permission. She has no money of her own. Ruthie isn't close with her brother, Luke, but Stella hates her brother. Hunter is cruel to her at home and at school. He's also nasty to Ruthie. He spies on the girls and reports their activities to his parents. Stella's family seems to have code names. I need to research Bertalda and Kuhleborn. Stella refers to herself as Undine and Ruthie is called Melusine. I'll have to look up all four of those names."

Olivia set the notebook aside and followed Haviland onto the deck. He trotted off to investigate an interesting scent in the dunes while Olivia gazed at the ocean for a long time. "They wanted to be mythical creatures. For the water to wash over them and turn them into something wild, beautiful, and free."

Standing there with the warm spring sunshine bathing her shoulders and face, Olivia suddenly wondered how the girls exchanged their letters. There were no envelopes and they were always folded into small, narrow rectangles. The shape seemed familiar to Olivia, but she couldn't place it.

"Is there an unread letter waiting to be collected? One of Ruthie's perhaps? There could be a clue in such a letter. A sign that she was suicidal. Or scared."

The idea spurred Olivia into finishing the last of Stella's correspondence to Ruthie.

When Olivia was done, she could feel the weight of Ruthie's absence in the pile of papers on her lap. Ruthie would never answer Stella's final letter. She couldn't sign off as Melusine or draw tiny mermaids around her signature. Her voice had been forever silenced.

A wave of sorrow washed over Olivia, but she refused to let it pull her under. She had to swim against the current, to use her anger to discover what had happened to Ruthie Holcomb.

After carefully arranging the letters into a neat pile and retying them with the blue ribbon, Olivia poured a second cup of coffee and opened her laptop to search for the code names.

Bertalda and Kuhleborn were from a novella called *Undine*, the story of a beautiful but soulless maiden. Undine, daughter of the King of the Sea, comes ashore to live with an old fisherman and his wife. She aspires to find true love and acquire an immortal soul. To her delight, she meets a handsome knight and the two are married. Bertalda, the knight's jilted fiancée, tries to ruin the couple's happiness as does Kuhleborn, Undine's uncle. Heeding the advice of these wicked individuals, Undine's husband betrays her and Undine is forced to kill him.

"Bellamy and Beauford Drummond are Bertalda and Kuhleborn," Olivia surmised. "They plot to destroy Undine's happiness, which is why Stella chose Undine as her nickname."

Melusine, Ruthie's nickname, was from a legend about a woman who turned into a mermaid once a week.

Gazing at a color illustration of Undine from the cover of an early nineteenth-century copy of the novella, Olivia suddenly realized that she had a very good idea of where the girls had left each other letters for so many years.

Jumping up, she raced to the back deck and shouted, "Haviland! Come in!"

When Rawlings came downstairs, still half-asleep and murmuring something about the lack of quiet, Olivia pressed a cup of coffee in his hand, kissed his stubbly cheek, and said, "I'm off to the library."

She left him standing at the bottom of the stairs, looking drowsy and confused.

Leona Fairchild had worked at the library for as long as Olivia could remember. She and Olivia's mother had been close friends, and Olivia saw Leona more as an aunt than the tireless mistress of the public library.

"It's been a long time since you were the first patron waiting to get inside," Leona said as she unlocked the front door and propped it open for Olivia and Haviland.

"I need to check someone's record." Olivia proffered a take-out coffee cup and a paper bag containing a chocolate hazelnut croissant from Decadence.

Leona gave Olivia a quizzical look. "Are these bribes?"

"Yes, but I don't think you'll mind bending the rules this time," Olivia said. "The patron is no longer living."

Relaxing somewhat, Leona led Olivia to the circulation desk and invited Haviland to come around behind the counter and make himself comfortable. Next, she booted up the computer and took a sip of her coffee. "Wow. This is the good stuff." She gestured at the ring on Olivia's left hand. "There's a German proverb that says coffee and love are best served hot. When's the wedding?"

"End of May," Olivia replied with a smile.

Leona studied her and Olivia tried not to squirm beneath the librarian's shrewd gaze. Leona knew almost everyone in town. Had she somehow crossed paths with Charles Wade? Did she already know Olivia's secret?

"Have you heard about the plans for the new bookstore? That it's supposed to have a café and a performance space?" Olivia asked with false nonchalance.

"It's all anyone can talk about." Leona's mouth twitched in amusement. "Suddenly, every man, woman, and child is an aspiring poet, hip-hop artist, or musician."

"Leona. The man who bought Through the Wardrobe is . . . he's . . ." Olivia found that she couldn't speak the words.

Leona put her hand, soft and age spotted, over Olivia's. "Camille told me about Charles. I was sorry to learn that he's come back to Oyster Bay. I never cared for the man. And for the record, you favor Willie Wade far more than Charles. You have Willie's toughness. Camille was my best friend and you inherited her best attributes, but she didn't possess half of your gumption. If she had, she might have lived a happier life."

Olivia felt a prick of familiar grief and nodded silently. "I don't want people to know Charles is my father. I don't want to be seen as an outsider ever again."

Leona patted Olivia's hand. "Is that what's troubling you? Silly girl. Put that out of your mind this minute. You're as much as part of this town as anyone else. Now, tell me whose borrowing history you need to see."

"Ruthie Holcomb's."

Leona's fingers sprawled across the keyboard. "But you said—"

"That she'd passed away, yes. Caitlyn and I found her on the beach. The cause of death is still unknown."

"But she was so young!" Leona drew back in shock. "I've known her since she was knee-high. What a terrible, terrible thing." After taking a moment to collect herself, Leona called up Ruthie's record. "She was very fond of a particular book. She borrowed it again and again. Year after year. Perhaps the illustrations inspired her own artwork." Leona looked stricken. "Her poor mother."

Olivia murmured something about helping Mrs. Holcomb and then peered at the results on the screen. One title appeared over and over. Jane Yolen's *Neptune Rising:*

Songs & Tales of the Undersea Folk. In fact, it was currently listed as having been checked out by Ruth Holcomb, and wasn't due back for another week.

"Would you mind showing me Stella Drummond's record?" Seeing that other patrons had entered the library, Olivia dropped her voice to a hushed whisper. "I want to see if she borrowed this book with the same consistency."

"I hope you plan on explaining yourself at some point," Leona said, but did as Olivia requested.

The Jane Yolen title appeared on Stella's history too. Dozens of times.

"Stella and Ruthie were two peas in a pod. It doesn't surprise me to find that they loved the same book. They met here at least once a week. They'd sit and read and whisper together for hours." Leona took a tissue from a box on the desk and dabbed her moist eyes. Grabbing a second tissue, she blew her nose. "Heavens. I'd better pull myself together. No one wants to see an old lady weeping."

A man approached the desk carrying a stack of suspense novels and Olivia touched Leona's shoulder. "I'm going to wander around the stacks. I have a sneaking suspicion that *Neptune Rising* never left the library."

If the book was still in the building, Olivia couldn't locate it under Y for Yolen.

She scanned the entire shelf and then paused to think. If Ruthie and Stella didn't want the book to be found, they'd hide it at a safe distance from where it was supposed to be shelved. She checked over a display of Hans Christian Andersen books, examined the books surrounding the copies of *The Little Mermaid*, and then moved to folktales and mythology. Her eyes traveled along the colorful spines and then she felt a thrill of excitement. For there, tucked between a copy of *Mermaid and Other Water Spirit Tales from Around the World* and *The Folklore and Mythology of Sacred Waters,* was the Jane Yolen book.

Olivia pulled *Neptune Rising* from the shelf and reverently examined the cover. It showed a forlorn young woman sitting on a rock cradling the head of a bearded merman. She flipped through several pages, too intent on her task to admire the illustrations. And then, on the inside back cover, she found what she'd been searching for. Sticking out from the library card pocket, which hadn't been used since the library went digital over a decade ago, was a letter.

Taking a deep breath, Olivia carried her prize to a secluded corner. She sat in a plush maroon chair in the young adult nook, gingerly unfolded the single sheaf of paper, and read.

Sister Undine,

Bertalda and Kuhleborn have finally lost it. They actually offered me money to stop talking to you. It's a ton of money!! Enough for you to get out of that house!! You can buy a place on the beach. You know my mom won't let me leave but I'll visit. B and K said I have to leave town right after I get the money. By the time I write again, I'll have it, so figure out what you want to pack and where you want to go!! You're going to be free Undine!! You can take moonlight swims and put seashells in your hair. You can work wherever you want. Eat whatever you want. Wear whatever you want. I'm SO happy!! I can't wait to hear how you snuck out and never looked back. I'll leave one more letter and then you'll have to send me real ones in the mail. But not too soon. They'll all be watching. And they'll be SO pissed!! Ha ha!! It's finally time. FREEDOM!!

Love, Melusine

"Sweet Lord," Olivia whispered and reread the letter. "Bellamy and Beauford Drummond tried to bribe Ruthie into leaving town. Why now? Why the urgency? It *must* have something to do with the time capsule. But what?"

A patron seated nearby looked up sharply and Olivia made a conciliatory gesture.

I need to show this to Rawlings right away, she thought and slid the letter into her handbag.

Leona was busy with another patron, so Olivia waved good-bye and then snapped her fingers for Haviland to heel.

Outside, Olivia pulled out her phone and saw that Rawlings had sent her a text.

Working on Michel's wedding gift, he'd written, and Olivia knew that he'd gone to his house to paint.

She found him in the garage wearing an old Home Depot apron filled with brushes of all shapes and sizes. The radio was set to the classic rock station and Rawlings was singing along to "Gimme Shelter" by the Rolling Stones at the top of his voice.

Haviland started to howl and Rawlings faltered for a moment, but then smiled and kept right on crooning. When the song was over, he turned the volume down and examined the brushes he'd been using as drumsticks as if he couldn't remember how they got in his hands.

"I'm almost done, so you can look if you want."

Olivia didn't spend much time at the house Rawlings had shared with his late wife, and she'd been there even less lately because he didn't want her to see his gift to Michel and Shelley before it was ready.

"Are you sure?" she asked, and he put down the brushes and pulled her in front of two canvases.

The first painting featured a fruit and vegetable stand at the farmer's market. A woman weighed tomatoes on a produce scale while her husband prepared to slide a bunch of carrots into a brown paper bag. The couple was surrounded by a rainbow of food. There was bright yellow corn, glossy red apples, velvety purple eggplants, baskets of green beans, and bins of white onions. In the background, a fish seller held out the catch of the day—a freckled sea bass—for a customer to inspect. The faces of the merchants were weathered and plain, and yet Rawlings had made them beautiful.

In the second painting, the food had made its way to a young couple's kitchen. A man and a woman were in the kitchen cooking supper. The man, who was smiling widely and had a plaid dish towel thrown over his shoulder, held a bowl filled with the farmer's plump tomatoes in one hand and a frying pan containing the sea bass in the other. The woman, who was chopping onions, was caught in the middle of a laugh. The counters were covered with spice containers, utensils, and a tattered recipe card. Steam rose from a pot on the stove and the scene was bursting with energy.

"These are incredible," Olivia said. "You managed to capture the pure joy of growing, selling, and preparing food. It's like a dance that moves from one painting to another. The colors, the vitality—they're incredible." She shook her head in awe. "Michel and Shelley are going to love these."

"I hope so," Rawlings said humbly. "I'd like to add more shading around the stove. After that, they can dry until Monday."

Olivia crossed the paint-splattered cement floor and switched off the radio. "I found something at the library. I think it's Ruthie's last letter to Stella. I figured out their codes names too. Bertalda and Kuhleborn are Beauford and Bellamy Drummond. Stella is Undine and Ruthie is Melusine." She held the letter out for Rawlings. "Sawyer, Beauford and Bellamy tried to bribe Ruthie shortly before her death. And there's more. Cheryl Holcomb told us that Ruthie had big dreams, but it didn't sound like she'd ever be allowed to follow them. Ruthie makes it clear that she isn't allowed to leave her mother. What if Cheryl found out about the bribe and insisted Ruthie give her the money?

Ruthie wanted Stella to have it. She wanted Stella to get away." Olivia forced herself to stop. "Just read."

Keeping his expression blank, Rawlings unfolded the letter. Olivia watched a crease appear on his forehead as he read. When he reached the end, he glanced at her and then returned to the beginning again. "Why bribe her?" he puzzled aloud. "Why did she pose a threat?"

"Ruthie says Beauford and Bellamy offered her a ton of money. That reeks of desperation. And this goes beyond parents disapproving of a friendship. Beauford and Bellamy crossed a line. Are you going to question them?"

Rawlings shook his head. "I can't. They're not even mentioned by name. Ruthie had no money on her when she died and you didn't find any in her room, right?"

Olivia admitted that she hadn't.

"Cheryl Holcomb didn't behave like she had a recent windfall either." Rawlings kicked the base of a nearby sawhorse in frustration. "I need something concrete. I can hardly accuse the Drummonds of a crime based on this." He waved the letter in the air. "Frankly, I'm not convinced myself."

"What if I show the letter to Stella? Maybe she can come up with a piece of hard evidence."

Rawlings considered the idea. "I don't know, Olivia. Based on what you told me, Miss Drummond is rather unstable. You'd have to tread very lightly."

"She might refuse to see me altogether," Olivia said, feeling dejected.

In fact, Stella did refuse. Olivia stopped by White Columns the next afternoon and asked for Stella. A housekeeper wielding a feather duster accepted the note and the bouquet of blue hydrangeas Olivia had brought for the young lady of the house, but refused to allow Olivia inside. Stymied, Olivia decided there was nothing to do until Stella made contact. She'd used Stella's code names and had written that she had important information to share about Melusine. Now, she could only wait and hope that Stella took the bait.

"Until then," she told Haviland on the way home, "we have a wedding to celebrate."

The First Presbyterian Church was filled to capacity on the last Monday in April. The afternoon sun streamed through the stained glass windows and lit the sanctuary with brilliant splashes of color.

The pews and altar were bedecked with sprays of iris, camellia, and daffodils, and the heady scent of lilac permeated the air. Organ music soared through the room, coming to roost in the rafters of the vaulted ceiling.

Shelley was stunning in an off-white strapless sweetheart gown with a trumpet skirt. Her hair was pulled back and she'd tucked a spray of baby's breath to the side of her French twist. Other than her pearl earrings, she wore no accessory and had chosen natural-looking makeup. She didn't need adornments. Her happiness made her beautiful.

The moment she reached the end of the aisle, Michel seized her right hand and kissed it fervently. Smiling at him, Shelley cupped his cheek with her free hand and wiped away a tear with her thumb. The guests released a collective sigh at this display of tenderness.

Pastor Jeffries began the ceremony with a call to prayer. Unlike the other guests, Olivia did not bow her head. Her gaze was drawn to the stained glass window of the angel and the child. This time, she didn't see herself in the child pressed against the woman's robe, but Ruthie Holcomb.

I hope an angel came for you, she thought before focusing on the bride and groom again.

The ceremony proceeded smoothly. An a cappella group sang an exquisite rendition of John Denver's "You Fill Up My Senses (Annie's Song)" and then invited everyone to join them in singing a rowdy version of the hymn "One More Step Along the World I Go."

By the end of the song, people were grinning and clapping and Pastor Jeffries had to settle everyone down in order to conduct the exchanging of vows. Unfortunately, Michel decided to write his own, and when he removed a stack of notecards from the pocket of his suit coat, several people groaned. Olivia listened for a full minute before her mind began to wander. As Michel went on and on, albeit with great passion, Olivia heard a noise in the back of the sanctuary.

Two policemen slipped inside and stood behind the last row of pews on the bride's side. They seemed to be searching for someone, so Olivia leaned over to Rawlings and whispered, "Without being too obvious, take a look at the men by the main door."

Rawlings stretched out his arm and, like a teenager in a movie theater, curled it around Olivia's shoulders while twisting his neck toward the back of the room. One of the officers caught his eye and held up his cell phone. Rawlings nodded and faced forward again. He subtly removed his phone from his pocket and read the text message. Olivia saw his jaw muscles tighten and then he closed his eyes and kept them shut for a full five seconds.

"What is it?" she whispered, feeling a knife-twist of alarm.

Michel had finally finished his vows, the rings had been exchanged, and Pastor Jeffries invited the couple to share their first kiss as husband and wife.

The moment the beaming newlyweds breezed down the aisle, making their way out of the sanctuary to the sound of raucous applause and cat cries, Rawlings pulled Olivia close. While everyone else watched the bride and groom make their jubilant exit, Rawlings pressed his forehead against Olivia's temple and held her tightly. "I have to go," he said in a low voice. "I'm sorry."

Olivia put her hand over his. "What's happened?"

Rawlings released a slow breath and Olivia felt like a huge weight had descended upon them. It wrapped around their bodies like a dense fog, blinding them to everything and everyone. Blotting out the light.

"I'm sorry," Rawlings repeated. "But Cheryl Holcomb is dead."

Chapter 11

The wine of Love is music,
And the feast of Love is song:
And when Love sits down to the banquet,
Love sits long.

—JAMES THOMSON

Olivia didn't remember leaving the sanctuary. She had a dim sense of the other guests throwing birdseed as the bride and groom hurried, hand in hand, to the vintage convertible parked in front of the church. She heard more shouts and applause and the clanking of something metal striking asphalt as Michel eased the car into traffic.

"Look!" someone cried. "Someone tied tiny pots and pans to the bumper. Isn't that darling?"

And then, somehow, Olivia found herself at The Boot Top. Entering the kitchen through the back entrance, she glanced around as if the place were altogether unfamiliar.

"Ms. Limoges! You're just in time. We literally *just* put the last glass on the champagne glass pyramid," a waitress declared. "It is *so* Great Gatsby in the dining room. Is Michel on his way?"

Before Olivia could reply, one of the sous chefs approached. "The buffet is ready too. We're using the domed chaffing dishes, so the food will stay warm. The rest of the kitchen staff left to shower and change, but I wanted to make sure everything met with your approval before I take off."

Olivia gave them both a vacant nod, and the waitress put a hand on her arm. "Are you okay, Ms. Limoges?"

"I heard something upsetting at the church, but it has nothing to do with the wedding." Olivia managed a reassuring smile. "The ceremony was really lovely. The bride was radiant and the groom, exuberant. Why don't you show me the magic created in my absence? The first of our guests will arrive any minute now."

The waitress practically skipped as she led Olivia out of the kitchen and into a dining room filled with dazzling candlelight, magnificent flowers, and a host of tantalizing aromas.

The scene before her was incredibly romantic. There were the yards of diaphanous white fabric hanging from the ceiling, silver candelabra, hundreds of tiny tea lights on each table, pearl napkin rings, beribboned chairs, and handmade place cards dangling from the lids of glass spice jars. The jars had been filled with sea salt for the men and sugar for the ladies, and each one came with a set of heart-shaped measuring spoons.

"This is a fairy tale setting brought to life," Olivia said, awestruck. "I've never seen so many candles. It looks like the stars fell from the sky onto our tables." She pointed at the ceiling. "Having those lanterns hanging beneath the gauzy fabric adds another touch of magic. Michel will be speechless."

"If we could only be so lucky," the waitress scoffed, but her eyes were shining with pleasure.

The room soon filled with wedding guests. They walked around admiring the décor and exalting over the incredible food. In their wedding finery, they looked like a flock of colorful birds. The candlelight increased the restaurant's elegance and gave everyone a glamorous air.

Olivia tried to enjoy herself, but felt too hollow inside to engage in small talk. Standing in the midst of luxury, she thought about Cheryl Holcomb's decrepit trailer. As Olivia watched the partygoers sip cocktails and dine on Lobster Thermidor, she recalled Cheryl's vacant refrigerator and the empty potato chip bags covering her scarred coffee table.

"I must offer my congratulations!" A woman suddenly appeared in front of Olivia. She had a cocktail in each hand. "I've never seen an elegant reception."

Olivia took in the woman's designer gown and heels and remembered Cheryl's shapeless housedress and cracked rubber flip-flops. Hoping that her expression didn't betray her thoughts, Olivia said, "Thank you, but I can't take the credit. My talented staff is responsible for this wondrous transformation."

"Well, Michel and Shelley are over the moon. And the rest of us are just happy to have been invited to the event of the season," the woman continued.

"The Secret Garden Party is more likely to earn that distinction," Olivia said pleasantly. Though she now thoroughly disliked and distrusted Bellamy Drummond, she still wanted to support the historical society. "Are you planning to attend?"

The woman nodded. "With that recommendation, how could I possibly miss it?"

"Be sure to tell your friends," Olivia said before turning away to speak with another guest. "It'll be an unforgettable evening."

As Olivia headed to the bar area to make sure Gabe had everything he needed, she took her cell phone from her satin evening bag and examined the blank screen for the third time. Rawlings had promised to update her on his whereabouts by text, but as the evening wore on, Olivia doubted he'd be making an appearance at the reception.

"What could be more important than my party?"

Michel teased, coming up behind Olivia and sliding his arm around her waist. "Are you sexting your man?"

"Not exactly. He was called out on a case," Olivia said with false cheerfulness. She wouldn't let anything spoil Michel's perfect evening, and in an attempt to change the subject, she pointed at the round table where the wedding cake was on display. "I've never seen a cake like that. It's so over-the-top that it could only be yours, my dear."

Michel laughed heartily. "The quilted fondant with the lapis beading is a bit much, I admit. But having the top tier shaped as a chef's hat? That was Shelley's idea. I had my doubts about all the flavors we wanted to accommodate, but we managed."

"And who decided to put chef hats and aprons on the fondant bride and groom? You?"

"Both of us." Michel grinned. "Cooking is more than a job to us. It's who we are." He glanced upward and clasped his hands together. "We wanted to celebrate the calling that brought us together all those years ago at culinary school. If it weren't for our love of food, we'd never have found each other. And to be completely honest, we wanted to show off a little. And it worked. Even *Maman* is looking forward to a slice and she doesn't care for sweets. Can you imagine? A Frenchwoman who doesn't like chocolate?"

"Having tasted my fair share of Shelley's desserts, I know we're in for a treat."

Michel beamed. "Allow me to whet your appetite." He led her closer to the cake. "The bottom tier is marble pound cake with a chocolate fudge filling, the next tier is an almond walnut cake with a filling of raspberry puree, and after that, we have a light-as-air red velvet cake with a Bavarian cream cheese filling."

"Which leaves the top tier."

"The chef's hat, yes." Michel proudly gazed at his creation "The pièce de résistance is made of hazelnut soaked chocolate devil's food cake with a Nutella filling." Michel inhaled. "Can you smell the buttercream? It reminds me of Shelley's perfume." Laughing, he accepted a glass of champagne from a waiter and kissed the young man on both cheeks. Without taking a sip of the bubbly, he placed his glass on the cake table, wrapped his arms around Olivia, and spun her in a circle. "You have made my every dream come true!"

"Stop it," Olivia protested, beating lightly on his chest and trying not to laugh. "You're confusing me with Shelley."

Releasing her, Michel plucked a freesia stem from a nearby centerpiece and tucked it behind her ear. "This place is a paradise on earth, Olivia. I cannot put my gratitude into words. Shelley and I will never be able to repay your generosity."

"Just promise you'll never quit," Olivia said and squeezed Michel's arm affectionately. "Stay in my kitchen and keep making my customers happy. If I lost you, I'd have to close the place down."

"I have everything I need right here," Michel said, and then drifted off to find his bride.

Eventually, Olivia took a break from the party to walk Haviland. Gabe had kept an eye on the poodle while Olivia was at church, but he'd been shut in Olivia's office for the reception. The moment she opened her office door, Haviland ran to the rear exit, eager to escape the din.

Together, the pair walked toward the harbor. Relishing the sudden quiet, Olivia inhaled a deep breath of sea air. She was grateful for the chance to gather her thoughts. And though she knew she had to return before Michel and Shelley cut the cake, the night was so lovely that she was tempted to linger by the docks.

While Haviland sniffed a pylon, Olivia stared out across the water to where a large freighter was making its slow passage northward. The ship was just a black smudge against the horizon. It seemed so far away and so solitary that it somehow reminded her of Luke Holcomb. How far offshore did he live and work, she wondered. And had he been told about his mother yet?

"You're all alone now," she whispered as she watched the ship. "You've barely had time to grieve for Ruthie. And when that phone call comes and you hear about your mother . . ." Tears pricked Olivia's eyes and she angrily blinked them away.

Haviland finally completed his olfactory inspection of the pylon and nuzzled Olivia's palm to get her attention. "I'll help Luke Holcomb," she swore to Haviland. "Somehow."

Her cell phone rang and she hurried to pull it out of her handbag.

"Hello," Rawlings said, imbuing the word with sorrow and fatigue.

Olivia wished she were with him. "How are you?"

"Confused," Rawlings said. "It appears that Mrs. Holcomb ingested too many pain pills. However, she left no note and was also in the middle of cooking. We found a burned lasagna in the oven. A neighbor told me that Luke Holcomb is due to arrive tomorrow and that Mrs. Holcomb was very much looking forward to seeing her son. Lasagna's his favorite supper, and Mrs. Holcomb wanted to have it ready ahead of time."

Olivia searched for the freighter's lights in the dark ocean and felt a wrench of pain on Luke Holcomb's behalf. "Does he know yet? About his mom?"

"I haven't been able to reach him," Rawlings said. "And now I think it might be more prudent to tell him once he's safely in Oyster Bay."

"Oh, Sawyer. This is awful." She gripped the phone tightly and tried to focus. "And Cheryl swallowing pills? I can't wrap my head around it. She was brokenhearted, but not despondent. And she wanted to know what happened to her daughter. I can't believe she would have deliberately taken her own life before having those answers." Olivia hesitated. "Unless she already knew what happened."

"She may have forced Ruthie to help pay bills, drive her

around, or promise not to move out, but do you think she would have harmed her daughter?"

Olivia had been asking herself the same question since she'd met Cheryl Holcomb. "I don't know. She was keeping *something* from us. I saw a flash of guilt in her eyes when she mentioned Ruthie's big plans."

"If Ruthie overdosed on her mother's pain medication, it would explain the guilt you saw on Mrs. Holcomb's face," Rawlings reasoned. "What I'm about to say next is for your ears only, Olivia, but two of Mrs. Holcomb's neighbors witnessed someone delivering flowers to Mrs. Holcomb last night. Neither neighbor saw the delivery person's car, which is strange."

"I'd say. That mobile home park is fairly remote. There's no way to get out there without a car and you could hardly put a floral arrangement on the back of a bike or motorcycle." Olivia's mind was buzzing. "I don't think the local florists deliver on Sundays either."

"Officer Cook will contact the florists within a fifty-mile radius, but I imagine you're right."

"Did anyone get a look at this guy?"

Rawlings sighed. "Not really. Black sweatshirt, jeans, and sneakers. It was drizzling, so the person had their hoodie pulled over their hair. The neighbors don't even know if it was a man or a woman. They got the impression of someone young, but the twentysomethings seem to dress alike these days."

"Dark-wash skinny jeans, faded T-shirts, and tennis shoes," Olivia said. "Did you find a note in the flower arrangement?"

"No. And this is going to sound unusual, but I'm sending you an image of the bouquet. Can you look at the picture and call me back with your immediate impression? I'm sorry to ask this of you in the middle of the reception, but I'm trying to gather as many details as I can while the scene is fresh."

Olivia assured him that she'd return to the party as soon

as they were done talking and hung up. A few seconds later, a text with an attachment came through. She enlarged the photograph and frowned.

"White lilies, carnations, and fern leaves. It looks like the kind of arrangement you'd see at a funeral home," she said when she had Rawlings on the line again.

"My thoughts exactly. And in that case, I should be able to trace the source of the flowers. They could merely be an expression of sympathy and the card was lost en route. Perhaps the deliveryman—let's just assume he's male for the moment—was dropped off at the entrance of the mobile home park, made his delivery, and left again without being seen."

"In the rain?" Olivia asked in disbelief. "Did the neighbors notice whether he entered Cheryl's home or not?"

Rawlings paused. "The woman facing Mrs. Holcomb's house claims that he went inside."

"I don't like the sound of that. People accept deliveries at the door. Either Cheryl knew the delivery person and invited him or her in, or she was forced to do so."

"There could be a less sinister explanation," Rawlings said. "For example, the flowers were too heavy for Mrs. Holcomb to manage, so she had the delivery person carry them inside."

"Did the neighbor see this person leave?"

"No." Rawlings couldn't conceal his frustration. "She had to break up a fight between her two boys, and by the time the dust settled, she assumed the deliveryman was long gone. My team is dusting the entire trailer for prints."

"They'll find mine."

"I already documented our visit to Mrs. Holcomb," Rawlings said. "We're looking for prints other than ours, Ruthie's, or Mrs. Holcomb's."

There was a second of dead air in the middle of his last line and Olivia realized that someone was trying to call her. She told Rawlings to hold on and checked the screen. "That's Gabe," she said. "It must be time to cut the cake."

"Give Michel and Shelley my best." Rawlings sighed. "I would have liked to have danced with you at least once," he whispered. "You look so beautiful in that blue dress."

And then he was gone.

Olivia turned back for The Boot Top, and Haviland fell into step behind her. The moon peeked out from behind a scattering of wispy clouds and cast its pale light over the midnight-blue silk of her gown. The fabric shone like fish scales, and Olivia was reminded of a corkboard covered with photographs of two girls pretending to be mermaids.

Rawlings stayed in town again, and when Olivia woke the next morning with a fuzzy head and stiff limbs, she felt like she'd barely slept. After letting Haviland out, she flopped on the sofa and stared at the ceiling fan, too tired to brew coffee.

Michel's reception had gone on until well after midnight. Olivia suspected the open bar had something to do with the revelers' reluctance to go home, but it was more than that. The atmosphere of gaiety permeating the party continued to renew itself as the hours passed. Even after the music wound down from a pulsating dance beat to the jazzy instrumental tunes played in coffee shops and bookstores, the energy levels remained high. Guests clustered in small groups and shared stories and soft laughter while the newlyweds moved from table to table, sharing their happiness with everyone.

Leaving Gabe in charge of the restaurant, Olivia had finally bade the couple good night and slipped away. She hadn't crawled into bed until after one in the morning and then, as tired as she was, hadn't been able to quiet her mind.

"Did Cheryl kill herself?" she asked Haviland, who was stretched across Rawlings's side of the bed. "Did she know something about Ruthie's death that she couldn't bear? Or that someone else couldn't risk having her know? Are either of these deaths connected to Beauford and Bellamy's bribe?" She stared at the shadows on her ceiling. "No matter what, I do think Cheryl Holcomb loved her daughter."

There was no one to argue this point. Haviland had fallen asleep almost instantly and was chasing his dream quarry—a sandpiper or a squirrel perhaps. His paws twitched and he moaned longingly, making Olivia wonder if his prey had gotten away. She watched him, his face bathed in moonlight, and wished she could escape as easily.

Now, lying on the sofa, Olivia closed her eyes and gave herself permission to doze off for a little while. The morning sun streamed through the windows, and like a cat, she felt relaxed and comforted by its warmth. She was on the verge of sleep when the ringing of a phone shattered the peace.

"You sound like I feel," Rawlings said when she picked up.

"It was a late night, but a good one for Michel and Shelley. How are you?"

"As confused as I was during our last conversation," Rawlings said. "Ruthie's tox screen results came in first thing this morning. She had drugs in her system—Oxycontin to be precise—but not enough to kill her. Not even enough to make her sick. I'm currently waiting on the full blood panel report. There was a powerful toxin in her body, but we couldn't identify it using the standard tox screen."

"Some sort of poison?"

"The ME believes it might be venom. We're all confounded, to say the least." Another voice mumbled in the background and Rawlings said, "I have to go. I sent a pair of officers to meet Luke Holcomb's flight and they've just arrived at the station."

Olivia closed her eyes and groaned softly. "That young man is about to hear that his mother is gone—that he's lost everyone. Can he handle that kind of shock? Most of us couldn't."

"I have a flask of whiskey in my desk for times like this," Rawlings said in a leaden voice. "And Cook's on his way to the kitchen to get us black coffee. I just hope it's strong enough." He paused and then whispered, "Jesus, I hope we're all strong enough."

Olivia offered what words of encouragement she could before hanging up. She then sank back against the sofa cushions feeling utterly powerless. And angry.

"Venom?" she shouted at the empty room. She thought of Ruthie's last letter and decided it was time to have another talk with Stella Drummond. After taking a quick shower, she dressed in jeans and a white blouse and drove to Grumpy's Diner. She needed to see a friendly face before heading to White Columns, and it had been too long since she'd tasted Dixie's wonderful coffee and seen her infectious smile.

"I gave you up for dead!" Dixie skated to an abrupt halt in front of Olivia's favorite window booth. "I know Laurel's a traitor, but I never expected *you* to eat at that bagel shop. Not since it changed hands anyway. My oldest boy saw you there, so don't try to deny it."

"Have you heard any rumors about the clientele?" Olivia asked after assuring Dixie that she wouldn't dream of eating a single item off the Bagels 'n' Beans menu.

Dixie grudgingly placed a cup of coffee on the table. She then stood with the carafe balanced on one hip and frowned at Olivia. "Why? What's goin' on? Does this have somethin' to do with Ruthie's death?"

"Maybe," Olivia said, reaching for the cream. "I honestly don't know."

"All I can tell you is that my regulars hate the place and the folks who hang out there."

Olivia nodded. "I can't see the two crowds mixing."

"That's because the folks who eat here at five in the mornin' actually work. Deep-sea fishin' charters? Booze cruises? Day trips to Ocracoke or Hatteras? Those bagel boys aren't exactly doin' hard labor, but their boats are nicer than anythin' the men I serve would dare to dream about. They could slave away their whole lives and never set foot on the floating palaces those spoiled brats are captainin'." Warming to her subject, Dixie slammed the carafe on the table, causing coffee to slosh over the rim of Olivia's cup. "Folks say that those kids don't know the first thing about navigatin' these waters. Or fishin' for that matter. So what are they doin' with their fancy boats?"

"I don't think they're in Oyster Bay to sell fish." Lowering her voice, Olivia shared her theory that the Golden Boys were running drugs. "But we have no proof. Can you spread the word that Rawlings needs help nailing these guys? Ask the shrimpers and the dockhands and anyone else you can think of to keep an eye out for suspicious activity on the water? It's going to take a village to put a stop to this."

Dixie wiped up the spill and promised Olivia she'd do anything to help. "I'll fetch you and Haviland some breakfast. I imagine you have a busy day."

Olivia nodded. "While we were talking, I realized that almost everyone I know would lend a hand to keep this town safe. I need to eat quickly, Dixie. I just figured out a way to flush Stella Drummond out into the open. It's imperative that I speak with her about Ruthie."

"I heard she hasn't left her house since she identified Ruthie's body. The poor girl." Dixie released a sympathetic sigh. "How do you plan to convince her to meet you?"

"I'm going to ask Leona Fairchild, the most honest person I know, to lie."

Leona removed her reading glasses and cleaned the lenses with the hem of her shirt. "Let me get this straight. You want me to call Stella Drummond and tell her that the book she requested is ready to be picked up?"

"Yes."

"Even though she hasn't put any materials on hold?"

Olivia squirmed under the librarian's steely gaze. Leona was the closest she had to a mother figure, and she hated to disappoint her in any way. "Yes. I found a note that Ruthie Holcomb wrote to Stella in the library's copy of *Undine*. It wasn't shelved correctly, and I believe the girls used that book to pass each other notes."

"Are you telling me that they've hidden books around this library for over a decade?" Leona was clearly put out by the idea that they'd flagrantly disrespected the Dewey decimal system.

"They didn't have much choice. Stella's parents are very controlling, and they didn't want her to hang out with Ruthie."

Leona scowled. "Why would they disapprove? Ruthie was a sweet girl. A quiet, sweet girl." She replaced her glasses and examined the computer screen. "I'll bend the truth just this once, Olivia. I trust you, and I know you wouldn't ask me to do this if it wasn't important."

Fifteen minutes later, Olivia saw Stella securing a periwinkle beach bike to the rack near the library's front entrance. "Here she is."

Olivia darted into Leona's office and waited for Leona to show Stella in.

When Stella entered, she was clutching the library's copy of *Undine* to her chest as if she were holding a life vest.

She probably feels like she's drowning, Olivia thought.

Grief was like that. She remembered all too well that sense of sinking into cold, numb darkness. The pressure of loss made it hard to breathe. But no matter how much Olivia longed to keep sinking, to escape from the pain, she always rose to the surface. The tug of life was too strong. Looking at Stella's wan face, Olivia hoped that the truth would help pull Stella from the depths and allow her the chance to tread water for a little while as she grieved.

"You." Stella stood by the door, looking warily at Olivia. "What do you want?"

Olivia was afraid she might bolt, and was thankful when Leona put a hand on Stella's arm. "I got to know your friend Ruthie over the years. She always showed me her latest works of art in case I wanted to add to my collection. See?" She gestured at the bookshelf behind her desk, and Olivia noticed several picture frames and a tissue box covered with seashells. "I was friends with Olivia's mother the way you were friends with Ruthie, so I understand what you're going through. I really do. Camille was young when she was taken from us. And I loved her. To live without her was like walking around with half of my heart. Is that how you feel?"

Keeping her eyes on the floor, Stella nodded.

"Olivia wants to help. Talk to her, Stella. And whenever you need a friend, you know where to find me." Leona backed out of the room and shut the door behind her.

Stella took two steps toward the empty chair across from Olivia. "You tricked me into coming."

"When you didn't respond to the note I left at White Columns, I had to resort to deception." Olivia held out Ruthie's letter. "I wanted you to see this as soon as possible. Ruthie left it in the book you have there."

Snatching the letter away, Stella shook with anger. "This is private!"

"Not if Ruthie was murdered, it isn't. If someone killed your best friend, then nothing's private anymore."

Stella's knees buckled and she practically fell into the chair. Taking a deep breath, she tenderly unfolded the letter. She read it hungrily, her eyes flying over the lines and her entire body curling inward, as if she wanted to absorb Ruthie's words into her skin. "Damn it, Ruthie. What were you thinking?" she murmured, crushing the letter against her chest.

"You didn't know about the bribe?"

Stella shook her head. "I had no clue. My parents never wanted us to hang out, but I can't believe they'd pay Ruthie to stop being my friend. They're so screwed up." She touched the letter with trembling fingers and uttered a crazed little laugh. "But Ruthie was going to screw *them*. She was going to take their money so I could get the hell out of here. This letter? It's like she found a way to come back and tell me that she was looking out for me right until the end." She glanced up, her eyes gleaming. "My parents should be arrested for blackmail. If Ruthie took the money and then got killed by some stoner thief—"

"Ruthie's letter isn't proof of anything. It implies that your parents—who aren't named because she used code words—offered her money to leave Oyster Bay," Olivia said gently. "There was no money in Ruthie's room, and it doesn't seem like her mom knew anything about it. If she did, she kept it secret."

"Mrs. Holcomb took *all* her secrets to the grave," Stella whispered furiously. "And who do you think sent her there? Ruthie's killer! She must have known something, like where the money was. And now, we'll probably never know." Stella began to withdraw inside herself, just as she did when Olivia spoke to her at White Columns.

"We need to find this person." Olivia reached over and seized Stella's hand. "You promised to make them pay for what they did to Ruthie. Do you want to keep that promise or not?"

Stella gaped at her.

"Listen, Stella. This whole mess began when the time capsule was discovered. When I peeked inside the capsule, I saw a copper box sealed with the Drummond Family seal. Then the box disappeared. I think your mother removed it before anyone else could see it, but I don't know why."

"Is the box about this big?" Stella motioned with her hands. "With a cotton flower stamped into the wax?"

Olivia's heart raced. "Yes! Have you seen it?"

Stella nodded. "I have no idea why the stuff inside scared my parents so much, but it did." Suddenly, her expression changed. Awareness flooded her face. "I think you're right. After that box was found, they acted weird. There was all this nervous whispering, but I don't know why . . ." She got to her feet and headed for the door.

"Wait!" Olivia called after her. "Where are you going?"

Stella paused just long enough to say, "Home. To get the box. I'd like to see if you can make sense of what's inside."

Chapter 12

Hope is the only good god remaining among mankind; the others have left and gone to Olympus.

—THEOGNIS OF MEGARA

Olivia decided to pass the time awaiting Stella's return critiquing the first chapter of Millay's next young adult novel. The opening paragraph described the young heroine's recurring nightmare in which she was unseated from her Wyvern in the midst of a heated battle. Pushed from her mount's back by a dragon rider's lance, Tessa fell from a great height, the cold air whipping her long braid as the dark and jagged mountains rushed up to meet her.

The anxiety of the scene was so well written that Olivia felt her own angst increase. Without making a single note, she returned the chapter to her purse and left Leona's office.

Haviland, who'd once again been invited to nap behind the circulation desk, made it clear that he would rather not be disturbed. When Olivia spoke his name, he signaled his reluctance to move by rolling onto his back and stretching his paws skyward.

"Stella rushed out like the building was on fire," Leona said. "Is everything all right?"

Olivia nodded. "She went home to get something and

will hopefully come straight back when she has it. I'm too restless to sit and wait. I thought Haviland and I could walk around out front, but he looks pretty content where he is."

Leona glanced down at the poodle and then handed Olivia a sheet of paper. "Take this outside instead. It's a list of the new titles we'll be featuring this month. You could reserve a few books before anyone else gets the chance." She grinned. "Bring some on your honeymoon."

"My honeymoon?" The word momentarily paralyzed Olivia. It struck her that she and Rawlings had never vacationed together. They'd had several long weekend trips to Savannah, Charleston, and Annapolis, but never spent more than four days away from Oyster Bay. "I hadn't given a honeymoon much thought. Sawyer and I are always so busy . . ."

"You'll only get married once, so make it memorable," Leona said. "I know you're not interested in bells and whistles. I don't see you marching down an aisle to Mendelssohn." She smiled and took Olivia's hand. "When you were a little girl, you reminded me of a sprite or a water nymph. You were tall and willowy with that cloud of white-gold hair. You hated to wear shoes and always had sand on your feet. Even in wintertime you smelled like the sea. Your wedding needs to fit your personality."

"I'm too old to be a sprite," Olivia said.

Leona shook her head. "To me, you'll always be that quiet, wild girl with the ocean-blue eyes. Maybe if you honeymoon at the right place, you can be her again for a few days."

Olivia pictured an island surrounded by glittering water. She saw Rawlings napping in a hammock—a book splayed across his belly and a hat covering his face—while Haviland splashed through the surf. She imagined wading into the ocean, her fingertips brushing the curling froth of waves as they rolled into the shore, and smiled.

"See?" Leona released Olivia's hand. "You're going to need that beach read."

Heeding the librarian's advice, Olivia took the flier to a

bench outside the front entrance. From this vantage point, she'd be able to see Stella bicycling toward her.

Olivia scanned the first group of titles on Leona's handout. The latest political thriller didn't capture her interest nor did a romantic suspense set in Alaska. However, when she read the blurb about a gothic novel featuring a peculiar Scottish family, a crumbling castle, and a terrible secret, she momentarily forgot about Stella.

When she did glance up from the book list, she saw a sleek Mercedes convertible pull into the empty spot next to her Range Rover. The driver was Charles Wade.

"I've been looking all over for you!" he shouted and strode over to her.

Olivia clenched her jaw. She didn't want to speak with him. She wanted him to leave so she could meet Stella alone and finally see what was hidden inside the mysterious copper box.

"You're a hard woman to find." Charles put his hands in his pockets and gave her a winsome smile. "Every time I dine at one of your restaurants, you're either working at the other location or running errands. I considered dropping by your house, but I didn't want your cop boyfriend to shoot me in the kneecap."

"The chief of police doesn't make a habit of firing his sidearm without provocation," Olivia said dryly. "What do you want?"

Charles gestured at the bench. "May I join you?" Without waiting for Olivia to respond, he sat beside her. He breathed in deeply through his nose and then exhaled loudly. "I feel twenty years younger. Must be the clean air and simple living. Sometimes it's good to be in a place where nothing happens."

Olivia had a flash of Ruthie's dead body on the beach. Oyster Bay had its dark side, but people like Charles didn't know it existed. She stared at him. "Is this some delayed midlife crisis? Are you trying to prove to the locals that you're unrecognizable as the son of a fisherman?" She swept her arm to indicate their surroundings. "Do you want to impress a bunch of people who don't remember or give a damn about you?"

Charles said nothing.

"No matter how much property you buy, you won't belong," Olivia continued.

A shadow passed over Charles's face. "But Willie did? Even though he was nothing but a drunken fisherman who coveted the woman I loved."

"Yes," Olivia said. "He had many faults, but he wasn't duplicitous. He didn't love me, but he still put food on the table and a roof overhead. When my mother's death crippled him, the people of this town swept in to help. They cooked us meals. Gave me rides home. They saw our suffering and understood. But you? They'll hear your accent and see your manicured fingers and know you for an outsider."

Charles shrugged. "Then I'll be the outsider who changes this place forever."

For the first time, Olivia heard an emptiness in his voice. A longing. Softening her stare, she turned her whole body to him and spoke gently. "What are you really looking for? I'd truly like to know."

Charles seemed taken aback by her change in demeanor. His cocky grin vanished and it seemed like a lifetime of disappointment appeared on his face, deepening the wrinkles around his mouth and the lines etched into his forehead. "I grew up wanting to be clean," he murmured. "I didn't want hands covered with rope burns and scars. I didn't want to smell like fish or have their scales stuck all over my skin and clothes." He examined his smooth palms. "My parents would work all day and then sit at the dinner table without saying a word. Their eyes were vacant. They rarely laughed. How can you be carefree or happy when every penny's been spent before you've even earned it?"

The question was rhetorical, but Charles seemed to be waiting for a reply, so Olivia mumbled, "I don't know."

"You live here. You've seen people like them, haven't you? Shuffling through each day like zombies?"

"At times," she said. "But I've also seen those same people shuck off their cares over a cold beer at Fish Nets. I've seen them shout and laugh when sharing stories with one another, and I've witnessed their courage and magnanimity of spirit during times of trial. The people here always come together. They don't hesitate. They're strong and fierce and brave. They know life is hard, but they also know how to celebrate small triumphs." She spread her hands. "I'm sorry that your parents couldn't do that. It makes me better understand why you wanted to leave."

Charles averted his eyes. "Was Camille happy? At least some of the time?"

"She was happiest here." Olivia pointed at the library. "And when she was with me. She was an amazing mother. I had a story and a lullaby each night. She cooked all of my meals and stuck little notes in my lunchbox. Most importantly, she . . ." Olivia had to pause to swallow the lump in her throat.

"Go on." Now it was Charles who spoke in a soft voice.

"She told me that I could do anything I set my mind to. She'd say, 'You shine brighter than any star. Yesterday and today and tomorrow.'" Olivia smiled at the memory. "She recited that to me once a day. And I believed her."

Charles gazed at the library's façade. "I'm glad you had each other. And I'm sorry that I left her." He turned back to Olivia. "And you."

"That doesn't matter now," Olivia said without ire. "But this town matters to me. If you ever cared about my mother, let it alone. She loved this place."

"I'm not the bad guy," he protested. "I saved the

bookstore for Camille. And for you. When I got wind that the former owner needed funds to keep the place afloat, I bailed him out. I knew the two of you were friends. Now that he's gone, I'd hoped you and I could be partners."

Olivia was stunned. "Partners?"

He pulled a business card from his pocket and handed it to Olivia. "In order for the bookstore to succeed long-term, it needs a chic café. You're a damn good restaurateur, and I thought we could embark on this venture together."

Olivia examined the card. "Biblio Tech Café." The O of "Biblio" was shaped into the round rim of a coffee cup. "Is this a play on the word *bibliothèque*?"

"I thought we'd pay homage to your French heritage. Doesn't *bibliothèque* mean library or bookcase?"

"It does." Olivia had to admit that she liked the name. "Are you envisioning an Internet café?"

"Not in the standard sense," Charles said and immediately became more animated. His eyes gleamed with boyish exuberance. "I thought we'd use technology to showcase books. It's kind of a reverse model. Far too often, people do their browsing at a bookstore and then go home and buy the book online. I'd like to put a stop to that trend and give Through the Wardrobe a chance of not just surviving, but flourishing."

Olivia was caught up by his enthusiasm. "And by making the bookstore a hip place to hang out, you'll earn customer loyalty."

"Exactly. Imagine a small screen on every café table. A book cover and short blurb fills the screen for maybe ten seconds. Then, another cover and blurb appears. The screens could feature certain genres like romance, mystery, or the hottest fiction titles—whatever. I'd leave those decisions to you and Jenna. That young woman has a good head on her shoulders."

"It would be like the meeting of two worlds," Olivia mused aloud, warming to the enterprise. "One half of the store would be filled with books, magazines, and educational materials. The children's play area and the cushy reading chairs would all remain. And then—"

"You step through an enormous stainless steel wardrobe into the café," Charles said dreamily. "The new space is sleek and modern. Wood and metal with an exposed brick wall and funky light fixtures. The coffee is amazing. The food is casual—sandwiches and salads—but very fresh and artistically presented."

Olivia was so immersed in the discussion that she almost failed to notice Stella pedaling straight for her. She blinked, pushing aside menu ideas like fried green tomato BLTs and shrimp Po Boys, and shot to her feet.

"I have to go," she said to a befuddled Charles. "But I like the sound of Biblio Tech. We can talk more later. How can I reach you?"

"Give me your phone," he said with the relaxed ease of someone used to being obeyed. "I'm just going to add myself to your contact list."

Olivia thrust her phone into his hand and then waved at Stella. "I'll meet you at the bike rack," she shouted. Her anxiety to relieve Stella of the object filling her teal backpack was nearly palpable. The moment Charles returned her phone, she promised to contact him soon and hurried off.

Stella seemed unsettled to find Olivia outside, sharing a bench with another person. "Who's that man?" she asked warily, eyeing Charles over Olivia's shoulder.

"A business associate," Olivia said airily. "He just happened to see me waiting and decided to stop and give me a status update on a building project."

"He's tall. Like you," Stella said, slipping the backpack from her shoulder. She held it by the handle until the black Mercedes left the parking lot. "My mom hid this in her closet, so she won't realize it's missing for a while. Not that I care. I hope she stresses out so badly that she jumps off a bridge. Of course, that still leaves my A-hole dad and brother." Stella proffered the backpack. "I don't know what this stuff means, but if you figure it out, you'll tell me, right?"

Olivia nodded. "I'll leave a letter in the back of the library book just like you and Ruthie used to—"

"I want those letters." Stella's face was suddenly dark with anger. "They were for Ruthie. I hate that you read them."

"I'd hate that too. And I'm sorry." Olivia tightened her hold on the backpack in case Stella tried to reclaim it. "I only wanted to help. And Stella? Ruthie was right to advise you to leave Oyster Bay. Go after that nanny job. Buy a little place near the water. Try to make some of your dreams come true. Do it for Ruthie."

Stella's eyes narrowed. "I'm *staying* for Ruthie. I'm staying because the only thing that matters is finding out who killed my best friend." Her voice rose with each statement. "I'm staying to make sure they get what they deserve!"

"I hear you," Olivia said softly. "But after the killer's been caught, will you think about starting your life over?"

"What life?" The words were a whisper. "Just take the box. I need to bring home some library books because my mom will check my backpack. But I'll come back every day to see if you've left me a note."

After removing the box from the backpack, Olivia followed Stella into the library. She headed for Leona's office while Stella approached the circulation desk. Olivia heard Stella say, "I need books on marine biology. Textbooks. With pictures."

Olivia didn't catch Leona's reply. The pull of the box was too strong. Heart racing, she shut Leona's door and placed the box on the desk blotter. And then, fingers trembling in anticipation, she raised the lid.

"You think the contents of this box have something to do with Ruthie's death?" Laurel asked.

She, Millay, and Olivia were gathered around the island in Harris's kitchen. It had been agonizing to wait for Laurel and Harris to get off work, but at least they could meet. Rawlings couldn't come at all. He'd finished a gut-wretching interview with Luke Holcomb and had driven the young man home. Then, he and Cook had sifted through Cheryl Holcomb's financial history and were presently searching for the unidentified floral delivery person.

"We e-mailed images of that bouquet to every flower shop and grocery store within an hour's drive," Rawlings told Olivia when she called to see if he could get away for an hour. "No one made that arrangement, but a customer could have purchased the flowers and done it themselves."

"What about the shops who deliver? Can they account for their employees' whereabouts on Sunday?" Olivia asked.

Rawlings sighed. "As we suspected, most of them are closed on Sundays. Two florists keep Sunday hours and that's only to fill funeral orders. In both cases, the florists are a husband-and-wife team and handle their own deliveries. I sent an officer to interview them in person, but I doubt either of them is our hooded deliveryman. I'm putting every resource into locating this person because my gut tells me that those flowers weren't given as an act of kindness."

"Maybe the Bayside Book Writers can find a clue." Olivia told him that she'd asked their friends to examine the obscure items inside the copper box. Rawlings wished her luck and promised to check in later.

Eager to begin, Olivia now laid a black-and-white photograph on the granite countertop. "Let's start with this," she said. "Harris, do you have a magnifying glass?"

"An awesome one. Hold on." Harris disappeared into the next room and returned carrying a small wooden case.

Millay eyed the case. "Seriously? You keep your magnifying glass in there?"

"This isn't some kid's toy," Harris said. "It's an LED lighted glass that can magnify an object up to ten times its original size. My parents got it when I was building my first computer from scratch."

"Just hand it over, Steve Jobs." Millay opened the case and passed Olivia the magnifying glass.

While Olivia studied the image, Laurel filled tumblers with iced tea from a pitcher in Harris's refrigerator. "Is this a family portrait?"

"If so, the head of the household looks like a pompous ass," Millay said. "Why does he get to wear a suit and sit in a chair while his wife stands behind him dressed in an apron and a cheesy cap? And the little girl between them looks scared. She's holding the woman's skirt as if she'll fly away if she lets go."

Olivia moved the magnifying glass over the man's face. "This is Nathaniel Drummond, the patriarch of the Drummond family. He's responsible for the wealth and social prominence the Drummonds enjoy today. He owned cotton plantations and later became a merchant. He purchased large tracts of land near the harbor—land that Beauford and Bellamy have since sold or now lease at exorbitant rates." She glanced at Millay. "And this woman is *not* Nathaniel Drummond's wife."

Laurel's eyes went wide. "How do you know?"

"I saw another photo just like this at the historical society," Olivia said. "It was in a bundle of portraits from the early nineteen hundreds that someone had placed in the time capsule. In his family portrait, Nathaniel wore the same suit, and his wife and daughter were elegantly dressed. They posed in a formal room and the wallpaper pattern featured the same cotton flower as the one stamped into this wax seal." She put a hand on the copper box, indicating the traces of green wax. "Beauford or Bellamy must have pried off the seal."

"Why?" Harris asked.

"That's what we need to find out." Olivia turned her attention to the photograph. "So who are these ladies?"

"With that apron and cap, I'd guess the woman was a maid." Millay elbowed Harris. "Get those lightning-fast fingers in gear and see if you can find images of maids." She looked at Olivia. "What year are we talking about?"

"The family portrait was dated 1910. Seven years before the time capsule was buried," Olivia said. "This photo was taken at White Columns."

Laurel grunted. "The Drummonds' ancestral home. That mansion could hold dozens of skeletons in its closets."

The friends continued to study the photograph while Harris searched for images on the computer. Within a few minutes, he swiveled the laptop around and said, "Here you go. Housekeeper's uniforms. According to this website on the history of domestic service in America, the housekeeper was in charge of the household. She bought the food, decided on menus, and oversaw the cleaning, laundry, and the rest of the staff."

"So is the little girl a lower-ranking maid?" Laurel puzzled.

"I think she's too young. Besides, she's holding a doll, not a feather duster." Millay borrowed the magnifying glass and held it over the girl's hip. "See?"

"I didn't notice that before. Both girl and doll have matching dresses, so the doll is almost camouflaged," Olivia said, peering at the tiny face. "Nathaniel's daughter had a doll in their family portrait too. A hand-painted bisque doll in a fancy lace frock. She had a curly blond wig and tiny pearl earrings."

"This looks like a German china doll. My grandmother had one just like it. I remember the white face and black hair," Laurel said, gesturing at the photograph. "Speaking of looks, the girl is a dead ringer for the housekeeper. Except for her eyes. She and Nathaniel Drummond have the same eyes."

"Oh, someone was a naughty boy." Harris wagged his finger. "But if he was sleeping with the help, why take a picture with her? Wouldn't he worry about his wife seeing this?"

"Maybe he kept the photo hidden," Olivia said. "Maybe he loved this woman. His expression is completely different from the portrait taken with his wife and daughter. His whole face is softer, more relaxed, and he's pivoting toward the woman and girl instead of away from them. In the family portrait, he's stiff and cold. They all look miserable. Here, they seem to be on the verge of smiling."

Laurel murmured in agreement. "And they're in the kitchen. The heart of the house."

"You can actually see through to the next room. Is that the wallpaper you were telling us about?" Harris repositioned the magnifying glass.

Olivia gave a nod and then sat back to think. As her friends sipped their tea, she stared into the middle distance.

"If Nathaniel Drummond had a long-term affair with this woman, and she bore him an illegitimate daughter, it would explain why the housekeeper's daughter has such a nice doll." Olivia shrugged. "But this is all conjecture."

Harris picked up the photo. "There's nothing written on the back?"

"Not that I could find." She watched him examine the blank surface with the magnifying glass.

"That's because you didn't have Inspector Gadget at your side. There's something here, all right. It was erased, but I can see the indentations." Smiling triumphantly, Harris pulled open a drawer and fished around for a pencil. He then laid the photo facedown on the counter and gently rubbed the side of the pencil across its surface. Pale letters emerged like the outlines of tiny ships in the fog.

Millay gazed at Harris. "You're the coolest nerd I've ever met."

"I know." Harris flashed her a grin and then squinted at the letters. "Emma and something Vance."

"Sadie," Millay said, peering at the wispy shapes. "Emma and Sadie Vance, 1910."

The names floated around the room. Everyone looked at the woman and the girl. They were no longer strangers from the past, but Emma and Sadie. Two people with a story to tell.

"Bellamy and Beauford must have been horrified to discover that Nathaniel wasn't exactly a pillar of society," Laurel said. "So they hid the box and this photograph out of shame. They haven't broken any laws."

"There's more." Olivia reached into the copper box and removed a yellowed document. "This is Nathaniel Drummond's will. Of a sort anyway."

"'Last Will and Testament of Nathaniel E. Drummond,'" Harris read aloud. His eyes traveled down the paper. "This will is useless. He doesn't actually leave anything to anyone. All those spaces are blank. And talk about your spidery handwriting." He pointed to the sole line on the paper. "Um, I have no idea what this means, but I can read it."

"Go on," Olivia prompted.

Harris cleared his throat importantly. "'For where your treasure is, there will your heart be also.'"

The friends exchanged confused glances.

Laurel placed the photograph next to the legal document. "The handwriting on the back of this picture and the will are a match. This line almost reads like some sort of postscript." She frowned in thought. "Or a riddle."

"Maybe Nathaniel Drummond was trying to send a message." Harris's eyes shone with excitement. "A message that he placed in the time capsule for posterity. Along with this photograph." He tapped his chin with his forefinger. "Do you know what I think?"

His friends waited for him to speak, barely breathing in their anticipation.

"I think this is a clue." Harris began typing into Google's search box. "I have no idea if it'll help us find out what happened to Ruthie or her mom, but Nathaniel's will mentions a seriously powerful word."

Olivia met his gaze and nodded. "Yes," she said. "Treasure."

Chapter 13

I once had a sweet little doll, dears,
The prettiest doll in the world;
Her cheeks were so red and so white, dears,
And her hair was so charmingly curled.
But I lost my poor little doll, dears,
As I played in the heath one day;
And I cried for more than a week, dears,
But I never could find where she lay.

—CHARLES KINGSLEY

"The line about treasure comes from the Bible," Olivia told Rawlings that night over dinner.

She had the photograph and Nathaniel Drummond's strange will spread out on the table between a salad bowl and an aluminum tray filled with Michel's Chicken Saltimbocca. After her meeting with the Bayside Book Writers, Olivia hadn't felt like cooking, so she'd called The Boot Top and placed a to-go order. The meal was still hot by the time Olivia returned home and placed it in front of Rawlings.

"It's hard to concentrate on Scripture when this chicken smells so good," Rawlings said, loading his fork. "Lunch seems like a distant memory."

"You eat. I'll talk," Olivia said. "Before our impromptu gathering broke up this afternoon, Harris researched the biblical reference. According to a website he found on interpreting the New Testament, the passage in which this line appears is about worldly treasures versus heavenly treasures." She filled a glass with red wine and handed it to Rawlings. "The gist of the message is that man cannot serve two masters. He can choose to spend his life acquiring material possessions, but loses his soul as a result. His other choice is to surrender his heart to God and thereby obtain the treasure of heaven."

"'For where your treasure is, there will your heart be also,'" Rawlings read the quote aloud. "So is Nathaniel Drummond trying to say that his worldly goods meant nothing? Is this a message of self-reproach? And why seal it in a separate box with a photograph of a woman who may or may not be his mistress?"

Olivia had been wondering the same thing. "I keep coming back to the size of the box. These two items could have been placed in a much smaller container. This was large enough to hold a pair of shoes."

Staring at the photograph, Rawlings continued to eat his meal. Olivia kept quiet, knowing he was turning over theories in his mind. Finally, he laid his fork down, pushed his plate aside, and folded his hands under his chin. "Let's say Bellamy Drummond did remove this prior to the official time capsule unveiling because she didn't want people to know about Nathaniel's affair. She hasn't committed a crime. What were you expecting to find, Olivia?"

Olivia thought back to the day in the church when the capsule was first discovered. "I want to know why Pastor Jeffries was frightened after he opened the time capsule. Why did he rush off to fetch Bellamy? There's something more to this than a cover-up of an old affair and I think it has to do with Nathaniel's will. His fortune was impressive back then, but nothing compared to what it is now. The Drummonds' real estate holdings alone are worth several million dollars."

"The only connection between Beauford and Bellamy Drummond and Ruthie Holcomb is a purported bribe. There's no proof of said bribe nor does the time capsule seem to fit anywhere in my investigation of the Holcomb women's deaths." Before Olivia could reply, Rawlings squeezed her hand to silence her. "I'm not dismissing the possibility that something underhanded has occurred, but the pieces of this jigsaw are so scattered that I can't form a lucid picture. The ME reports are equally enigmatic."

Olivia buttered a heel of French bread and tore off a piece. "What did he cite as cause of death for Cheryl Holcomb?"

"Suspected heart failure. Same as Ruthie. The symptoms are nearly identical. He expects Oxycontin to appear on Mrs. Holcomb's tox screen results, but he's also asked for the blood panels on both women to be given high-priority status." Rawlings ran his hands through his salt-and-pepper hair. "He shares in our confusion and frustration. He knows something is off with both Holcomb cases, but he can't identify what it is. Remember how I mentioned that Ruthie had cyanosis of the index finger?"

"Yes. It gave her skin a bluish appearance due to decreased blood flow."

Rawlings nodded. "That's right. Well, Mrs. Holcomb's finger also showed cyanosis. That's not coincidence. There's foul play involved, but I don't know the extent of it."

Olivia chewed her bread, her gaze repeatedly straying to the photograph of Nathaniel, Emma, and Sadie. The way Sadie held on to Emma's dress reminded Olivia of the young girl and the angel from the stained glass window of the Presbyterian Church. How often had that child changed faces since Olivia had first noticed her? She'd seen herself and her mother in the rainbow of glass, but then the girl had become Caitlyn, Ruthie, and Sadie. Little girls in need of comfort. Little girls in need of guidance, love, and perhaps most of all, protection.

Caitlyn had her parents to protect her, but what of the others? Ruthie's father had died when she was young, and her mother had been unwell for years. Sadie's father, if Nathaniel was her father, couldn't acknowledge their relationship, so how could she have felt loved and protected by a man who already had a legitimate daughter?

"Nathaniel Drummond looks happy here," Olivia murmured, her eyes fixed on the trio in the photograph. "He loved them. They loved him. This was his second family. The one he wasn't supposed to have, but did. He didn't regret his liaison with Emma. He secretly celebrated it. Otherwise, why risk taking this picture? Why capture the three of them together? If his contemporaries saw this, he would have been ruined."

"He was a bigamist," Rawlings said. "Not in the traditional sense—I'm assuming he didn't marry Emma—but for all intents and purposes, he had two wives and two daughters."

Olivia closed her eyes and pictured the photograph of Nathaniel with Martha and Josephine. And then her eyes flew open. "Both of his girls had dolls. Perhaps they were gifts from Nathaniel? Josephine's was in the time capsule. Maybe Sadie's was too."

Rawlings gestured at the copper box. "You think Sadie's doll was inside along with Nathaniel's cryptic message and this photograph?"

"I do." Olivia felt suddenly energized. "I'm not sure why, but I'll have to contact Stella tomorrow and ask her to look for Sadie's doll. Harris has already scanned both the will and the photo, so I might as well have Stella return the originals to her mother's hiding place. I'd rather let Bellamy believe that her secret—whatever that might be—is safe for the moment."

"Is it wise to exchange missives with Stella?" Rawlings gave Olivia a tender look. "I know you mean well, but perhaps this cloak-and-dagger approach isn't good for a young woman who's already on edge."

Olivia shook her head. "I disagree. Stella needs to act. She needs to feel like she's participating in solving the riddle of Ruthie's death." Olivia placed the paper and photograph back in the copper box and pushed the lid on tight. "Otherwise, she'll sit in her room, lost in her grief. My hope is that she gains enough energy to keep moving forward after this investigation is over. But she needs to play a part, to have an impact on this case, in order to move on with her life."

Rawlings was silent for a long moment. Finally, he nodded.

The couple discussed other topics over bowls of lemon sorbet. They talked about Millay's return to Bagels 'n' Beans following her fake arrest, and how, according to Millay, the regulars had received her warmly. In fact, Hunter Drummond had asked her to be his date for the Secret Garden Party Gala.

"All of the Bayside Book Writers will be there," Olivia said. "Harris told me earlier that he's invited the young woman he met in Texas to visit for the weekend."

"Emily, right? He mentioned her the other night when we went out for that beer." Rawlings smiled. "I'm hope it works out between them. She sounds like a keeper."

Olivia wondered if Harris could maintain a relationship with another woman now that he'd be hanging out with Millay on a regular basis. "What do you think of Harris becoming a police officer?"

Rawlings shrugged. "As long as he stays behind a desk, he'd be an excellent addition to my team. I just can't see him using a sidearm."

"Not a real one anyway." Olivia grinned. "I can easily imagine him playing one of those video games with the big plastic guns. He can probably mow down zombies like a pro."

Laughing, Rawlings got to his feet and lurched across the kitchen floor, moaning.

When Haviland raced over to him and sniffed his legs, Olivia said, "He thinks you're drunk."

"It's your fault. You kept topping off my wine." Rawlings raised a brow. "Are you planning to take advantage of me?"

"Absolutely," Olivia said. Joining him by the sink, she

wrapped her arms around his neck. "Leave the dishes. We'll do them later."

Rawlings tossed his utensils aside and cupped Olivia's face in his hands. "Much, much later," he whispered and then bent to kiss her.

Because the garden party fell on a Saturday, the Bayside Book Writers decided to hold their weekly critique session on Friday night. They planned to critique both Millay's chapter and Olivia's short story at the same time so Olivia could decide whether or not to shelve her historical novel and focus on her new project. Olivia was anxious to hear their thoughts on her piece about the lighthouse keeper, having injected more feeling into the story than she'd ever put in her novel.

By Thursday, Olivia's head was filled with ideas for more stories. After jotting down a few ideas, she dropped by the library to see if Stella had left a reply inside *Neptune Rising*. The day before, Olivia had left a note in the pocket asking Stella to search for the doll pictured in the old photograph. She also told Stella that the copper box was in Leona's office and suggested she return it before her mother realized it was missing.

"Too late," Stella had written in the letter Olivia found inside the book. "They know I took the box. To punish me, they're shipping me to my aunt in Atlanta. If I don't go, they'll say I'm suicidal and check me into the psych ward. My dad is driving me to the Raleigh airport tomorrow night and my jackass brother is supposed to watch me until then, so this might be my last chance to contact you. I haven't found the doll yet. If I find it, I'll hide it under the pier where you found Ruthie. Don't give up on her! S—"

Olivia traced Stella's initial with her fingertip. "You're not Undine anymore," she murmured sadly. Stella's fantasies had died along with her best friend.

"Did you find what you were looking for?" Leona asked when Olivia returned to the circulation desk.

"Yes, but Beauford and Bellamy are sending Stella away." She frowned. "I'm worried about her."

"Me too," Leona said. "There's something ancient about her eyes now. A look more befitting a wizened old widow than a young woman in the prime of her life."

Olivia knew exactly what she meant. "Maybe going to a new city will be good for Stella." The statement lacked conviction, but she pressed on nonetheless. "A fresh start."

"Maybe," Leona said.

"Have you shelved the books she returned?" Olivia asked.

Leona seemed surprised by the question. "Not yet. We're still shelving fiction, and the books she borrowed were all nonfiction. Big marine biology hardbacks." She gestured at the cart behind her. "Would you like to see them?"

Olivia came around the desk and examined the spines of the three books Stella had returned earlier that day. Leona was right. The material didn't seem to fit Stella's reading profile. Judging by the titles on her borrowing history, Stella preferred stories of mythical sea creatures to factual essays on ecosystems, but this time she'd selected two textbooks. One was called *Marine Biology* and the other, *Marine Pharmacology*. The third book was a National Geographic publication entitled *Citizens of the Sea: Wondrous Creatures from the Census of Marine Life*.

"Your brother's field," Olivia murmured. "What were you looking for, Stella?" Pulling the three hardcover books from the cart, Olivia placed them in front of Leona. "Can I borrow these? I'd like to figure out why Stella took a sudden interest in marine biology."

"Of course." She scanned the barcodes and stacked the books neatly on the counter. "Too bad Haviland doesn't wear a saddle. It would be so handy to place things in a doggie saddlebag."

More than happy to join in the librarian's attempt at levity, Olivia looked at Haviland. "No one can beat the Swiss when it comes to canine porters. What could top a brandy barrel attached to a dog collar?"

Leona smiled. "An apocryphal image, to be sure, but one I like to believe is based in truth. Could you imagine being lost in the Alps in the middle of a blizzard some two hundred years ago when suddenly an enormous dog appears through a curtain of snow, providing you with a shot of liquor and the hope of rescue?"

Both women gazed at Haviland fondly. The poodle sensed their eyes on him and got to his feet, his tail wagging merrily.

"He rescued me. There was no blizzard, but I was definitely lost," Olivia said, stroking the fur on top of Haviland's head. "He taught me that it's worth the risk to love, even if it means making oneself vulnerable." She gathered the marine biology books in her arms and tucked Stella's letter in her purse.

"We could all use a Haviland," Leona said and turned away to help another patron.

On the way home, Olivia passed a roadside produce stand. The sight of it sparked an idea for another short story, and since she'd already finished critiquing Millay's chapter, she carried her laptop into the kitchen and brewed a cup of coffee. Sitting at the table, she tried to create another story as rich in detail and feeling as the one about the lighthouse keeper.

To her delight, the writing flowed as easily as it had with that first story. Olivia's girlhood memories of the old woman who ran the fruit stand near her elementary school were remarkably vivid. As she typed, she could almost smell the vine-ripe peaches and hear the woman's musical voice.

The fruit seller's name was Rosalie. As a child, Olivia found it strange that such a work-worn woman should bear such a lovely name. But she liked Rosalie. Everyone did.

Rosalie was jolly, often to the point of silliness. She told jokes that Olivia didn't get but sent Camille into peals of laughter.

Rosalie could also juggle any kind of fruit. Olivia had seen her juggle two apples, a banana, and a plum while hopping on one foot and singing a song called "Backwater Blues." At the end of the song, she'd catch the plum in her nearly toothless mouth and let the rest of the fruit drop into her apron. The apron had two pockets that Rosalie kept stocked with peppermint candies for her customers' children.

Rosalie lived with her sister and her sister's large family. She'd never married and had once told Olivia's mother that, when she was a young woman, she'd fallen in love with a man she could never be with. His name was Valentino. She said that she'd given him her heart and could never get it back.

Then, without warning, Rosalie vanished. Her sister, who rarely smiled and certainly never sang or juggled, took over the fruit stand.

"What happened to Rosalie?" Olivia asked one day while her mother paid for their tomatoes, corn, and strawberries.

"She ran off with a man," the sister said derisively. "And at her age! He's a widower, an Italian, and a *Catholic*," she added. "My daddy is spinnin' in his grave. He was a Baptist preacher, you know. He wouldn't let Rosalie walk out with her Italian when he was alive, but there's no one to stop her now."

"No, there isn't," Camille had agreed, and Olivia could tell her mother was fighting to keep a straight face. Safely inside the car, Camille had clapped her hands. "Good for you, Rosalie!" she cried. "Good for you."

As for Olivia, she thought the names "Rosalie" and "Valentino" sounded very nice together. However, she missed Rosalie's cheerfulness and her peppermint candies.

Olivia spent all afternoon writing Rosalie's story. As before, she was so wrapped up in her memories that the hours passed unheeded. It took the ringing of the phone and an automated message about car insurance to jar her back to the present.

Stretching, she saved her work and got up to let Haviland out.

"I'll go with you, Captain," she said and slipped on an old pair of sneakers. She considered taking the metal detector along on their walk, but when she realized that the afternoon was already passing into evening, she decided to leave it behind.

As she strolled along the sand, the past retreated like a turtle drawing into its shell. Images of Rosalie were replaced by thoughts of Ruthie and Cheryl Holcomb. And of Stella.

Olivia tried to mentally organize what she knew about the Holcombs, the Drummonds, and the time capsule, but there were too many incongruent details. Why had Pastor Jeffries looked frightened the day the time capsule was found? What kind of toxin had killed Ruthie? If Beauford and Bellamy Drummond had really tried to bribe Ruthie, then where was the money? Had Sadie's doll been inside the copper box?

Eventually, the unanswered questions destroyed the tranquility of her walk. This irked her, especially because it was a picture-perfect evening. The air bore hints of an early summer, dozens of shorebirds scurried along the damp sand, and striations of peach and pink were appearing low on the horizon. Still, she turned back for home.

Rawlings had called while she was out and left her a message saying that he planned to work through dinner. The ME had received Ruthie's blood panel results and wanted to review them immediately.

Olivia felt a rush of hope. Perhaps Rawlings would come away from the meeting with a solid lead.

"I think we'll go into town for supper," she told Haviland. At the sound of the word, he lifted his ears and smiled.

She drove to The Bayside Crab House and was both pleased and annoyed that there was no available parking anywhere near the restaurant. She could hear bluegrass music coming from the eatery's spacious back deck and knew that dozens of people were sitting at the picnic tables, enjoying crab legs and lobster tail and the view of boats moored in the harbor.

Inside, she found the manager's office empty. Kim had gone home early to help Caitlyn with a school project and Hudson was up to his neck in dinner orders.

"The season has started!" he shouted boisterously and then barked a command at a line cook. Everyone in the kitchen was red-faced from exertion, the heat from the ovens, and the steam rising from the enormous pots on the stovetop.

Olivia sat on a stool and ate Caesar salad with grilled shrimp while her brother talked about his family. He cooked and chopped and plated, yelled at his staff, and shared new menu ideas with Olivia.

Haviland was served fresh fish mixed with greens on the small fenced patio area reserved for the staff. When he was done eating, he spent thirty minutes sniffing every inch of the area and then pressed his nose against the door screen.

"Ms. Limoges? I think your dog needs to go," the dishwasher said, pointing at Haviland.

"Yes, it looks that way," she said and thanked Hudson for the food and for chatting with her in the middle of his hectic dinner shift.

After leaving The Bayside Crab House, she led Haviland to the public beach access near the pier where she and Caitlyn had found Ruthie Holcomb. She didn't expect to find an antique doll tied to one of the pier's beams, but she felt compelled to check.

"With Stella leaving tomorrow, we're running out of time to discover what secrets are hidden inside White Columns," she told Haviland.

The poodle, who'd been staring straight ahead with an

unusual intensity, abruptly slowed his pace and issued a low growl.

"What's gotten your hackles up, Captain?" Olivia asked, peering into the gloom.

Unlike the day they'd found Ruthie, the entire beach was covered in shadow. The sky had gone dark and the water was a bruised blue. Only the sand gleamed with the pale light of a high half-moon. There was just enough illumination for Olivia to recognize the shape of a person sitting close to where Ruthie had lain.

"Go away," a male voice said. His tone was more weary than threatening.

Olivia was tempted to comply. It was far from wise to approach a stranger in the dark, but she had Haviland and she suspected she knew the man's identity.

"Luke? Luke Holcomb?"

"Go away," he muttered and raised a bottle to his lips.

Ignoring his request, Olivia advanced. "My niece and I found Ruthie," she said gently. "I came here to pay my respects. I couldn't think of another place to go."

The man released a low, guttural groan and Haviland responded by baring his teeth.

"Easy, Captain." Olivia put a hand on the poodle's head. She edged closer to the man she assumed was Luke. "Can we sit for a minute?"

"You might catch something if you do," he said, his speech slightly slurred.

The breeze carried the scent of sweat and beer to Olivia's nostrils, so she sat several yards upwind of the man. "What would I catch?"

"Our family curse. Seems to be spreading." He took another swig from the bottle. "I'm probably next."

Olivia found it disconcerting to be speaking with someone whose face was veiled in shadow. It made the man's voice seem very far away and strangely close at the same time. "Because of what happened to your sister and your mother?"

He made a noise that was part-laugh, part-sob. "Not just them. Every Holcomb—going back for decades. We never have money. We never have nice houses or cars. What we've got is bad health, crap jobs, and zero luck. Our lives are hell from the get-go." He threw the bottle at a pylon and missed. It landed in the sand with a nearly imperceptible thud.

Haviland trotted over to investigate the projectile and Olivia used the distraction to glance up at the wood overhead. She'd planned to use the mini flashlight on her key chain to examine the pier's underbelly, but she didn't dare do so now.

"I can see why you feel cursed," she said. "I've felt that way myself, but that was when I was much younger than you. If I'd known about whiskey then, I would have been the world's youngest alcoholic."

Her comment had the desired effect. Luke froze in the act of opening another beer bottle and set it in the sand.

"The neighbors keep asking me what I'm going to do next," he said, fixing his gaze on the water. "How the hell should I know? I barely made it through high school, but I don't need a college degree to know that something bad happened to my mom and sister. Two heart attacks? Nah, I don't think so. No way they were both accidents. No way my sister OD'd or had a bum ticker. But if someone did this to them, I can't figure out why. We haven't got anything worth taking. Never have." He reached out his hand, silently imploring Haviland to come closer. The poodle did so hesitantly, and was rewarded with a scratch between the ears. "I always wanted a dog. No room for one in that dump we called our house. And no pets are allowed on the rig."

Olivia wanted to offer this broken young man words of comfort, but all she could think of were useless platitudes. Luke Holcomb had lost his entire family. What could she possibly say to make him feel better?

"If you stay in Oyster Bay, you could adopt a dog from the shelter. You could save each other."

Luke stroked the fur on Haviland's back. "I'll probably have to sell the trailer. Even with the bit of money I sent Mom, she still wasn't getting by. She should have told me they were so hard up. Ruthie and I were never close, but knowing that she was taking painkillers because she couldn't afford to go to the dentist? That's messed up. It's such a goddamn waste." He kicked at the sand in frustration. "Nothing ever changes. Lots of Holcombs have tried to better themselves, have fought for a better life, but there is no better life. Not for us. Ruthie and I were idiots to believe we'd be different."

"I'm sorry," Olivia whispered. She couldn't think of anything else to say.

Luke got to his feet, swayed a little, and grabbed a nearby pylon for support. "Yeah," he murmured drunkenly. "Me too."

And then he stumbled off down the beach, a hunched shape disappearing into the dark.

Chapter 14

Strange to me, sounds the wind that blows
By the masthead, in the lonely night.
Maybe 'tis the sea whistling—feigning joy
To hide its fright.

—THOMAS ERNEST HULME

Olivia couldn't believe it was Friday. Stella would be leaving Oyster Bay today for an unknown amount of time, and her impending departure was weighing heavily on Olivia.

"If only I had something concrete to tell her," she complained to Rawlings over a breakfast of oatmeal mixed with banana slices and honey. "I hate that she has to go with her questions unanswered."

"I know we were pleasantly preoccupied last night, but do you remember what I said about the ME's findings?" Rawlings asked.

Olivia nodded. "That the toxin was biological, not chemical, which means its origins are natural and not synthetic." She put a hand on the stack of marine biology books on the kitchen table. "What does Hunter collect during his trips around Florida and the Caribbean? Is he harvesting toxic marine creatures?"

"I don't know, but I'd like find out." Rawlings topped off his coffee. "I plan to drop by the Drummonds' place this afternoon for a casual chat, and I've asked Harris to visit Hunter's employer, MarineBioPharm. They have a location in Research Triangle Park, and it was Harris's idea to apply for a job there when he first began to gather information on Hunter Drummond. Their HR department wanted to line up an interview within a day of receiving Harris's online application, but he's kept them at arm's length until now."

"What about Emily? Isn't she flying in from Texas today?"

"Harris will first meet with MarineBioPharm and then head to the airport. I'm hoping that he'll have a lead to share with us tonight."

Olivia pulled Stella's letter from between the pages of one of the marine biology textbooks. "Stella left this for me yesterday." She passed it to Rawlings and gave him a minute to read before pressing on. "Why do you think Beauford and Bellamy are reacting so dramatically? As both you and Laurel pointed out, they broke no laws removing items from the time capsule. Stella must know more than she confided to me."

Rawlings stared at the letter, his eyes glassy and unfocused. Olivia knew that his thoughts were drifting beyond the words on the page. "Stella's parents are either genuinely concerned for her state of mind or they've grown weary of her accusations. The third option is—"

"That she's a threat? Is she a threat because she won't stop searching for the truth?" Olivia asked. "It took Ruthie's death for Stella to come out from her shell, and I bet her parents are mighty displeased by her contrary behavior. Honestly, I don't believe Stella will go to Atlanta of her own volition. And since she's not a minor, how could her parents have her committed?"

"The Drummonds are very influential," Rawlings said. "If they assert that Stella poses a danger to herself, the hospital will have no choice but to admit her and have her evaluated. If she then shares her theory that her family tried to bribe her best friend into leaving town, she could very well be diagnosed as delusional or what-have-you."

Olivia dropped her empty cereal bowl in the sink and it clattered noisily against the basin. "How could they treat their own child like this? It's a shunning, plain and simple."

"A shunning? Yes, I suppose it is." Rawlings frowned and gestured at the library books. "I wonder if she found what she was looking for in these volumes. I can try to speak with her, but I doubt her parents will let me see her and I can't force the issue. I still have no grounds to exert my authority." He sighed in frustration. "According to this letter, Stella will be closely watched until she leaves for the airport."

"If she has something important to share, she'll find a way to get a message to me," Olivia said. "Stella used to be a dreamer. She used to be immature and timid. But that girl doesn't exist anymore. She's gone."

Rawlings pushed back his chair and collected his keys and phone. "You survived a tragedy," he said, coming to stand beside her. "It changed you, but here you are. People are amazingly resilient. Stella can move on. She's out from under her parents' thumb and there's nothing tying her to this town. She can seek her future. Just like you did." He kissed her and left for work.

"But I came back," Olivia said to the empty kitchen. "I couldn't sever the cord tying me to this place. It was too strong."

She went out to the deck, inviting Haviland to join her. After telling him to go play, Olivia stood gazing across the wide swath of dunes toward the lighthouse keeper's cottage. The small clapboard house had once been her girlhood home. It had been filled with so many unwanted memories that Olivia had had to renovate the entire structure from foundation to roof. It wasn't simply a cosmetic improvement. She'd been exorcizing ghosts. Olivia hadn't been able to move forward until she'd let go of the past, until the love of a few precious people gave her the courage to believe in the future. She wondered if Stella would ever return to the place where she'd known such grief. If so, would she find what Olivia had found? Peace. Finally.

"There's no peace without closure," Olivia said into the salt-laden wind, letting it carry her wish over sand and sea. "I must try to get that for her."

That evening, over lackluster Chinese takeout, the Bayside Book Writers shared their observations and recommendations with Millay.

"I'm not sure how to verbalize this," Laurel began, her eyes fixed on her notes.

She was always reluctant to criticize, but Millay nudged Laurel with the toe of her leather boot and said, "Out with it."

Laurel gave her a nervous glance and then nodded. "Well, I thought it was much darker in tone than your first book. And Tessa is different too. She's unsure of herself. I miss her fearlessness."

"Yeah, she's more basket case than bad-ass," Harris said bluntly. "Too many nightmares. Too much indecision. This isn't the Tessa we saw in the final scene of your previous book. At the end, she's learned how to fight like a Wyvern rider. And she was conflicted because she doesn't know if she can betray those people as she originally planned. It was deep stuff. Exciting stuff."

"In the beginning of this book, she's bogged down by doubt, but you never tell the reader why," Olivia said. "The chapter doesn't even mention the Wyvern riders, so I'm not sure where she is or what she's doing. She has compelling and descriptive nightmares, but I don't see how they connect to the plot."

Millay turned to Rawlings. "What about you? Do you think Tessa needs a dose of shock therapy?"

"So far, this book reads like a standalone. It just doesn't seem connected to your first novel. Tessa's different. The narrative voice is different. It seems to lack direction." He held out his hands, palms up, as if in apology, and gave Millay a sympathetic look. "How do you feel about what you wrote?"

"It's crap," Millay said. "Absolute crap. The pressure and anxiety you're sensing? It's all mine. It's not Tessa's. And it started immediately after I signed my contract."

Olivia was surprised by Millay's hangdog expression. "You make a three-book deal sound like torture."

"It kind of is," Millay muttered. "I'm being dramatic, but I'm not enjoying the whole publishing experience. I thought it would be so cool." She pointed at a stack of books on the coffee table. "But what I'm discovering is that after you write a novel—after you pour everything you have into the story—you hand it over to an agent, an editor, a sales team, an art team, and boom! It's gone. It's not yours anymore."

Laurel frowned. "Are you having issues with your editor?"

Millay shrugged. "Some of her suggestions are great, but there are scenes she wants me to change that will totally alter how readers view Tessa. I'm having a problem with that. My agent says that the author-editor relationship is all about trust and that ours will develop in time, but I'm not so sure."

"That sucks," Harris said. "How much veto power do you have?"

"Not enough." Millay shook her head in defeat. "I found that out when my editor e-mailed a sketch of my cover. It shows Tessa standing on the edge of a cliff. She's wearing a semitransparent white robe that belongs in a Victoria's Secret catalog, and her hair is blowing in the wind. Seriously, all she needs now is Leonardo DiCaprio and a spot on the bow of the *Titanic*. It's totally cheesy. There isn't a weapon or gryphon in sight—only a lame dragon silhouette in the upper corner."

"Sounds very Dungeons and Dragons," Harris said, and Olivia was pretty sure he meant it as a compliment.

Laurel put her hand on Millay's. "The scene on the cliff was very powerful. That's probably why your publisher wants to emphasize it. You have this young innocent girl who'll either be pushed to her death or saved by a young Wyvern. The tension of that moment is palpable. I remember it as if I read it yesterday."

Everyone else murmured in agreement.

"None of us can quite understand what you're going through, but it sounds like you need to separate the business side of your writing from the creative side," Rawlings said softly. "Stop thinking about the book you've already written for now. There may be some bumps in the road on its way to publication, but we all believe it'll be a smash hit. Concentrate on Tessa now. What does *she* want?"

Millay seemed startled by the question, but she immediately turned thoughtful. "Tessa wants to earn the trust of the Wyvern riders. Her people will need allies in the near future, and she's come to respect this strange clan. But her feelings about their prince are complicated. She's definitely attracted to him, but she's too proud to ask for his help and too inept at relationships to express how she feels. Therefore, she pours all her energy into prepping for the enemy on the horizon."

"There's your first chapter," Olivia said.

Millay's expression instantly transformed. Her doubt vanished like a morning mist being burned by the sun. She sat up straighter, her eyes shining. "You're right. Tessa wouldn't waste time wringing her hands and pacing the halls. She'd strap on her quiver, grab her bow, and meet every challenge with a war cry that could shatter glass." Reaching over, she grabbed Laurel's copy of her chapter and crumpled it into a tight ball. "Thanks, guys. My mind was full of fuzz, but that's gone. I know exactly what to write now." She smiled happily. "Let's move on to Olivia's awesome story."

Laurel raised her glass of chardonnay in Olivia's honor. "It's the best thing you've written. I made a few tweaks here and there, but they were minor. Overall, I loved every word."

"Me too," Millay said. "I felt like I got close to this guy right away. The whole piece was simple but emotional, and you didn't take the touchy-feeling stuff too far. I think having the narrative voice be that of a young girl added to the sincerity of the story. She saw this man plainly—his ugliness and his beauty—all at once."

"Well said," Harris said. "But am I the only one who wanted more? I wanted to know what was going to happen next. Maybe you should write a whole novel around this character. I'm not done with him yet."

Rawlings shook his head. "No, that wouldn't work. The lighthouse keeper resonates because we only have a powerful glimpse of him. It's meant to be a glimpse."

"That's true." Laurel waved a printout of Olivia's story in the air. "I didn't have his entire history and I had no idea what would become of him, but I was still satisfied by what I'd been given. It made me wonder which character we'd get to meet next."

Unable to conceal her pleasure and relief, Olivia thanked her friends for their feedback. She was eager to introduce them to Rosalie, but knew she'd have to wait a few weeks until it was her turn to be critiqued again.

"Speaking of fictional characters, where's your cowgirl?" Millay asked Harris.

"Her name is Emily," Harris said. "And she's at my place looking over one of my work projects. I've been stuck on a section of code and she's incredibly good at—" He stopped. "I won't bore you with cybergeek talk. Let's just say she's totally into code riddles and probably isn't missing me a bit right now."

Millay smirked. "Sounds like true love."

"Actually, it sounds like a good partnership." Rawlings opened a beer and offered it to Harris. "You've had quite a day. Now that our critique session is done, can you tell us about your interview?"

Waving off the beer, Harris helped himself to a Coke. "Emily doesn't drink, so when she's around, I don't either." He poured the soda over ice and settled deeper into the sofa. "Let me start by saying that if I didn't already have a job in a great town, I'd be pretty tempted to join the MarineBioPharm team. Of course, doing IT work for them wouldn't be half as exciting as designing game software, but the campus is like something out of a sci-fi novel."

"Like Google's?" Millay asked.

"Better," Harris whispered and Millay whistled in surprise and admiration. "Everything is sparkling chrome and white surfaces," Harris continued. "You feel like taking your shoes off in the research labs."

Rawlings leaned forward a little. "What did you learn about their medical research?"

"It's both extensive and impressive," Harris said. "They're working on all kinds of cool stuff like using jellyfish toxins to kill drug-resistant bacteria or cancer cells. They've identified a strain of sea anemone toxin that can actually arrest the development of multiple sclerosis. That one's awaiting FDA approval but should make MBP, as the employees call the company, a boatload of money."

Olivia was struck by how the word "toxin" had such a positive meaning in this light. One day, toxins might be used to cure MS, but toxins had also killed Ruthie and Cheryl Holcomb. "Stella borrowed several books on marine biology from the library. I think she was looking for the plant or animal toxins that were used to poison her friend."

Laurel's jaw dropped. "Wait a minute. Isn't that what Hunter does? Collect marine specimens?"

"Come on, people." Millay got up and headed into the tiny kitchen. "Are we accusing him of being a drug runner or a jellyfish smuggler?"

Everyone turned to Harris, who raised his hands in protest. "There was no way I could mention Hunter during my fake interview. It might have gotten back to him, and then he'd know I'd been snooping around."

"That would probably spell the end of Millay's garden party date," Rawlings pointed out. "Right now, she's our best hope of discovering what Hunter Drummond is really transporting in his floating lab."

Harris asked Millay to grab the bowl of pretzels on her way back to the sitting area. He ate a handful and then gulped down half a glass of soda. "Speaking of labs, MBP has recently opened a small medical research lab in James City."

"That's right near New Bern," Laurel said. "I wonder if Hunter's been making deliveries to that lab." She ran her hands through her hair. "If only Stella had more time to poke around."

Olivia glanced at Rawlings. "How was your visit to White Columns?"

"I wasn't there in an official capacity," Rawlings explained to the rest of the group. "I told Mr. and Mrs. Drummond that I'd come to see if Stella could shed light on the names 'Bertalda' and 'Kuhleborn.' I showed them Ruthie's letter—the one mentioning the bribe—and watched closely for a reaction. I saw brief flashes of alarm on both of their faces, but that was all."

Olivia could feel her anger rising. "Did they let you speak with Stella?"

Rawlings shook his head. "Mrs. Drummond said that Stella was unavailable because she was in her room, packing for her trip to Atlanta. She made it very clear that it was an inconvenient time for me to be calling because she was preoccupied with garden party preparations. The place was crawling with landscapers, florists, and cleaners—you'd think Michel's wedding was happening all over again."

"So it was a wasted visit," Millay grumbled.

"Not exactly," Rawlings said. "First of all, Stella wasn't in her room. While I was talking with her parents, I saw her creep down the stairs. She was dressed in jeans and the same Kelly-green T-shirt the landscapers were wearing. She headed for the back of the house, and later, when I was getting in my car, I spotted her riding a bike toward the harbor."

Olivia's pulse quickened. "Was she carrying anything?"

He nodded. "A backpack. And she was pedaling as if her life depended on it."

Olivia didn't need to hear another word. She bolted to her feet, stuffed her papers in her bag, and clapped her hands to wake her dozing poodle.

"Where's the fire?" Millay asked.

"Stella must have found the doll," Olivia said, gesturing for Rawlings to hurry.

Laurel and Harris exchanged befuddled glances.

"I'll tell you in the car. Come on! We need to get to town." Olivia pulled open the door and waved at her friends. "Let's go! Someone's bound to notice an antique doll tied to the underside of the pier."

Harris decided to take his own car because he wanted to get back to Emily as soon as they were done with their unusual errand. Rawlings rode with him, while Laurel, Millay, and Haviland piled into the Range Rover.

Olivia drove well above the speed limit. As she raced toward town, she told her friends why she believed the copper box might have contained Sadie's doll.

"Why would Nathaniel Drummond put a toy in the time capsule?" Laurel puzzled.

"I think he was trying to show his descendants that he cared about Emma and Sadie. I believe something else was in that copper box. We're not seeing the complete picture because an object or objects were removed." Olivia reduced her speed as she approached the downtown business district. "Stella must have discovered where these things were hidden. That's why she snuck out of the house. And why she had her backpack."

Olivia parked at the beach access lot and opened the passenger door for Haviland. When he jumped out, he gave Olivia a look as if to say, "This place again?"

Too impatient to wait for Harris and Rawlings to catch up, Olivia retrieved a pair of flashlights from the emergency kit in the trunk and handed one to Laurel. The wind blew her hair into her face and she impatiently pushed it away and raised her eyes to the sky.

Laurel followed her gaze. "I think it's going to rain."

"Then we'd better hurry," Olivia said.

Millay fell in place beside Olivia. "Hey, these boots were made for walking, but not this fast." She pointed at the pier. "How would Stella get a doll up there anyway?"

"She could use a life-saving hook from the lifeguard stand," Olivia said. "Stella and Ruthie spent so much time at this beach that I'm sure she thought this through."

The three women strode forward in silence. The wind was at their backs, propelling them as they walked. It snapped the fabric of their clothes and whistled over the waves.

Olivia glanced to the west. Inland, the sky was still clear. The stars were huddled around the moon like frightened children sitting close to a campfire. Over the ocean, miles away yet, the storm loomed. Thick, dark clouds hung so low that it was hard to separate sky from sea.

Picking up her pace, Olivia led her friends under the pier.

"My hair's in tangles," Laurel complained and tried to rake through the knotty strands with her fingers.

"It's very nineteen eighties," Millay said. "You just need some huge shoulder pads and parachute pants."

Ignoring her friends, Olivia directed her flashlight beam upward, illuminating the beams.

Laurel followed suit. She and Millay focused their gazes

on a different section of the pier and only paused when they heard Harris calling to them from down the beach.

"I can't hear him over the wind," Laurel said.

Olivia continued with her search, but she was beginning to lose hope. There was nothing above the sand where Ruthie died, and though the shadows kept tricking her into believing she'd spotted something solid, a shift of the flashlight beam would quickly prove otherwise.

"Damn it," she muttered angrily. Standing where Ruthie's body had lain brought the injustice of the young woman's death, Cheryl Holcomb's death, Stella's grief, and Luke's despair to the forefront of Olivia's mind. Nothing else existed in this moment but the empty beams and her memory of finding Ruthie on a beautiful spring morning not so long ago.

"Anything?" Rawlings's voice jarred her back to the present. She turned to him and shook her head despondently.

"There's nothing at this end!" Laurel called.

Rawlings touched Olivia's arm. "We should go."

Olivia pivoted so that she faced the dark, roiling water. She stared at it for a full minute, as if the answer waited beneath its inscrutable surface.

And then it came to her.

"The tide," she whispered, moving past where Laurel and Millay stood with their arms crossed over their chests. "It's come in since this afternoon. If Stella wanted to make sure others wouldn't notice the doll . . ." She dropped to the sand and began to take off her shoes and socks.

"What are you doing?" Harris asked.

Olivia rolled up her pants and waded into the water. It was cold. The wet sand hampered her progress and the current tried to push her off balance. Haviland splashed along next to her, and by the time the water was up to her knees, he was swimming at her side.

"Olivia!" Rawlings shouted. Seconds later, his powerful

Maglite illuminated the beams above her. "Anything there?"

The cold water seemed to sink into Olivia's veins, freezing all hope. She saw nothing but shadows.

She waited for several heartbeats, as if a delay might change the outcome, and a gust of wind nearly knocked her sideways. Whirling her arms, she stiffened and looked up, but didn't fall. Instead, she caught a flash of white. An object wedged between two planks and a beam at the very edge of the pier.

Moving directly under the spot, she pointed her flashlight directly at the white smudge. A round face with red painted lips stared down at her. Olivia didn't recognize it as the china doll in the old photograph. It looked like a disembodied head. An ugly, disfigured thing with black eyes. A doll with a cracked face.

But it was Sadie's doll. And now, nearly a century after Nathaniel Drummond had packed it into a copper box, Stella Drummond had snuck out of her house to bring it here. The doll mattered.

She might be fractured. She might even be broken. But she must be important, Olivia thought wildly.

"Harris!" she shouted into the wind. "Bring me a hook!"

Chapter 15

Unworthy offspring brag the most about their worthy descendants.

—DANISH PROVERB

Olivia was waiting by the front door of Circa, Oyster Bay's only antique store, at quarter to ten. The store wouldn't open for another fifteen minutes, but Olivia hoped to catch the proprietor before his first customers arrived.

Like her, Fred Yoder placed great value on punctuality. The lights went on at nine fifty, and as soon as Olivia saw Fred move behind the counter to switch on the register, she rapped lightly on the door.

He glanced up and smiled. From somewhere inside the shop, a dog started to yip excitedly. Haviland replied in a succession of impatient, high-pitched barks, his tail wagging furiously.

"Be patient, Captain," Olivia said. "You'll see Duncan in a moment."

As soon as Fred opened the door, his Westie darted between his legs and raced out to the sidewalk. Duncan gave Olivia a brief nudge on the ankle with his black nose before launching himself at Haviland. The two dogs sniffed and snorted and grunted at each other and Olivia couldn't help but laugh.

"You'd think they hadn't been together for months," she said. "We just met at the park two weeks ago."

"Maybe time passes differently for canine BFFs," Fred said, coaxing Duncan back inside and ushering both Westie and visitors into the kitchen. Haviland was more than happy to comply. He knew that Fred kept a stocked treat jar next to the paper towel holder and clearly expected to receive a midmorning snack. Sitting on his haunches directly below the treat jar, he exchanged eager glances with Duncan before fixing his hopeful gaze on Fred.

"Haviland's in for a pleasant surprise," Fred said, prying off the jar's airtight lid. "I ordered a fresh supply of Himalayan dog chews." He offered a treat to each dog. "They're made of boiled yak and cow milk and last for hours. Of course, Haviland might finish his sooner because this size is meant for smaller dogs, but since you're carrying a bundle, I sense that you're going to need my full attention."

Olivia nodded. "I'm sorry to drop in minutes before you're about to open, but it's important."

Fred waved her off. "You're my friend. I'd be glad to see you even if this place were packed to the rafters with paying customers. Besides, no one else brings me such intriguing pieces." He arched a brow. "Is this object connected to another of the chief's cases?"

"At this point, it's just a girl's keepsake," Olivia said. "A girl who's been gone for a long time. And yet I'm desperately hoping it could be more than that." She proffered the doll, which had been swaddled in diapers until it resembled the mummified body of a small animal.

"Someone knows how to protect a delicate antique." Fred scrutinized the packaging with an expert eye. "Diapers are far superior to bubble wrap."

Olivia watched as he used a box cutter to carefully sever the tape securing the bundle. "I can't take credit for the wrapping. Laurel had a box of diapers in the back of her car that she was going to donate. It was a good thing too, because this doll looks like she's been to hell and back."

"Let's see what we have," Fred said.

Though she wanted to be right at Fred's elbow, Olivia gave him room to work. She took a seat at the small kitchen table while the dogs stretched out on the floor and munched noisily on their treats. Fred peeled the layers of diaper away and the doll's cracked face appeared. "Looks like a German china doll," he said, his finger probing the diagonal fissure running from the doll's forehead, across its nose, and down to the bottom of its right cheek. "Deep hairline here. I've seen damage like this on china heads many times." Gingerly, he pulled the doll free of its white cocoon. "I'd say this was her original dress. It's in remarkable condition."

Olivia produced the copy of the photograph showing Nathaniel Drummond and Emma and Sadie Vance. "Here's what the doll looked like in her prime. The girl holding her is Sadie."

Fred took his reading glasses out of his shirt pocket and slid them on. Holding the image at arm's length, he smiled. "The doll is dressed just like Miss Sadie." He pushed his glasses over his forehead and gave Olivia a curious look. "Do you know this family?"

Olivia pointed at the man in the chair. "This is Nathaniel Drummond. He's the patriarch of the Oyster Bay Drummonds. I'm sure you've met Beauford and Bellamy. I know they're antique connoisseurs."

"They most certainly are. Bellamy has excellent taste," Fred said approvingly. "Excellent and expensive."

The Drummonds likely numbered among Fred's best customers. "Yes," she said tactfully. "Their home is filled with lovely things."

"Many of which were purchased in this shop." He gave her a satisfied wink and then gently turned the doll over and began undoing the buttons on the back of its dress. "This always feels a bit creepy—a grown man removing a doll's clothes. I never quite get used to it." He indicated the MADE IN GERMANY stamp on the doll's shoulder. "This is your customary German china doll design. China head, bisque arms and legs, sawdust-stuffed cloth body. Jointed shoulders and hips. Painted hair, facial features, and shoes."

Olivia motioned at the dress. "May I? I've already disrobed her once."

"Be my guest." Fred stepped aside. "Most of the dolls I come across from this era have newer dresses because the original ones fell apart. It's even rarer for them to still have their original undergarments." He shook his head. "I'm sounding creepy again."

After pushing the ivory-colored camisole up to the doll's shoulders, Olivia slid off the lace-trimmed pantaloons and pointed at the shredded stitches in the pink fabric of the doll's back. "Is this normal?"

Fred frowned. "No. The stitches are too big and they don't match the fabric. I'd hazard a guess that someone added them post manufacture."

"Why would anyone do that?"

Stroking his chin, Fred gazed off into the middle distance. "I once read a book, oh, what was it?" He shrugged. "A Perry Mason novel maybe. I don't remember the whole story, but a clue was hidden inside the body of a doll."

They both stared down at the china doll. "The thought crossed my mind, but these seams have been cut," Olivia murmured unhappily. "So I assume the clue, if there was one, has already been removed. I also squeezed the soft center of her body, but didn't feel anything inside."

Fred nodded, but he didn't seem to be listening. His fingers progressed down the doll's torso, gently pinching and probing. They traveled down the doll's arms and then moved from its hip to its left leg. When he reached its right leg, he paused. He made a curious noise that prompted Olivia to ask, "Is something there?"

"Maybe. I need my special tweezers." Instead of putting the doll on the table, he handed it to Olivia. She found herself cradling it as if it were a real baby. "I'd better unlock the front door before I operate. Be right back." He smiled at Olivia and left the room. Moments later, he returned holding a pair of tweezers with long, rubber-coated tips. "They weren't exactly lined up outside, but if a customer does come in, don't let Duncan dash into the shop and lick them to death."

"I won't," Olivia promised, though she doubted she'd react very quickly. She was far too riveted by the sight of the tweezers disappearing into the doll's body cavity.

Fred closed his eyes and became so absorbed in his task that Olivia could no longer hear him breathe. Finally, he released a "Gotcha!" and grinned.

Olivia leaned forward as Fred eased a tiny metal cylinder from the sawdust stuffing. It looked like a miniature cigar tube. He brushed off the sawdust and then fumbled for his glasses, transferring the sawdust to his hair. "Something's been engraved on the side. See?" He pivoted the metal tube so that it caught the light.

Squinting, Olivia read the first few words aloud, "'For where your treasure is . . .'" She trailed off.

"'There will your heart be also,'" Fred finished reading the text. He tilted the tube until its rubber stopper faced upward. Giving it a little tug, he pulled it free and offered the tube to Olivia. "Can you fit your finger in there?"

She tried to stick her pinkie into the opening but it was too narrow. "Do you have a flashlight?"

Fred had just produced a slim penlight from a kitchen drawer when the bells above the shop door tinkled. Duncan dropped his treat and shot from the room in a flash of white fur. Haviland was on his feet, but looked to Olivia for permission before following his friend.

"Stay," she told the poodle and took the penlight from Fred.

He gestured toward the front. "I'd better save that customer from Duncan. If a flawless diamond is wedged down at the bottom of that thing, just scream so I know you've found the treasure."

Olivia aimed the light into the tube's interior. She stared and stared, unwilling to believe her eyes. Finally, she lowered both arms and sighed. "Empty." She looked once more, just to be sure, and felt like weeping.

Setting the tube and the flashlight on the table next to the doll, she sat in her chair like a stone. The line of Scripture ran through her head over and over again. "Where was your heart, Nathaniel?" she whispered in despair. "What was your treasure?"

Fred reentered the kitchen a few minutes later. "No diamonds, I take it?"

Olivia rubbed her temples. "I don't know what I expected. I probably read too much into this photograph." She stared at it for a long moment and then touched the black-and-white faces with her fingertips. "I was so positive that Nathaniel cared about this woman and child that I convinced myself that he tried to send his descendants a message using this doll." She raised her eyes to meet Fred's kind gaze. "Do I sound crazy?"

He gave her a friendly pat on the shoulder. "When we start digging around in other people's pasts, it often turns out that we were looking for something in ourselves all along."

"I don't understand."

He looked at the photograph. "Are you trying to solve a mystery about a father and a daughter?"

Olivia nodded.

After a brief hesitation, Fred pointed at Sadie. "Are you searching for her father?" He lowered his voice and fixed his gaze on Olivia. "Or for yours?" And before Olivia could speak, he put his fingers to his lips. "Charles Wade has been to the shop several times. In fact, he's my first customer of the day and is standing by the jewelry display case as we speak."

Feeling a rush of embarrassment, anger, and betrayal, Olivia stuffed the rubber stopper back into the tube and began roughly rewrapping the doll. She didn't look at Fred and was too flustered to respond to his comment.

"I didn't mean to upset you, Olivia," Fred said softly. "Stay back here as long as you'd like. Have a cup of coffee. Take a moment to think things through. I'll be right on the other side of the wall if you need me."

Olivia followed his advice. She wasn't hiding from Charles, but she wanted to take a good hard look at herself and her motives. She needed to determine if she'd grabbed hold of a wild theory and run with it just because her biological father had arrived in Oyster Bay supposedly hoping to establish a relationship with her.

"No, it must be more than that," she argued, directing her words at the doll. "There's a *reason* Nathaniel Drummond sealed that copper box for posterity. He wrote that line of Scripture on a blank will for a *reason*. And the same quote was engraved in that tube and placed inside Sadie's doll for a reason. He wanted people to see this photograph of Emma and Sadie. And you." She touched the doll's face, tracing its bow-shaped mouth and round chin. "Was Sadie the treasure of his heart? Is that why he chose you to bear his message?"

She heard the bells above the front door chime again and wondered if another customer had entered or if Charles had left.

"Come on, Haviland. Let's see if the coast is clear."

Gathering the doll in her arms, Olivia left the kitchen and was surprised to find the shop empty except for a young Asian couple examining a Chippendale sideboard. There was no sign of Charles or Fred.

Suddenly, Fred's head popped up from behind the counter. He wore a look of triumph. Waving a tape measure in the air, he came around the counter and handed it to the couple. "Take your time," he told them, shooing Duncan away from the sideboard. "I'll be waxing the grandfather clock if you need me."

Olivia felt a rush of affection for Fred Yoder. He always knew when to give people their space. When he joined her by the clock carrying a chamois cloth and a tin of beeswax, Olivia held out her hands, offering to hold the wax as he worked. "Did Charles tell you that he's my biological father?" she asked.

"No," Fred said. "I overheard Charles and Dixie talking at the diner. I was at the next booth, and wasn't even trying to eavesdrop. Scout's honor. I was completely immersed in the latest issue of *Antiques and Fine Arts* and was rather annoyed when Dixie started berating my neighbor."

"Why?"

Fred applied the wax and moved the cloth over the clock case in small, gentle circles. "She warned him not to play around with your feelings. She told him that if he really wanted to act like a father, he'd do his best to protect what you care about. For a diminutive woman, Dixie can be quite terrifying." He shook his head in wonder. "I was afraid to pour syrup on my pancakes because my hand was unsteady—and I wasn't the one being threatened."

Olivia had no trouble imagining the scene. "How did Charles respond?"

"He said that he only had so much time to make things right with you and that it meant a great deal to him to win your approval. He assured Dixie that he'd acquired Through the Wardrobe because the bookstore was important to you." Fred stopped waxing and looked at Olivia. "He sounded sincere. Yes, he's pushy. He has too much swagger for my taste, but I don't think he's a bad man."

Olivia glanced at the young couple. The wife seemed to be trying to convince her husband to buy the piece, but he kept pointing at the price tag and showing her an image on his phone. "I think Pottery Barn might steal this sale if you don't get over there."

Fred glanced at the couple and then faced Olivia again. He was smiling. "I'm not worried about Pottery Barn. If he loves her, he'll buy her that sideboard because she has her heart set on it. This isn't the first time they've shopped at Circa, so I know he loves her. However, he doesn't like to be rushed. They'll probably have lunch and come back this afternoon."

"And Charles?" Olivia indicated a display of crystal decanters and sterling silver liquor tags. "What does he collect?"

"This and that," Fred said enigmatically and then relented. "His interests focus mostly on nautical objects. He also asked me to track down some architectural pieces for the bookstore's new café. He said that he wanted to blend items with a local flavor with those having a more modern, industrial feel. So far, I've found several anchors and a ship's wheel."

Olivia tried to envision how the nautical items would work in the café and realized that she was eager to speak with Charles about his renovation plans. "Before he left the store, did he happen to say where he was headed? I'm thinking of partnering with him on this bookstore project."

Fred smiled. "I think he'll be very pleased. And he did mention that he was on his way to Through the Wardrobe. He's meeting with the contractor in thirty minutes."

"Thank you, Fred. You're always willing to help."

"Hey, that's what friends do." He put a hand on the bundle containing the doll. "And I'm sorry that she wasn't carrying any hidden treasure. Let's just hope she brought joy to the little girl in that photo. That's the purpose she was meant to serve, after all."

Olivia nodded and held the bundle closer to her chest. She called softly to Haviland, and as the poodle loped out of the kitchen, the young couple motioned to Fred.

"Could you place this piece on hold?" Olivia heard the wife ask. "My husband and I want to talk about it over lunch. We'll be back with our decision later this afternoon."

"Certainly," Fred said. He turned and winked at Olivia.

Olivia grinned. Fred Yoder's instincts were as finely tuned as a concert piano, and she was fortunate to number him among her friends.

Tucking the doll under one arm, she left the shop, got into her Range Rover, and drove to the bookstore. As she stared at the familiar brick building, she hoped her own instincts were half as sharp.

Late that afternoon, as she and Rawlings got ready for the Secret Garden Party, Olivia shared Charles's renovations ideas with him and explained her involvement in the project. Sadie's doll sat, momentarily forgotten, on top of Olivia's bureau. It was Olivia's plan to serendipitously return the doll sometime during the tour of the Drummonds' gardens. Because the final object from Nathaniel Drummond's copper box failed to yield a clue to back up Stella's claims that her family was responsible for Ruthie Holcomb's death, Olivia decided to put the whole affair out of her mind. For one evening anyway.

It was easier than she thought to focus all her attention on the upcoming party. The afternoon's warmth lingered and the sky was a lovely shade of hydrangea blue. Attired in his new tux, Rawlings was the epitome of a distinguished, middle-aged gentleman. When he stepped up behind Olivia to zip her floor-length black gown, he planted a featherlight kiss at the base of her neck.

"I can get you out of this dress just as quickly as I helped you in," he whispered, running his hands over her bare arms. He then spun her around. "Let me look at you."

Olivia did as he commanded, watching as he took in her gown. With its one-shoulder silhouette, delicate ruching, and long skirt, the dress conjured up old Hollywood glamour. Olivia wore no accessories, inviting the eye to fall upon the Swarovski crystal peacock brooch on her right shoulder. The blues and greens of the peacock's feathers sparkled like the ocean in moonlight.

"In a few weeks, the most beautiful woman I've ever seen will be legally mine," Rawlings said, drinking in the sight of her.

Olivia smiled and reached for him. "I'm already yours. A wedding is just you and I exchanging words in front of witnesses. It's a ceremony. A pretty one. But no event could capture what I feel for you. Those feelings are as wide and fathomless as the sea."

Rawlings smiled. "I think you just wrote your vows."

Olivia waved him off. "We're not doing that, are we? The standard vows are fine."

"We're supposed to be writers." Rawlings polished a cufflink with a handkerchief. "We should create something unique. Just a line or two." He took Olivia's hands in his. "Two lines each. We can—"

Olivia stopped his speech by kissing him.

"We're going to be late," she said when they finally broke apart.

Rawlings smiled. "Two lines," he whispered and then offered Olivia his arm to escort her downstairs. "Now tell me more about Uncle Charles. I thought you disliked him, distrusted him, and couldn't wait to see the last of him. What changed?"

Olivia turned. Here it was: her chance to tell Rawlings the truth. She just had to open her mouth and say that Charles Wade wasn't her uncle. He was her father.

As she searched for the words, her gaze fell on her nightstand, where her starfish necklace sat curled in a little porcelain dish. The necklace had been her mother's and Olivia wore it every day. Instinctively, she put her fingers to the soft depression in her neck where the starfish pendant usually rested. Touching bare skin instead of cool silver, Olivia felt a dull ache. Her mother, the person she'd loved more than anyone in the world, had been in love with Charles Wade. He'd chosen his other family over Camille, just as Nathaniel Drummond had chosen his wife and daughter over Emma and Sadie. Nathaniel's flimsy attempt to send a message one hundred years later angered Olivia and she couldn't help but wonder if she was truly willing to let Charles make amends.

"What is it?" Rawlings looked at her with tender concern.

"I'm not sure if I should trust him, but I'm going to try," Olivia finally said. "I believe in his vision for the bookstore, and because of that, I want Charles Wade to prove himself an honorable man."

Rawlings nodded. "With you involved in the project, it's not solely in the hands of an outsider. Everyone will have confidence in the endeavor if they know you're on board."

Olivia gave him a grateful smile. "In that case, I'm glad I signed on as an equal partner today. I had my reservations, but you just dispelled them. Come on, I'll buy you a drink to show my gratitude."

The couple descended to the first floor, where Haviland waited expectantly. "You're having a sleepover with Caitlyn and Anders this evening," Olivia told the poodle. "They've been looking forward to it all week."

Haviland barked, picked up his favorite ball, and trotted into the kitchen.

Rawlings opened the door and hesitated. Still holding on to Olivia's arm, he said, "Will you be all right? Hobnobbing with Beauford and Bellamy Drummond after how they've treated their daughter?"

"I have to be," Olivia said. "There isn't much more I can do to help catch Ruthie's killer. The time capsule clues have led to a dead end, but I'll be damned if I'm going to let my feelings for Beauford and Bellamy interfere with our only chance of stopping the influx of drugs into Oyster Bay. It's all up to Millay now. My job is to play the part of supportive benefactor. I'll admire Bellamy's camellia bushes and garden statuary. I'll compliment her on her dress and the time capsule display and no one will know that the entire time I'm fawning over her I'm fantasizing about wrapping my hands around her neck."

"Can you refrain from voicing murderous threats tonight?" Rawlings asked, and Olivia suspected he was only half jesting. "Remember, I have a role to play too—that of solicitous civil servant. I want everyone to be at ease. If the Drummonds really tried to bribe Ruthie or have hidden time capsule items to protect their wealth and reputation, they probably believe they've gotten away with it. With an open bar and Mr. and Mrs. Drummonds' incredible arrogance, one of them might make a mistake. I also plan to be watching very closely for the tiniest crack in Hunter Drummond's façade. And I'll be listening carefully for the slightest misstep in speech. If he slips up, I imagine it will be toward the end of the evening after the fatigue and alcohol set in, so we might have a very long night ahead of us."

Olivia glanced out at the ocean and sighed. "I doubt anything out of the ordinary will occur. I know these people. This world. Tonight will be about big houses, showy gardens, and overdressed couples overindulging in food and liquor. The guests will compete in the scavenger hunt, eat and drink themselves silly, dance beneath the stars, and write a few checks. Then the evening will come to a close. Parts of it will be wonderful because I'm with you, but otherwise, the whole event is rather predictable."

"Two people have already been murdered," Rawlings reminded her softly. "There's no telling what can happen next."

Chapter 16

'Twas twilight, and I bade you go,
But still you held me fast;
It was the time of roses,
We pluck'd them as we pass'd.

—THOMAS HOOD

The gardens at twilight were magical. Night encroached as people strolled down gravel paths and velvety lawns. The air was perfumed with the heady aroma of gardenia and the subtler fragrances of Confederate jasmine, newly turned soil, and damp grass. Birds twittered from their nests in ancient magnolia and oak trees, but the shrill rasping of bats could be heard too. Wind chimes played tuneless melodies and insects hummed in the shadows.

The secluded gardens, hidden from view behind high walls or dense hedges, seemed to belong to another place and time. White fairy lights were strung across picket fences and the enchanted guests moved slowly, whispering to each other and pointing skyward as the first stars appeared. Couples who hadn't exchanged an intimate gesture for months found themselves holding hands. Others sat, knee-to-knee, on stone benches beneath arbors resplendent with wisteria blossoms.

Tall candle stands lined the garden paths. In their soft

light, the guests became transformed. The women were as beautiful as brides, and the men looked taller and stronger. The secret gardens of Oyster Bay put all who moved through them under a spell.

Olivia was more than willing to surrender to the moment. She and Rawlings had begun their tour at White Columns, where they'd lingered by the back door until the closest volunteer became preoccupied showing a guest a fountain featuring a pair of intertwined seahorses. Olivia slipped inside the house, put the doll in a dresser drawer in Stella's room, and then quickly rejoined Rawlings.

"We can focus on enjoying ourselves now," Olivia said, smiling at him.

She and Rawlings toured all six gardens. They took their time, relishing the lovely tranquility of the candlelit pathways. Neither of them felt like talking. It was enough to be together as the sky darkened and stars sparked to life overhead. Olivia could feel a loosening of her body and sensed that Rawlings was also relaxing for the first time in weeks. At the last garden, he waited until they were alone before leading her under a bronze arch covered with Carolina jessamine. Rawlings reached out, plucked one of the yellow flowers from its vine, and placed it in Olivia's hand. He then pulled her close and kissed her. The kiss was long and tender, and Olivia felt its warmth move through her.

They sat together in silence, listening to the garden's night music. Eventually, Rawlings took Olivia by the arm, and as they started walking toward the historical society, he began to sing very softly.

But surely you see My Lady
Out in the garden there
Rivaling the glittering sunshine
With a glory of golden hair.

Olivia smiled. "A kiss and a serenade? This *is* a magical evening."

When they reached Hanover House, the sight of Beauford and Bellamy Drummond dimmed some of her merriment. The couple stood on either side of the front door of the historical society exchanging handshakes and air kisses with the guests.

Rawlings slid his arm around Olivia's waist and gave her a little squeeze, as if to remind her that they both had parts to play and that it was time to get into character.

While Beauford reviewed the rules for the scavenger hunt with Rawlings, Olivia praised Bellamy for her decision to hold the Secret Garden Party in the evening. "The gardens have been completely transformed. It's like discovering an exotic oasis in the middle of Oyster Bay."

Bellamy beamed. "I know! I felt as though I'd stepped through a magic portal and appeared in the distant past. I could easily picture my ancestors meandering through the gardens at White Columns." She smiled dreamily. "I could almost hear the swish of gowns and the tap, tap of a walking stick on the bricks."

Olivia imagined Nathaniel Drummond taking a turn in the garden with his wife and daughter. She had no trouble visualizing Josephine and Martha, their chins lifted at a haughty angle, but she couldn't picture Nathaniel's face. She'd seen two photographs of him and his expression had changed markedly from one sitting to another. The portraits had captured different sides of him. The first showed Nathaniel as the respectable businessman and patriarch. But Olivia believed that the second photograph portrayed the real man—the man with the smiling eyes.

"You'd better hurry," Bellamy said, snapping Olivia out of her reverie. "You're the last couple to start the scavenger hunt and the competition is fierce. The winner gets a luxury cruise to the Mexican Riviera. You could win a free honeymoon trip."

Olivia and Rawlings exchanged an amused glance and headed inside. They immediately ran into Laurel and her husband, Steve.

"You're good at this," she overheard Steve say to Laurel as he filled in an answer on the scavenger hunt sheet.

Laurel, who wore a dress of champagne-colored silk, caught Olivia's eye and gave her a conspiratorial wink. She then whispered something in Steve's ear and, after her husband vanished into the next room, drew closer to Olivia and Rawlings. "Any luck with the doll?" she whispered.

"No. If there was a clue hidden inside, someone beat us to it." Olivia was about to fill Laurel in on her visit to Circa when Harris entered the hallway. He was holding a clipboard in one hand and had his free hand clasped around the wrist of a slim young woman with a pixie-like face and short, spiky blond hair.

"You're here!" Harris exclaimed when he noticed his friends. "Everyone, this is Emily."

Emily smiled widely. "I've heard so much about all of you that I feel like I've known you for ages already."

When Olivia moved to shake her hand, Emily pushed it aside and hugged her instead. She repeated the gesture with Laurel and Rawlings and then stepped back, laughing. "Sorry, I'm a hugger. I know I don't look like one with the punk rock hair and tattoos, but I am."

Laurel raised her brows. "And I love your hair, but where are the tattoos?"

Considering Emily's short strapless dress left very little skin concealed, Olivia assumed the tattoos were well hidden.

Emily blushed prettily. "Right here." She turned her hands palms up, revealing a blue, green, and purple dragonfly on each wrist. One had been captured in flight while the other rested on a cattail stalk. "I've always liked dragonflies," she said. "When I was a kid, my parents called me Little Dragonfly because I was never still. Did you know that the Native Americans believed that dragonflies were the purest of all creatures because they ate the wind? *I* love them because they teach us that change is to be embraced, not feared." She lowered her hands and laughed. "I am totally babbling, aren't I? Sorry. I do that when I'm nervous."

Olivia took an instant liking to Emily. "My mother used to read me this wonderful picture book. The girl in the story found a secret fairy village in the woods by following the flight of a dragonfly. I chased after them like crazy after that but, alas, never saw a fairy." Olivia gestured to the back of the house. "The bar's set up on the patio. Why don't we go outside and order drinks?"

"Fine by me," Harris said. "Emily and I have totally nailed this scavenger hunt. Whatever we couldn't locate in the house we found on the Internet."

"Cheater." Pretending to be appalled, Laurel swatted Harris on the arm with her clutch.

The group exited the house and made for the bar, where the three bartenders were working at a furious pace. The first poured champagne or chardonnay while a second served either cucumber gimlets or mint juleps. The third was filling a row of chilled martini glasses with what he described as a pink hibiscus martini.

"It's either that or the elderflower tequila slipper," a woman in front of Olivia told her husband.

The man frowned. "I don't want to drink flowers. Can't I have a whiskey and soda?"

Olivia silently agreed with the man, but seeing as there was no whiskey, she chose champagne. Laurel ordered two mint juleps while Rawlings opted for the gimlet. Emily and Harris skipped the cocktails altogether and asked for glasses of cranberry juice garnished with sugared limes.

"Has anyone seen Millay?" Rawlings asked.

"Not yet," Laurel said. "And I'm trying not to worry." She took a sip from each of the mint juleps she carried and then, seeing as everyone was watching her, grinned. "Don't want to spill any while I'm tracking down my husband."

After Laurel disappeared into the house, Olivia and Rawlings sat on the low brick wall surrounding the patio and chatted with Harris and Emily. Emily told them that she came from a large, noisy family.

"I have five siblings," she said.

When Olivia told her that she was an only child, Emily shook her head in amazement. "I can't even imagine what that must have been like. My brothers and sisters and I are always competing. We all want to stand out in a crowd. One of my brothers is an actor, another is a district attorney, and my favorite sister is a two-time Olympian. She was a member of USA's shooting team."

Rawlings looked impressed. As he and Emily reminisced about their first experiences with firearms, Harris patted his flat stomach and said, "Seeing as the only weapon I ever owned was a cap gun, I'm going on the hunt for some snacks."

Offering to join him, Olivia followed Harris to a buffet table loaded with sliced cheese, caviar, bruschetta, pâté, bacon-wrapped shrimp, and fruit. She filled a plate to share with Rawlings, and while Harris piled shrimp on his own plate, she said, "Emily's great. She's smart, pretty, and easy to talk to."

Harris nodded. "I'm really glad she's here. She's the kind of person who always sees a bright side to everything. I told her about our investigation because she has this crazy ability to analyze and organize information, and I was hoping she'd have one of her famous breakthroughs. No luck there, but she did say that Hunter Drummond was the type of guy who'd brag to impress a girl playing hard to get, so I hope Millay is stringing him along like a kid with a yo-yo."

"Seeing as that's her modus operandi, I'm not too concerned. Besides, Hunter isn't her type, so it'll be easy for her to act disinterested." Too late, Olivia realized that her comment might be hurtful to Harris. He hadn't been Millay's type either, but they'd dated for a long time. In the end, Millay had broken Harris's heart, and Olivia hated that she'd reminded him of what was best forgotten.

When she opened her mouth to apologize, Harris raised his hand to stop her. "I'm good. Really. I'll always love Millay. She's amazing. But I don't have to be in love with her. There are other awesome girls out there. I have one with me tonight."

"Yes, you do," Olivia said, and together, they carried their plates back to Rawlings and Emily.

The foursome ate and talked until the lights came up on the makeshift stage at the far end of the garden. A group of musicians attired in black and white sat waiting for a cue from Bellamy Drummond, the mistress of ceremonies. She gazed out at the guests with a satisfied purse of her lips. Pivoting, she signaled to the conductor. He held up a yellow rose boutonniere and slid it through the buttonhole of his left lapel. The other men in the band followed his lead while the women placed combs decorated with yellow roses in their hair.

Adorned with flowers, the band began to play a soft rendition of "I Get a Kick Out of You," while Bellamy asked the guests to locate their place cards and be seated. Because Olivia had written a large check to the historical society, she was hosting her own table. When she and Rawlings, Laurel and Steve, and Harris and Emily had settled into their chairs, their circle still felt incomplete. Millay's absence left a gap, and Olivia found herself scanning the rest of the tables in search of her.

"I see her," Rawlings said as if reading Olivia's mind. "To the right of the stage."

Millay stood between a pair of boxwood bushes, looking

restless and bored. She held a pair of stiletto heels in one hand and a champagne bottle in the other. She'd traded in her customary miniskirt for a slinky scarlet dress and wore her hair in loose curls. As Olivia watched, Millay flashed Hunter Drummond a coy smile. He immediately inched closer, as if he'd waited a lifetime to earn a smile from a woman as captivating as Millay.

Casually, Millay handed Hunter the champagne. He tilted the bottle back and drank deeply, and she laughed, pretending to be pleased by his rashness.

Harris, who was talking to Emily about some video game, abruptly stopped speaking. Seeing Millay, he muttered a little "Oh," and then turned back to Emily. "That's Millay. In the red dress at the end of the garden path. And there's Little Lord Fauntleroy in the tux beside her."

Emily darted a brief glance at Millay. "Looks like she's working her magic. But we'd better not stare. We don't want to blow her cover."

There wasn't a trace of jealousy in Emily's voice. Olivia smiled at her and said, "You're absolutely right. And Millay had better find another place to flirt, because the song's almost over and Bellamy's heading for the microphone again. I doubt she'd approve of her precious son chugging champagne in front of these prestigious guests."

Bellamy led the audience in a round of applause for the band and then held out a top hat. "Before we enjoy our meal on this lovely spring evening, I have a few announcements to make. First, I'd like to recognize the volunteers who've made this event possible. If you're wearing a yellow rose, would you please stand?" Bellamy clapped for several seconds before continuing. "Our volunteers are coming around to show you the newest items available for purchase in our gift shop. I think you'll be especially taken with the reproductions of the photographs found inside our time capsule. We've had these made into postcards, notecards, framed prints, and coffee cups. Of course, anyone donating to the historical society fund at the gold or platinum level will receive a gift basket with a sample of our shop's finest products." She smiled at the crowd. "Who could resist such an offer?"

A female volunteer appeared in the space between Laurel and Steve's chairs and placed several items on the table. Laurel was clearly enamored with the historic images of downtown Oyster Bay and made her husband promise to purchase several prints after dinner.

"I'm fine with that," he said. "But there's no way I'll agree to be a sponsor. Who the hell would hand over that kind of money to preserve an old building? The stock market is a much better investment."

"Is it?" Olivia murmured under her breath and curbed an impulse to accidentally spill her drink onto Steve's lap.

She's your friend's husband, she chided herself. *And Laurel swears that he's trying to change, to be more supportive and attentive.*

As if to prove his wife right, Steve put his arm around Laurel and told her that he'd be glad to treat her to anything she wanted in the gift shop. He then squeezed her shoulders and said, "But I want to dance with you first. Deal?"

"Deal," she replied and kissed him.

Onstage, Bellamy was recapping the successes of the past year while outlining future goals for the historical society. She faltered only once, and that was when her gaze fell upon Hunter as he pulled out a chair for Millay at what was clearly the head table.

Harris caught Bellamy's brief stammer and grinned. "I guess Mommy didn't put the gold stamp of approval on her baby boy's date."

"And that isn't even the Millay we know and love," Rawlings added. "I barely recognize her as this diva. I think I prefer her in black boots and Hello Kitty hair clips."

"Hello Kitty rocks," Emily declared and they all laughed.

At the end of Bellamy's speech, she waved the top hat

containing the correct scavenger hunt entries and asked a volunteer to draw a name.

The volunteer pulled out a piece of paper and frowned. After shooting an uncertain glance at Bellamy, she leaned into the microphone and cried, "Dale Arden and Flash Gordon!"

Harris and Emily jumped up, exchanged a complicated series of high-fives, and hurried to the stage. After accepting an envelope from Bellamy, Harris put his arm around Emily's back and dipped her low to the floor. When he raised her to her feet, she threw her arms around his neck and kissed him to the sound of boisterous applause.

Olivia flicked her eyes at Millay, but she wasn't even looking at the stage. Somehow she'd tied her napkin around her wrists and was proffering her bound hands to Hunter. His mouth curved into a lascivious grin, and she responded by whispering something in his ear. As he listened, Hunter ran his finger along the ridge of Millay's shoulder and down the slope of her back. Suddenly, he stiffened, and even from where she sat, Olivia could see Beauford Drummond's censorious glare. Gently pushing Millay away, Hunter straightened his crooked bow tie and ran his fingers through his hair.

"She's not very subtle," Rawlings said to Olivia. "Maybe the champagne has clouded her judgment."

"Millay knows how to make it seem like she's drinking far more than she actually is. I've seen this performance before." Olivia focused her gaze on the salad a waiter had just placed in front of her. "I have complete faith in her."

Rawlings had barely speared an avocado slice with his fork when Harris signaled to him. "Don't look now, but Millay just stormed off."

Of course, having been told not to look, they all proceeded to do just that. Olivia caught a flash of red as Millay vanished into the house, and when she glanced back at Hunter, he was shaking his head at his father. And then he pushed back from the table, dropped his napkin on his salad plate, and followed in Millay's wake.

"She's good." Emily nodded in approval. "Hunter is totally blowing off that older man. Is that his dad?" When Harris told her that she was correct, she smiled excitedly. "That means Millay has power over Hunter. He's choosing her over family."

"Let's hope she takes advantage of her temporary power," Laurel said.

Steve, who'd been preoccupied helping a waitress locate a dropped knife, turned to his wife. "What are you guys talking about?"

"We're providing a running commentary about Millay's date. We can't tell whether or not she's having a good time." Laurel passed her husband the bread basket. "Remember those Asiago cheese rolls we had the last time we were at The Boot Top? Presto! Here they are!"

While Steve helped himself to several rolls, Rawlings leaned close to Olivia. "Do you think Millay's all right? If she teases Hunter too much, takes the flirtation too far . . ." Rawlings's expression was calm, but his fingers pressed into the skin of Olivia's forearm.

"If you chase after Millay, the jig will be up. Hunter knows you're the chief of police," Olivia said. "Let me go. I can pretend to be en route to the ladies' room."

Rawlings considered this. "Okay, but you'd better hurry. Beauford is conferring with his wife, and Bellamy doesn't look too happy."

Olivia glanced at their host and hostess. While everyone else was sampling the main course—glazed Cornish Hens stuffed with wild rice and apricots—the Drummonds weren't even seated. They'd moved away from their table and were speaking, heads discreetly bent, near a garden bed brimming with white anemones. Illuminated by candlelight, the flowers glowed like tiny stars against the dark foliage of a massive rhododendron. As Olivia watched,

Bellamy stomped on one of the plants, flattening it beneath her pointed heel.

Bellamy's anger was almost palpable and Olivia knew she didn't dare tarry another second.

"Excuse me," she told her friends and got to her feet with what she hoped was a leisurely air.

Inside, the house hummed with noise. The caterers were using the kitchen as both a plating station and a storage area for dirty dishes. Party guests headed to and from the restrooms, and a handful of women, who didn't seem to be aware that their gourmet meals were growing cold outside, were chatting over what Olivia assumed was their third or fourth round of cocktails in the dining room.

She meandered through the rooms on the main floor, but found neither Millay nor Hunter.

"I wish Haviland were here," she said to herself and mounted the stairs. "He'd find Millay in a heartbeat."

Glancing around to make sure no one was watching, Olivia hurriedly ascended to the second floor.

At the top, she paused to listen for the sounds of voices, but she only heard the din from the waitstaff below and the partygoers outside.

She decided to search at the front of the house and move backward, beginning with the study where she'd first seen the photograph of Nathaniel, Martha, and Josephine. The room was cordoned off and there was a STAFF ONLY sign attached to the door. Ignoring the sign, Olivia entered and cast a quick glance around the empty room. She was about to leave when she noticed that the closet door was ajar. Despite her urgency to find Millay, Olivia felt compelled to peer into the closet. Office supplies and cleaning products took up the shelf space, but next to a tin of furniture wax was a thick book with a glossy cover that clearly didn't belong with the rest of the old, leather-bound volumes displayed in the study's bookcase.

"Another marine biology textbook?" Olivia asked the

silent room and picked up the book. Flipping through it, she noticed a scrap of paper tucked between two pages detailing the medicinal uses of snails.

"Is this what you'd been looking for when you checked out those library books, Stella?" Olivia whispered.

She read the section on snails rapidly, but thoroughly, and by the time she finished, beads of perspiration were dotting her forehead and adrenaline was surging through her body.

"Is it possible?" she murmured. Returning the book to the shelf, she realized that a strange, slightly rotten odor was coming from deeper inside the closet. There was a rectangular object on the floor, shrouded by a black cloth. Olivia whipped off the cloth to reveal a fish tank occupied by a pair of snails.

Dropping to her knees, she reopened the book to the marked page, and compared the illustration to the animals in the tank.

"How cruel," she hissed, slammed the book shut, and strode out of the room.

Olivia had just reached the top of the stairs when Millay appeared in the hall, firmly closing a door behind her. She was flushed, but her eyes glimmered with triumph.

"Are you okay?" Olivia whispered softly. Millay nodded and Olivia gestured for her to accompany her downstairs.

When they reached the bottom, Olivia continued out the front door to the porch. She stopped by a potted fern, inhaled a deep lungful of air, and tried to calm her racing mind.

Millay didn't give her the chance. Thrusting her hands into the air, she raised her face skyward and pronounced, "I got him. I *totally* got him! The chief can nail the bastard to the wall." Her voice trembled with a mixture of excitement and indignation. "I know exactly how Hunter's getting the drugs into Oyster Bay. That smug son of a bitch is going down."

"I certainly hope so." Olivia spoke in a low voice. "I

believe he's complicit in the murders of Ruthie and Cheryl Holcomb."

"What?" Millay's dark eyes widened and she dropped her hands.

Olivia clutched the textbook tightly against her chest. "I'm dying to hear everything you learned and to tell you what I discovered, but we need to get Rawlings." Olivia turned to go and then stopped and faced Millay again. "Where's Hunter?"

"In the back bedroom thinking unpleasant thoughts so he can walk around in public again." Millay said and, seeing as Olivia didn't understand, added, "He's pitching a tent."

"Oh. Fine. Let's go." Olivia took Millay by the wrist. Intending to cut through the house and out to the patio, the two women stepped into the hallway and froze. Hunter stood in the middle of the staircase looking down at his parents while both Bellamy and Beauford scowled up at their son with overt disapproval.

At the sound of the door opening, the Drummonds shifted their gazes to the two women. Three sets of eyes radiated cold fury.

"Have you ladies lost your way?" Bellamy asked in a soft and dangerous voice. Her eyes went to the book pressed against Olivia's chest.

"I saw Millay come inside and thought I'd take a moment to talk with her alone," Olivia said breezily. "We're in a writers' group together."

None of the Drummonds replied. They continued to stare at Olivia and Millay with unconcealed rage.

"Well, we'd better get back to our food," Olivia said and made to walk past Beauford and Bellamy, but Beauford blocked her path. And then, with lightning quickness, Hunter leapt down the stairs and grabbed Millay by the elbow. He twisted her arm until she was forced to face him.

A waiter bearing an empty tray hurried past their small

group on his way out of the kitchen, and for a long, surreal moment, no one spoke. No one moved. It was as if a nightmare on the verge of unfolding had been put on hold.

The instant the waiter disappeared, Millay tried to shrug Hunter off, but he refused to loosen his grip.

"Let the lady go," a man commanded. "I'm not gonna ask you twice."

Olivia turned to see Luke Holcomb darkening the doorway of the room to the left of the hallway. He was swaying slightly and Olivia saw a wink of a metal flask peeking from his hip pocket. But her eyes didn't linger on the flask. She was far more captivated by the pistol in Luke's right hand. As she watched, shocked into silence, he raised his weapon and pointed it at Hunter's chest. He then pulled the hammer back and released a soft sigh. It was such a small sound, but it frightened Olivia more than the sight of the flask or the gun.

The sound said that Luke Holcomb was prepared to cross a line. He'd come to the garden party intent on killing someone, Olivia was certain of that. And the sigh was a signal that he was seconds away from completing that mission.

Olivia saw the pistol, smelled the odor of whiskey and sweat, and heard the sigh, but she also felt his anguish. It poured out of his rent heart and filled the narrow hallway with an impenetrable shadow of sorrow and pain.

Olivia stared at Luke and waited for him to pull the trigger.

Chapter 17

She goes but softly, but she goeth sure;
She stumbles not, as stronger
creatures do:
Her journey's shorter, so she may endure
Better than they which do much
farther go.

—JOHN BUNYAN, "UPON A SNAIL"

"Stop!" Beauford shouted, though it was clear that Luke was beyond hearing. His eyes were fixed on Hunter Drummond. He didn't acknowledge Beauford or anyone else in the room.

And then a strange thing happened.

Bellamy began to laugh.

The sound was so incongruent with the dire circumstances that it caught Luke's attention. His gaze shifted, as did everyone else's, and came to rest on Bellamy.

"Mom?" Hunter croaked in astonishment.

"That gun is from the time capsule display." Bellamy pointed at the revolver. "It hasn't been cleaned or fired in a hundred years. I doubt that this inebriated hillbilly had the foresight to locate the correct ammunition for an antique revolver. I locked the bullets in the study, so unless our boy genius thought to buy his own, he's pointing an unloaded pistol at you, son."

Olivia could hear the air escape through Hunter's lips,

and one glance at Luke proved that Bellamy's assumption was accurate.

Millay, who'd managed to pull free from Hunter's grasp, pointed at Bellamy. "That's a relief, Mrs. Drummond. If Hunter was dead, he couldn't spend the best years of his life behind bars. Olivia and I know what your scumbag son has done to the Holcombs." She turned to Luke. "Come with me. We need to get Chief Rawlings. This Southern prince is going down."

Bellamy laughed again. "You should crawl back under the rock where Hunter found you before I have you arrested for aiding and abetting this piece of trailer trash." She flicked her wrist at Luke. "As for you, that gun belongs under glass for the *civilized* people of this town to enjoy. I suppose the handle is covered with greasy fingerprints and smells like a locker room. I'll need to clean it on Monday and have the lock on the display case repaired, as if my to-do list wasn't long enough already." She frowned in annoyance. "You Holcombs are like vermin. Always underfoot. Always getting in the way."

Luke's face tightened in fury and he raised the gun in the air, wielding it like a club. But as his arm rose, Hunter's shot forward and he drove his fist into Luke's solar plexus with such force that Luke dropped the revolver and doubled over.

"That's enough!" Olivia cried sharply. "Millay, get the chief. Go out the front door. Go!"

Millay didn't hesitate. Hunter made to grab her again, but she moved too fast.

"Mom!" Hunter yelled in a panic. "We need to do something!"

"No, we don't," she replied calmly. "Let the girl point her filthy finger at us. We have nothing to hide." Bellamy turned to Olivia. "I'm surprised by the company you keep, Ms. Limoges. Perhaps *you* should retrieve your fiancé. He can handcuff our uninvited guest." She directed her haughty gaze at Luke.

"Leaving you free to murder him? I don't think so," a female voice hissed from behind Bellamy.

Pivoting, Bellamy gasped. Beauford and Hunter also released guttural noises of surprise.

Stella stood by a dark cavity. She'd clearly been hiding in a secret nook beneath the stairs. She was dressed in a long, gauzy cobalt skirt and teal camisole. Strings of costume pearls hung from her neck, and both wrists were covered with seashell bracelets. Her brown hair had been dyed royal blue and was pulled back over one ear and held in place by a mother-of-pearl comb. She wore no shoes and her cheeks and eyelids sparkled with blue and silver. She'd transformed into her mermaid persona. She was Undine. Otherworldly, wild, and beautiful.

And she held a revolver that was identical to the one Luke had stolen from the time capsule exhibit.

"What are you doing here?" Bellamy seethed. "You deceitful, disobedient girl. How dare you? And what in heaven's name are you wearing?"

Beauford put his hands on his hips and puffed out his chest, his brows creased in anger. "You're supposed to be in Atlanta. Your aunt must be worried out of her mind. And what the devil are you doing with that gun?"

"Nothing," Bellamy scoffed. "She's not much brighter than the hick over there."

Stella looked down at the gun and then at her mother. "I'm holding a Colt SAA revolver made in 1910. Considered the last of the cowboy era, this firearm is easy to clean and happens to be in excellent shape. I knew where you put the bullets and had no problem loading this gun while you and Dad and my precious brother were getting gussied up."

Olivia's eyes never left Stella's face. "You're here to protect Luke?" she asked, struggling to make the connections she'd fail to make until now. "This all started when your mother found Nathaniel Drummond's will, didn't it?"

Beauford took a step toward Stella. "You keep your mouth shut, Stella. You're in enough trouble as it is."

She gazed at her father as if she'd never seen him before. "I'm not in Atlanta because you and Mom made Hunter murder my best friend and my best friend's mother. I'm here because I made Ruthie a promise. I'm here for revenge."

Without warning, Beauford Drummond suddenly charged at his daughter. He put his head down and thrust his shoulders forward like a bull and moved with surprising quickness.

Stella opened her mouth to scream, but Beauford barreled into her, knocking her sideways before she could make a sound. They both went down. Stella's right arm struck the plank floor and the gun went off with a deafening report. The blast echoed in the hallway, bouncing off the walls and high ceilings.

Following the direction of the bullet's path, Olivia turned to see a red stain bloom in the middle of Hunter's belly before he covered the wound with his hands and sank to his knees.

"*Hunter!*" Bellamy shrieked and rushed to his side. "He didn't do it!" she screamed, ripping off her jacket. Her voice was shrill with terror. "It was *me!* It was *me!*"

Ignoring his daughter, Beauford clambered to his feet. "Shut up and help him, Bellamy!" He stared at his wife with a glazed expression as she balled up her jacket and pressed it over Hunter's stomach. "Jesus," Beauford whispered. His face turned ashen and he reached over his daughter's sprawled form to grab the banister for support.

Olivia tossed the textbook she was holding on a hall table and grabbed Beauford's arm, forcing him to lean hard on her. "Call 911," she told Beauford. "If you want to save your son, you'll go and make the call. Go," she repeated, pivoting an unresponsive Beauford and giving him a shove in the back.

When Olivia glanced down at Stella again, the young woman was sitting up. She rubbed the base of her skull with her left hand and gazed at the gun in her other hand with a mixture of horror and wonder.

"It's over now, Stella." Olivia spoke very softly, her voice belying the tremors of shock running through her body. She squatted down next to her. "It's over. You don't need to do anything else. You kept your promise."

Stella still hadn't released her grip on the pistol, and Olivia had no way of knowing if she'd discharge the gun again. She knew she had to choose her words very carefully. "Are you okay?" she whispered.

Stella blinked, as if waking for a long sleep, and leaned her head on Olivia's shoulder. "I had to save him. They were going to kill him next."

"Because of the will?" Olivia asked.

Stella nodded and Olivia put an arm around her back. "Come on, honey. Let's find another place to talk."

Olivia raised her eyes and saw Rawlings and Officer Cook racing toward her, the thud of their footsteps mingling with Bellamy's anguished cries and Hunter's moans of pain.

Cook reached for Stella, but Olivia shook her head, silently begging him not to touch her. "Stella," she said. "I want you to put the gun on the floor. Very gently. Okay?"

Stella complied instantly. She put the Colt on the rug and placed her hand in Olivia's. When Olivia helped her to her feet, she wobbled slightly and Cook shot out an arm to steady her. "I'd like to get her outside. She needs fresh air," Olivia said to Cook. "I think she has a great deal to tell us, but not here."

Cook was obviously torn. His training told him to follow protocol. In this situation, he should secure the weapon, cuff the suspect, Mirandize her, and lead her to his cruiser.

Olivia held his eyes and did her best to convey the importance of handling Stella with care. "She was trying to save Luke Holcomb's life. I'd like to hear why he was in danger, wouldn't you?"

Cook never had the chance to respond. Rawlings, who had two fingers pressed against Hunter's neck, called for his junior officer to request immediate backup. "And then I want you to keep the public out of this area. Grant access to the paramedics only." He then looked at Bellamy. "Keep applying pressure. You're doing great."

In response to this reassurance, Bellamy finally ceased her keening. Her eyes swept the room and landed on her daughter. Her face became a mask of rage and hatred. "*You* should be bleeding to death. *You!* Not *him!* You've brought me nothing but shame. Your whole life has been a waste! A waste of time and energy and—"

"Focus on your son, Mrs. Drummond," Rawlings interjected. "He needs all of your attention."

Mercifully, Bellamy listened to him.

Cook pulled out his phone and headed for the back door to stop a waitress from entering the hallway. Without his support on her arm, Stella sagged against Olivia. Half dragging Stella out the front door, Olivia guided her to a rocking chair and eased her into it. Olivia drew up another chair and took Stella's hands in her own.

"Did you find something inside Sadie's doll?" she asked softly. "When I examined her, I noticed that her seams had been cut and sewn with different thread. What was inside that doll, Stella?"

Stella stared out at the street, where the flashing lights of an ambulance illuminated the horizon. "Nathaniel Drummond's will. His *real* will. And a letter to his heirs. My mom found the will first and showed it to my dad. It's why they acted so weird after the time capsule was found. That thing changed everything . . ."

A letter to his heirs, Olivia thought and then gasped.

"Were the Holcombs the heirs to Nathaniel Drummond's fortune?"

Stella nodded weakly. "All along, Ruthie was family. *My* family. No wonder we felt like sisters. Sadie was Ruthie's great-great grandmother or something like that. And Josephine was mine."

"Two daughters with the same father. Two girls borne by different mothers," Olivia murmured in awe.

"Yes," said Stella. "In his original will, Nathaniel split everything between Sadie and Josephine, but when he got really sick, Martha Drummond destroyed that will and had another one drawn up naming her as sole beneficiary. She then forged her husband's signature and their attorney notarized it. According to the letter Nathaniel put in the metal tube inside the doll, Martha told everyone that he was too sick to write, talk, or receive visitors. That's also when she kicked Emma and Sadie out of the house." Stella curled her hands into fists. "Nathaniel only managed to get the copper box in the time capsule by giving it to the minister when his wife wasn't in the room."

Olivia fixed on the word "minister." "If the attorney notarized the forged will, then Nathanial must have given the minister a copy of the original. And if Nathaniel was really that ill, the minister must have been the one to hide it inside the doll. He and Nathaniel may have chosen that line of Scripture together. I wonder how many copies of that original will existed . . ."

The outside world faded as Olivia was swept up in a vision of Nathaniel Drummond in his bed. She imagined sweat dampening his brow and pictured his sallow skin. She could almost feel his anguish—his desperate desire to use the last of his strength to send a message through time—to tell the truth about his double life. "Sadie was the treasure of his heart," Olivia said. "And Nathaniel meant for her to inherit half his fortune."

"Do you realize what they did? First Martha and then

my own family? Ruthie should have lived a totally different life." Stella released a strangled sob. "A nice house, pretty clothes, a college education. Regular doctor and dentist checkups. She and her mom and Luke are Sadie's descendants. She should have had my life. But with a family who loved her."

Olivia squeezed Stella's hands. "You knew they'd go after Luke because he's the last of Sadie's descendants."

Stella exhaled in relief. Someone understood. Someone believed her. Tears slipped down her cheeks and landed on Olivia's forearms. "I couldn't save Ruthie, but I wasn't going to let them get to Luke."

"I saw the textbook in the study in the historical society. Was it one of Hunter's?" Stella nodded absently and Olivia continued. "He brought those snails to Oyster Bay. Poisonous cone snails. But it sounds like your mother used them to kill Ruthie and Cheryl."

"It was all her idea. Hunter brought the snails on his boat and kept them in his room. He locks it with a key, so I couldn't search it. And of course, Dad went along with everything. He'd do anything to avoid a scandal or have to give up one of his sports cars or European vacations." Stella twisted one of her shell bracelets. "Only someone who knew Ruthie could murder her using a snail. Its shell was so beautiful. Ruthie must have thought she'd found an amazing prize. For someone who had nothing, finding that perfect, beautiful shell was like getting a gift from the sea." Stella's voice sounded dreamy when she spoke next. "It was like all the stories we told each other. A magic shell that could grant wishes."

Crying now, Stella sagged against Olivia.

"Ever since I was a girl, I believed the ocean brought me things," Olivia whispered, stroking Stella's brittle blue hair. "I still believe. It led me to Ruthie. And from there, to you. I will never abandon you, Stella. You will never be alone."

She held Stella for a long time, rocking her softly and murmuring words of comfort to her.

Noises erupted around them, but the women didn't move. Neither the blaring sirens, nor the thumping of heavy treads on the porch, nor the shouts and commotion going on just inside the front door interrupted their embrace. Only Rawlings, who laid his hand lightly on Olivia's shoulder, finally managed to get through to them.

"Are you two all right?" he asked. "Miss Drummond? Are you hurt?"

"I feel nothing," she muttered. But she raised her head and wiped her cheeks. Rawlings held out a handkerchief and Stella looked at it for a long moment, as if she'd been given something precious, as if the kindness of being offered a small white square of cloth was so monumental that she wanted to imprint it in her memory.

"I need to hear everything, Miss Drummond," Rawlings said in a hushed, patient tone. "The whole story. Do you think you can tell me tonight? Are you up for it?"

Stella glanced at Olivia. "Will you stay with me?"

Olivia saw the tear tracks in Stella's glittery makeup and the smudges of black mascara under her eyes. The blue shadow was all but gone and she looked both young and vulnerable and ancient and jaded. "The whole time," Olivia promised.

Together, she and Rawlings walked Stella to the Range Rover. Olivia retrieved the extra sweater she kept in the car and helped Stella into it, dressing her as a mother might dress a child. As soon as Rawlings was settled in the backseat, Olivia pulled around the ambulance, with its blinding lights and open rear doors, and left the historical society, with its clusters of gawking partygoers, behind.

Chapter 18

Fear follows crime, and is its punishment.

—VOLTAIRE

At the police station, Rawlings bypassed the interview rooms and led the women to the conference room.

"We need to get you warm, Miss Drummond. I'll be right back," he said and left. He returned shortly with Officer Cook, a steaming coffee carafe, and two blankets. He set the carafe down and handed a blanket to Stella. "Fresh out of the package." He smiled kindly. "They're not made of the softest material on earth, but they'll do in a pinch."

Cook placed a digital recorder and a notepad and pen in the center of the table and began to pour coffee into paper cups. Watching him, Olivia suddenly realized that he was clad in the black-and-white uniform of the waitstaff.

"I didn't noticed you at the party," she said.

He seemed pleased by the remark. "That was the idea. For me to blend in. My waiter duties weren't very demanding. All I did was walk around with a water pitcher. Most of the guests were only interested in their cocktails, so I was able to keep an eye on things."

"I'm glad you were there," Olivia said, accepting a cup

of coffee. She put the cup in front of Stella and passed her the sugar and creamer packets. Stella stared off in the middle distance without tasting her drink.

Rawlings Mirandized Stella and then asked if she wanted to phone an attorney. Stella waived the right to seek legal counsel and agreed to have her statement recorded. Though she spoke in a weary monotone, Olivia sensed that Stella was ready to unburden herself.

Rawlings turned on the recorder and stated the date, the time, and the names of the people in the room. The moment he paused, Stella said, "I wanted to shoot my brother because I thought he was a murderer. Turns out, he was only helping my mother do the dirty work."

Olivia expected Rawlings to direct the course of the conversation, but he didn't. He simply looked at Stella and waited for her to continue. Everything about his expression and posture let her know that she had his undivided attention.

"Hunter's job is to collect toxic marine animals and plants," she continued.

"For MarineBioPharm?" Rawlings asked.

"Yeah." Stella took a sip of coffee. "The animals are kept alive in tanks on my brother's boat. I went aboard with a crewmember the day after Hunter got home and noticed a tank with snails. They had really beautiful shells." She stared down at her cup. "I was thinking how much Ruthie would love a few of those shells, so I asked the crewmember if he could get me some, but he said that if he stuck his hand in the tank, he'd be dead before suppertime."

Olivia thought about the library books Stella had borrowed. "After Ruthie died, you checked out the marine biology textbooks to research the cone snail, didn't you? You knew that, among all the things your brother collected, the snail thing would be the one Ruthie would pick up."

"Exactly." Stella's mouth tightened into a thin line. "Of course, the one she grabbed still had the snail inside."

Rawlings leaned a fraction closer. "I'm not familiar with this snail. Can you tell me why it's so dangerous?"

Stella turned to Cook. "Could I have another cup? And a pencil?"

Cook was quick to oblige.

"Pretend this is the snail." Stella turned the cup over and tapped it. She then snapped the pencil in two and hid the smaller piece under the cup. "See this sugar packet? This is a fish. It swims by the snail and bam!" The pencil shot out from under the cup and struck the sugar packet. "The snail has this thing called a proboscis. It's basically a harpoon filled with venom and can sting the fish multiple times. The fish becomes paralyzed and then the snail eats it."

"That explains the cyanosis of the victims' index fingers," Olivia added. It's where the snail harpooned them. Where the snail's venom entered their bodies."

Rawlings picked up the sugar packet. "But a fish is small." He glanced between Stella and Olivia. "Are you saying that the toxin is just as lethal to humans?"

When Stella didn't answer right away, Olivia said, "I don't know as much as Stella on the subject, but I read the pages she had marked in the book. According to that textbook, not all cone snails are deadly, but the ones that attack fish can kill us just as quickly."

Rousing, Stella took a sip of coffee and grimaced. Tearing open several sugar packets, she dumped them in her coffee and watched them dissolve. "Their venom is really potent. Hunter's company is developing it as a medicine to control pain. Of course, he collects most of his samples illegally and sells them to MarineBioPharm off the books." Stella began to tear the empty sugar packets into pieces. "My seemingly perfect brother is a liar, thief, and an accessory to murder. I hope he dies on the operating table while my parents cry their eyes out in the waiting room."

Instead of responding, Rawlings wrote something on

his notepad and passed it to Cook. Cook scanned the lines, nodded, and left the room.

"Officer Cook is going to acquire search warrants for your brother's boat and your family home. It would save time if you could point me in the right direction. What should we be looking for at White Columns?"

Stella didn't answer. She continued to shred the sugar packets until tiny pieces of white paper were stuck to her fingertips. It looked as if she'd been catching snowflakes.

"Help me, Miss Drummond," Rawlings said. "I'm still not seeing the full picture. I'm afraid you're the only person who can tell me exactly what happened to your friend. And why it happened."

"Millay and I can be of assistance too," Olivia said. "Millay says she has a pretty clear idea of how Hunter smuggled drugs into Oyster Bay and I know that Bellamy Drummond killed Ruthie and Cheryl Holcomb because of what she found in the time capsule. Bellamy left the snail on the beach for Ruthie to find."

While Olivia spoke, Stella sagged in her chair. It was plain to see that the fight had gone out of her. She'd accidentally shot her brother. Her mother had killed her best friend, and her father had approved of the plan. Stella had found a way back home to save Luke Holcomb's life, and having accomplished her goal, she was bone weary. The night's revelations had taken a toll on her.

"You called her Melusine," Rawlings said very quietly. "She was like a sister to you. I know you're exhausted, Stella. You've been through hell. But I also know that you loved Ruthie, and that love is stronger than any other power on earth." He waited a heartbeat and then continued. "I think she was the only person in this world who made you happy. So give her the ending she deserves, Stella. Be her hero."

"Undine," Olivia whispered into Stella's ear. "Be Undine and tell the chief about the will."

Stella drew the blanket over her face and Olivia feared she'd made a grave error in bringing up the secret name Stella and Ruthie had used in their secret communications. But after a long moment, Stella lowered the blanket and nodded.

"My parents found Nathaniel Drummond's original will and a letter inside the doll he put in the time capsule. Not Josephine's doll. Nathaniel had another daughter. Sadie. Yes, the mighty patriarch of the Drummond Empire was a total scumbag." She grunted in disgust. "I knew they'd found a doll and a photo that upset them both. I overheard them arguing about the 'best course of action.' I was still too out of it because of what happened to Ruthie to care about the doll." She glanced at Olivia. "It wasn't until I saw you at the library that I wanted to find out what my parents were hiding."

Stella went on to describe the contents of the will and the letter while Rawlings took notes and bobbed his head to show that he was listening.

"So your mother placed the cone snail in Ruthie's path because of Nathaniel Drummond's will? How do you know it was her and not your father or brother?"

"Hunter was busy committing other crimes, and while my dad talks a big game, he isn't a man of action. But he and my mom must have worked the plan out together, because after Ruthie and her mom were dead, they acted like high school sweethearts. They haven't been that nice to each other in years. And though Hunter's always been perfect in their eyes, they've treated him like he could walk on water ever since he showed up early for his visit."

Stella gestured at the shredded cup. "With Ruthie, Mrs. Holcomb, and Luke gone, none of Sadie's descendants would be left to claim their rightful share of Nathaniel's fortune. In his will, Nathaniel left half of his assets to Josephine and Sadie or to their descendants if his daughters were unable to claim their inheritance. He must have known

Sadie wouldn't see a dime during her lifetime, so he tried to make things right with her children's children."

Rawlings frowned. "But why wouldn't your parents simply destroy the will? Why resort to murder?"

"Because Nathaniel was a crafty man," Olivia said. "In the letter, he refers to there being multiple copies of the will. Even if they burned or shredded the one from the doll, there may have been others." She turned to Stella. "Is that right?"

Stella's mouth curved into a wry smile. "Nathaniel hid other copies throughout White Columns. It says so in the letter, which was hidden in my father's desk. He has one of those desks with a secret niche, but I've known about it since I was a kid. I found it right before we were supposed to leave for the airport."

"Where did he hide the other copies?" Olivia asked breathlessly.

"Well, that's where the ink of the letter is completely smudged. It's almost impossible to read. *Almost.* I studied that thing at every angle and finally made out the word 'bed.' I figured Nathaniel had to hide the other copies close by. He was too weak to go far and it sounds like his wife watched him like a prison guard. I also have his original bed. The thought creeps me out now, but it ended up giving me the proof I needed to nail my family." Her voice quavered and she paused to get it under control. "I found another copy of the will. I pried off the carving of a cotton flower in the headboard and there was a space behind it. Nathaniel had stored the will inside a glass jar."

The cotton flower. The Drummond family seal. It was *important all along*, Olivia thought and cast a glance at Rawlings, but his gaze was fixed on Stella. "And where is that document now?" he asked.

"In a display case at the historical society," Stella said. "It also held the Colt." She shook her head. "I never imagined Luke would take the other gun. I should have locked the case again, but I had to get back to my hiding place under the stairs before anyone saw me. I had to stop my mom. You see, the housekeeper left Hunter's room unlocked today, and when I saw the cone snails in his fish tank, I assumed my mother was going after Luke next. I wasn't going to let her hurt anyone else."

Rawlings, who'd been taking notes while Stella talked, tapped his chin with the end of his pen. "Even if Martha Drummond forged her husband's signature on a will he hadn't had drawn up, the crime happened in 1917. It would be very difficult to prove that the will he hid inside Sadie's doll was the original and even harder to contest the forged will in court." He examined his notes. "And there would only be a court case if the Holcombs were made aware of the original will and told that their distant relatives—Sadie's children—had been tricked out of their inheritance. I'm not doubting you, Stella, but it seems like a stretch that your mother, with your father and brother acting as accessories, would kill three people to prevent what could be a circumstantial threat to their security."

Stella shook her head. "All I know is that from the moment that time capsule was dug up, my parents became basket cases. They tried to hide it, but I knew they were scared. They drank and fought and called my brother home. They needed him to deliver the murder weapon, and since he has no moral code whatsoever, he agreed."

Rawlings nodded. Next, he had her painstakingly create a timeline of events, dating from the day Bellamy was called into the church right up until Stella passed through the security gate at Raleigh's airport, only to exit the terminal fifteen minutes later and climb into the shuttle she'd booked the night before using her mother's credit card.

Rawlings only interrupted her once to ask, "What about your aunt? Wasn't she concerned when you didn't show up in Atlanta?"

"I sent her a text from my mother's phone saying that I

wouldn't arrive until Sunday. I even sent her a new itinerary with my flights and added a comment about how I'd been so unruly before leaving for the airport that I'd had to be sedated." She wiped the paper bits still clinging to her fingers on the blanket. "I knew my aunt would buy it."

Now that Rawlings had satisfied his questions leading up to the shooting, he slowed his pace even further, asking Stella what she'd heard from her nook under the stairs and if she was cognizant that Luke Holcomb would show up at the garden party. She said that she was as surprised as everyone else by his presence.

As they continued to rehash the evening's events, Rawlings got Stella a new cup and poured her more coffee. Eventually, Olivia tuned out their conversation. She couldn't get past his use of the word "circumstantial." Even with Nathaniel's original will in hand, the case against the Drummonds wasn't solid enough. Everything came back to the subject of the time capsule. The ruination of two families had begun with its discovery, but there were still questions that had to be answered.

Olivia returned to the moment when she'd stood in the church cloakroom with Michel and watched Pastor Jeffries open the lid. She remembered his expression. She remembered the fear in his eyes. And suddenly, Olivia knew that she'd found the missing piece to the puzzle. Ruthie's death had been foreshadowed in those brief seconds when Pastor Jeffries had read the inventory sheet and seen Nathaniel Drummond's name listed on it. The destruction of one family and the unraveling of another hadn't started with Bellamy Drummond. It had started with a man of God. A man who made a terrible choice—a choice that Ruthie and Cheryl Holcomb paid for with their lives. A man whose ancestor had once been the minister of the church he now presided over.

Olivia gestured at the recorder, frantically signaling for Rawlings to turn it off. Raising his brows in question, he pressed the stop button. "I know you're spread thin with officers at the hospital, the historical society, and obtaining search warrants, but you need to send someone from your team to the First Presbyterian Church right away."

"Why?" Rawlings asked.

"Because I believe Bellamy and Beauford have known about Nathaniel's original will for a long time. And I don't think they were the only ones who profited from Martha's forgery. You need to question Pastor Jeffries. His family played a role in this charade too."

Stella gave Olivia a sharp look. "What do you mean?"

"Nathaniel Drummond entrusted the copper box to a minister. Pastor Jeffries told me that Jeffries men have led the church for over a century, and Bellamy mentioned that the Drummonds had always attended First Presbyterian. She also added that the pastor approached her family before anyone else when the church needed funds." She spread her hands. "Why would Mr. and Mrs. Drummond be the first people the church called upon? Because they were wealthy? Yes. But perhaps also because Beauford and Bellamy were indebted to Pastor Jeffries."

"For what?" Stella asked, clearly not liking the idea of the kindly pastor being complicit in the crimes her family had committed.

"I think they were indebted to him for his silence," Olivia said, gazing intently at Rawlings. "But the time has come for him to talk."

Two weeks later, Olivia sat alone in the sanctuary of the First Presbyterian Church. The cloakroom project was nearly finished, and the workmen had left for the day. Olivia was glad to have the place to herself. It gave her the chance to gaze upon the stained glass angel and child before the window restorations got under way.

Following Bellamy and Beauford Drummond's incarcerations, there'd been no one to provide the necessary funds to return the stained glass windows to their original glory. The idea of them falling into further disrepair gnawed at Olivia, so not long after the new pastor arrived to take Pastor Jeffries's place, Olivia knocked on his office door and presented him with a very large check.

"You're offering this sizable donation, but have no affiliation with the church?" The boyish-looking pastor was clearly puzzled. "I'd love to accept it, because the windows are spectacular and should be preserved, but I want to make sure you've thought this through."

Olivia liked that Pastor Daniels didn't just take the money, shake her hand, and send her on her way. She liked that he wanted to pause and reflect first. It showed integrity on his part. "I'm doing this because of a particular window in the sanctuary," she confessed. "The one with the angel and child. It reminds me of many mothers and daughters. At first, I saw my mother in the angel's face. And in the child, I saw myself. But over the past month, the child has become other children. Lost girls with names like Ruthie. And Stella. Children who didn't get the love and protection they deserved. Children who needed to be shielded beneath an angel's wing."

The young pastor nodded. He'd been listening with a quiet intensity that reminded Olivia of Rawlings. "It's my favorite window too. This might sound far-fetched, but it's one of the reasons I took this job. When I came to visit, I saw my little sister in that girl's face. She died when I was nine. At first, the resemblance made me sad because it brought back the pain of losing her. But the more I sat in front of it, the more I was comforted by the scene. It was then that I knew I'd been called here."

Olivia understood that feeling all too well. After years of wandering, she too had been called home. Smiling warmly at Pastor Daniels, she said, "Welcome to Oyster Bay."

Now, the day before her wedding, Olivia sat in the stiff pew, her face bathed in soft morning light. Patches of gold, white, and green from the window fell across her skin. She closed her eyes, feeling weary, but peaceful. She and her community had survived another ordeal, another trial by fire, and were slowly getting on with the business of living.

Olivia had come to the sanctuary to reflect on what had happened, but also to sort out how she felt about her mother. It had taken the standoff between Stella and her parents for Olivia to recognize that she was angry with Camille Limoges. Limoges. The name Olivia had taken after leaving Oyster Bay to live with her maternal grandmohter. The name that had made her an heiress. The name that Olivia wanted because it connected her to her mother. To Camille. Olivia felt angry and betrayed and needed a quiet place to process these feelings. In the end, she realized that her mother had married Willie Wade to protect her unborn child—that she'd sacrificed her own chance at happiness to keep Olivia safe. Holding both palms to the light, Olivia watched as the multicolored sunbeams set her skin aglow. She sat there for a long time, picturing her mother's face and holding a rainbow in her cupped hands.

"I hope I'm not disturbing you," a hushed voice broke the silence.

Olivia turned to find Charles Wade standing in the aisle. Though disappointed to have her solitude spoiled, she gestured at the empty cushion next to her.

The pew creaked as Charles lowered his weight onto the seat. He lifted his gaze to the angel and child and stared at the pair until his eyes watered. "She looks like Camille," he whispered. "That child could be you."

"I saw it that way too," Olivia said. "But my mother was no angel. She married a man she didn't love to avoid giving birth to an illegitimate child. That was a mistake. For her. For him. And for me."

"She was trying to protect you," Charles said. "And my brother, for all of his faults, tried to be a father to you."

Olivia thought of Sadie, of how she and her mother had

been thrown out into the street when Nathaniel Drummond was too weak to stop his wife from evicting them.

"It's strange to hear you defend him," Olivia said. "Whenever you've talked about him, it's always been with a mixture of dislike and disrespect."

"I liked to think that I was better than him. But I'm not." Charles twisted his wedding ring around his finger and sighed. "Sandra, my wife, has asked for a divorce."

Surprised by the turn in the conversation, Olivia shifted in her seat. The pew had suddenly grown uncomfortable. "I'm sorry to hear that."

"It was bound to happen," Charles continued. "Especially after I told her about you and Camille. I think she knew about Camille. She knew that someone else had claimed the best parts of me. Through the years, Camille haunted our marriage. I just couldn't let her go."

Olivia looked at the window again. "What will you do?"

Charles shrugged. "Give Sandra whatever she asks for. She was a good wife and mother. I chose her over Camille, but I married her for the wrong reasons. Career advancement doesn't make for the best foundation in a relationship." He moved the ring to his right hand. "I plan to stay here until the bookstore's finished. After that, who knows?"

At that moment, Pastor Daniels entered the sanctuary, waved at Olivia, and went out through the side door.

Charles followed him with his eyes. "He looks like he should be in high school."

"He's young, but he'll be a refreshing change for this congregation. The former pastor stepped down and will probably face criminal charges."

Charles frowned. "Was he involved in the Holcomb murders? I've been following the stories in the *Gazette,* but I don't remember reading anything about a pastor."

"Not all the details have been made public," Olivia said. "Pastor Jeffries possessed a diary written by his great-grandfather, who was also a pastor of this church. The diary contained evidence that the last will and testament of Nathaniel Drummond, the patriarch of the Drummond family, was a forgery. Pastor Jeffries used the diary to blackmail Beauford and Bellamy into financing the church's most expensive projects. The chief reviewed records going back over twenty years. Whenever the church has had a need, the Drummonds have always stepped up as the first and most generous of donors. Whether it was purchasing a new organ or a suite of office equipment for the pastor's staff, they never failed to write big checks."

"Why not just bump him off?" Charles asked casually. "It sounds like these people would do anything to preserve their wealth and position."

Olivia found that a curious remark coming from someone who valued those things as much as the Drummonds, but kept the thought to herself. "From what I understand, Pastor Jeffries had insurance. Immediately after the time capsule was discovered, he gave a copy of Nathaniel's will to a nameless individual for safekeeping. In the event of the pastor's untimely death, the will would be handed over to the authorities."

Charles jerked his thumb over his shoulder. "Was the cloakroom renovation one of the many projects Beauford and Bellamy funded?"

Olivia nodded. "The project that led to the discovery of the time capsule. If only that lead box had remained safely inside the walls, two innocent women would still be alive."

"At least he looked after this old place," Charles said. "It's very peaceful."

An image of Ruthie's body beneath the pier swam to the surface of Olivia's thoughts, and she shook her head angrily. "The pastor's job was to look after the people of this community and he completely failed in his duty. Jeffries must have known that Ruthie Holcomb's death was no accident, but he never came forward. And after Cheryl was killed, it was unconscionable for him to remain silent.

He was willing to sacrifice truth and justice for the preservation of this building, but his lack of judgment will haunt him the rest of his life. In hopes of a leaner sentence, Beauford Drummond admitted everything to the chief. He gave up his wife, his son, and the pastor, leaving Jeffries no choice but to make a full confession and hand the diary over to the authorities."

Charles whistled softly. "Unbelievable. And what happened to the Drummond boy? The one who was shot by his sister?"

Involuntarily, Olivia's hand went to her belly. "He survived, but he's paralyzed from the waist down." She shook her head. "And though Stella shot him by accident, I don't think she feels too sorry for him. Hunter had always been cruel to both her and Ruthie. I read Ruthie's letters to Stella, so I know. Not only did he bully Stella every chance he could, but he ratted on her to his mother whenever possible. I had no idea he was such a bastard under that charming veneer. After Ruthie died, he seemed genuinely concerned for his sister's well-being. But it was just an act, a part played for my sake."

"Do you think she'll ever forgive her brother?"

"I can't say," Olivia answered after a moment's reflection. "After all, he was instrumental in the murder of her best friend. He was responsible for bringing the cone snails to Oyster Bay. However, it was Bellamy Drummond who placed the snail on the beach and watched as Ruthie Holcomb picked it up. She watched as Ruthie was stung on the hand. She watched her collapse in the sand. And then she just walked away, leaving that young woman to die a horrible death. Not long after that, she borrowed one of Hunter's hooded sweatshirts and brought flowers to Ruthie's mother. She pretended to offer sympathy and apologized for treating Ruthie so abhorrently for years. Because it was raining and Cheryl had a kind heart, she invited Bellamy inside. Bellamy repaid that kindness by placing a cone snail in Cheryl's hand."

Charles grimaced. "And Stella? What's in store for her?"

"She faces jail time, I'm afraid. She showed up at the party with a gun and admitted that she planned to use it. True, she wanted to save Luke Holcomb, but she still has to face the consequences of taking the law into her own hands." Olivia smiled a little. "I doubt she'll be incarcerated for long and I don't think she minds it one bit. She sought justice for the person she loved most and she got it. I think she's willing to accept the price she has to pay for keeping the promise she made to Ruthie."

Charles exhaled loudly. "The decisions we make . . . I could have been more loving to my kids too. I was never around. Too busy working or schmoozing with potential clients. Sandra raised my children and now they're basically strangers."

"You can change that," Olivia said gently. "When the bookstore's finished, maybe you should go back to New York and work on your relationship with them."

"Maybe," Charles said and then hesitantly touched Olivia's hand. "I'd like to spend some time with you first. I'm glad that we'll be reinventing Through the Wardrobe together." Smiling, he gestured at the window. "You'll be in white tomorrow. A beautiful bride."

Olivia felt a warning bell go off. Was Charles on the verge of inviting himself to her wedding? "How did you know?"

Ignoring the question, Charles got to his feet and pulled out a tissue-wrapped object from his pocket. Holding it gently in his palm, he sat back down again. "Is that the pendant I gave Camille?" He pointed at the depression between Olivia's collarbone where the silver starfish nestled.

Her fingers instinctively closed around the pendant. "Yes. I had one too, but mine's gone now."

Charles must have seen the pain flash in her eyes, for he didn't ask what had become of her necklace. "To answer your question, I learned your wedding date from Fred

Yoder," he said. "Though he refused to tell me a thing until he knew my motive. The man's a loyal as a hound." Charles laughed. "I like the guy. He's a savvy businessman and a good friend to you."

"And what was your motive?" Olivia asked quietly.

"I wanted you to have something special for your wedding—something that Camille might have given you. So I had this made. Fred helped me find the starfish and put me in touch with a silversmith and a jeweler. I hope you like it." He offered her the tissue-wrapped package.

Olivia peeled back the tissue and gasped. Cushioned in the white paper was a tortoiseshell hair comb topped by a cluster of small starfish. Unlike her pendant, these starfish were of white gold and were covered with tiny diamonds and sapphires. As Olivia tilted the comb, admiring the exquisite workmanship, the diamonds glinted in the light. "It's lovely," she whispered and was on the verge of telling Charles she couldn't accept such a costly gift when she looked at his face. His eyes shone with delight, and when he exhaled softly in relief—a caress of air that brushed Olivia's cheek—she felt a rush of shame.

"Thank you," she said. "This is incredibly thoughtful of you."

Charles beamed. "A one-of-a-kind woman should have a one-of-a-kind accessory on her wedding day."

"And she should have her family beside her," Olivia said quietly. "I'd like you to be there. I know it's last minute, but . . ." She trailed off, hoping he'd readily accept.

Charles was clearly stunned by the invitation. Pointing at the hair comb, he said, "I wasn't trying to bribe you into including me. I just wanted to wish you well."

"I believe you. And you should save your well-wishing for tomorrow evening." She laid her hand over his, noting how the shapes of his nails and fingers were similar to those belonging to the man she had always thought of as her father. However, Charles's hands were smooth and clean while Willie's had been covered with scars and burns—the marks of a fisherman's life etched into a canvas of salt-weathered skin. Willie was gone, but his twin brother had returned—a prodigal son looking to make amends. Olivia squeezed his hand and then excused herself, saying she had much to see to before her big day.

On her way out of the sanctuary, Olivia glanced back to where her biological father sat alone, staring at a window of an angel and a little girl. There was only one thing she left to do. She needed to tell Rawlings the truth about Charles Wade.

Chapter 19

Secrets are things we give to others to keep for us.

—ELBERT HUBBARD

The Bayside Book Writers gathered that night to discuss the latest chapter of Laurel's novel, *The Wife*. From the beginning, the title had failed to captivate them, and Laurel was hoping her friends could help her think of a new one.

"We've only read half of the book, so it's hard to come up with a title that captures the whole project. What if you summarized it for us?" Olivia suggested. "Like you were writing a blurb for the back cover."

"I'm not sure I can." Frowning, Laurel turned to Millay. "Did you have to write your own back cover material?"

"Nope. My publisher took care of that. It was pretty good too. Lots of alliteration and catchy phrases."

Laurel groaned and Haviland, who was resting at her feet, echoed the sound.

"Forget about the blurb," Harris said. "Pretend your book's just been published and you're doing a signing at Through the Wardrobe. I'm a stranger and I come up to you and ask what your novel's about. What would you say to me?"

"That it's the story of a woman who's trying to discover her identity beyond that of being a wife and mother. She's known as 'the wife' by everyone in her husband's law firm and as 'the twins' mother' by the women in the community. No one calls her by her first name, and she's fighting to be her own person while still caring for her family."

Rawlings opened his notebook. "It's a good thing we're exploring new titles tonight. I went on Amazon and found that *The Wife* has been taken already by a well-known novelist."

"Can't use *The Good Wife* either," Harris said.

Olivia gestured at Harris's laptop. "Maybe we should see if any of our titles are available."

As it turned out, established authors had recently used *The Lost Wife*, *The Silent Wife*, *The Ordinary Wife*, and *The Reliable Wife*. They came across similar roadblocks when combining the words "wife" and "mother" until finally Rawlings called a halt to the search.

"Laurel's character would hate this," he said. "We're pigeonholing her."

"But we have to call her something and we don't know her name," Millay protested. "Laurel won't tell the reader what it is."

Laurel shook her head. "Not until the end. The wife has to finish this journey of discovery before she grabs the microphone at her husband's company Christmas party and shouts it at the top of her lungs. Basically, she loses it in front of everyone."

"Cool," Harris said with a smile.

"So I don't want to use her name until that scene."

Olivia nodded. "I like that idea. But what about a nickname? Something her mother called her? Or her best friend from childhood?"

Laurel gazed out the window, where the first stars of the evening were appearing above a glassy sea. "Like Undine. Or Melusine."

A silence descended over the group, and was only broken by the sound of Haviland sighing in his sleep.

"I can't get my mind off Stella," Laurel whispered. "I went to see her at the women's correctional facility." She looked at Olivia. "I didn't know that you'd been several times already."

"I made her a promise," Olivia said. "And I intend to keep it."

"Which was?" Millay wanted to know.

Olivia also glanced at the ocean. "That I wouldn't desert her. That she'd never be alone."

Harris raised his can of soda in salute. "How is she?"

"Surprisingly content," Olivia said. "She's in what many would consider a country club correctional facility. I don't think she'll be there long, but she's making the best of it. She's made some friends and loves working in both the library and the vegetable garden. She's also been researching the nuances of the laws of inheritance. She plans to help Luke Holcomb claim his rightful share of her family fortune. She comes into her trust fund in about eighteen months and is determined to give Luke half of her money. The two of them have been talking about starting a business together."

Millay grinned. "That would be like a Capulet working with a Montague."

"Way to throw in a Shakespearean comparison." Harris exchanged a high five with Millay.

The friends meandered off topic for a little while longer, until Rawlings quietly suggested they finish the business at hand by at least providing Laurel with a working title. However, Laurel politely rejected his plan.

"I'm not ready for this," she insisted. "Seriously, I'll worry about the title when the book is done. I'm positive that it'll come to me at the end." She put a hand over her heart. "I'm sorry if I wasted your time and creative talent, but this title is like wine. It needs to age a little to be any good."

"Speaking of vino, let's open a bottle of bubbly and toast our soon-to-be newlyweds!" Harris exclaimed, jumping off the sofa and bounding into the kitchen.

Laurel stood up and moved next to Rawlings, who had risen to help himself to more cheese and crackers. "Can I tell them your other good news? It'll be in the paper in the morning and after that, well, it'll be everywhere."

Olivia gave Rawlings a curious look. He smiled at her and then turned to Laurel. "All right. But it's not *my* good news. There were at least a dozen officers from the police department involved. As well as Coast Guard officers. And Millay. Though for her protection, she's remaining anonymous."

At the sound of her name, Millay paused in the act of lining up plastic champagne flutes. "Me?"

"Because of you, we were able to crack Hunter Drummond's code," Rawlings said. "Without the information you secured, we couldn't have helped the Coast Guard—"

"With the biggest drug bust in the state's history!" Laurel cried, clapping and bouncing on her toes like the cheerleader she once was.

Harris, who had the champagne bottle in his hands, said, "Stop! I need to hear this from the beginning. When was the bust?"

"This afternoon," Rawlings said. "The Golden Boys, as everyone's now calling them, motored out to sea for their pickup. They took delivery of *twenty tons* of marijuana. Next, they followed what has become their usual protocol: They split up. Some of the Golden Boys delivered their cache to fishing trawlers, many of which were operated by local fishermen, while the others served as decoys. As they had many times before, the fishing vessels docked and unloaded their cargo of fresh fish or shrimp, along with the drugs hidden beneath the catch of the day. The Golden Boys didn't deal the drugs. Once the product made land in Oyster Bay, they were done. Their job was transportation and distribution, not sales."

"Their only role was to transfer the drugs from ship to ship?" Olivia asked.

"Their job was to get them onshore through any means," Rawlings said. "Nine times out of ten, they motored out with the sole purpose of performing decoy operations. They invested a great deal of time giving law enforcement the runaround and have wasted a great deal of manpower and resources. But today, they brought in several tons of marijuana. Everything had been leading up to this major delivery, and the DEA seized the product of a year's worth of careful planning by the Golden Boys and their cohorts."

Millay's mouth hung open. "Why did they go ahead with it? Hunter was their leader and he's in a prison hospital."

"Someone else took his place," Rawlings said. "Master Drummond had already established a protocol, and all the Golden Boys had to do was follow it."

Olivia was confused. "Let me get this straight. The drugs were on real fishing vessels all along?"

Rawlings nodded. "The Golden Boys were the brains. The white-collar criminals. They didn't do any heavy lifting or run the big risks. They micromanaged and were paid handsomely for their work. And they believed they were invincible."

"Until they met Millay," Laurel said proudly. "She broke the code."

Millay was staring at Rawlings in astonishment. "I did?"

"The night of the garden party, you told me how Hunter had boasted that he'd never get caught because he was smarter than the people chasing him. The phrase that caught my attention was Hunter's assertion that he had 'more book learning.' It stuck in my mind."

"Mine too." Millay's gaze grew distant, and Olivia knew her friend was back at the party, pretending to be enraptured as Hunter Drummond tried to impress her. "When he said that the secret to success was doing things by the book, I guessed that he and his punk friends must have created a code using a particular book."

Harris was leaning over the counter in his eagerness to hear the rest of the story. "And? What was it?"

"A nautical first-aid manual." Rawlings pulled a red-and-white paperback from his leather satchel. "Hunter was in charge of communications. He'd send each Golden Boy a text with two page numbers and two topic headings. The page numbers turned out to be degrees of longitude and latitude, and the information listed below the topic heading told them if they'd be receiving drugs from ships at sea, running a decoy operation, or transferring drugs to a local fishing vessel. Petty Officer Lindsay Parker cracked their code in under an hour. It had to be simple enough for both the Golden Boys and our local fishermen to follow, so it didn't prove too much of a challenge for a young woman of her talents."

Olivia flipped through the first-aid manual. "Can you give me an example?"

Rawlings waited for the rest of the group to gather around the book. "If Hunter sent me a text with the numbers thirty-five and seventy-five, I'd end up west of Ocracoke Island. The topic on page thirty-five is 'Life-Threatening Emergencies.' The catchphrase is 'Arrange immediate evacuation.' That's code for a pickup. A ship is waiting for me at the given coordinates and I'm to collect a supply of marijuana."

"Awesome!" Harris exclaimed. "This is like real spy stuff."

Millay gestured for the book. "I want to be a Golden Boy."

"Okay." Rawlings smiled. "Find the code on page seventy-five under the topic 'Bleeding and Shock.'"

With Laurel, Olivia, and Harris looking over her shoulder, Millay scanned the page and grinned. "Here!" She pointed at a sentence. "This says, 'Bring the patient ashore.' I'd bet the contents of a Saturday night tip jar that it's a code for giving the fishermen the go-ahead to approach land. After reading this, they'd know it was safe to dock with the contraband."

Rawlings nodded. "Armed with this information—thanks to you, Millay—we intercepted a text sent to one of Hunter Drummond's associates. According to Hunter, this would have been his replacement's first smuggling attempt, so we convinced the young man to work for us rather than risk facing jail time."

"You turned him from the dark side," Harris said, impressed. "But what a cheap move on Hunter's part—to sell out a compadre like that. Man, he has no honor."

Laurel turned to Harris. "That's no big shock. Even as a criminal, he led a double life. I know because I interviewed him this morning. He actually got involved with the drug cartel about a year ago after he was caught illegally collecting specimens in the Gulf of Mexico to sell to MarineBio-Pharm. A representative from the cartel bailed him out of jail and recruited him. It all happened so quickly that Hunter's parents never knew he'd been arrested. And they certainly never knew he was running a drug operation along the entire Southern coastline."

Millay shook her fists in the air. "Weren't his pockets filled with enough money? Why did he agree to Beauford and Bellamy's insane proposal to kill the Holcombs? He was already loaded."

"It wasn't just about the money," Olivia said. "You heard the scorn in Bellamy's voice when she spoke to Luke. Or whenever she mentioned Ruthie's name. The Drummonds would have done anything to keep their blood ties to the Holcombs a secret and to protect their reputation as one of Oyster Bay's foremost families. Wealth, history, and tradition were the gods Bellamy and Beauford worshiped. The Holcombs were a threat to all three of those deities. Not only that, but they had no idea how many copies of Nathaniel Drummond's original will existed or where they'd been hidden. The only way to guarantee their status quo was to eliminate Sadie Vance's heirs."

"But Hunter wasn't under his parents' thumb, and yet, he brought that cone snail to them knowing how its venom worked," Harris spluttered. "I watched a video of that snail attacking a fish. Knowing the same thing happened to Ruthie and her mother . . ." He shook his head as if chasing the images away.

"At least he knows what paralysis is like," Millay murmured darkly. "Even if it's only partial. That's what the snail's venom does, right? Paralyzes the diaphragms of victims until they can no longer breathe? Personally, I think Hunter got off easy. He can't feel. What he really deserves is a lifetime of pain."

"The young man has done everything in his power to cooperate with us," Rawlings said softly. "And I don't think he got off easy. In fact, I believe he's just begun to suffer. He once lived a charmed life. A shallow one built on a foundation of arrogance and greed. Now, he views tomorrow with nothing but despair and fear. He'll never walk again. His father will be incarcerated for years while his mother will live out the rest of her days in prison. And his sister refuses to answer his letters."

Sensing a hint of censure in his voice, Olivia frowned. "Can you blame her?"

Rawlings looked at her, and in his green eyes she saw the depths of kindness and compassion that set him apart from every man she'd known. "No. But maybe when enough time has passed, after the sharp edges of pain have dulled, a brother will ask for his sister's forgiveness and she'll give it to him. I have to hold on to that hope. I have to believe that something good can come from this tragedy. If I don't believe that, then all the terrible things I've seen and all the terrible news I've had to break—it would weigh too much. It would pull me under the surface."

Moved by his words, Olivia took his hand and held it in

both of hers. "You're right," she said. "Sometimes the only way we can heal is to forgive those who've hurt us. Especially if they're family. We owe it to them to try to understand. To give them hope that it isn't too late."

Harris stared at her in befuddlement. "Are we still talking about Stella?"

"No." Olivia hadn't taken her eyes from Rawlings's face. "Sawyer, Charles Wade isn't my uncle. He's my father. And I've invited him to our wedding."

The rest of the writers exchanged brief looks of surprise, but no one spoke.

Olivia didn't notice. For her, there was only Rawlings and the expressions flitting across his face. Disbelief, confusion, hurt, and finally, acceptance.

"I've known for a while," she said, answering the question he was bound to ask. "I didn't tell any of you"—she quickly glanced around her circle of friends—"because I was afraid you'd see me differently. I'd no longer be the daughter of an alcoholic fisherman, but the daughter of a rich businessman. I didn't want that. I'm still me. And I still belong here." She waved to incorporate the lighthouse, the ocean, and the small town across the harbor. To her embarrassment, tears sprang to her eyes. "I didn't want to be the product of a lie. But I am. I'm the result of a woman who loved a man named Charles Wade, but ended up marrying his twin brother, Willie, to avoid giving birth to a fatherless child."

Laurel reached out to touch Olivia, but Olivia shied away. She needed to say her piece and she didn't deserve their understanding. Not until she'd told them everything.

"I also kept this secret because I didn't want to lose Hudson. I was alone for such a long time, and then Hudson and Kim and their kids became my family." She looked at her friends, drinking in each beloved face. "As have all of you."

Turning to Rawlings again, she spoke in a near whisper.

"And then there was you, Sawyer. The person I'd been searching for all of my life. I found you. Or you found me. Either way, I suddenly had so much to lose. Everything, in fact."

"We don't love you because of your DNA, you silly woman," Millay said and thrust a paper towel at Olivia. "No one cares who your parents were. We care about you."

"And that will never change," Laurel added.

Wiping her face with the paper towel, Olivia recalled how Rawlings had offered Stella his handkerchief so she could dry her tears. She remembered the expression of gratitude on Stella's face and how patiently Rawlings had waited for her to speak, for her to be ready to share her story with him.

"I'm sorry I didn't tell you sooner," Olivia said to him. "I just couldn't get the words out."

"Well, now you have," he said, and she saw only warmth and tenderness in his eyes.

She sagged in relief. It was going to be all right. She'd told him and nothing had changed. He hadn't gotten angry or called off the wedding or walked out the door. He'd simply stood there and listened.

And then he smiled and opened his arms to her.

Chapter 20

This is love: to fly toward a secret sky, to cause a hundred veils to fall each moment. First to let go of life. Finally, to take a step without feet.

—Rumi

In the hours leading up to her sunset ceremony, Olivia went about her business like it was any other Saturday. She started the day by taking Haviland for an especially long walk on the beach. With her metal detector slung over her shoulder, she and her poodle crossed the stretch of sand where she and Rawlings and their loved ones would later stand.

Watching Haviland splash beside her in the surf, Olivia realized that she wasn't the slightest bit nervous. In fact, she felt extraordinarily calm. As she passed under the shadow of the lighthouse, she glanced up at the looming structure. For once, images from her past didn't flood her mind. She saw only the sunlight winking off the glass—a daytime beacon for those searching for a safe place to land.

With the lighthouse well behind her, Olivia turned on the metal detector and slipped the headphones over her sun-warmed hair. She slowed her pace, swinging the arm of detector back and forth and listening to its familiar chirps and blips. She and Haviland continued on until they reached the narrow spit of land jutting out into the sea.

Olivia usually left the metal detector behind when walking along the rock-lined finger of beach, but she brought it with her today. She spent a long time gazing out over the water, watching the container ships lumber along the liquid highway. Closer to shore, the triangular sails of yachts shone a bright white in the sunshine. The ocean was dazzling. From her vantage point, Olivia could see exactly where the blue green of the shallows gave way to a dark navy blue as the bottom fell away.

"To the place where the water is deep and cold. Down, down to the kingdom of Undine and Melusine," Olivia said, pushing a strand of hair from her eyes. The wind was stronger out on the jetty. As it pushed at her hair again, Olivia caught the scent of summer: hot, salty, and humid. Standing on that narrow bit of land, she contentedly mused over when to take a vacation with Rawlings.

"Of course, you'll be coming along," Olivia told Haviland and caressed the fur on top of his head. Haviland's tongue hung from his mouth and his brown eyes were smiling. Olivia had already stopped once to give him a water break, but she sensed the poodle was almost ready to go home.

"You're dreaming of second breakfast, I suppose." She gave him a final scratch and then took her headphones from around her neck and placed them over her ears. "Lead the way, Captain."

The pair made it halfway back to the beach when the metal detector let loose a series of shrill bleeps. Olivia was tempted to ignore the sounds, but she hadn't found anything interesting in months and couldn't help but wonder if the sea had something special to offer her on this, her wedding day.

She put the device down and shrugged off her backpack. Retrieving her folding shovel, she dug a layer of surface sand and coaxed it into her sieve. Pressing the loose sand through the holes, she was left with nothing but shell and stone fragments. She repeated the motion several times, knowing that treasure hunting required both patience and perseverance.

Moving the head of the metal detector over the area again, she heard its excited cry. The object was still embedded in the ground. She needed to dig deeper.

"Would you like to help or are you supervising?" she asked Haviland. The poodle appeared to give her question serious consideration before putting his front paws in the hole and clawing at the sand.

Again and again, Olivia scooped sand into her sieve but didn't find anything man-made. The sun beat down on her neck and shoulders and she shifted her position, wondering what Rawlings would make of a sunburnt bride. But she knew he wouldn't care if she showed up as red as a lobster and as freckled as a trunkfish. He loved her. He loved her so much that he had called in every possible favor to give her a very special wedding gift. She smiled just thinking about it, and of what he'd done to grant her wish.

"Last scoop," she promised Haviland, suddenly anxious to return home. She wanted to sit in the cool kitchen with Rawlings, to hold on to the morning's peace and quiet a little while longer. They could sit at the table and have one more cup of coffee before they separated to run errands, field phone calls, and attend to last-minute details.

Pushing the sand around inside the bowl of the sieve, Olivia watched the grains stream through the holes, rapidly at first and then more slowly, like a faucet being turned off. When the sand was gone, what remained was a pile of small rocks and shells. And something else.

Olivia picked up a conical object and turned it this way and that. The yellow wink of metal hinted at gold, but she'd been fooled before.

"What do we have here?" She scratched at the brown crust until a tiny loop of gold revealed itself. "A charm?"

Haviland sat down and waited patiently. Olivia continued scraping and then suddenly gasped. Haviland instantly moved closer to her, sniffing worriedly and releasing a single whine of concern.

"It's all right, Captain. Look," she whispered, holding the gold object in her palm. "It's a shell. A little conch shell."

Putting the charm in her pocket, she slid the shovel and sieve into her backpack. Then, she leaned over the rocky divide between sea and sand and plunged her hands into the water, washing them clean.

"That was the best one yet. Thank you." She pressed her hands together and smiled at the waves. They seemed to gently hum and whisper in reply.

And then she stood and walked down the beach. She was eager for home, for coffee, and for Rawlings.

"We're here!" Laurel knocked on Olivia's bedroom door. "Is it safe to enter?"

"In other words, are all of your bits covered?" Millay added.

Olivia crossed the room and flung open the door. "I'm as decent as I'll ever be."

Laurel's hands flew to her mouth. "Decent? You're stunning!"

Millay nodded. "Seriously, I can't even think of a snide remark. You look really pretty."

"Pretty?" Laurel scoffed. "Girls with ribbons in their hair are pretty. Olivia looks like a Greek goddess. A short-haired Aphrodite."

Olivia shook her head. "I might love the ocean, but I wasn't born inside a seashell. But that reminds me. Come see what I found on my walk this morning."

She led her friends into the bathroom, where the conch charm was soaking in a pickle jar filled with water. "I boiled it in distilled water first, and then cleaned it with soap. This soak is to remove the soap residue. I'm going to put it in my ultrasonic cleaner next, but thought I'd better get dressed before I was late to my own wedding."

"And you could hardly claim to have been stuck in traffic," Laurel said, bending over the jar. "I can't believe you found a shell. After everything that's happened . . ."

"Everything related to shells, you mean," Millay finished for her.

The two women exchanged silent glances of understanding, and Olivia was tempted to embrace them both. They'd been through so much over the years, she and these women, and she loved them like sisters. And in that moment, she was able to imagine the terrible, penetrating pain Stella must have felt upon losing Ruthie.

"What will you do with it?" Millay asked, her eyes on the little gold charm.

"You'll see," Olivia said and then gestured at the starfish comb Charles had given her. "I keep putting that in crooked. Can you help me?"

Laurel grinned. "I feel like your maid of honor. Or matron, I guess." She picked up the comb. "This looks old. And your dress is probably new, so you're partway there. How about the something borrowed and something blue?"

"I don't pay attention to that stuff," Olivia said.

"You're planning to dismiss hundreds of years of tradition?" Laurel was genuinely mortified.

Olivia held very still while Laurel worked the comb through her hair. "Were you aware that the idea behind something borrowed and something new came from a nineteenth-century superstition about battling the Evil Eye? The Evil Eye rendered women barren. As you well know, I'd be perfectly fine with that outcome."

Millay let out a loud laugh.

"But the blue part is important. Blue is a symbol of loyalty," Laurel persisted, ignoring Millay. "Don't you want to be seen as true-blue?"

Olivia shrugged. "I'm supposed to put a six-pence in my shoe for prosperity too, but since I'll be barefoot, I'd say this whole poem is blown to hell."

"Such language from our blushing bride," Millay said approvingly. "I've got you covered on the silver and the blue. I have just what you need in my bag."

Laurel gestured at Millay's satchel. Emblazoned with a pattern of skulls and crossbones and a dozen hand-sewn patches, the bag had always been a repository for a host of unusual items.

"I'm afraid to see what she pulls out of there," Laurel murmured.

Millay's hand disappeared into her bag, followed by her wrist and most of her forearm. "Don't worry," she said. "I'll keep the lewd photos of old boyfriends safely hidden."

Olivia glanced at her in the mirror. "Speaking of old boyfriends, is everything okay between you and Harris?"

Millay shrugged. "It was weird when he first came back." She paused in her rummaging. "I felt this weird tug inside me. It was like . . . I think it was grief." The last word was barely audible. Then, she shrugged again. "But it was stupid to feel that way. We didn't work when we dated and we work as friends. I love the guy and I'm happy he came back, but I'm not in love with him. Besides, Emily's cool. She and I talked for a long time the Sunday after the Secret Garden Party. I'm glad Harris picked her and not some yuppie cheerleader. No offense, Laurel."

Laurel poked Millay in the side, forcing her to jump. "Where's your man, by the way? I thought you were seeing some hot drummer."

"Even if we were serious, which we're not, I wouldn't want him here," Millay said, finally withdrawing a bottle of nail polish from her bag. "Today is about celebrating with my friends, not my secret life of wantonness and depravity."

"It's supposed to be secret?" Olivia quipped, and they all laughed.

"Stick out your feet, Cinderella," Millay commanded. "This covers your blue and your silver-in-your-shoe themes." She tilted the bottle of iridescent polish upside-down. "It even has an ocean-themed name. See? Twilight Pool."

Olivia watched as Millay expertly painted her toes with a layer of shimmery polish. Laurel fiddled with the hair comb a few more times and then stepped back to let Olivia examine the results.

"I think it's time," Laurel said softly. "You're ready." She put her hands over her heart. "I can't believe it. You're getting married!"

"Stop bouncing, Laurel. You'll wear a hole in the floor," Millay chided and then smiled at Olivia. "I'm going to allow myself one cheesy remark and only because it's your wedding day." She paused. "I'm happy for you, Olivia. And for the chief. You two are good together. You make me believe that maybe, just maybe, there's someone out there for me too. It doesn't have to be now. Probably shouldn't be. But you've proven that it's worth it to let people in. Every once in a while, it's worth the risk."

Olivia touched Millay's smooth cheek. "It's terrifying. But yes, for the people who matter most, we should let our guard down. It's the only way love can get in."

Laurel reached for the tissue box on Olivia's nightstand. "Oh! Look what the two of you have done. My makeup will be ruined before we even get to the beach!"

Downstairs, the guests were spread out between the living room and the deck. Michel and Shelley were standing by the fireplace talking to Hudson and Kim while Caitlyn and Anders sat on the sofa, shaking Haviland's paw and plying him with treats. Fred Yoder and Leona Fairchild peered into the curio cabinet at the far end of the room, seemingly engrossed by the objets d'art within, and Jeannie, Rawlings's sister, was introducing her husband to both Charles Wade and Steve Hobbs. Harris and Officer Cook were conversing by the bookcase, and Rawlings was outside with Pastor Daniels.

Olivia stood on the bottom step and watched as Rawlings swept his arm from left to right, indicating the ocean and the small coastal town, and then clapped the younger man on the back.

"Is your fiancé abusing a man of the cloth?" Millay teased.

Olivia smiled. "Actually, I think we're witnessing a display of male bonding. Rawlings is making friends with Pastor Daniels. We'd originally planned on using a justice of the peace, but the moment I met the pastor, I wanted him to marry us."

"Is he old enough to have graduated from seminary?" Millay wanted to know.

"You shouldn't talk," Laurel said. "I'm surprised people don't ask to see *your* ID before you serve them beer or shots of whiskey."

Millay snorted. "Honey, my customers are a 'don't ask, don't tell' kind of crowd. That's why I love them."

Leaving her two friends to chat about Millay's customers, Olivia moved through the room, graciously thanking people for coming and exchanging hugs with all of the women and a fair share of the men.

"Is Dixie here?" she asked Michel after he'd kissed her on both cheeks and gushed over her appearance.

"She's in the kitchen," he said and then narrowed his eyes in suspicion. "What do you have up your sleeve, *ma chérie*? There isn't a chafing dish or champagne bottle in sight. Is Grumpy catering this affair?"

Patting her head chef on the sleeve, Olivia said, "The food and beverages, like many things this evening, will be a surprise."

"Speaking of surprises," came Rawlings's voice from behind Olivia. "Your wedding gift has arrived. Come with me."

Rawlings led her through the kitchen and out to the driveway. An Oyster Bay police cruiser was idling alongside Olivia's Range Rover, but as soon as the officer behind the wheel caught sight of Rawlings, he leapt out of the car and opened the rear door, behaving more like a chauffeur than a decorated policeman.

Luke Holcomb got out first and then hurriedly turned to offer his hand to the other passenger. And then, Stella Drummond alighted from the car. She stood still for several seconds, gripping Luke's hand and squinting as the beams from the low sun lit her face. Eventually, her eyes found Olivia. She smiled at first, but then glanced uncertainly at her billowy white sundress and silver sandals.

"You're beautiful," Olivia said loudly and held out her right hand. Without letting go of Luke's hand, Stella strode forward to clasp Olivia's. The three of them formed a little circle in the sunlight. Olivia caught the shy smiles passing between Luke and Stella and her heart swelled with happiness. Stella had been granted only a few hours of supervised freedom, but it was enough. Tonight, she would dance and be merry. Tonight, Olivia would continue to honor her promise. She would never leave Stella alone.

"Come inside," she said to Stella and Luke.

Upon seeing the new arrivals, Laurel and Millay cried out in surprise and delight. Harris bounded forward to welcome Luke with an awkward half hug. He then settled for a handshake, and within minutes, Stella and Luke were being greeted and included in conversations and jokes by the rest of the wedding guests.

Olivia put her arms around Rawlings. "Thank you," she whispered and kissed him.

"Aren't you supposed to exchange vows before you start making out?"

Olivia released Rawlings and looked down to see Dixie, who was clad in a lace tank top, a white tutu, and silver roller skates.

"You'll have to fix your lipstick now," Dixie said and pointed to her own shimmering lips. "You can borrow mine if you want. This stuff will outlast the apocalypse."

Grumpy gave Olivia a thumbs-up over his wife's head. "We're good to go."

When Rawlings opened his mouth to ask what Grumpy meant, Olivia looped her arm through his and said, "What do you say? Should we get married?"

"We should," Rawlings agreed and rounded up the guests.

The section of beach at the end of the dune path looked as it always did with one exception: a large twig arch covered with jasmine vines, magnolia blossoms, scallop shells, and silver starfish had been set in the damp sand. The tails of the white satin bows tied on either side of the arch fluttered in the breeze, and the scent of jasmine floated in the warm air.

"How gorgeous!" Laurel exclaimed softly and pressed closer to her husband.

Millay, who was walking companionably alongside Harris, murmured, "I think Luke's interested in more than Stella's trust fund."

Olivia glanced to her right, where Luke and Stella were making their way over the dunes. They were holding hands and laughing. Looking at them, Olivia wanted to laugh too. She'd wanted Stella to be with her tonight more than she could say. And yet when she'd explained to Rawlings that Stella's inclusion would bring her joy, he'd immediately understood.

"It'll help us heal," he'd said. "All of us."

"Yes, but it's more than that." She'd held out the guest list for their wedding, which was scribbled on a notepad next to the kitchen phone, and affectionately touched each name with her fingertip. "These people—these quirky, smart, funny, infuriating, incredible people—are our family. Yours and mine. Stella and Luke are ours now too. For better or for worse, they're ours."

Rawlings had nodded and smiled at her with the same tenderness she now saw in his eyes. Walking next to him, their strides perfectly matched, she wondered why she hadn't been in more of a hurry to join her life with his.

Better late than never, she thought as they stopped under the arch and turned to face each other.

Pastor Daniels waited for the rest of the guests to gather around and then asked everyone to be still for a moment of silent prayer.

The guests bowed their heads, but Olivia and Rawlings looked at each other. Behind them, the sun hung low in the sky. It glowed a fiery gold, burnishing the sea, the sand, and the people gathered there with a radiant glow.

The ceremony was short and poignantly sweet. There was no music save for the hum of the waves and the whistle of the breeze. And when it was time for Olivia and Rawlings to speak their vows, Rawlings took both of Olivia's hands in his and said, "You and I were a story waiting to be written."

Olivia said, "You were the word on the tip of my tongue."

"The memory I'd yet to make."

Seeing the love shining from Rawlings's eyes, Olivia spoke her next line in a voice choked with emotion. "As long as the ocean meets the shore, I will share your story."

He squeezed her hands to stop his own from trembling. "As long as the sky meets the sea, I will share your story."

"You and I were a story waiting to be written," they said in unison. "We were in each other all along."

They shared their first kiss as man and wife to boisterous applause, shouts, and whoops from their friends. And then, from somewhere in the distance, came the sound of music.

"What is that?" someone asked.

The guests turned back toward the house, looking for the source of the strong, clear notes. "It's a trumpet," said Michel. "I think it's coming closer."

Another trumpet joined the first. And then another.

From around the corner of the lighthouse keeper's cottage, a man with a steel drum hanging from a cord around his neck appeared. Behind him were two more drummers.

Suddenly, musicians dressed in bright red Hawaiian shirts were approaching from every direction. Musicians with guitars and bass guitars. Musicians playing the saxophone and trombone. A man with a bongo drum. A woman with a portable keyboard. And with them, dressed in yellow and orange Hawaiian shirts, came the waitstaff from The Boot Top Bistro. Swaying to the beat of the reggae band's rendition of "I Can't Help Falling in Love," they moved through the cluster of stunned and delighted guests, passing out tequila sunrises and fragrant leis.

Gabe, who'd created an entire array of special cocktails for his employer's wedding, served the bride and groom theirs in cups shaped like pineapples. After congratulating them both, he moved aside to allow one of the hostesses to place a lei around Olivia's neck. The hostess approached Rawlings next, but instead of giving him a flower necklace, she presented him a blue Hawaiian shirt with a pattern of white hibiscus blossoms. "This is from your wife," she said, indicating the shirt, the band, and the cocktail in his hand.

Admiring the shirt, he turned to Olivia and said, "You *do* love me."

He put on his new Hawaiian shirt behind the cover of a pair of burly waiters, who stood shoulder-to-shoulder and folded their arms across their chests, sending a silent and mockingly severe message not to disturb the groom. When he emerged from behind the waiters, the guests clapped and whistled. Pivoting, Rawlings tossed his white dress shirt over his head as if it were a bridal bouquet. Harris caught it and glanced around, dumbfounded, while men thumped him on the back and women squeezed his cheek.

Even Millay joined in the fun. She put the dress shirt over Harris's head so that it looked like a veil and shrieked when he dragged her into the surf and splashed her with salt water. Haviland, who'd begun barking as soon as the band had struck its first note, gave a yip of glee and joined Harris and Millay in the surf. Caitlyn and Anders rushed after the poodle and he pranced along the waterline, trying to entice them into a game of chase.

Rawlings smoothed the front of his new shirt and grinned with pleasure. The band members, who'd congregated near the end of the path, struck up the opening notes of their song again. Rawlings recognized his cue and pulled Olivia into his arms. "Dance with me," he whispered, drawing her even closer.

"For the rest of my life," she whispered back.

As Rawlings held her, Olivia rested her head on his shoulder. Flushed with happiness, she held the man she loved and stared at the setting sun. It was only a half circle above the horizon now, but still had the power to produce a shimmering road of pink and orange over the waves.

Olivia gazed at the golden path and imagined dolphins leaping through the diamond light. Or mermaids. She could picture a mermaid moving just below the surface, swimming with her face to the sky in hopes of catching a glimpse of the evening's first star.

But then Olivia felt Rawlings's hand on her lower back and she turned away from the water. Looking around, she realized that magic did exist. Not in treasure chests or undersea castles, but in the faces of the people she loved. And in the stories they created together.

The music and laughter called to her, tugging at her heart like the tide. The sound was sweeter than any siren's song, and Olivia Limoges was more than happy to surrender to its melody.

Dear Reader,

Thank you for spending time with Olivia Limoges, the Bayside Book Writers, and the rest of the colorful characters living in Oyster Bay, North Carolina.

If you're looking for another cozy, captivating read, I'd like to invite you to visit a rather unusual and intriguing small town. Havenwood, the fictional hamlet featured in my Charmed Pie Shoppe Mysteries, is located in an isolated corner of northwest Georgia. Home to heroine Ella Mae LeFaye, a pastry chef with an uncanny ability to enchant the food she makes, Havenwood is filled with quaint shops, delightful eateries, and a population of magical residents.

In the next installment of the Charmed Pie Shoppe Mysteries, Lemon Pies and Little White Lies, *Ella Mae and her employees are preparing for History in the Baking, a one-of-a-kind pie celebration. This historic event will include bake-offs, cooking demonstrations, lectures on the history of pie, and pie-eating contests. People from all over the country will travel to Havenwood to pay homage to America's favorite pastry.*

Unfortunately, several unwelcome guests will also make the trip. And one of them is a murderer.

To whet your appetite, turn the page for a preview of the next Charmed Pie Shoppe Mystery, Lemon Pies and Little White Lies, *coming April 2015 from Berkley Prime Crime.*

Thank you for reading and supporting cozy mysteries!

Your Friend,
Ellery Adams

Ella Mae pressed chocolate cookie crumbs into the bottom of a springform pan with deft, quick motions. She then moved to her commercial stovetop and gave the marshmallow cream simmering in the saucepan a gentle stir. Satisfied, she turned the burner off and set the saucepan in a stainless steel bowl filled with ice. When the marshmallow cream was sufficiently cooled, Ella Mae reached for the liquor bottles on the worktable and poured small amounts of crème de menthe and white crème de cacao into the fluffy mixture. Next, she squeezed in four drops of green food coloring and watched the white and green spiral around the tip of her wooden spoon before the green finally overpowered the white. She continued to stir until all traces of white were gone.

"Green as an Irish meadow," she declared to the empty room.

Ella Mae's mind began to wander. She thought of all the things she needed to accomplish that day and of the endless list of tasks still awaiting her. When she glanced down at the saucepan again, she frowned. She couldn't remember if she'd added the crème de menthe.

Shrugging, she grabbed the glass liquor bottle and added a generous splash to the white mixture. After giving it a good stir, she leaned over the pan and inhaled deeply.

"Minty fresh," she murmured to herself and wiped at a drip running down the liquor bottle with the hem of her apron.

Feeling pleased with her morning's work so far, Ella Mae hummed as she entered the walk-in freezer to fetch her beater attachment and a large mixing bowl. The cold air permeated the warm cocoon of marshmallow and mint that enveloped the entire kitchen and Ella Mae shivered. She didn't want to feel. She didn't want to think. She just wanted to bake, cook, and plate and repeat those steps over and over until it was time to close The Charmed Pie Shoppe for the day. After that, she could collect Chewy, her Jack Russell terrier, from doggie daycare and go home. HGTV and The Food Network awaited her there. As did her cooking magazines and page after page of glossy photographs and new recipes.

The oven timer beeped and Ella Mae backed out of the freezer, dropped the cold beaters and bowl on the counter, and pulled on a pair of oven mitts. She transferred six shepherd's pies, a trio of potato and green onion pies, and a dozen corned beef hand pies to the cooking racks. The scent of hot, buttery crust and fresh spices settled on her shoulders like a shawl, but she didn't pause to savor the aromas.

Instead, she poured heavy cream into the chilled bowl, attached the beater to her commercial mixer, and switched on the appliance. She stared at the white liquid as it frothed and churned in the bowl while her right hand involuntarily slid into her apron pocket and touched the letter nestled inside.

"No! I can't," she said, withdrawing her hand with the swiftness of someone whose fingers have come too close to the fire. "I have a business to run. I'm on the Council of Elders. Everyone's looking to me for answers. I need to stay focused."

Ella Mae's stomach growled and she removed one of the steaming shepherd's pies from the cooling rack and cut herself a thick wedge. While the mixer whirred, she savored every bite of pie. She had so little time to sit and enjoy a meal these days that she decided to take a few, precious minutes to enjoy this one. When her pie was done, she raised her coffee cup to her mouth and drained the tepid liquid. She then reached out to set the cup on the table, but her eyes strayed to the window above the kitchen sink and she missed. The cup fell, and when it struck the kitchen floor and smashed into pieces, Ella Mae shouted, "*Opa!*" She'd survived so much over the past two years and wasn't about to let a broken cup bother her.

Turning her attention back to the whipped cream, she cursed. She switched off the mixer, dipped the beater in the cream, and raised it again. In lieu of stiff peaks, the mixture was grainy. For the first time in her life, Ella Mae had overbeaten the cream.

"I'll just add a little sugar," she said, heading for the dry goods shelf. Grabbing the sugar container, she pried off the lid and scooped out a heaping tablespoonful. "A spoonful of sugar makes the medicine go down," she sang and dumped the sugar into the cream. She turned on the mixer again and finally achieved the desired result. At last, she folded the rescued whipped cream into the green marshmallow mixture and then poured the whole thing over the chocolate cookie crumb crust.

She carried the pie to the freezer and placed it at the end of a row of a dozen green pies. "That should be plenty for take-out orders and afternoon tea. I hope I made enough four-leaf clover cookies."

Back at the worktable, she saw that Reba or Jenny had left her an order ticket and dumped a pile of dirty dishes in the sink. The lunch rush was over, but there were still customers in the dining room. The Charmed Pie Shoppe had become so popular with locals and tourists alike that people often had to wait until two o'clock for a table. And since afternoon tea service started at three, Ella Mae baked and plated for hours in a row. She rarely left the kitchen, taking brief coffee or meal breaks perched on a stool next to the dishwasher. From this vantage point, she could stare out across the small rear parking area and over the Dumpster to the block beyond. On a clear day, she could see the roof of the fire station, its shingled gray gable rising a few feet above the brick building housing Havenwood Insurance. At certain times, the sun would hit the fire station's Dalmatian weathervane just right and it would wink like a star. Ella Mae would gaze at the glowing copper and think of Hugh.

"Hugh's gone," she told herself and read the order ticket once more.

She plated a generous wedge of shepherd's pie with a side of field greens and was just spooning charred corn salad into a bowl to go along with a serving of corned beef hand pies when she heard the blare of a car alarm.

Ella Mae didn't pay much attention to the wailing until a second alarm sounded. And then a third. The noise was fairly loud and Ella Mae guessed that the cars were parked nearby. She barely had time to register this thought before voices raised in angry shouts added to the cacophony. Ella Mae couldn't tell what had made the people so upset, but she knew either Reba or Jenny would inform her sooner or later.

She didn't have to wait long.

Reba burst through the swing doors and cried, "Do you hear that devil's racket outside?" She put her hands on her hips and surveyed Ella Mae. "Mr. Jenkins just drove on the wrong side of the street. He scraped four parked cars from bumper to bumper, takin' off their side mirrors as he passed, and then plowed through the Longwoods' picket fence, flattenin' their collection of garden gnomes as he went. Mrs. Longwood is fit to be tied."

Ella Mae glanced toward the window. "Oh."

"That's all you have to say?" Reba pulled a red licorice stick from her apron pocket and shook it at Ella Mae. "What did you put in that leprechaun pie? Mr. Jenkins had two pieces."

Ella Mae feigned great interest in the parsley on the cutting board. "Are you asking if I enchanted our Saint Patrick's Day dessert?"

"You know damn well I am!" Reba snapped. "Seein' as you transfer your emotions into the food you make, I'd like to know what you *put* in those pies."

Shaking her head, Ella Mae said, "Nothing. I've been deliberately trying not to use magic when I'm . . ."

"Down in the dumps?" Reba narrowed her eyes and bit into her licorice stick. "Or just plain drunk?" In a flash, she closed the space between herself and Ella Mae just in time to catch Ella Mae's next exhalation. "You smell like a peppermint patty dipped in paint thinner. How much of that mint liquor have you had?"

Ella Mae felt her cheeks grow warm. She walked to the sink, turned the faucet on, and held a dirty dish under the water. "I haven't had a drop. I wiped the bottle with my apron, which is why I smell like I do."

Reba grabbed the plate and loaded it into the dishwasher. "I hope so. You've always been a glass of vino after work kind of girl."

"I still am. Though sometimes I have two, but that started when Hugh left," Ella Mae said.

"I know you miss him, but it's not like you two broke up. He told you he needed to travel—to search for a way to reclaim his lost powers—and you said you understood. It's only been a month and he's sent you letters. I see you readin' and rereadin' them." Reba frowned. "Is that why you put too much booze into your pies? I'm assumin' that's what happened because you've been real distracted lately."

"It was a mistake, and I only messed up a few pies. Not all of them. I didn't think I'd added that much more. I guess my magic somehow amplified the effects," Ella Mae said and continued to wash dishes. The steam from the water rose in diaphanous plumes around her face, masking her anguished expression.

"I'm going to deliver those orders and then I'm coming back here to pinch you," Reba warned.

"You already pinched me for luck today. And guess what? It didn't work."

Reba left with the food. When she returned, she turned off the faucet and took Ella Mae's red, water-wrinkled hands in her own. "What's got you so sad?"

With a resigned sigh, Ella Mae withdrew Hugh's letter and placed it in Reba's palm. Reba had just unfolded it when Jenny Upton, The Charmed Pie Shoppe's newest waitress, entered the kitchen.

"Where are those chocolate coins?" She frantically scanned the room, her gaze passing right over Ella Mae and Reba. "The ones wrapped in gold foil? I need them and I need them now."

Ella Mae heard the note of desperation in Jenny's voice. "I thought we made plenty of Saint Patty's Day gift bags for the customers." She pursed her lips. "But let me think. I ordered those gold-wrapped chocolate coins in bulk and they came packaged inside a cardboard treasure chest. That's where I put the extras."

"Then lead me to that treasure chest. And they're not for a customer. They're for me," Jenny added. "I had to give *every* customer a zap of energy before they left. They all had the leprechaun pie and were as tipsy as sailors on furlough. I was afraid to let them drive or cross the street on foot." She jerked her thumb toward the front of the store. "Look what happened when Mr. Jenkins got behind the wheel. Unfortunately for him and a hundred lawn gnomes, he paid his bill and slipped outside before I could touch him. And if I don't eat some chocolate, I won't be able to zap *you*, Ella Mae."

Ella Mae scowled. She was Jenny's boss, not some naughty child who could be pinched by one employee and given magical doses of energy by another. She whipped her head around to chastise Jenny, but stumbled over the leg of the closest stool. Putting both hands on the seat to steady herself, she suddenly remembered having placed the extra chocolate coins between containers of cocoa powder and confectioner's sugar. Plunking down onto the stool, she waved at the dry goods rack. "The treasure chest is on the second shelf from the floor."

By this time, Reba had finished reading the letter and had placed it on the worktable where Ella Mae did most of her prep work. Two sharp knives were resting on the wooden surface and Reba's hand closed over the paring knife. Her lips were compressed into a thin line and Ella Mae knew she was angry.

Jenny drew alongside Reba and dumped the treasure chest on the table. "Here," she said, handing Reba a chocolate. "You look like you could use some candy."

"I never leave home without it," Reba said, taking a fresh licorice twist out of her apron pocket. She tore off an end and chewed furiously while Jenny unwrapped a dozen coins as if her life depended on it.

While the two women devoured their confections, Ella Mae stared at Hugh's letter. She then slid off the stool and fetched a ball of dough from the walk-in. Shoving the knives and letter to the side, she dusted the surface of the worktable with flour and reached for her rolling pin. She freed the dough from its plastic wrap and began rolling it out, forcing it to grow wider and thinner, wider and thinner.

"Okay. Between the chocolate and the three cans of Mountain Dew I chugged on the front porch, I'm starting to feel like myself again," Jenny said. "Are you ready, Ella Mae?"

"Just clear the fog in the poor girl's head," Reba said. "She's had some discouragin' news and I want to talk it over with her."

Before Ella Mae could protest, Jenny put a hand on her shoulder and squeezed. A jolt shot through Ella Mae's body. For a brief, delicious moment, her blood turned to liquid sunshine—white hot and radiant—and hummed in her veins. Her fatigue evaporated like chimney smoke swept away by the wind and her mind was sharp and focused. "Thanks, Jenny," she said, smiling gratefully. "I'm still in awe of your gift."

"Yours isn't too shabby either." Jenny pointed at the round circle of dough. "By influencing people's emotions, you can alter their behavior. Talk about powerful." She smiled. "So what's going into this pie?"

Ella Mae transferred the dough into a buttered pie dish. "My heart."

Reba and Jenny exchanged worried glances as Ella Mae placed the dish in the oven.

"What happened?" Jenny asked.

"Hugh wrote that he hadn't found what he was looking for in England or Scotland so he's heading to Ireland. If that doesn't pan out, he's going to Greece. He's put his assistant manager in charge of Canine to Five, informed the fire department that he's no longer available to volunteer, and said that I shouldn't wait for him—that he's not coming back until he's the man he was before I . . ." She trailed off.

"Before the source of his power was taken and used for the common good," Reba finished for her.

Ella Mae threw out her hands in exasperation. "But he doesn't know that! He doesn't know what I am. I couldn't sit him down and say, 'Hugh, you're in love with a magical being. Not only can I make charmed pies, but I can also command butterflies. And according to some ancient prophecy, I'm the Clover Queen, a position that means I'm responsible for the safety and well-being of lots of enchanted people.'"

"Of course you couldn't tell him." Reba tenderly brushed

a strand of hair off Ella Mae's cheek. "He isn't like us. Sweetheart, he never will be one of us."

Ella Mae nodded. "I know that, but I love him. I've loved him for most of my life. Since I knew how to love. And no matter what he said in this letter, I'll wait. If it takes twenty years, then so be it. I have to hold on to the hope that, one day, I can be completely honest with him and that he'll be able to forgive me for what I did to him."

"What kind of existence will you have pining for him for twenty years?" Reba asked very softly.

Ella Mae faced her friends. "I don't plan on pining. You see, I'm going to bury everything I feel for Hugh into this pie. And then, I'm going to freeze it. I hope it'll be like pausing a movie—that it'll give me the freedom to focus on work and the rest of the people I care about."

Jenny looked doubtful. "Is that possible? Can you really transfer enough of your feelings that you actually stop, well, feeling?"

"When it comes to these particular emotions, I have to try," Ella Mae said, sounding like her strong, determined self again. "Hugh's wasn't the only letter I received in today's mail. The township committee has accepted my proposal to have The Charmed Pie Shoppe sponsor Havenwood's Founder's Day celebration."

Reba arched a brow. "Why would we want to do that?"

"Because it gives us an unprecedented chance to gather our kind from all over the country. If I can convince Elders from other communities to meet, we can discuss how to unite, grow stronger, and break a very old curse."

Jenny pumped her fist in the air. "Yes!"

"Founder's Day is the first of May. Beltane. Our biggest party. A celebration I dream about all year," Reba said, her eyes gleaming. "And with all these visitors, we'll have hundreds of magical people in our grove. Good-lookin', half-naked men from all over the country dancin' around a bonfire. Tall Texans with cowboy hats, bronze-bodied surfers from California, men from the Dakotas who know how to keep a girl warm at night." She grinned at Ella Mae. "This is your best idea ever."

"Make sure to leave a few half-naked men for me," Jenny said and then issued a wistful sigh. "Too bad May is weeks and weeks away."

Ella Mae waved her hand around the pie shop. "Don't worry. With all we have to do to prepare for this event, the time will pass with lightning quickness."

"Speaking of which, I'd better zip back to the dining room and check on our customers," Jenny said and rushed off.

Ella Mae removed the pie dish from the oven and set it on a cooling rack. She then retrieved raspberries, heavy whipping cream, and a bar of white chocolate from the walk-in. She dropped the items on the counter and went to the dry goods shelves for a bottle of orange liqueur, a package of unflavored gelatin, and a jar of currant jam.

Reba eyed the liquor bottle warily. "What are you doin' with that?"

"Mixing it with the gelatin, cream, and chocolate. And I'm not serving it to our patrons." She crossed the first and second fingers of her right hand and held them over her heart. "Promise."

Satisfied, Reba crossed the room and opened one of the swing doors a crack. "Only two tables are occupied," she said. "I think the rest of the customers raced outside to watch Mrs. Longwood soak Mr. Jenkins with her garden hose."

"That poor man," Ella Mae said, pausing in the act of breaking the bar of white chocolate into small pieces. "I'm responsible for the damage to the parked cars and to Mrs. Longwood's gnomes, not him. What if he's given a breathalyzer test? He could be in big trouble. He might lose his license. Or worse."

Reba shook her head. "I called Officer Wallace and told her exactly what happened. She's going to help us out. Her report will make it sound like Mr. Jenkins's car malfunctioned. Leak in the brake line or that sort of thing. His insurance company will cover the damage and my buddy at the body shop will mess with those brake lines long before the insurance rep shows up."

"Thank goodness for Officer Wallace. I never realized what an advantage it could be to have one of our kind on the police force."

"She's not the first person to relocate to Havenwood because of you," Reba said. "Thousands of folks would give half a lung to live in a place where they can renew their powers anytime they want. You've changed the rules, honey. And I have a feelin' you're just gettin' started." She picked up the bottle of orange liqueur. "You can't afford to be distracted. Your life isn't your own anymore."

Ella Mae knew Reba spoke the truth. "You're right," she said. "On both counts. Let me finish with this pie and then I'll be fine. Really, I will. But I have to do this alone, okay?"

Reba searched her face. "Okay, then. But remember, Jenny and I are just on the other side of those doors if you need us."

When she was gone, Ella Mae placed Hugh's letter in the pie dish. She unfolded it so she could see his familiar handwriting on the thin airmail paper. She traced the letters of his name, one at a time, silently pledging to love him as long as she lived. "But the part of my heart that you claimed needs to hibernate. I don't know when I'll see you again, and like Reba said, my life isn't my own. It belongs to the people of Havenwood, and they don't need a lovesick girl leading them. They need a woman. Fierce and fearless."

Ella Mae beat more cream, creating picture-perfect stiff peaks before folding the whipped cream into the chocolate mixture. As she gently worked her rubber spatula through the pie filling, she closed her eyes and thought of Hugh. Memories flashed through her mind like a high-speed slideshow. There were images from the recent past: Hugh asleep in her bed, his Great Dane stretched out across his feet; Hugh frying bacon; Hugh frowning over a crossword puzzle; Hugh leaning in to kiss her. And then she went back further in time—to the first moment she'd seen him. He was still a boy then, and she, a shy and awkward girl. Despite her youth, Ella Mae's heart had tripped over itself when Hugh turned his bright blue gaze in her direction. She'd felt a rush of heat, of terror, and a longing she didn't fully understand.

"I understand it now," she whispered and then poured the creamy white filling over the letter.

While waiting for the filling to set, Ella Mae tidied the kitchen and washed the raspberries. She then melted a small bowlful of red currant jam and dropped the berries into the ruby liquid. Using her fingertips, she tenderly coated each berry and then removed the pie dish from the refrigerator. Gingerly pinching a raspberry between her fingers, she inhaled the sweet scents of chocolate and jam, and as she gently pressed the berry into the filling, she willed her memories of Hugh's touch to enter the fruit. She repeated this act over and over, transferring into each berry the feel of his hands, the sound of his voice, his musical laughter, the hunger in his kisses, the glint of humor in his brilliant blue eyes, and the way his body moved when he danced. She pictured how he swam like a dolphin, the way he rolled on the ground when he played with his dog, and how he stood, taut and rigid as a steel beam, directing water from a fire hose at a wall of angry flames. She put all the things she felt about this remarkable man—the man she'd loved for most of her life—into the pie.

Feeling oddly vacant, Ella Mae dropped a handful of dark chocolate morsels and two tablespoons of butter in a glass bowl and cooked them in a microwave. Pouring the melted chocolate into a pastry bag, she piped dark hearts over the surface of the berries. The hearts overlapped until they were unrecognizable, but if Ella Mae looked very closely, she could follow the path of the lines and see the shapes she'd created.

She continued to pipe until the chocolate was gone. With a weary sigh, she sealed the pie in an airtight container and put it on a high shelf in the freezer.

By the time Reba returned with the first of the teatime orders, Ella Mae was ready to work again.

"Are you all right?" Reba asked.

"I will be," Ella Mae said and smiled.

Reba nodded. "I believe it. While you plate this order, why don't you tell me what you have in mind for this Founder's Day event? We should focus on the future now."

"Yes," Ella Mae agreed. Taking a deep breath, she prepared to leave the past behind. "My idea is for us to host a one-of-a-kind celebration of pie. It'll be called History in the Baking. We'll invite cooks from across the nation to participate and encourage them to bring friends and family along. There will be pie bake-offs, presentations, lectures, cooking classes, and large cash prizes."

Reba's brows shot up her forehead. "Where's the cash comin' from? Not from my salary, I hope."

"No." Ella Mae laughed. "We'll charge every contestant a registration fee and I've already asked the manager of Lake Havenwood resort about using their kitchen for classes and their auditorium for the presentations. He was willing to waive the fee for these facilities, seeing as our event is likely to ensure new bookings and plenty of advertising for his hotel."

"I don't get the history part," Reba said and started to slice a leprechaun pie into even wedges.

"Pies have a long and rich history," Ella Mae began. "Ancient Egyptian bakers made a form of pie dough, but the Greeks were the first civilization to produce a real pie. Of course, the pies were of the savory variety for centuries.

The dough was just a container to hold a protein-packed filling. It wasn't until the fifteen hundreds that the bakers began experimenting with fruit pies."

Reba still looked puzzled. "So the contestants bake an old recipe—a really old recipe—and then talk about that country's culture?"

"Exactly. You could make a Roman mussel pie, for example. Of course, only the wealthy Romans could afford mussels, so you'd have to explain what the different classes of that period would use as their filling. For extra impact, you could dress like a Roman."

Shaking her head, Reba said, "Not a chance. You can't hide enough weapons under a toga. Give me a kimono. Or one of those medieval gowns. Do you know how many throwing stars I could tuck inside those bell sleeves?"

Ella Mae laughed again and was surprised by the levity of the sound. She felt much lighter, as if a burden had been lifted. With a shock, she realized the transfer had worked. She'd used her gifts to store her longing for Hugh in a white chocolate mousse raspberry pie. She could think of him now without feeling that needle-sharp ache in the center of her chest. Her love was intact, but it was a love without pain. It was more like the memory of love. Pure, sweet, and distant.

"Anyway," she continued animatedly. "The contestants don't have to restrict their recipes to foods made in ancient times. America has a storied pie-making history. Pie has always been very important to this nation."

Reba loaded her serving tray with the completed orders. "Shoot, everybody knows that. I bet there wouldn't have been an America if the pilgrims hadn't made pumpkin pie for the natives durin' the very first Thanksgiving."

"There wasn't any pumpkin pie," said Jenny, who'd entered the room in time to catch Reba's last remark. "That's a total myth. They ate fowl and venison at the inaugural Thanksgiving. There might have been a savory pie, but definitely no pumpkin."

"All right, Einstein. You stay here and trade history lessons with Ella Mae. I need to serve my customers." With a scowl, Reba left the kitchen.

When she was gone, both Ella Mae and Jenny stifled laughter behind their hands.

"She really hates being corrected," Jenny said. "And I don't dare press a point with her. The woman has a whole arsenal of weapons concealed under her clothes. She might be smaller and older than me, but she could kick my butt from now until Tuesday."

Ella Mae retrieved a plastic bag filled with sugar cookie dough from the walk-in and began to roll it out on the worktable. "Reba's been my bodyguard since I was born. I've never seen anyone fight like her. She's almost fifty, but her reflexes are quicker than those of a pissed-off rattlesnake."

"I'm glad she saves her venom for our enemies," Jenny said. "Though it would be nice if we didn't have enemies for a spell. I'd like to enjoy a peaceful spring."

At that moment, one of Ella Mae's aunts burst through the swing doors, leaving them to flap wildly in her wake.

"You need to come with me!" Aunt Verena bellowed.

Ella Mae was unfazed by her aunt's tone and volume. The oldest of the famed LeFaye sisters didn't possess an indoor voice. She was also accustomed to people leaping to obey her. When Ella Mae didn't, Aunt Verena pointed at the cookie dough and said, "Put down that rolling pin. We need to go!"

"It's the middle of tea service," Ella Mae protested. "I can't just—"

"Yes, you can!"

Reba entered with another order ticket. "What's goin' on?"

"Can you take over for Ella Mae for a few minutes?" Though Verena towered over Reba and was nearly double her girth, she spoke to her with deference and affection. Reba might not be a LeFaye, but she was still family. "There's something she needs to see."

Reba nodded and turned to Ella Mae. "You'd best listen to your aunt."

Knowing that Aunt Verena wouldn't insist unless it was extremely important, Ella Mae untied her peach apron, hung it on a wall hook, and quickly washed her hands. "I hope you aren't the bearer of bad news," she said, reaching for the dish towel. "It's a holiday, after all. We're supposed to wear green, pick four-leaf clovers, and look for pots of gold at the end of rainbows. We're supposed to be merry."

Verena looked pained. "Honey, there's nothing to be merry about. And there's nothing to celebrate. This news is beyond bad. And things are about to get worse."

And with that, she turned and pushed on the swing doors with such force that Ella Mae thought they'd fly right off their hinges.